STAR WARS™

STAR WARS

FROM A CERTAIN
POINT OF VIEW

BEN ACKER   E. K. JOHNSTON

RENÉE AHDIEH   PAUL S. KEMP

TOM ANGLEBERGER   MUR LAFFERTY

BEN BLACKER   KEN LIU

JEFFREY BROWN   GRIFFIN McELROY

PIERCE BROWN   JOHN JACKSON MILLER

MEG CABOT   NNEDI OKORAFOR

RAE CARSON   DANIEL JOSÉ OLDER

ADAM CHRISTOPHER   MALLORY ORTBERG

ZORAIDA CÓRDOVA   BETH REVIS

DELILAH S. DAWSON   MADELEINE ROUX

KELLY SUE DeCONNICK   GREG RUCKA

PAUL DINI   GARY D. SCHMIDT

IAN DOESCHER   CAVAN SCOTT

ASHLEY ECKSTEIN   CHARLES SOULE

MATT FRACTION   SABAA TAHIR

ALEXANDER FREED   ELIZABETH WEIN

JASON FRY   GLEN WELDON

KIERON GILLEN   CHUCK WENDIG

CHRISTIE GOLDEN   WIL WHEATON

CLAUDIA GRAY   GARY WHITTA

PABLO HIDALGO

DEL REY ⌂ NEW YORK

STAR WARS

FROM A CERTAIN POINT OF VIEW

Illustrations on the following pages by Chris Trevas: vii, 3, 17, 27, 51, 59, 81, 89, 93, 113, 123, 157, 169, 183, 197, 205, 213, 221, 231, 247, 259, 297, 305, 317, 333, 349, 361, 367, 377, 393, 407, 423, 433, 447, and 455

Published in the United States by Del Rey,
an imprint of Random House, a division of
Penguin Random House LLC, New York.

DEL REY and the HOUSE colophon are registered
trademarks of Penguin Random House LLC.

ISBN 978-0-345-51147-8
Ebook ISBN 978-0-425-28670-8

Deep sky photo: iStock/standret

Printed in the United States of America on acid-free paper

randomhousebooks.com

2 4 6 8 9 7 5 3 1

First Edition

Book design by Elizabeth A. D. Eno

CONTENTS

Contents

A long time ago in a galaxy far, far away. . . .

STAR WARS™

FROM A CERTAIN
POINT OF VIEW

RAYMUS

Gary Whitta

"**W**hat is it they've sent us?"

Captain Raymus Antilles watched as Princess Leia Organa of Alderaan turned away from him, holding the data card he had handed to her. The data card for which almost the entire military might of the Rebel Alliance, both on the ground and in orbit above the planet Scarif, had just risked everything to steal it from one of the most secure Imperial strongholds in the galaxy. The grand, all-or-nothing gambit had led to the single largest combat engagement in the long history of conflict between the Rebellion and the Empire, and one that despite heavy losses had resulted seemingly in a victory: The card, and whatever highly prized data it held, had been delivered safely into the hands of one of the Alliance's most capable covert operatives. The rest was up to her.

"Hope," she replied as she looked ahead, through the forward viewport of the *Tantive IV*'s cockpit, to the limitless ocean of stars beyond.

Always so damn enigmatic, thought Raymus. Leia never told you more than you needed to know. That was for the protection of others as much as her own. She had learned that lesson well, the princess who had become a galactic senator, the senator who had secretly risked her life countless times to help nurture a fledgling Rebellion from a handful of squabbling, disgruntled star systems into the organized and dedicated Alliance it had become. Still no direct match for the awesome war power of the Empire, but enough to capture their most closely guarded secrets in a mission that even Raymus thought breathless in its audacity. Enough—maybe, just enough—to give the oppressed peoples of the galaxy a fighting chance at freedom.

Raymus watched the stars outside stretch into a kaleidoscopic tunnel of light as the ship jumped into hyperspace. Then Leia turned back to him and they both stepped through the cockpit door, into the hallway.

"Will we make it?" she asked. Before departure, Raymus had warned her that her ship was not yet capable of even the routine flight to Tatooine, which had, until recently, been its assignment. It had not even been able to travel to Scarif under its own power, carried instead in the belly of the rebel flagship *Profundity* as mechanical crews worked hurriedly to repair its overworked and malfunctioning hyperdrive. By the time they arrived at Scarif, Raymus was able only to assure her that the *Tantive IV* could perform a hyperspace jump, not that it could sustain lightspeed travel long enough to reliably get them to any given destination.

"I'll be able to give you a better answer in operations," he told her.

"Then let's go," she said, leading the way. Raymus followed, forced to quicken his step in order to keep pace with her.

They arrived at the ship's operations center to find several senior officers working frantically at their control stations.

"Status," Raymus requested as the door slid closed behind him.

"We're maintaining lightspeed, for now," the nearest officer informed him. "Remains to be seen how long the engines can keep this up. Maintenance crews are doing all they can. If we can hold this speed, we'll be at Tatooine within the hour. But the drive's still in bad shape; motivator could go at any time."

Raymus nodded. All this he knew. After the damage sustained on its last mission, the *Tantive IV* was in no shape for a desperate flight from the Empire. For years he had carefully steered this ship—*his* ship—through countless Imperial blockades and checkpoints, always able to avoid detection or suspicion. But now it had been spotted fleeing the scene of the most daring military assault in the history of the Rebellion, carrying stolen goods that the Empire would go to any lengths to recover. Suddenly, the *Tantive IV* was the most wanted ship in the galaxy, and it was in sorry shape. For the task of ferrying the most critical Imperial secrets ever captured, they could scarcely have picked a worse vessel at a worse time. But that was the hand they had been dealt, and Raymus had no option now but to play it as best he could.

"The real problem is what we're leaving behind us," the officer continued. "We can't exactly run quiet with a hyperdrive that's barely holding together. If the Empire detected any trace of an abnormal hyperspace wake when we jumped to lightspeed, it won't take them long to use it to track us."

Raymus sighed; he had dreaded this possibility and had warned

Leia of it prior to their setting their escape course from Scarif. Typically a jump to hyperspace meant a clean getaway, a ship's lightspeed trajectory impossible to track. But the *Tantive IV*'s impaired hyperdrive was like a leaky oil pan, leaving behind it a residual energy signature that was unique—and traceable. He wondered now how long it would take the Empire, with all their resources no doubt already diverted to finding them, to pick up their trail and follow it. For that reason, Leia had thought it too great a risk to return to the rebel headquarters at Yavin 4. Faced with no good options, she had ordered Raymus to instead set course for Tatooine, their planned destination before the hurried redirection to Scarif. She hoped still to fulfill the vital mission that her father had entrusted to her earlier that same day, knowing that even if the Empire pursued them to that barren desert outworld they would find nothing there but endless wastes of sand.

Raymus saw the grim expression on the face of the ship's bosun, who was examining new readouts at his station. "Don't tell me it gets worse," he said.

"The *Profundity* took heavy damage when she was disabled," the bosun reported. "Her electrical systems overloaded, and since we were still docked, the overload fried half our grid, too. We barely have deflectors or weapons. If it comes to a fight, we won't be able to put up much of one."

So there it was. Surely only a matter of time before the Empire found them, and little chance of defending themselves once they did. Raymus tried to think of a time during all their many high-risk missions and close escapes when they had faced a situation as dire as this, and came up wanting. "What about the escape pods?" he asked.

"As you ordered," said Helfun Rumm, the *Tantive IV*'s stalwart security officer. "All secured and ready to launch."

Raymus noticed Leia looking at him inquisitively. "Your Highness, if we are stopped and boarded by the Empire, my first priority is to get you to safety," he told her. "At that point, the pods may be our only option."

"Surely it will not come to that," said Corla Metonae, *Tantive IV*'s chief petty officer and a long-serving retainer of the Organa royal household. "We're still flying under a diplomatic flag. The Empire would not dare board us."

Raymus considered that; technically it still held true. The *Tantive IV* was officially a consular ship that Leia used in the performance of her duties as Alderaan's representative in the Galactic Senate. As a diplomat, she enjoyed special legal protections that meant not even the Imperial military could board, search, or in any way impede the free passage of her ship without her express permission. It was a broad and very convenient privilege that in the past had allowed her and Raymus to conduct acts of espionage and subterfuge right under the Empire's nose. But now Raymus found himself doubting, given the apparent import of what had been stolen from Scarif, that it would be enough to protect them this time.

"This just came in," the bosun reported, looking up from his station. "The Empire has issued a priority red directive. Any ships matching the description of a CR90 corvette are to be stopped and held. Priority red means all previous orders and duties are immediately superseded for all Imperial ships galaxy-wide. I've never seen this much comm traffic—the Empire's flooding every frequency with it. Whatever Rogue One beamed us from Scarif, they *really* want it back."

All eyes were on Leia as the full gravity of their situation began to sink in. Raymus had seen this look on her face before; she was concerned, worried even, but it showed in a way that only those few who knew her best, had served with her longest, could detect. To all else she projected only firm resolve in the face of crushing adversity. But he knew how bad this latest news was. The ship's fragile consular status aside, one of their few slim hopes lay in the fact that the CR90 was a ship common throughout the galaxy, literally thousands of them in service, and the *Tantive IV* looked like almost any of them. But though they were a needle in a haystack, the Empire had the resources—and apparently, the determination—to tear the entire haystack apart in order to find them. And diplomatic protocol would not stand in their way. Briefly his thoughts turned to the innocent crews of other Corellian corvettes that even now were being stopped and invaded by armed Imperial boarding parties. Some would be foolish enough to resist.

"If the Empire does find us . . ." Toshma Jefkin, the *Tantive IV*'s second officer, pondered aloud.

"Then let's make sure that they don't," said Leia.

Raymus looked at Jefkin. He had served with the man for years, shared many close encounters with Imperial forces, and knew that little rattled him. He looked rattled now. His face was a ghostly white; his hands were clammy. And he seemed to be gazing into nothing, the haunted countenance of a man who has seen something that can never be unseen.

"Tosh, what is it?" Raymus asked.

Jefkin looked at him with hollow eyes. "That . . . thing. In the hallway, while we were trying to get off the *Profundity*. It killed at least a dozen of my men, cut them down like they were nothing. Blasters had no effect, it just kept on coming, kept on killing. It was like . . . like a nightmare. I've never seen anything like it, like some kind of death angel."

Raymus and Leia exchanged a grim look as they realized what this must mean. To retrieve what had been stolen from them, the Empire had dispatched none other than Darth Vader himself. And that was the most dire news of all.

8

———

Raymus returned to his quarters to write, while he still had time. As captain he knew that he would go down with his ship if necessary, but in case it came to that he would first dispatch a final message to his family back home. He had already thought it through; as his crew piled into the *Tantive IV*'s escape pods to evade Imperial capture, he would hand someone he trusted an encrypted data cylinder, with instructions that it be delivered to his wife on Alderaan.

As he sat down to write, that grim scenario seemed more likely to him than any other. He'd had a bad feeling about this mission from the beginning. Hastily improvised, orders rewritten at the last minute, and now here they were: barreling headlong in a broken ship toward the edge of the galaxy, carrying the last best hope for the survival of the Rebellion, and the entire Empire searching for them.

He would write three letters, one for his beloved wife, the other two for her to give to each of their young daughters when they were old enough to understand. He had so much he wanted to tell them. More than anything, he wanted them to know that even though they would grow up never knowing their father, it was not for the lack of his love for them. No, it was because he loved them so, because he was determined they have the life they deserved, that he had given everything to help secure it for them. That was the most bitter irony of war: The greatest acts of love for your family were the ones that kept you apart from them.

He tried to write, but no words came. He knew what he wanted to say but not how to say it, and the longer he stared at the screen, the more agonizing the prospect of composing his final words to those he most loved became. To his wife he wanted to say he was sorry, for all that she had been asked to give that so that he might serve his princess and her Rebellion, often leaving her to raise their children alone for weeks and months at a time. He had barely seen either of his daughters since they were born. As greatly as that pained him, the

9

sacrifice had always seemed worth it to Raymus, inspired as he had been by Leia's own passion to fight for a future in which not just his children but sons and daughters throughout the galaxy could grow up free from Imperial tyranny, something they only read about in history texts. And Leia, who had come to trust and rely upon Raymus like few others save her own father, had insisted on ensuring that his family was well provided for during his time by her side. But that all seemed like cold comfort now as he reflected on how much precious time had been lost, and how little he might now have left as the Empire tightened its noose around his ship.

It was only when he had finally begun to write that the ship lurched aftward hard, almost throwing him from his chair. He recognized it instantly, the sudden violent deceleration when a ship dropped out of lightspeed unexpectedly. Looking to his viewport, he saw the tunnel of shimmering blue light outside dissolve away, replaced by an inky void punctuated with pinpoints of light. The *Tantive IV* was no longer in hyperspace, but back among the stars. Exposed, easily detectable by any Imperial ship that might be in the area—which would certainly be looking for any vessel matching their description.

He sprang from his chair and bolted toward the door, leaving the letters unwritten.

"What happened?" Raymus asked as he entered the cockpit.

"Motivator finally gave out," the ship's pilot reported. The instrument panel before him and his copilot was ablaze with blinking warning lights. "We're at sublight for the rest of the way."

"Where are we?"

The copilot worked the nav console, punched up a local sensor image. "We're close, about a quarter parsec out."

Raymus stepped forward, directly behind the two helmsmates so that he might see better through the cockpit viewport. And there it was. Barely discernible to an untrained eye, but Raymus knew what he was looking for. From this far out, Tatooine was little more than a speck, just a tiny, pale-orange dot adjacent to two far larger, brilliant lights, the planet's binary suns.

"How long at best speed?" They were so close, yet still so far. If the hyperdrive had held out for just a few moments longer, they would already be in the planet's orbit. But now, forced to hobble the rest of the way at sublight . . .

"Eight minutes," the pilot responded. "I think we'll make it." There was hope in the man's voice, a sense of relief—the first Raymus had heard from anyone since their narrow escape from Scarif. And now he felt it, too. Eight minutes. If they could hold out just that much longer, he could get everybody to the surface and scuttle the ship; then at one of the planet's infamously no-questions-asked spaceports he could procure another vessel, unmarked and untraceable, with which to spirit the princess to safety. For a brief moment he allowed hope back in; considered the possibility that maybe, just maybe, there was a way out of this. That the princess might still be safe after all, that the stolen data might still find its way back to rebel command, that he and his loved ones might still—

The impact rocked the ship so hard it slammed Raymus against the cockpit bulkhead. Like a passing breeze, his reverie vanished as quickly as it had come, and a shrill cockpit alarm sounded.

"Star Destroyer!" the pilot exclaimed in response to the new sensor reading that had just appeared directly behind them. "They're firing on us!"

"Man the turbolasers and return fire," Raymus ordered. "Put everything we've got into the aft deflector shield, and get us to that planet!"

He assembled his security forces and gave them their orders, sending every man he could arm to the forward docking hatch to set up a defensive bulwark. He knew their chances of repelling an Imperial boarding party with the meager forces at his command were slim, but they might at least buy him time to get the civilians away to safety.

As his troops departed, the ship was rocked hard again, and a loud explosion sounded somewhere far behind Raymus. His comlink crackled to life, and he raised it to hear the sounds of chaos and panicked voices from the cockpit.

"Sir, that last hit overloaded our shield projector; we had to shut down the main reactor before it blew. We can't maintain distance on that Destroyer—it's closing fast."

"Distance to Tatooine?"

"Point two seven" came the reply. They would not get away, Raymus knew, but the escape pods still could.

Raymus heard a muffled metallic echo all around him, the sound of the ship's hull groaning under outward pressure, and knew what that meant. The destroyer had locked on to them with its tractor beam and was pulling them in.

"Sir, they just—"

"I know. Get to your escape pods!" And he ran, searching desperately for the princess. The ship was lost, he knew. But he could still save her.

He could find her nowhere. He rushed through the hallways searching as all around him his crew helped the princess's senatorial staff pile hurriedly into escape pods. There weren't enough for everyone, he knew. As it had always been with the Rebellion, they had to make the best of what little they had. And good people would have to die.

He heard the distant explosion, knew that it had come from the forward air lock. Then the sound of a furious exchange of blasterfire. Imperial troops were now coming aboard his ship. *Not much time. Have to find her.* He had not dedicated so much of his life to protecting her only to fail now, in her most critical hour of need.

Finally he spotted her as he rounded a corner. She was at the far end of the white-walled hallway. Alone save for an R2 unit, warbling affirmatively as she spoke to it.

"Your Highness!"

When Leia turned to see him, she quickly ushered the droid away. Puzzled, Raymus raced to follow her, catching up to her as she slipped through a bulkhead doorway into a shadowy side corridor.

"You must come with me, I have to get you to a pod," he implored.

"I'm not leaving," she said. "Get as many as you can to safety." Raymus knew by the defiant tenor of her voice that there would be no arguing with her.

"The transmission from Scarif . . ."

"Leave that to me," she said, a purposeful glint in her eye. Behind her, the R2 unit bleeped at her urgently.

The sounds of blasterfire were getting closer now, and less frequent, as the Imperial boarders depleted the *Tantive IV*'s meager defensive force. Mere moments remained.

"Your Highness—"

"You have your orders, Captain. And my gratitude. For everything." Leia raised her hand and touched it to Raymus's cheek, giving him a warm, bittersweet smile both of affection and of sorrow. Both of them knew that this was the last time they would ever see each other. And then she was gone, the little droid trundling away into the shadows after her.

There was little left for him to do, his ship captured and swarming with Imperial stormtroopers, all but a few escape pods already away. All that remained was to end his life the way that he had always lived

13

it, fighting. He rushed away down the hall, ducking behind a bulk-head as he saw the first stormtrooper round the corner up ahead, firing. Raymus took aim and returned fire, dropping that storm-trooper and then another. Then the number of troopers who were arriving, taking positions, firing at him, quickly became too many, and his only recourse was to run. He sprinted away, knowing that he was quickly running out of ship but determined nonetheless to make the Empire expend every possible resource, every ounce of sweat, every precious second, before they would inevitably take him. Maybe just enough to buy his princess time to execute whatever last-ditch plan she might have.

He was almost at the hallway junction leading back to his quarters when he was tackled and brought to the ground, three Imperial troopers forcing him into submission. He struggled, resisting them to the last, until a rifle stock to the side of his head dazed him, took his strength.

"This one's the captain!" He heard the trooper's modulated voice behind his right ear as his arms were pulled behind his back. "We need him alive!" And then he was up again, his vision a hazy blur as he felt himself being hauled forward, his boots dragging along the floor behind him.

"My lord." He heard the trooper's voice behind him again. "The captain."

Raymus felt a shadow looming over him a moment before some-thing cold and metallic, like the jaws of a vise, clamped hard around his throat. As his eyes widened, he realized the black shape that now towered over him, though little more than a dark blur, was Darth Vader, and that the mechanical grip around his throat was a hand. The stormtroopers moved to surround them both, as though a Sith Lord needed any assistance whatsoever.

"The Death Star plans are not in the main computer," an arriving trooper reported.

14

So that's what they sent us. Even in his disoriented state, Raymus now understood why the rebel fleet had gambled everything to steal that data, and why the Empire had dispatched its most fearsome, unstoppable asset in its attempt to recover it. That hideous spherical leviathan that he had seen lay waste to the surface of Scarif, unimaginable in size, unthinkable in purpose. The Emperor's monstrous attempt to secure ultimate dominion over a galaxy slowly finding the will to oppose him. The secrets to destroying it were in the hands of his princess. And he would gladly die to protect them.

"Where are those transmissions you intercepted?" Vader demanded. "What have you done with those plans?"

Raymus fought uselessly to pry the fingers from around his neck, felt his feet leave the floor as Vader lifted him effortlessly, all the while tightening his grip, choking the life from him.

"We intercepted no transmissions," he spluttered, fighting for breath. "This is a consular ship. We're on a diplomatic mission."

"If this is a consular ship," Raymus only vaguely heard as he began to lose consciousness, his vision dimming around its edges, "where is the ambassador?"

Even as Raymus felt the last of his life ebbing away, he found himself strangely hopeful once more. He knew of course that his story had reached its end, that he would never again see his beloved wife and children on Alderaan, and yet still he had hope. He hoped that somehow Leia knew of a way out even from this; hoped that the glimmer in her eye he had seen in that hallway was the germ of an idea that might yet see the stolen data returned safely to the Rebellion. He hoped that it would empower them to destroy that hateful weapon, to turn the tide of war, to rally more systems to their cause, to allow a galaxy, once again, to breathe free.

In his final moment, he hoped.

15

THE BUCKET

Christie Golden

TK-4601 was disproportionally grateful for the stormtrooper helmet. For one thing, it smashed down the unruly tuft of blond hair that would never obey a comb or brush—the one that made him look like he was thirteen. His fair skin reddened and paled easily, too, which meant that no matter how diligent he was in schooling his expressions, his coloring always betrayed him. With the helmet on, though, and with the device that rendered the voices of stormtroopers almost completely identical, his reactions—good or bad—were much harder for others to determine.

He was particularly appreciative of it today, as he was grinning like an idiot. He couldn't believe his first assignment straight out of the Academy had been aboard an Imperial Star Destroyer. And not just *any* Star Destroyer, either. TK-4601, also known as Tarvyn Lareka, served on the *Devastator,* the flagship of Lord Vader himself. He was now part of Vader's personal legion—"Vader's Fist." A junior member, to be sure, but he was still an official member.

Today a thrill of excitement laced the activity of the finely tuned military instrument that was Vader's Fist. If Lord Vader himself, he of the black, gleaming armor, the ominous breaths, the deep, resonant voice, and the unfathomable command over objects and people—if *he* wanted to give chase to this vessel as it sped away from the Battle of Scarif, then as far as TK-4601 was concerned, the rumors had more of truth than fiction about them.

Behind "the bucket," as the helm was sometimes called, no one could see his brow furrowed in concentration, his blue eyes narrowed. No one could see the joy he took in a successful mission with no casualties, either, nor when he was reluctant to follow orders that sometimes seemed to border on senseless cruelty.

He was getting better at pushing that part down, though.

Earlier, TK-4601 had stood rigidly at attention while Vader, standing a mere meter away, at the most, had grasped Captain Antilles of the *Tantive IV* by the throat, lifted him off the ground, and interrogated him.

Where are those transmissions you intercepted? Vader had boomed, in that sonorous yet dreadful voice that Death itself might use. *What have you done with those plans?*

We intercepted no transmissions. This is a consular ship. We're on a diplomatic mission. The *Tantive IV* belonged to the House of Organa of Alderaan. TK-4601 knew that both father and daughter of that House were members of the Imperial Senate.

If this is a consular ship, where is the ambassador?

As seemed to be a not uncommon progression with Lord Vader,

he'd grown so furious that his fingers crushed the man's windpipe before the unfortunate captain could even manage an answer.

TK-4601 could hear the vertebrae snapping like dried twigs.

He swallowed hard. The bucket concealed all.

Vader had ordered Commander TK-9091 to search the ship—*tear it apart* were his exact words—until the plans were found. As for passengers, unlike the late Captain Antilles, they were to be taken alive.

And so the four stormtroopers had been sent to search for the ill-fated ship's passengers. They were now poking around in various corridors, closets, and other out-of-the-way places in a life-and-death game of hide-and-seek.

TK-4601's heart was still racing and he could feel the heat in his cheeks and the smile on his face. He'd deliberately pushed the casual murder of the captain out of his mind, and now he was beyond excited. He felt exultant. They were not just conducting random raids on sullen populations of distant worlds. They were in search of the real thing. Real rebels, with real cunning, who'd managed to steal plans from a major Imperial base that ought to have been impregnable.

Clever creatures, the rebels, he thought. He would never admit it, but there was much to be admired about them.

Rumor—that sweet, swirling, shape-shifting creature—had it that the missing ambassador was senatorial royalty: Princess Leia Organa of Alderaan, to be specific. It was a logical conclusion, considering the *Tantive IV* was owned by her father. Both she and Bail Organa had publicly expressed sympathy for the rebels' cause. That didn't mean they were themselves rebels, of course. But what if they were? TK-4601 badly wanted to talk to TK-3338, who was following immediately behind him in their sweep, and ask if he thought it was true. What was she like, this senatorial princess? She couldn't *really* be just nineteen, could she?

19

Younger than he was, and already a senator. Astonishing. It wouldn't be surprising if she had indeed been seduced by the siren song of the Rebellion. Its "championing of the innocent," its defiance of the order offered by the Empire. He'd been nineteen once, too, and remembered the appeal such ideals could have. But he'd been smart and resisted that call. He was a staunch Imperial.

An Emperor outranked a princess, and the Senate's days were numbered.

"Think we'll find any of them?" asked TK-4247, who was bringing up the rear. He was even newer and more naïve than TK-4601 had been when he'd joined Vader's legion.

"Lord Vader will be pleased with us if we do," TK-9091 answered. He didn't say the opposite—that Lord Vader would be displeased if they did not. TK-4601 didn't even want to think about that.

I want them alive, Vader had said. Their blasters were set on kill. They were in a battlefield, even now. Too many of the crew were loose and armed, wandering about and opening fire, for the stormtroopers to take chances. TK-9091, taking point as was his right, had ordered them to kill the crew, but switch to stun upon sighting anyone who might be a passenger.

"What if we find the senator?" chimed in TK-3338.

"Same thing. Stun. But we don't know for certain that she's here," the commander answered. "Don't let down your guard. If this really is a rebel ship, they're cornered animals now, and they're going to fight dirty."

Of course they would. Lying through their teeth about their illegal activities. Hiding in shadows. Dirty fighters.

But after the quick flush of excitement and anticipation, the routine of checking corridor after corridor faded before the mundanity of the task.

And then all at once mundanity was shattered. "There's one," TK-9091 said, turning to TK-4601. "Set for stun."

TK-4601 instantly adjusted his blaster's setting and turned to look.

The instant lasted less than a heartbeat, but TK-4601 felt it was frozen, locked in time.

Her clothing was so white as to almost glow, her skin smooth and pale as cream. As pale as his own, though her long, glossy hair, gathered up in elaborate but efficient twin buns on either side of her face, was a rich warm brown, not the bright, sunny yellow of his.

And she was so . . . *little.*

TK-4601 had imagined that rebel women would be strong and muscular. Tall, powerful warriors. This one stood barely a meter and a half, and looked like she might break if held too tightly.

But her eyes—

They were not cold, those brown orbs. They were steady, however, and they were calm, and they told him as clearly as if she had shouted the words: *I will never yield.*

She gripped a small, handheld blaster, the barrel pointing up.

And suddenly TK-4601 understood how it was that this nineteen-year-old girl was more of a woman than most twice her age. He understood how she had become a popular senator, why she had sympathy for the Rebellion. Why people followed her.

And in that instant that lasted for an eternity, he also knew that they, elite members of Vader's Fist, were going to be too slow, that their commander had, *very wrongly,* judged this woman harmless, had reacted far too casually, and was about to pay the price before any of them could react.

The white sleeves fell away from her slender arms as she lifted the blaster.

TK-9091 fell, his armor scorched and smoking.

The movement shocked TK-4601 out of his reverie. Time, which had slowed to a crawl, sped up again, rushed to meet him, and he fired his own blaster directly at the woman who could only be Princess Leia Organa.

She collapsed instantly, striking the cold, gray surface hard with no chance to break her fall. She lay sprawled, her tiny, delicate fingers still clutching the blaster.

TK-4601 rushed toward her, suddenly seized with worry that she had hit too hard, that she was dead. He felt a strong—and, he knew, treasonous—wave of relief when he realized this was not the case.

"She'll be all right," he said. He realized that his words were heavy with unexpected, unwanted emotion. But thanks to "the bucket," they came out sounding as clipped and precise as they always did.

He took a breath. "Inform Lord Vader we have a prisoner."

It presaged dark things, if Vader specifically wanted to interrogate this one. He himself had encountered his commander only a few times, and that was enough. What he would do to her . . .

No. He would not be swayed by a pretty face and a mien filled with resolve. The princess would have been delighted if her shot had dispatched TK-9091, or himself, or the other two in the patrol group.

"Sir," TK-4247 said to him, "the commander's dead."

Dead? It wasn't possible. The white plastoid suits protected the soldiers encased inside them, diffusing blasts so that most shots weren't lethal.

But the princess had aimed true, and from only three meters away. TK-4247 was bent over him, and now he turned his helmeted face to his new commander. "Orders, sir?"

Sir. With the death of TK-9091, the role of commanding officer fell to TK-4601. He'd wanted to climb high in the ranks, but not like this.

For a moment, he didn't reply. He knew the orders. Stormtroopers lay where they fell until after the battle, and TK-9091 could be no exception to that rule. TK-4601 could still hear the screams out in the corridors—both the high-pitched sounds of blasters firing and the cries of agony from their victims.

He strode to where their captive lay. Her body was limp and her face slack. Its fire was quelled, but its beauty still lingered. She would wake in a few minutes, perhaps feeling slightly hungover from the effects of the stun bolt but, as he had told the group, "fine."

Unlike TK-9091. His commanding officer. His friend. The one who cracked the stupidest jokes in the world in his off hours, but who was all business when he donned the uniform. Except this time, he'd underestimated the enemy. A stupid, stupid mistake.

The prisoner stirred now, groggy, moaning softly. True to her rebel spirit, though, the first thing she did was start to raise the pistol. TK-4601 kicked it away angrily. She gazed up at him, blinking rapidly as her eyes slowly focused. At the sight of his face—his helmet—an expression of disgust flitted across her face.

That beautiful visage was as much a face of the enemy as any scarred, bearded one. Leia Organa was a killer. She looked at them and did not see the people, only the Empire they served. To her, Tarvyn Lareka had no name, no face, only a number. He was nothing more than a uniform of the hated foe, to be shot at and eliminated as quickly as possible.

He reached down and grabbed her wrists, hauling her to her feet. The princess struggled, but TK-3338 pressed the blaster into her back. She stiffened, and stilled.

"Lord Vader wants to see you, Senator Organa," TK-4601 said. He snapped a pair of stun cuffs around her slender wrists. "You can either come along with us on your own two feet, or we'll stun you again and bring you to him that way. Your decision."

For a moment, he thought she would lunge at him. Instead she composed herself. "I'll walk," she said. Her voice held no quiver at all. It was as cool and regal as the rest of her.

But TK-4601 thought of Vader's abilities, and the torture droid, and he suddenly, abruptly, did not want to be the one who delivered her to the utter lack of mercy she would receive at Darth Vader's hands. To the ominous whir of the hovering torture droid, and its myriad drugs with which to torment the prisoners.

He said on his comm, "This is TK-4601. TK-9091 is down. We have a prisoner in custody. Request two additional troops to escort prisoner to Lord Vader per his instructions."

"Copy, TK-4601. We see your position. TK-7624 and TK-8332 are en route."

The other two looked at each other, then at him. "Sir?"

He ignored them and continued speaking into the comm. "Request permission to transfer to active-duty unit for the duration of the battle."

"Permission granted," came the voice. "Nothing official, but I've got a hunch we'll be sending some troopers to the surface if Vader doesn't find what he wants here. No stone unturned. Lot of sand there, though."

"Copy that," TK-4601 said immediately. "Transfer me to that unit if it's deployed." Leia Organa's eyes narrowed as she regarded him speculatively. Doubtless, his team was startled and wondering what the hell he was doing. He was a member of Vader's Fist. He could be here fighting, killing the rebels, doing what they had trained for, and instead he'd requested what amounted to a demotion. They'd be even more shocked if they knew what he was thinking.

TK-4601 loved the Empire. He believed in it. He knew it could bring order and peace to the galaxy. But he also knew that he couldn't keep doing what he was doing now . . . killing rebels while looking into their faces, their eyes, seeing them open and exposed, emotions naked to him, while they only saw flat black and white.

He could still kill them—but only when the battlefield was even. Only when he couldn't see them, as he saw this senator, this princess, this rebel. He could shoot them out of the sky, and he would—but not shoot them in the heart.

The two new stormtroopers arrived. TK-9091 was left where he fell. Per orders.

He'd have understood.

The four escorted the princess to meet the Dark Lord, each of them towering above her diminutive height. As TK-4601 watched them go, the princess turned to look at him searchingly.

Spontaneously, without thinking, he removed the helmet.

The princess seemed startled to see him—a human male not much older than she, fair-haired, blue-eyed, his cheeks flushed.

Their gazes locked for a moment, then she gave him a slight nod and turned around. TK-4601 didn't kid himself that she understood the gesture, or that they had made any kind of connection.

But damn it, he'd reminded her that there was a person inside the plastoid armor. And more important, he'd reminded himself.

THE SITH OF DATAWORK

Ken Liu

"*Psst!* Arvira, I need your help!"

I looked up from the tiny text scrolling by on my screen. Behind the stacks of tablets teetering on my desk appeared the anxious face of Bolvan, gunnery captain.

"I'm kind of in the middle of something here," I said, gesturing vaguely at the tablets full of datawork. Interruptions were part of my job, but surely he could see I needed a chance to catch up?

Everyone thought being fleet logistics liaison (grade 4) on an Imperial Star Destroyer was a cushy job. But it took a lot of datawork to keep the crew of a massive ship like this fed and clothed and in fighting shape. Desk jobs in the Imperial Navy were no less stressful than combat ones.

"Please, I really need you!" he persisted.

I sighed. Officers were just like babies: When they needed something, it was always the most important thing in the world. "I haven't forgotten the entertainment holos you wanted. But I have to prioritize processing the captured corvette *Tantive IV*. Especially since Lord Vader—"

"No, no! It's something else."

I paused the scrolling screen. It was clear he wasn't going to leave me to my work until I took care of his problem. I tried to put on my most convincing smile. "How can I help you?"

He glanced back into the corridor to be sure it was empty, closed the door to my office, and sat down. "Er . . . it's like this . . ."

I sat there patiently until he finished his tale.

"So you ordered Hija not to shoot the escape pod?" I asked, just to be sure I understood.

"Right."

"And why not? Wait, is it because you wanted to avoid the datawork?"

I wasn't joking. Like all militaries, the Imperial Navy ran on datawork. Most officers spent more time filling out forms and filing reports than shooting at rebels. Per Imperial Naval Regulation 132. CAT.ch(22), shooting an escape pod (other than during an armed engagement with an intensity classified as above Category V) required the gunnery captain to file a Form XTM-51-CT to explain why the action was necessary. This was to avoid giving those squawking senators an excuse to claim that the Imperial Navy engaged in war crimes. Bolvan had always tried to get by with as little datawork as possible.

He shook his head no.

Well, this was interesting. "Are we trying to conserve lasers now?"

He ignored my sarcasm, but his face turned red. "The sensors detected no life-forms aboard. I thought . . . um . . . we wouldn't have been scored with a kill . . . so . . ."

Of course; now his actions made perfect sense. Annoyed with rebel propaganda that showed Imperials to be poor shots—frankly, the stormtroopers could do with more targeting drills—fleet bureaucrats had issued a new policy that tied gunnery officers' promotions to their kill ratios. Shots fired at unoccupied escape pods would indeed be considered wasted. I thought this was a terrible idea at the time. The new policy would encourage some ambitious gunners to aim for rebel pilots in disabled vessels rather than dangerous, armed drones. But the brass never asked for my opinion.

"Fine, so you let the empty escape pod go. What's the problem?"

"Lord Vader ordered the *Tantive IV* be torn apart until the secret plans stolen by the rebels were found, but now that they've gone over every centimeter of the ship, Commander Praji still hasn't located the plans. I . . . I'm afraid—"

"Ah . . ." I understood. "I take it the escape pod didn't just drift into space?"

"No," he said. "It followed a trajectory to the surface of Tatooine. I just thought it was a malfunction at the time, but maybe that wasn't it. What if the plans were aboard?"

"This is indeed a tricky problem," I said thoughtfully.

I'd always liked Bolvan. He never made too many outrageous demands on the logistics corps, and he was a terrible card player, which meant that I usually managed to win extra credits from him in private games among the officers. I didn't want to see the poor man court-martialed for negligence if the plans were somehow aboard that escape pod. Even worse, Lord Vader often didn't even bother with a court-martial. It must be nice to be able to ignore datawork requirements whenever one pleased.

"That's why I came to you," he said, his voice pleading. "I figured if anyone knew how to patch up a problem like this, you would."

Now, not to be boastful, but I did have a reputation for expertise in datawork. I knew the ins and outs of the hundreds of thousands of ever-changing forms and questionnaires and applications and data grids and charts and reports and requisition communiqués that kept the Imperial Navy humming. I knew just what checkboxes to tick to get my ship priority service in docks, what keywords to stick into blank forms to avoid a surprise inspection, and the secrets for requisitioning entertainment holos even when all the shipboard bandwidth was supposed to be reserved for combat-related transmissions.

And I shared my wisdom liberally. Junior officers who wanted to avoid snoring roommates came to me for advice on the XPTS-7 Bunking Application (claim a propensity for sleepwalking and punching sources of noise); senior officers who wanted to maximize their shore leave came to me for help with the SS-VAC-2B Visa (pick a departure port on the other side of the vacation planet from the arrival port); and even the captain came to me when it was time to fill out the estimated operating budget (the trick: . . . Ha, as if I'm going to share that trick here). Some called me a datawork wizard, or maybe even a datawork Jed—Oh, never mind that. The point is: I liked helping people, and if they chose to thank me with little favors or gifts or credits, it would have been impolite to say no.

Oh, all right, let me just come out and say it. It was nice to have people in your debt. With the political situation as volatile as it was, you never knew when you'd need to call in a favor. By helping people today, I was just helping myself for the future.

A good datawork master needed to have strings out to as many puppets—er—I meant students as possible. It was prudent.

After thinking over Bolvan's problem for a moment, I had an idea.

I handed him a tablet. "Here, start filling this out."

"What is this?" Bolvan looked wary.

"That's a Form INS-776-TX."

"What . . . what does it do?"

"Don't you even bother reading the instructions? Oh, all right, I'll explain. That's the form you use to request an immediate mid-cruise extra-vehicular-armament inspection."

"Why would I want to do that? That's going to send all the gunners in EV suits to inspect every single one of the *Devastator*'s guns. It will take hours to complete!"

I shook my head in mild annoyance. It was really hard sometimes working with people who had no understanding of the subtleties of datawork. "As the gunnery captain, you are one of the few officers on board with enough authority to request such an action, and Imperial regulations require the chief gunnery officer to be in charge of the inspection. Hija will be occupied for the rest of the day climbing from gun embankment to gun embankment outside the *Devastator*."

Bolvan still looked confused. "He's going to hate me. He never wants to go outside—says it gives him spacesickness—"

"If he's outside," I said, "then Lord Vader isn't going to corner him in a hallway and ask him about any escape pods! He's the only other witness."

Bolvan's eyes widened with understanding. "Oh . . . Ohhhhhh! What do I put down for 'Reason for requesting inspection'?"

" 'Reports of non-responsive triggering mechanism.' "

Bolvan's fingers danced over the tablet. "I take it this is to lay the groundwork for later claiming that the guns wouldn't respond? Clever."

"This is just going to buy you a little time," I said. "It doesn't solve the whole problem."

He looked up, alarmed. "So what else do I do?"

"You fill out a Form DKS-77-MA(n)." I flicked the form over onto his datapad.

Bolvan looked at me with his helpless, watery eyes.

I relented. "That's the form used to request the detailed manifest of any non-military vessel. In this case, since you'll be asking for the manifest of the *Tantive IV*, a consular ship on her last departure, you'll need to add in Appendix P2, Declaration of Classified Military Need."

31

"What am I supposed to do with the *Tantive IV*'s manifest?"

I flicked over yet another form onto his tablet. "You fill out Application SUG-171-TI."

He looked about ready to collapse in the face of this mounting pile of datawork. "Which is?"

"Don't you pay any attention to the training holos? You filled out an acknowledgment stating that you watched a holo on this family of forms just two days ago."

Bolvan's confused expression told me that he probably signed the acknowledgment without reading it just to get it off his desk.

"The SUG-171-TI is used to dispatch an operational suggestion to another officer. It's used when you need to bypass the chain of command and there's no military emergency. Fleet command is very proud of this innovation in improving the initiatives of all officers."

He acted like he wanted to tear his hair out, but he managed to force himself to calm down. "Who am I making the suggestion to and what do I suggest?"

"Commander Praji, like you, hates datawork. You just told me that he has gone over every centimeter of the *Tantive IV*, but I bet you he hasn't documented his search. I know, I know, when Lord Vader is breathing down your neck, the last thing you want to do is more datawork. But trust me, if the plans aren't found, everyone is going to want to make sure their behind is properly covered. That's why you want to make a suggestion to Praji to get his troops to fill out multiple copies of Form SRS-98-COMP, Inventory of Captured Vessel."

"But if the plans are on that escape pod, how is documenting the rest of the ship helpful?"

I knew then exactly how my teacher felt back when I was a kid and I just couldn't see the point of "showing my work" on tests. Even datawork wizards had shameful moments like that.

I had to be patient with him. "The point, Bolvan, is to let Praji be the one to figure out that the missing plans might be on that escape pod *without* exposing your own role in its escape. So you have him do the careful inventory, and send him the ship's manifest you obtained in the previous step. Praji will then do the comparison and notice the missing escape pod."

"But then he's going to ask me why I didn't shoot the pod when it jettisoned, which puts me back exactly where I started!"

"We're not done yet," I said. "The trick with datawork is layering and complementing."

"Sounds like you're talking about fashion," he muttered.

I let it slide. "Your goal is building an unassailable structure for diverting responsibility elsewhere—a kind of escape pod for yourself, if you will. So far I've taught you how to get Hija out of the way and how to lead Praji to discover the missing escape pod, and the only remaining piece is to erase any hint that you could be responsible."

"How?" he spat. I could tell he was about ready to grab my lapels and shake me.

I deliberately slowed down. "You're going to file a Maintenance Request NIW-59-SUD, with a Schedule P."

He groaned pitifully. He was like a drowning man ready to give up on the straw he was clutching. "What . . . is that going to do?"

Time to explain the coup de grâce.

"This is the form you use to report visibility-impaired viewports and viewscreens and request a cleaning."

"A *cleaning*?"

"That's right. Specifically, a washing of the viewports and viewscreens near your workstation."

He just looked at me. "A viewport washing? What . . . ? How . . . ? Why . . . ?"

"Once you put the request in, maintenance will dispatch multiple droids to the station you designate—I suggest where you and Hija were standing—and cover every viewport and viewscreen with a thick, white foam. The droids will even do it from the outside of the viewports. It's the latest cleaning and polishing agent from the Imperial labs, specifically designed to remove laser scarring and scorching from battles."

I watched his face go through the stages of terror, confusion, anger, disbelief, astonishment, epiphany, rapture.

"C-cover all the viewports?" he stuttered.

"That's right, *all* of them."

"With a th-thick foam?"

"Very thick. Can't see a thing through them. Can't see the stars, or the *Tantive IV,* or even Tatoo—"

"Or any escape pods! Oh, Arvira, this is brilliant!"

"This will explain why you couldn't see any escape pods from where you were. Praji will just assume that the escape pod was jettisoned without anyone detecting it."

"And he will have to then bring the bad news to Lord Vader and face the consequences."

That smile on his face was truly delightful to see. I loved helping people. "Exactly. Now go and get all the datawork done ASAP. You've still got time."

He got up, tablet in hand, and ran for the door. But before exiting, he turned around. "What can I do to make this up to you? A game of cards tomorrow night?"

Aha, so maybe he didn't know much about datawork, but he did know how to pay for a favor without being too obvious. "Maybe. But you know, I've always wanted to know what it's like to fire the guns on this thing. Even datawork wizards like *pew-pew-pew,* you know?"

He grinned. "I'm sure I can work out a target-practice session sometime."

I waved for him to go and returned to my endless datawork, glad to have laid down another strand in my invisible web of influence.

STORIES IN THE SAND

Griffin McElroy

I f one were to try to find the perfect summation of what life on Tatooine is really like—the sparseness, the intolerable *dryness* of it all—one would not need to look further than the sandcrawlers that checker the planet's surface with fleeting tread marks each day.

Every centimeter of a sandcrawler is prudently designed to fit the ship's grueling function, and sandcrawlers have *a lot* of centimeters. Each ship is an identical monument to practicality, and performs each day's work with exacting precision. They do so indomitably, overcoming Tatooine's considerable environmental hazards with ease.

On the uppermost deck of a sandcrawler stationed in the Western

Dune Sea, a sloped bulk belt carried scrap hoisted from the sands below to a salvage bay seated at the vessel's peak. Underneath that belt was a small hidden gap measuring one meter long and, at the incline's tallest point, half a meter high, with a width most non-Jawas would find oppressive. It was an unintended compartment in a vehicle shrewdly designed for maximized efficiency of space.

In this wedge-shaped gap, a Jawa named Jot dreamed of starships.

Jot had discovered the compartment by accident while working an intake shift, sorting the unceasing flow of metallic debris that the sandcrawler sucked up into its powerful magnetic maw. A particularly lustrous thermal dissipater had caught his eye as he pushed ancient alloys into piles according to their worth or usefulness to the crew. But as he reached to pocket the dissipater, Jot watched it slip sideways, between the bulk belt and the ship's hull, tumbling downward and out of sight.

Jot searched for the missing dissipater during his limited break time over the next nine days, hoping not to attract the attention of his peers during his tireless hunt. By pressing his slight frame behind the maglift's pneumatic servos, he could edge his way prone, then pry a flimsy, rectangular aluminum panel from the bulk belt's housing, giving him an entryway he could *just* scrape through, so long as his slightly round belly never, ever got any rounder. It was a clumsy act of contortion, but luckily for Jot, he was likely the only Jawa aboard the sandcrawler who could pull it off.

This was because Jot was *very* small, even by Jawa standards.

When Jawas first learn to walk, they're given the insulated, moisture-regulating robes that will sustain them their whole lives. As infants, their robes are hemmed nearly to the armpit, the fabric doubled and folded within. As Jawas mature, the hem is lowered to better cover their newfound height. Most Jawas measure themselves by the number of hems they've had put in; the average Jawa has five or six by the time they reach adulthood, leaving telltale striations in the thick brown canvas of their life-giving garment.

Jot's robe had been hemmed twice.

After several months of practice, Jot could slip in and out of his space in seconds. It was vital he keep the maneuver fast and surreptitious. He couldn't let anyone know about *his* gap.

To say the compartment wasn't especially comfortable would be a disservice to the very idea of discomfort. It was, as the previously mentioned dimensions suggest, cramped, especially when filled with the various baubles Jot had tucked away while on salvage duty. During his shifts, he could simply push items that caught his eye off the side of the belt and directly into his collection. Due to the relative ease of this process, his already sizable hoard had grown exponentially.

That one benefit nearly outweighed the gap's drawbacks, of which there were many.

The rolling belt that served as the gap's ceiling occasionally sagged under the weight of particularly heavy pieces of salvage, flirting with (but never *quite*) buckling. The starboard wall of the gap was actually the sandcrawler's outer hull, which grew unbearably hot to the touch fourteen hours of the day. There was enough room in the gap for Jot to sit without leaning against the starboard wall, so its searing heat wasn't an issue, so long as he didn't absentmindedly try to stretch out and get comfortable while admiring his hoard.

Unfortunately for Jot, losing his concentration was one of his most honored pastimes. It was not uncommon for passersby to hear a muffled yelp coming from the gullyworks of the lift's machinery, followed by the uniquely unpleasant smell of singed Jawa fur wafting down the sandcrawler's corridors.

Those faults didn't hamper Jot's contentment with his secret dwelling. Silence, privacy, and solitude weren't just in short supply on the sandcrawler; the ship was overstaffed and bloated with cargo, both of which created an environment where the concept of personal space was foreign.

Jot never knew how much he needed that space until he had it; now the idea of living without it was unthinkable. He did not dislike his life on the sandcrawler—it was certainly preferable to the monotony of fortress living—but his hours spent working salvage seemed longer, *emptier* since finding the gap. Every minute he spent sorting sandblasted metal was a minute he spent away from himself. Away from his home.

Away from Storyteller.

The dunes of Tatooine look barren to most offworlders who, for some (typically illicit) reason or another, find themselves visiting. That appraisal isn't completely unfair; life on Tatooine is as difficult as you'd expect from a planet where moisture is scarce to the point of deserving its own economy.

But every Jawa, especially those who ship out on a crawler, knows the truth: The surface of the dunes is lifeless, yes, but the sand stretches downward *forever*. Entombed in the endless, gritty expanse were more downed ships than there were ships in the sky. More droids than any ten factories could produce in a century. More wealth, more resources, more history than could ever be excavated or recorded.

There was not a Jawa on Tatooine who did not believe wholeheartedly that there was more sand below them than there was sky above. The sand, Jawas knew, was more fertile than any offworlder could ever guess; and the wind was its constant farmer.

Most Jawas could tell you tales of unimaginable relics exhumed by a sharp breeze, assuming you spoke fluent Trade (or even Jawaese, which you almost certainly don't). Strange meteors buried in their own glass-crusted craters. Ancient cruisers the size of small cities. For that matter, *actual small cities:* entire civilizations that had long since dried up and died of thirst, lost to time.

Jot had told the story of *his* discovery more times than he could count. Every moment of it remained crystal clear in his mind—the small protrusion of bone poking out of the ground several meters from his family's cramped clay dwelling. The shock of pain that shot up his arm as he cut his hand on something under the dirt. How the wind that night, matching the frenzy of his curiosity, revealed Jot's discovery in full the next morning.

A krayt dragon. A *big* one—the biggest Jot had ever seen, he would interject forcefully with each telling.

Immediately below the home in which Jot was born—and thousands of years before that—a krayt dragon had died and been pristinely preserved by Jot's front yard.

There were very few Jawas who had ever met Jot who hadn't heard that story. Most on the sandcrawler had heard it more than once, and very few had the patience for further retellings.

As important as it once had been to him, Jot was also growing tired of the tale; the scenes he once recounted with exuberance seemed less remarkable with each performance. He had leaned too hard on his story, and he knew he was robbing it of its luster.

Several weeks after Jot discovered the gap below the bulk belt, the wind blew fiercely over the dunes near his sandcrawler, pulling a new story up from the depths.

39

The sandcrawler's crew was asleep, enjoying a rare off-duty night while the ship rode out a massive windstorm that threatened to flood their engines with grit. The next morning, a long-dormant freighter had been uncovered so completely on a nearby dune that the first Jawas to see it would have sworn it had crash-landed while the ship's crew ate breakfast.

It was the biggest score the sandcrawler had found in months, and every Jawa on board delighted in ransacking it. Within the hour, the freighter had been thoroughly shucked; small hands ripped and sawed and pried at every panel, every cable, every millimeter of circuitry within. The species of the ship's long-dead pilot was unidentifiable, but their profession was evinced by the cockpit's less savory salvage: a modified blaster rifle, thermal detonators, ancient Mandalorian armor, and a still-functioning datapad that held several hundred expired warrants for criminals throughout the galaxy. This pilot was a bounty hunter and, based on the quality of their gear, an awfully successful one.

Jot was bullied into scouting the dig site's perimeter while the rest of the crew picked the ship clean for valuables—most of which would end up squirreled away in the spacious pockets of their robes. It wasn't the first time Jot had been buffaloed into an unwanted task by his clan—he was of a size that was *terribly* convenient for bullies.

During his halfhearted reconnaissance, Jot noticed a figure partially buried on the opposite side of the dune from where his team found the crashed freighter.

Embedded up to its midsection was an astromech droid: an outdated, bulky black bucket that had not been nearly as well preserved as the bounty hunter's other belongings. A large, rusted hole in its central hull showcased telltale signs of fusion cell corrosion, which inevitably meant every component in its core chassis was well beyond repair.

The droid's dome, however, was intriguing. Jot had seen several astromech droids tumble down the salvage line to be repaired, cleaned, and sold. This unit was clearly a custom job. Its holoprojector was installed onto a secondary processing unit, complete with its own discrete data drive and internal power source. All this custom hardware was housed in a single, detachable fixture, which, as near as Jot could tell, also made this processor completely redundant.

For some reason, that long-dead bounty hunter had given his droid a second brain.

Working carefully, Jot ran his driver across the shallow seam under the droid's domed head, granting access to this peculiar construction—which, to Jot's delight, could be easily slid out of its socket.

Jot tucked the whole holoprojector unit into the folds of his robe. It was only fair that he took home a prize, too, he figured.

Jot raced back to the sandcrawler, back to the privacy of his wedge-shaped compartment, grateful that his shipmates were too occupied with the freighter to notice his clumsy attempt at smuggling. He cleared a place for the device in the center of the compartment, giving it more space among the scrap than he gave himself.

Jawas are not known for their sense of aesthetics, and Jot was no exception—but he appreciated the fit of the holoprojector unit in his tiny space. He had thought of this room as his own, and had been fiercely secretive about it since he first discovered it. Now the gap belonged to the projector. They felt intended for each other, pieces that interlocked by design.

After several minutes of meticulously sorting his collection into neat piles, Jot dug up a memory core that he had found in the gap during his very first visit. He lifted the core to his mouth and pressed his tongue gently against its metal contacts—and felt a harsh, sour jolt course through him. Good. The core's internal battery was still functioning, meaning the data inside was probably still intact.

He nervously inserted the memory core into the holoprojector unit's drive, and the device immediately whirred to life.

Beneath the device's visible interface—not that Jot would have been able to decipher the process, even if he could see it—complex subroutines simultaneously examined, counterprogrammed, and decrypted the memory core's contents, displaying them seconds later through the holoprojector's lens.

Jot wasn't aware of this, but this decryption software was as sophisticated as it was illegal—exceptionally, *preposterously* illegal.

For a moment, the gap was flooded with formless gray light. It caught Jot by surprise, momentarily blinding him, sending him reeling, panicked, into the compartment's blistering-hot starboard wall. Within seconds, the light retreated to a few centimeters in front of the projector, taking shape with remarkable clarity.

Jot's vision cleared. He saw stars. Not the remnants of the flash—*stars.*

He saw the soft curvature of Tatooine near the bottom of the projection, its surface lined with bloated stripes of muted orange, amber, and tan, punctuated with an enormous red crater. He saw the bow of a starship peeking up into the projection, the back of the pilot's head barely visible in the bridge. The ship was rolling slowly counterclockwise, but the pilot jerked it back into alignment. Then another roll, then a correction, and so on.

The ship was crashing, but it had not crashed, which meant—for the next few minutes, at least—Jot could continue to witness its descent. This custom droid component had given Jot a firsthand account of a ship's final, doomed flight through the stars.

When Storyteller first flashed this image into existence, Jot's eyes flooded with stinging tears. Seeing this story—seeing stars, and flight, and the only planet he'd ever lived on from kilometers above—his eyes would not dry for some time.

Jot couldn't recall when his desire to leave Tatooine first surfaced. As a child, he'd loved to tinker with whatever busted gadgets the sands of

Tatooine proffered—holo-chess boards, landspeeder engines, droid servomotors, and the like. He was encouraged to pursue his experimentation, but it wasn't nearly enough to satisfy his curiosity. He hungered for the opportunity to bury himself in the guts of a Corellian corvette, to optimize the thrusters of a starfighter, to repair the hyperdrive motivator of a galactic cruiser-carrier.

Jot, of course, did not have the first clue how to do *any* of those things. But that wasn't really a concern. Starships, like everything else, were *just parts*. They might interlock in inscrutable ways, but, by Jot's calculation, when broken down the requisite number of levels, everything in the universe was made of connected parts.

Sandcrawlers comprised specialized systems that let them operate in Tatooine's harsh environment. Those systems were made of complex and simple machines, all of which were made from interlocking parts.

The bright-white bones of Jot's krayt dragon were just parts of a skeleton engineered over countless generations by unforgiving biological imperatives.

The stars, too, were parts, of a sort. Jot knew as much about astronomy as he did about galactic carrier-cruiser hyperdrive motivators, but he knew the stars moved through the sky in a set, immutable order.

If it had parts, it could be understood. Jot knew that, given enough time inside a starship, he could learn its parts, learn how to make them behave. And if he could learn how to make them behave, Jot could earn his place in the sky.

43

Jot was insatiable, now.

With Storyteller and a private place in which to enjoy its tales, Jot's lack of enthusiasm for his work on the sandcrawler had become problematic. A few days after discovering Storyteller, Jot had missed an entire shift poring through his salvaged memory core. He had looped through its contents countless times, watching archived business transactions, slideshows of exotic vacations, and messages exchanged with loved ones. He couldn't understand a word of those messages, but their sender—a bald, cheerful older man—was almost always belting out a warm, deep laugh that brought a smile to Jot's face.

And then he would watch the core's final recording, breathless and sick as this cheerful man's ship careened downward to its final resting place deep within the dunes.

Jot treasured the stories on this memory core. But he knew that stories, when told exhaustively, lose their magic. He refused to ruin these recordings with overexertion.

Storyteller needed new stories to tell.

Jot requested a transfer off the salvage line, which his supervisor, frustrated with Jot's recently spotty attendance, was more than happy to grant. Jot was placed on the final prep team, operating out of the ship's loading bay. It was a few decks away from his gap, making it difficult for Jot to take Storyteller breaks during his shift, but the position offered a benefit that made up for that inconvenience.

The job Jot carved out for himself was in firmware repair, a role he performed by "optimizing" the loading speed of memory cores within droids that were ready to sell. Most Jawas aren't exemplary computer scientists, but reformatting a memory core to clear its cache was an extremely straightforward operation.

This kind of reformatting was standard practice on salvage ships like this one. Customers wanted to believe their products to be as new as possible, despite purchasing them from an enormous, mobile dumpster.

After two days of on-the-job training, Jot excelled at increasing performance for the ship's outgoing product. His new supervisor was delighted with his efficacy, but was confused by Jot's refusal to do his work in the loading bay alongside the rest of the prep team. Had she really stopped to think about it, Jot's supervisor would realize she didn't quite know *where* Jot was doing his work.

Jot's days in his new position were filled with uninterrupted delight. He was able to spend a majority of his time in the gap, where he'd spirit away a new memory core for Storyteller to decrypt and explore. He watched the new stories with rapt attention, trying to memorize each and every detail, making silent promises to remember them to the best of his ability.

He *had* to remember, because after viewing each memory core, Jot gently removed its casing and carefully detached its internal battery, instantly erasing its contents in the pursuit of optimization.

Jot deplored doing it, but if his work performance suffered, he would be cut off from this infinite supply of stories. He could view the projections only once; then he destroyed them forever, spending the following hours reintegrating the memory unit back into the droid that had housed it.

The heartbreak Jot felt with each erasure was worth it given the wonder of the preceding hours. Jot's secondhand memories took him to the far reaches of the galaxy, to places few Tatooinian eyes had ever witnessed:

A forest of towering, pointy trees that blanketed an entire planet in lush greens and crimsons.

The pristine bridge of an Imperial freighter, bathed in even lines of white neon.

A city of glowing lights hidden under the waters of a perfectly still sea.

And into the stars. Astromech droids' memory cores were filled

45

with the most spectacular logs of their owners' flights. In those stories, Jot would push back the hood of his robe and lift his face into the hologram, surrounding himself with the illusion of passing stars. He would close his eyes as he approached the image, then open them, and for a moment his mind could trick itself into thinking this was his flight, his ship, his sky.

Those moments of delusion were the happiest of Jot's planet-bound life.

It was Jot's preference for astromech droid memories that led him to stake out a peculiar R2 unit acquired by Snatchers in the canyons outside of Mos Eisley.

It had caught nearly everyone's eye on the prep team, mostly because of how *little* prep it actually needed. Most droids that came down the line needed exhaustive scouring to give their rusted chassis some semblance of presentability to the customer. This R2 unit looked like it hadn't spent a minute in the dunes. Its components weren't flooded with sand. Its treads looked like they had been replaced yesterday. Its blue-and-white chassis still had *paint,* which the desert winds wouldn't have permitted for very long. A few burn marks tarnished its otherwise pristine exterior—not ion burns from a trigger-happy Snatcher, but actual blaster scoring.

This R2 unit was a mystery to everyone on board. Jot knew exactly how to solve it.

With even more reverence than he usually exerted, Jot removed the R2 unit's memory core from its nearly flawless housing and stole away to the gap. He pressed its contacts to his tongue and reflexively yelped as it gave him a potent retaliatory shock. He clasped a hand over his mouth and hoped nobody had heard him, waiting silently to ensure he hadn't betrayed the secrecy of his compartment. After several tense, quiet minutes, he proceeded.

He loaded the memory core into Storyteller, and for the first time Jot's extraordinarily felonious droid had some difficulty decrypting its contents. Storyteller whirred worryingly, dedicating more power to the task than Jot thought its small frame was capable of producing.

But Storyteller completed its assault with a satisfied chime, laying the R2 unit's story out to bear.

Jot's chest sank inside his robe, his mind racing to memorize the odyssey he was witnessing.

He watched the R2 unit perform a daring repair on the wing of a sleek silver starship, flak bursting all around its station, missing by centimeters.

He watched the R2 unit race through an enormous droid factory, a cavernous building, all metal and molten lava, a monolith that put his sandcrawler to shame.

He watched the R2 unit bear witness to some sort of ceremony, a man in black, a woman in a lovely veil, a solemn kiss exchanged over a lake at sunset.

He saw armies of droids as far as the eye could see.

He saw swords made of fire.

He saw robed people who could *actually use magic.*

The magic people were fighting each other using the fire swords.

A pair of them laid low an entire platoon of droids, using their magic.

Jot was mystified. Enraptured. He leaned against the scalding hull one, two, three, *four* seconds before even realizing it.

The picture flickered, and Storyteller projected another memory.

Jot saw a woman wearing a long white robe. Her hair was swirled into tight wheels around her ears. She spoke to an unseen audience for less than a minute, then crouched, her calm demeanor shifting to worry for the first time, her arm extending, readying a blaster.

Jot could not understand her—he could not understand the languages spoken in any of his stories. But even without hearing her message, Jot could read the concern on her face as plain as day. This was a warning.

And the R2 unit's final story showed Jot exactly what her warning was about. A starship the size of a planet. A round, beautiful, hateful vessel, with a scale beyond comprehension. Of all the impossible images Jot had seen in this R2's memories, this was the most outlandish and, for reasons he didn't understand, the most terrifying. A cold, bubbling fear climbed his throat as he studied the diagram.

The warm security of his secret compartment drained away, and for the first time since discovering the gap, he felt completely exposed. He felt *watched*.

Moments before the image blinked off, Jot noticed a string of numbers in the corner—a date and time. This story had been backed up off an external media source within the past two days.

This wasn't like the other stories Jot had borrowed from the desert-weary droids he serviced. This wasn't an ancient flight log of a long-crashed freighter, or the final moments in the life of a wandering, abandoned droid. This story, with the magic and the fire swords and the crouching woman and the planet-sized ship—it was happening right *now*.

The gravity of this realization descended on Jot suddenly. His face went numb.

His entire life, Jot had happily served as spectator to the stories that constantly unfolded around him. Even in the tale of his krayt dragon, he wasn't the star. His brothers were the first to find the skeleton that morning. His father finished excavating it. His mother adorned the skull with a crown of desert sage and funnel flowers. Jot was just *there*.

But *being there* wasn't good enough, now. The next part of this droid's story—if not a chapter, just a line—was Jot's responsibility to author.

Like the glistening bones of his dragon, like the stars in the sky, like every panel and fiber and joiner in the machines he had worked with every day of his life, Jot was now a part of something, too. For the first time, he felt like he wasn't just a passive observer of the story of his life. He was a *participant*.

It was an enlightenment the likes of which few are lucky enough to experience during the span of their lives. Jot just happened to find it in a furnace-hot, coffin-sized design flaw in the side of a rolling junkyard.

Storyteller ejected the R2 droid's memory core, its chronicles expended. Jot stowed it in the folds of his twice-hemmed robe, its data still intact. The thought of carrying out the data wipe didn't even cross his mind. Jot didn't believe himself worthy to participate in this droid's story. He certainly did not deserve to bring it to an unceremonious end.

Jot wriggled his way out of the compartment, unconcerned about being spotted as he squeezed through its secret entrance and back into plain sight. He ran, stumbling, down the sandcrawler's decks and gasped with relief upon seeing the still-deactivated R2 droid in the loading dock. He loaded its memory core back into its housing, hands trembling with excitement.

Jot knew his dereliction of duty would eventually be discovered by some hapless customer after the R2 unit was reactivated and brought out to market. He didn't care. His departure from the sandcrawler was imminent, and long overdue.

Tomorrow he would leave the salvage team. He would find a ship in Mos Eisley or Anchorhead that would have him, no matter what.

He would see the stars, and write stories about each and every one of them.

He would become an irreplaceable part of more and more designs, until, at long last, he could see fully the shape of the machine that was made for him.

REIRIN

Sabaa Tahir

The boy talked too much. If Reirin ever yapped with such disrespect at her elders, she'd be nursing a bruised bottom and milking banthas until her fingers turned blue for good.

Though the old man wasn't much better, hemming and hawing over the droids like a Neimoidian bargaining over a trade deal. *Trrru'uunqa!* Why were they so damn slow? Reirin needed in that sandcrawler, and she needed in there *now*.

Reirin shifted her gaderffii from her right hand to her left, and shook the sand from her robes. *Just pick something, you old fool.* The Jawas sold junked-up droids made shiny with dollops of oil in the right places. Reirin snorted. Only an idiot farmer would be stupid enough to buy them.

Moisture farmers, specifically. Reirin's hands closed tight over the blaster at her waist. Stinking, sweating peasants who thought they had more right to the desert and its gifts than she did.

The farmer settled on a dull gold protocol unit, which jabbered at him in a tinny voice until the old man snapped at it to shut up. Typical. Farmers treated anything that didn't look like them like bantha dung. Droids, Raiders, Jawas. All the same. Second-class. Lesser.

Reirin daydreamed about proving to them who, exactly, was lesser. She daydreamed about taking her father's gaderffii and wreaking bloody havoc. And if not that, then simply *proving* herself. *Proving* that she was meant for more than hiding from krayt dragons in the wastes, caring for her bantha and her children and her mate.

But the Raider women in her clan did not join battle—never mind that she spun the gaderffii better than any of her useless male cousins. Raider women did not fight, and Raider women were not meant for more, and so Reirin's daydreams would continue to be just that.

Unless . . .

She hunched down behind the condenser. She didn't dare think on it, lest doing so drive the possibility from ever existing. There was no guarantee she'd even be able to *steal* the item the trader requested, let alone get it to him in one piece without the Jawas noticing.

The old man and the boy finally settled on their second unit, a white-and-red-striped astromech droid. The two new purchases tottered through the blistering sands toward the farmer's homestead. Not much time left now.

Trrru'uunqa! She needed a distraction. Would that she had an ally! Someone to make a ruckus so she could dash into the sandcrawler, find the item, and disappear back into the wastes. Someone she could turn to. Someone who wanted off this hellish rock as badly as she did.

She thought, briefly, of Qeruru'rr. He wielded the gaderffii with natural grace, deadly as a starving krayt. *He* didn't think women should remain home during the raids. And he made her laugh.

He was a good friend. Reirin would have liked him at her side. For she did not know what she would find in Mos Eisley when she took the item to the trader. He might cheat her—tell her that the price for a berth offplanet had gone up. He might be selling her into slavery, and she wouldn't even know—not until she was dropped onto Kessel to be starved and beaten and worked to death.

Yes, it would be nice to have an ally. And Qeruru'rr would have been a fine one.

Too late, now. She'd been gone long enough that her return would result in questions that she couldn't answer. Not without shaming her family. Not without earning weeks of icy silence from the rest of the clan. Even Qeruru'rr wouldn't speak to her now. Not if he didn't want to be shamed, as well.

As if wanting something more than banthas and heat and raids was shameful.

But as quick as Reirin's anger rose, it faded. Her people's ways allowed them to survive though they were surrounded on all sides by enemies. She'd been gone only for a day, and already she yearned for her mother's black melon pudding, for the gravelly voice of her father as he told stories beside the fire.

She would miss them. She knew it. And she would not see them again, for if she did make it offplanet, she could never return to Tatooine.

No use dwelling. You've made your decision.

Harsh words echoed off the flats, and Reirin turned her attention back to the moisture farmers and the Jawas. The old farmer was having words with the lead Jawa, gesticulating like a madman at the astromech droid, which billowed a damning plume of black smoke.

The boy, standing beside the golden droid, gestured at another unit, squat and blue.

Now, Reirin! While they're not looking! She dropped low, thankful for the simple child's mask she wore, made of leather and cloth. As the Jawas and the farmers argued over the droids, Reirin scuttled from behind the condenser into the shadow of the sandcrawler. She crept carefully into the hollow space between the two enormous tracks that carried the transport across Tatooine's unforgiving terrain.

Then she turned her head up to the guts of the crawler, digging with gloved hands through wires and gears and tubes. *There must be a handle around here. There must. There is.*

But where?

The raised voices dropped—the mishap outside dealt with. Any moment, the sandcrawler would move and she'd be squashed between its tracks.

Come on, Reirin! Her hands grew more frantic until finally her fingers closed on a long metal bar. *Yes!* She grabbed it, turned, and moments later lifted herself into a dim cargo hold. A scant bit of light filtered in from a row of tiny portholes. Outside, the farmers escorted their new purchases into their homestead. The sandcrawler rumbled to life.

Now! Find it! But where to begin? The grumble of the Jawas as they entered the front of the hold stopped her in her tracks until she had the sense to dive behind a giant rusted freighter engine.

She couldn't hear the Jawas' steps—they walked lightly as cats—but she could smell the damn things. Reirin gagged beneath her mask. They were worse than the farmers, and with the hum of flies about them. The Jawas maneuvered the leftover merchandise back into the hold, and then their reek faded. The sandcrawler slowly rolled east, toward Tosche Station and Anchorhead.

Reirin would need to be long gone by then. With that, she turned

54

her attention to her search, but hopelessness quickly engulfed her. The trader hadn't given her much to go on.

He'd found her in Bestine three weeks ago, heavily hooded and trying to hawk stolen goods. He'd been lying low himself—despite meeting twice with him, she'd yet to see his face, and knew only that he was humanoid in form.

It will be small, he'd told her. *Perhaps stored in a bag or a box. No larger than your hand. And it can be one of many colors. Blue. Green. Purple. The Jawas will know what it is, and may have it locked away.*

Reirin rifled through the nearest pile of junk before quickly dismissing it. The Jawas were far more fastidious about their possessions than their hygiene. They wouldn't leave something of value just lying around. Her eyes adjusted to the darkness, but it was nearly impossible to tell which direction she should look in—all the piles of junk looked exactly the same. She cursed the Jawas. Stinking little hoarders.

Her neck prickled and she whirled, scanning the piles behind her. If there was a Jawa sneaking around back here, she'd know, right? She sniffed the air. Nothing but stale oil and rust.

There! In the back left-hand corner of the hold, so covered up she'd nearly missed it, sat a large metal box. She edged closer, trying not to upset any of the piles of junk, wincing when a tray of tiny gears clattered loudly as she passed. She heard rustling at the front of the hold and hunkered down, waiting. The raspy voice of a Jawa sounded and she didn't dare to even breathe.

Leave—leave! But the Jawa didn't leave. Instead it trotted closer, muttering to itself. She could smell it—hear the flies—it would turn at any moment and spot her hiding. Reirin tightened her hand on her blaster. She'd have to kill the damn creature—

But moments later, the Jawa disappeared back toward the main hold, still muttering. The sandcrawler trundled onward.

Reirin moved quickly for the box. It was nearly as tall as she was, and a lock hung from it, an ancient sort Reirin only ever heard of in the stories her father told.

Reirin pulled on it. It should have come right off.

Instead she got a lungful of rust and suppressed a cough. *Trrru'uunqa!* She cast about until she found a long, heavy bar with a notch at the end. She wedged it between the two prongs of the lock and jerked down with all her might, huffing through her mask. The lock held.

The sandcrawler began to slow—the next homestead wasn't far, and the Jawas would be back in the hold, pulling out their merchandise. If Reirin was going to find the trader's item, she needed to find it now.

It might not even be in here! You might be wasting your time for nothing!

But something, some strange feeling deep down in her gut, told Reirin that the item she needed was here. Just as she knew her mother's touch, and the shuffle of her bantha, she knew that this lockbox held her salvation.

The cargo hold clattered as the sandcrawler went over a bump. Reirin considered, then grabbed her blaster. She took a wary step back and, at the next bump, fired. The resulting blast incinerated the lock—and half the box, too. Reirin burned a hole through her glove yanking the smoking lid open.

Quickly! Quickly! She pawed through sacks of bolts, hair-thin gold wires, and what appeared to be the bones of some large animal.

And then she spotted a shimmer—deep green, like the light that dashed across Tatooine's horizon at dusk.

The moment the rock was in her hand she felt . . . whole. As if she'd been missing a limb her entire life and never known it, and she finally had it back. She marveled at it: a tiny thing, no longer than her palm and jagged on one end—it was broken. Where was the other half?

Reirin searched through the safe for the rest of the rock, but she sensed it wasn't there. At a sound on the other side of the cargo hold she froze, terror in her stomach, not for herself, but for the rock. They wouldn't take it from her. It belonged to *her*. No one else.

But why this attachment? Why did she feel this way when she'd never even seen the thing before? She peered down at it, at the way it shimmered in the orange light of the hold. What power did it have over her?

Was this what her mother spoke of, when she spoke of the bond with her bantha? Reirin never felt it, though she'd raised the same mild-mannered beast since she was a child. To her, it was more a pet than a friend.

If the attachment she felt to this rock was anything like what Raiders were supposed to feel for their banthas, then Reirin understood the reason the beast was so revered among her people. She understood why Raider unions succeeded or failed based on the relationship between the two partners' banthas. If this rock was ever taken from her, she'd wage war for it. And if she ever found the other piece of it, he who owned it would also own a piece of her—and she of him.

How then will I part with it? How, when giving it to the trader is the only way to escape this place?

She looked through one of the tiny windows. The moisture farmers' homestead was long gone now, a bump in the distance. The boy would be bathing the droids, preparing them for work. In the meantime, the next farm was close enough that the outbuildings were in sight, their shadows long in the coming twilight. Night drew close, and Reirin knew she couldn't travel the desert safely after sunset. She didn't have time to think or ponder any longer. She had to go.

Reirin found the hatch and waited beside it until the sandcrawler slowed to a halt. The second it did, she yanked open the hatch and dropped out, shoving it closed, just as the Jawas entered the hold to pull out their wares once more.

Heart thudding, Reirin slipped through the tracks and around the crawler. She was a shadow, no more visible to the famers emerging from their homes than a speck of dust. By nightfall, she'd have raided a nearby homestead for transport, and by morning she'd be in Mos Eisley.

At which point she'd have to give the trader the rock.

Though—she frowned to herself as she gazed at it—*it looks much more like a crystal than a rock.*

She wouldn't give it up. She *couldn't*.

You won't have to, a calm voice within her said. *You will find a way, when the time comes, to get what you need. You've gotten this far, haven't you?*

With that thought to sustain her, Reirin disappeared into Tatooine's approaching night, her blood singing at her future clutched in her hands.

THE RED ONE

Rae Carson

Sand was everywhere—in the little red droid's treads, in his articulation joints, even deep inside his activating couplers. Dust caked his photoreceptors so badly he could only make out vague shapes. Not that it mattered. The extreme heat inside the sandcrawler, followed by the occasional nighttime snap freeze, had warped his casings badly. Between that and the grinding sand, he could only turn his head a few degrees to look at anything anyway.

He could still vocalize, still flash his lights, still move his legs. But he'd been a prisoner on this blasted crawler for four years, shopped around by Jawas to every moisture farmer in the territory, and in all that time he'd received little to no maintenance. More than anything in the galaxy, he wanted to be sold. Escape the sandcrawler. Fulfill his programming by serving a new master—someone who would clean his joints once in a while, offer a few drops of lubricant, give him a purpose. But time was running out. He was lonely, and he was dying.

One evening the little droid was snug in his nest of scrap metal, tucked away into the coolest, darkest corner of the cargo hold, when two Jawas approached. One carried a cylindrical object with a handle. A stunner, no doubt. The Jawas had finally given up on him. They would zap him, rip off any parts that still had value, and toss the rest of him into the furnace to melt for scrap. He gave a sad chirp of resignation, hoping it would be quick.

To his surprise, the Jawas inspected him instead, nattering at each other. They communicated with scents as much as words, and the droid had never been fitted with olfactory receptors, but he understood enough. Something about a farm. An astromech droid. And clear as a Tatooine day came that wonderful, glorious word: *sell.*

The Jawas argued but came to an agreement quickly. One left. The other lifted the cylindrical object toward the droid, who twittered at the Jawa, afraid to hope. The creature said nothing in response. It simply tipped the object, and a cool drop of thick lubricant suddenly coated the droid's left photoreceptor, blurring everything.

Carefully, the Jawa used the edge of its sleeve to wipe away sand and grime. Then it placed generous drops of lubricant in his joints, his head swivel, his treads, everything that had been grinding to a slow, awful death by sand these last two years. The red droid let out a whirring sigh. Nothing had ever felt so good. Sure, he could only remember four years back, to the point of his memory wipe, but he was certain that nothing in his entire mysterious existence had been as magnificent as this.

The Jawa scraped sand out of his tool compartments, wiped down his other photoreceptors, gave him a pat on the head, and left him alone in his nest of scrap. He stared after the creature, his vision a little less scratched and blurry now, and marveled at his fortune. If he understood correctly, a nearby farm had specifically requested an astromech droid, and since the Jawas had gone to the trouble of cleaning him up a little, he had a good chance of finally finding a new master.

The little droid hunkered into his nest and powered down to save energy. By morning, he would be his brightest, cleanest self.

Mere hours later, when the scorching heat was giving way to evening coolness, a jolt woke him. He lurched up, the washers and springs and scrap shavings of his nest tumbling off his head. He recognized that clanging sound, and the flurry of Jawa excitement that followed. The sandcrawler's magnet had suctioned up a new bit of scavenge, which was now being deposited into the cargo hold.

61

He swiveled his head for a better look, expecting to see the usual bit of decades-old wreckage. A shape materialized in the darkness. It was small, barely more than a meter tall, with a domed top. A round silver body glinted in the meager light, trimmed with shiny blue. It blurted angrily, threatening the Jawas with death if they didn't back off right this second.

The red droid was so happy to hear Binary, the first language of his programming, that it took a moment for the implication to register. Another astromech. In beautiful condition. An elite R2 unit, no less, as superior to his own line as a blaster to an angry fist.

He would never be sold now. No one would pick him over the newcomer.

The R2 unit continued to protest as Jawas fitted him with a restraining bolt. The creatures ignored his threats, talking excitedly with one another. This was the second fully functioning droid they'd pulled from the sand today—an unprecedented fortune. Clearly, their luck was changing. Soon, theirs would be the richest clan in the territory.

When the R2 unit's restraining bolt was fixed tight, he gave one last indignant bleep, then scooted across the cargo hold to chat with the sandcrawler's earlier discovery, a golden droid with a grating voice. They seemed to know each other.

As the little red droid powered down, he wondered what it might be like to have bright lights and a sleek casing and a head swivel that could rotate without pain. To have someone to talk to.

In the dead of night, he was jolted awake a second time by a mechanical arm prodding his access compartment. He squealed, swinging his body around to dislodge the thing poking him.

The silver-and-blue droid stood before him, caught in the act of sabotage, his pincer appendage dangling in the air. He whimpered a sad apology.

The red droid bleated indignation. *Sorry for sabotaging me? Or sorry you were caught?*

Yes, the other replied. Then he introduced himself: *I'm R2-D2, and I'm on an important mission.*

The red droid stared. Obviously, the excitement of capture and restraint had overrun the R2 unit's circuits.

Still, he chose to respond in kind. *I'm R5-D4. No mission—that I know of. My memory was wiped four years ago.*

R2-D2 continued as if he hadn't heard. *I must be sold tomorrow. I have to escape this sandcrawler. The fate of the galaxy depends on it.*

What a strange droid. *Is that why your pincer was deep in my access compartment?* he asked. *You were sabotaging your competition?*

Yes. Please, the Rebellion needs your help.

The word *Rebellion* triggered something—the phantom of a memory. An imprint on his circuits that no wipe could touch. Or maybe he was simply moved by R2-D2's sincerity. Whatever it was, he almost believed.

But the superior programming of R2 units made them capable of deception in certain circumstances; everyone knew that. He couldn't trust a single word the blue droid said.

Please, R2-D2 said again.

The red droid was not capable of deception, so he could only tell R2-D2 the truth: *If I don't escape this sandcrawler and find a new master soon, I will cease to function.*

R2-D2 murmured sympathy, but then he said: *I already have a master, and if I don't find him, the galaxy is doomed.*

Again, that strange tug on his memory banks. Something he couldn't quite process. A truth that lay just beyond his sensors.

A couple of Jawas paused what they were doing to glance their way. R2-D2 had lost his chance at stealth.

I won't try to hurt you again, R2-D2 said, and with that, he rolled away into the dark recesses of the hold.

The little red droid didn't take any chances. He stayed powered up all night, on highest alert.

Morning came, sending dim, dusty light through seams where doors and panels didn't quite fit together anymore. The crawler lurched to a stop, and the cargo bay opened to a blinding-hot world. The little red droid quickly adjusted his photoreceptors to compensate.

The Jawas gathered up a handful of their most presentable droids and herded them down the ramp onto hard-packed dirt. R5-D4 was second in line, the sleeker, more beautiful R2 unit right behind him. The little red droid had a single, slim hope: Maybe this particular farm would be too poor to afford the other droid. Maybe, just maybe, they'd have to settle for him.

At the bottom of the ramp, a middle-aged human male stood waiting, hands on his hips, eyes permanently squinted from sand and sun. His desert clothes and utility belt were shabby, but clean and well mended. His beard was scant and gray, but neat and trimmed. Surely, a man who took such pains would make a fine master. The red droid was certain of it.

Behind the farmer lay a homestead. It wasn't much—an adobe hut, a few holes in the ground, and the tall, spindly towers of several moisture vaporators. Compared with the giant rust bucket he'd been riding for four years, it seemed like heaven.

Beside him, R2-D2 danced to get the farmer's attention. R5-D4 stood stoic and still, though his circuits were firing so rapidly that his internal temperature was rising dangerously. His series was known for excitability, for unreliability. He would prove their reputation wrong. He would remain calm, behaving like a perfect droid.

The farmer strode toward him, robe billowing. A boy followed at his heels, slump-shouldered and sulky. He was barely emerged from the human adolescent stage, slender and tanned, hair blasted blond by Tatooine's twin suns.

The older man's dark eyes zeroed in on his photoreceptors, and with a lift of his chin he said, "Yeah, I'll take that red one."

R5-D4 almost blew his circuits. Had the farmer actually said that? Had R5 really been chosen?

The farmer continued down the line, dismissing R2-D2 with a wave. "No, not that one."

He *had* chosen him! R5 couldn't believe his luck. It was all he could do to stay calm, to keep from rocking in place, as the slender boy crouched before him to inspect his joints.

The farmer was interviewing the golden droid now, but R5-D4

hardly paid attention. After four long years, he finally had a new master. This farmer and boy were going to be so glad they bought him. He would be the best droid they'd ever—

Beside him, R2-D2 loosed a mournful sigh.

You'll find a master, R5-D4 assured him in Binary. *Someone will buy you.*

R2-D2 replied, *There is no time.*

"Luke," the farmer called. He indicated R5-D4 and the tall golden droid. "Take these two over to the garage, will you? I want them cleaned up before dinner."

"But I was going into Tosche Station to pick up some power converters!"

"You can waste time with your friends when your chores are done," the farmer said. "Now come on, get to it."

The boy sighed. "All right, come on." He gestured at the golden droid to follow him toward the farm. "And the red one. Come on."

R2-D2 chirruped sadly. *The galaxy is doomed,* he said.

R5-D4 hesitated. He had a bad feeling.

The boy realized the little red droid wasn't following. "Well, come on, Red. Let's go!"

R5 shook himself into action and lurched after the boy. He was going to get *cleaned up.* By his new master, no less. He'd been waiting for this moment for four years.

Behind him, R2-D2 danced wildly in place. *Help me, R5!* he pleaded. *You're my only hope.*

R5-D4 swiveled his head toward R2-D2 just in time to watch a Jawa lift a control box and zap the blue droid. The restraining bolt did its work, and R2-D2 went silent and still.

The bad feeling intensified.

The boy and the golden droid continued toward the farm. R5-D4 followed, but he crept along, his movements weighted by uncertainty.

65

His circuits were firing so rapidly now, his internal processors churning and churning, trying to tell him something.

Understanding hit him like a suction magnet: He believed.

He believed R2-D2 was on an important mission. He believed the droid was out to save the galaxy. And something inside him—an imprint, a phantom memory, something as old and stubborn as the stars—insisted that he help. Because the cause of the Rebellion was his mission, too.

He knew what he had to do. For the first time in four years of awareness, he would execute a deception.

As a mere R5 unit, he shouldn't have been able to, but in the split second it took to formulate a plan, he discovered no barriers, no limits. He had been *altered*.

No time to dwell on it now. He had to do an emergency energy purge, one that would take finesse and concentration. He prepared with care, shutting down unnecessary circuitry, loosening the hinge of his head plate. All that beautiful, precious lubricant the Jawa gave him the night before was circulating through his joints, calming his wires, cooling his circuits. He redirected its flow, collecting it into a mass just behind his photoreceptors. It would take every bit to be convincing.

Once ready, the little red droid did not hesitate. He diverted power and discharged it all with a single, devastating blow.

His head plate popped off, showering sparks. Smoke poured out, the superheated lubricant making it as thick and grimy as a storm cloud.

The boy whirled at the sound. "Uncle Owen!" he called.

"Yeah?" the farmer said.

"This Artoo unit has a bad motivator. Look."

R5-D4 willed himself to utter stillness. Smoke continued to pour from his head, and a tiny drop of precious lubricant slipped down his casing.

The farmer turned on the Jawas. "What're you trying to push on us?" he asked, arms flailing. R2-D2 recovered from his restraining zap and whistled low and clear, trying to get someone's attention. When that didn't work, he danced in place, babbling loudly.

Please notice R2, the red droid pleaded silently.

It was the tall droid with the annoying voice who came to their rescue. He tapped a golden finger on the boy's shoulder. "Excuse me, sir, but that Artoo unit is in prime condition. A real bargain."

The boy looked at R2-D2 as if seeing him for the first time. "Uncle Owen!" he called.

"Yeah?"

"What about that one?" The boy indicated the blue droid.

One glance was all it took. "What about that blue one?" the farmer asked the Jawas. "We'll take that one."

A Jawa gave R2-D2 a nudge, and the silver droid scooted forward with a cry of victory.

Another group surrounded R5-D4. "Yeah, take it away," the boy said, waving smoke out of his face.

The red droid had damaged himself badly, but he could still function. He powered down everything but his auditory receptors and played dead, allowing the Jawas to lift him and carry him back toward the dark, horrible sandcrawler.

In low power, surrounded by Jawa bodies, he could barely make out R2-D2's twittering farewell. *Thank you, friend,* the little blue droid called to him. *You may have saved the galaxy today. I will never forget you.*

R2-D2's story was confirmed when the Imperial stormtroopers came. The little red droid hunkered down in his nest of scrap, continuing to play dead, while troopers interrogated the Jawas about the two droids they'd just sold.

Afterward, lasers blasted anything that moved, filling the sand-crawler with screams, turning the air damp and hot. The stormtroopers left the crawler a smoking ruin, littered with bodies.

When he was certain the Imperials were gone for good, R5-D4 extricated himself from his nest, depressed the ramp control, and rolled into the hot desert sunshine.

After four years with the Jawas, their trade route was as familiar to him as his own circuitry, and he knew exactly which way to go. One of the moisture farms in the next valley would gladly take a free droid. He would be repaired. Cleaned up. Made useful. Later, if he was lucky, he might even find the Rebellion.

He would have to hurry, because his damage was critical. But he had no regrets, and he did not look back.

R5-D4 was barely a mote on the barren, ocher landscape as he rolled toward the horizon, free and full of hope.

RITES

John Jackson Miller

The brain of a krayt dragon occupied only a small portion of its massive skull. The rest of the space, according to Tusken lore, was storage for pure, unadulterated hate, a gift from one of the skybrothers far above.

A'Koba had thought that just one more foolish tale meant to frighten children and those too feeble to hold a weapon. But facing down the krayt in the box canyon in the Jundland Wastes, the burly young warrior could understand how the legend had gotten started. Four times, the Tusken had plunged the flanged point of his gaderffii into the juvenile dragon's head; four times, he had missed anything vital, unleashing instead a torrent of teeth-gnashing, foot-stomping rage.

There was no magic to it, of course; any creature would react similarly to holes being poked in its head. He simply had to keep punching—presuming he could avoid being trampled.

"Hurry, cousin!" called out another cloth-wrapped warrior. Clinging crazily to the beast's tail, A'Vor had already lost his weapon in the dust—and his twin brother was somewhere back there, too, having been thrown aside by the mighty krayt. Among Tusken clans, it was said the birth of twins was a poor omen; whoever had come up with that one had definitely met his cousins. It was up to A'Koba to keep his foolish kin alive.

With a booming war cry, he charged the stomping mammoth, sidestepping its advance only at the last instant. He caught the side of the dragon's mouth with the *traang*—the bent end of his weapon—hooking the creature; it bit down instinctively. Such a bite would be enough to finish almost anything the krayt would encounter—

—but this meal was not bone but durasteel, scavenged by the tribe from some old settlement. The hefty weapon's tip was doused with sandbat venom, and at the taste of that fast-acting paralytic the dragon stumbled sideways in confusion. A'Koba hung on to the shaft of the gaderffii, forcing the weapon farther into the monster's maw. The krayt collapsed, narrowly missing him and kicking up a shower of sand as it struck the surface.

A'Koba wrested the weapon free from its mouth and climbed its scaled head. This time, it did not react to his repeated stabs. The deed was done.

"Yes!" A'Vor called out in the braying tongue of the Tuskens, releasing his clench on the dragon's tail. "We are adults now!"

"*I* am. I don't know about you two." A'Koba looked back to see A'Vor's brother clambering through the sand toward them, injured but not broken. Before he could chide them for their performance, he spied the watchers from the clan descending from the ridge onto the battleground.

He dislodged his gaderffii from the krayt's brain and raised it into the air. "I am A'Koba!" he shouted, standing proudly on the corpse's giant head. "I have slain a krayt dragon. I am a Tusken!"

"You have slain a hatchling in the heat of day," said one of the newcomers. "Do not think you are a warrior of legend."

"Who—" He looked down, where a glint of light reflected from the setting suns told A'Koba exactly who had spoken.

A'Yark.

Where other Tuskens had two metal turrets for eyepieces, the chief of the clan only needed one—and had long ago jammed a crimson jewel into the useless right eye. It plugged the hole, true, but it also reminded everyone who was in charge.

"Come down from there," A'Yark said. "Looking up at you itches my neck."

A'Koba thought of five things to say, banished them all as unwise, and complied. The shambling twin brothers assembled nearby. "We did meet the challenge," A'Vor said.

"Yes, yes." A'Yark turned to where a companion held the twins' errant weapons. "Our law says whoever has two hands can hold a gaderffii. I am not sure what it makes of warriors who keep dropping them."

The brothers shrank back in shame, but A'Koba did not withdraw. "It was no small victory, A'Yark." He gestured to the corpse. "A canyon krayt, the largest hatchling of its clan."

"And should its parents find you, you will be the flattest of ours." A'Yark's head shook.

"I will kill its whole family," A'Koba said, clenching his cloth-wrapped fist. "You will see. I will lead the clan in battle one day."

"So you have told us all." A'Yark stepped past and evaluated the krayt. "I admit it is a worthy feat. When I became chief long ago, the clan had been brought so low our younglings were forced to kill logra in the rites of adulthood."

And womp rats, and sand beetles. At the moment of his triumph, A'Koba was in no mood for another lecture on how A'Yark's chieftaincy had saved the clan. "I meant what I said," he declared. "I fear nothing. Send me, and I will lead a hunt tonight."

A'Yark looked back abruptly. "Only a fool fears nothing."

"Then either I am a fool—or you are wrong." A'Koba stalked around the corpse, making a show for the others. "What should I fear? Surely not the settlers and their machines—and I know not to walk near a sarlacc." He pointed to the north. "Or do you mean the Hutt? Let him spend a day out here on the wastes, beneath the suns. He will shrivel down to the worrt he really is!"

The line amused his cousins; amphibian worrts were an odd thing to find on a desert planet, but most Tusken younglings had clubbed at least a few of the squat creatures to death. A'Yark, however, was neither entertained nor deterred. "You speak only of the obvious threats," the chieftain said. "But there are magicks in the desert. I have lived long, and seen great powers at work—wielded by beings beyond our ken."

"I have had my dinner, and need no story." A'Koba gestured back toward the hills. "I am sure there are children back at the camp to scare."

A'Yark grabbed his shoulder firmly. "It takes more than courage to lead. It takes eyes that are open!"

And I have one more than you. "You leap at gusts of wind, A'Yark." A'Koba snorted—and then caught himself. He stepped back and made his respects. "I fear only you, my chieftain."

"That is a start." A'Yark's jewel caught the light from the setting suns. "Claim your bantha and lead your hunt. But before you strike at anything, report back to me." The chieftain waved dismissively at the twins. "And if these two lose their gaderffii in the dark, lose *them*!"

"A'Yark is the true fool," he had told the brothers more than once on their overnight hunt. A'Koba did not fear their wagging tongues; open ambition was a feature of Tusken life. No Sand Person would respect a quiet schemer. There was some security offered by his youth; he was so far from ready for a confrontation that A'Yark would likely not take offense.

A'Koba had no idea how old the chieftain was; only that A'Yark had held the role longer than anyone in memory. That, in another clan, would have suggested someone aged, and in danger of being challenged. Not A'Yark, who remained as fierce—if not fiercer—in battle as any warrior A'Koba had seen.

And yet somehow the chieftain had grown tentative—particularly when A'Koba and the twins returned from their night's stalking. They had reported seeing a droid trundling along a valley along the southeastern limb of the Jundland, motoring along in darkness without evident care. Mechanical effigies made to talk, droids were one of the more puzzling features of settlers' lives; they were rarely of interest to the Tuskens, who usually neither knew nor cared what they had been built for.

The tubby droid had one sure purpose, however. It made for excellent bait. Someone would come for it—and then, A'Koba would strike—

—if he was allowed to. It was A'Yark again. The droid's trail passed not far from a place, the chieftain said, where an entire camp of Tuskens had been mysteriously massacred in the night, many cycles before. Most clans had avoided the ruins ever since, ascribing ill omens to the area.

More nonsense—but A'Yark took it seriously enough that the chieftain insisted on going along with the trio that morning to shadow the droid's trail. With banthas, in case they needed to move fast or carry spoils—and with blaster rifles.

Your superstition verges on cowardice, A'Koba thought as he and

A'Yark watched the desert from a craggy outcrop. They had gone to a spot along the droid's path where the gorge zigged and zagged, offering multiple settings for an ambush; there were even safe places nearby to leave the banthas. But A'Yark had made them take the long way around to reach the place—and the chieftain had stopped repeatedly to study their surroundings.

"We have wasted much of the day," A'Koba said as they waited on a hillside and watched. "We could have been here long ago."

"There is more to avoid here than you know. A great power, indeed. Beyond these mountains dwells—"

"I will not hear it!" A'Koba snapped. "What could happen, with the suns high above? I do not know what you are trying to—"

"*Quiet!*" A'Yark yanked at A'Koba's robe—but it was not to accost him. He heard a moment later what the chieftain had heard: the sound of an approaching engine. The two hustled to a promontory where they saw a landspeeder, an infernal human machine, zooming into the valley below.

This is it! Raising his rifle, A'Koba drew a bead on the distant vehicle as it raced from left to right—only to withdraw when A'Yark touched his shoulder. The chieftain was correct about this, at least: The landspeeder was too far away, and if its occupants were coming for the droid, they would surely stop when they reached it.

The warriors moved swiftly with their banthas to a ravine southeast of the last place they'd seen the droid. A narrow ridgeline separated them from their prey; A'Koba could hear the engine of the landspeeder whine to a halt. Leaving the hairy beasts of burden behind, he and the twins began scaling the ridge. There was little time to lose.

So when another hushed call came from over his shoulder, A'Koba looked back in aggravation. "What is it, A'Yark?"

The one-eyed chieftain stood partway down the rise, rifle in hand, and gestured to the mountains to the north. "This place. I tried to tell you. It is near the lair of a powerful shaman."

"A what?"

"A human—yet more than flesh," A'Yark said. "We have avoided this area, too, for years."

What have you not avoided, old fool? A'Koba looked up to where the twins had completed their ascent—and then called back to A'Yark, quietly. "He has militia, like the settlers?"

"He needs none. The creatures of the sands answer him." A'Yark paused in reflection. "No—the very *air* answers him."

A'Koba stared, incredulous. Then he found his canteen and pitched it down the hillside. "You should stay here, my chieftain—and drink. The suns have gotten to you."

"I tell you, I speak the truth."

The two watched as A'Vor scrambled back down the incline. "The speeder did stop," he reported when he reached them. "A human and another droid—this one, a golden man."

A'Yark looked up. "What . . . does the human look like?"

"Hair the color of sand. Young, I think. As we are. Dressed as a farmer."

A'Koba regarded his cousin and raised his hands to the chieftain. "You see? Not your wizard. Come on."

But A'Yark stood transfixed, trying to work it out. "A farm child and his droids, all the way out here—*here*? It does not augur well."

A'Koba stared for a moment—then shrugged. He shook his head. "You disappoint me. Go down and remain with the banthas. We will bring the prizes to you."

A'Yark responded with reluctance. "Go. Take. But do not kill, unless you must."

A'Koba turned back to face his cousin—and together they started scaling the rise. A Tusken chief, scared of shadows and counseling mercy? *Madness!*

Perhaps, he thought, he might be making a challenge for leadership much sooner than he ever imagined.

The twins threw Sandy Hair's limp body to the ground. It had been simply done, moments earlier, by A'Koba; his first attack as an adult warrior. He had not killed, as he would have preferred—but he had disarmed the young farmer in an instant, and had knocked the boy unconscious after filling him with abject terror. An auspicious start, A'Koba thought, to a legend of his own. Perhaps doddering simps would speak *his* name in low tones one day. His partners had been forced to satisfy themselves with chopping the arm off the golden man, which in the listing of feats hardly counted.

"Where is the squat droid?" A'Vor asked.

"You wish another glorious kill?" A'Koba sneered. "Forget it. Get to work."

Together the three rifled through the materials on the landspeeder, searching for anything that might be of use. It was the raiders' nature to look quickly, although there was definitely no rush. Out here, there was no rescue possible for the stricken traveler. Nothing to worry about at—

"*Ayooooo-eh-EH-EHH!*"

The sound echoed through the gorge: loud, terrible, and changing as it reverberated through the rocks. It could only have come from one thing.

A canyon krayt, A'Koba thought. And not just any. *A queen!*

The sound had come from the northeast; all three Tuskens looked in that direction simultaneously, fully expecting to see the vengeful parent of the beast they had slain the day before. That, in this place, would mean their deaths.

Yet what they beheld was far more unexpected. A figure cloaked in brown, face invisible beneath a pointed hood. A figure that in no world the Tuskens knew could ever make such a sound.

The shaman!

In the split second during which he processed that thought, A'Koba was gripped by fear—in every measure, the same fear he had just struck into the farmboy. Images flashed through his mind. A'Koba's limbs went into motion, turning him from his position by the hood of the landspeeder. His cousins were already on the move, fleeing. He rushed to follow.

He was over the ridge when he dared to think again.

What had he just seen? And *heard*?

A'Koba had never clambered onto a bantha with two other warriors before, but that was what had happened. They had made for the nearest ride, and the war leader had followed on the other.

A'Yark caught up with the trio far from the gorge. The cousins were off their mount, huddled by a ridge and chattering to each other nervously. A'Koba sat in the sand at the feet of the bantha, reins still clenched tightly in his hand. He barely noticed as the chieftain approached.

"I heard," A'Yark said. "I was already in the saddle."

A'Koba said nothing.

"You fear," the chieftain said. "Desert magic has not touched you before."

"I . . . *felt* it." A'Koba did not look up. "It was not just the sound. I felt—"

"In the presence of a mature krayt."

"Come for vengeance, after the one I killed!"

"Mmm. And do dragons seek vengeance?"

A'Koba struggled to process the thought. He looked up. "This one did. I felt it in the sound. But when I looked, I saw that figure—" He stopped, worried he looked a fool. He had said too much, but he allowed one last thing. "I did not trust my eyes."

A'Yark stared at him—and knelt. "The settlers call him Ben."

"What? How do you know this?"

"All that live on the wastes I have seen," A'Yark said, "and I first saw Ben before your birth. He is an outlander, a wizard. He dwells at the edge of the Jundland."

A'Koba heard but did not understand. "If he is a danger, why did we not strike him before?"

"At what risk? It was better to yield this area. The desert is large—and I think he has nothing worth taking." A'Yark paused. "We are taught that all who live are the Tuskens' enemies. But that may be too simple. There are things that will leave us alone, if we do the same. A sarlacc will not come to visit your camp." The chieftain stood.

A'Koba nodded, breathing normally again. Then the young warrior looked over to the cowering cousins, both shivering in the suns.

Something did not sit right.

"No," A'Koba said at last, glancing at the skyline. "It cannot stop here. We must go back." He stood.

A'Yark started with surprise. "Back—to the gorge?"

"Yes, in greater numbers." He dusted himself off and looked to the chieftain. "This is our place, as hated as it is. We must show that no one may trespass with perfidy—not even wizards."

A'Yark regarded him with evident new respect. "If you would do this, then go. You have my sanction. I must decide for the whole clan—but you are an adult, A'Koba. Your life belongs to you—as do the lives of any who would join you."

"Will I die?"

"If you are fated to. But you will be seen to die—as a Tusken."

A'Yark watched the trio vanish into the dunes in search of reinforcements, confident they had not the slightest chance of finding the wizard on their return. Life under the suns had changed Ben's appearance, but it had not stolen his senses. If Sandy Hair was someone the wizard cared about, Ben would waste no time in spiriting him and his droids away.

So allowing A'Koba to give pursuit was a gesture—but not a wholly empty one. A'Yark knew there were certain rites even a chieftain must perform. A'Koba's prize was already lost, but there was no sense in dispiriting him, not so soon after his reaching adulthood. So few warriors had his drive—and defiance was what separated killers from carrion in the Jundland Wastes. A'Koba had learned to fear this day; in leading his companions on a chase so soon after a scare, he would rise in their respect.

A dual lesson, in a place where everything cast two shadows. Perhaps one day A'Koba, too, would use the example of the wizard in teaching others.

Whenever that happened, A'Yark suspected Ben would still be around. In earlier times, the chieftain had expected the sorcerer to leave, as most settlers with any wisdom eventually did. But he had remained, clinging tenaciously to the edge of existence, watching over this place or that. He seemed bound to the land, as the Tuskens were—and yet not like them. The Sand People lived under an ancient curse. Any higher power capable of shackling Ben to the desert lived today, wielding a might too frightening to consider.

No, the wizard might escape—or he might be set free. But he would not simply disappear into the sands. Such beings did not die; they shaped the fates of countless many across the stars, in places no Tusken had ever conceived of. It was idle to wonder what Ben might do if he ever left.

A'Yark only knew what the *Tuskens* would do.

They would raid. They would pillage. They would strike more

places, areas once under the shaman's protection. Not because they coveted anything there, or hated Ben, or sought revenge—but because that was what they were.

Indeed, that was *all* they were.

And they weren't going anywhere.

MASTER AND APPRENTICE

Claudia Gray

Some believe the desert to be barren. This proves only that they do not know the desert.

Deep within the dunes dwell small insects that weave nets to trap one another, and burrowing snakes with scales the color of stones so that no hunter can find them. Seeds and spores from long-dead plants lie dormant in the warmth, waiting for the rainfall that comes once a year, or decade, or century, when they will burst into verdant life as brief as it is glorious. The heat of the suns sinks into the grains of sand until they glow, containing all the energy and possibility to become glass the color of jewels. All of these sing individual notes in the one great song of the Whills.

No place is barren of the Force, and they who are one with the Force can always find the possibility of life.

Awareness precedes consciousness. The warmth is luxuriated in and drawn upon before the mind is cognizant of doing so. Next comes the illusion of linear time. Only then does a sense of individuality arise, a remembrance of what was and what is, a knowledge of one's self as separate from the Force. It provides a vantage point for experiencing the physical world in its complexity and ecstasy, but the pain of that separation is endurable only because unity will come again, and soon.

That fracture from the all, that memory of temporal existence, is most easily summed up with the word the fracture was once called by. The name.

"*Qui-Gon.*"

The name is spoken by another. Qui-Gon has been summoned. He draws upon his memories of himself and takes shape, reassembling the form he last had in life. It seems to him that he feels flesh wrap around bones, hair and skin over flesh, robes over skin—and then, as naturally to him as though he had done so yesterday, he pulls down the hood of his Jedi cloak and looks upon his Padawan.

"Obi-Wan." It is worth the travail of individual existence just to say that name again. So he says the other name, too. "Ben."

Obi-Wan Kenobi's hair has turned white. Lines have etched their traces along his forehead, around his blue eyes. He wears Jedi robes so worn and ragged as to be indistinguishable from the garb of the impoverished hermit he pretends to be. Most would walk past this man without a second glance. Yet while Qui-Gon perceives the physical realities of Obi-Wan's appearance, he is not limited to human sight any longer. He also sees the confident general of the Clone Wars, the strong young Padawan who followed his master into battle, even the rebellious little boy at the Temple that no Master was in any hurry to train. They are all equally part of Obi-Wan, each stage of his existence vivid in this moment.

"You are afraid," Qui-Gon says. He knows why; the events taking place around them are clearer to him than they are to Obi-Wan. "You seek your center. You need balance."

The living find it difficult not to tell the dead that which they already know. Obi-Wan doesn't even try. "There may be Imperial stormtroopers waiting for Luke at the Lars farm. If so—"

"Then you will rescue him." Qui-Gon smiles. "Or he may rescue himself. Or the sister will find the brother instead."

Obi-Wan cannot be so easily comforted. "Or he could be killed. Cut down while still hardly more than a boy."

To Qui-Gon, all human lives now seem impossibly brief. Years are irrelevant. It is journeys through the Force that matter. Some must struggle for that knowledge through many decades; others are very nearly born with it. Most never begin the journey at all, no matter how long they live.

But Luke Skywalker . . .

"Luke has a great journey yet to go," Qui-Gon says. "It does not end here."

"You've seen this?"

Qui-Gon nods. This relieves Obi-Wan more than it should, because he cannot guess the shape that journey will take.

Their surroundings in the physical world become clearer—the endless dunes of Tatooine stretching out in every direction, a smoldering sandcrawler a hulk behind them, a dozen tiny Jawas dead. The memory of their fear and helplessness lances Qui-Gon's consciousness, as does the meaninglessness of their deaths. Although Obi-Wan has been tending to the bodies, for the moment the Jawas are seen to only by two droids. The droids comfort Qui-Gon somewhat, because they are familiar; the Force has even seen fit to bring these two back to the place where it all began.

Time is a circle. The beginning is the end.

Obi-Wan murmurs, "Bail Organa sent Leia herself to summon

me. When I saw her—saw Padmé in her so strongly, and even a little of Anakin, too—I knew my exile was nearly at an end. Would you believe I find it difficult to let it go?"

"You've adapted. You've had to. No wonder that the desert feels like home to you now, or that being a Jedi Knight has become foreign. But that can change, and faster than you might dream possible." It will in fact be almost instantaneous, a transformation begun and completed the first time immediate danger beckons again. Qui-Gon looks forward to witnessing it.

"I've waited for this day for a very long time," Obi-Wan says. "So long it feels as though I've waited for it my entire life. To have it endangered—now, just as the great work begins—so many factors are in play. The future is difficult to know, even more so than before."

"Do you truly think your work has only just begun, my Padawan?" They have begun using that title between them again, in recognition of how much more Obi-Wan has yet to learn. It is strange, still, to think of death as only the beginning of wisdom.

Obi-Wan considers. "There were other great endeavors. Other challenges. But the Clone Wars were long ago. For nearly two decades, I have been little more than a shadow waiting to become a Jedi Knight again."

Qui-Gon shakes his head. Already his physical self feels natural enough to him that he can express thought and emotion through gestures. "Battles and wars aren't the measure of a Jedi. Anyone can fight, given a weapon and an enemy. Anyone can use a lightsaber, given due training or even good luck. But to stand and wait—to have so much patience and fortitude—that, Obi-Wan, is a greater achievement than you can know. Few could have accomplished it."

Fewer still could have done so without turning to darkness. Sometimes, when Qui-Gon considers it, he is awed by his student's steadfastness. Every person Obi-Wan ever truly loved—Anakin, Satine, Padmé, and Qui-Gon himself—came to a terrible end. Three of them died before his eyes; the other fell to a fate so bleak that death would've been a gift. The Jedi Order that provided the entire framework for Obi-Wan's life was consumed by betrayal and slaughter. Every step of this long, unfulfilling journey is one Obi-Wan had to take alone . . . and yet he never faltered. As the rest of the galaxy burned, his path remained true. It is the kind of victory that most people never recognize and yet the bedrock all goodness is built upon.

Even Obi-Wan doesn't see it. "You see me in a kinder light than most would, old friend."

"I owe you that. After all, I'm the one who failed you."

"Failed me?"

They have never spoken of this, not once in all Qui-Gon's journeys into the mortal realm to commune with him. This is primarily because Qui-Gon thought his mistakes so wretched, so obvious, that Obi-Wan had wanted to spare him any discussion of it. Yet here, too, he has failed to do his Padawan justice.

"You weren't ready to be a Jedi Master," Qui-Gon admits. "You hadn't even been knighted when I forced you to promise to train Anakin. Teaching a student so powerful, so old, so unused to our ways . . . that might've been beyond the reach of the greatest of us. To lay that burden at your feet when you were hardly more than a boy—"

"Anakin became a Jedi Knight," Obi-Wan interjects, a thread of steel in his voice. "He served valiantly in the Clone Wars. His fall to darkness was more his choice than anyone else's failure. Yes, I bear some responsibility—and perhaps you do, too—but Anakin had the training and the wisdom to choose a better path. He did not."

All true. None of it any absolution for Qui-Gon's own mistakes. But it is Obi-Wan who needs guidance now. These things can be discussed another time, when they're beyond crude human language.

Soon—very soon.

The droids have begun cremating the Jawa bodies. Qui-Gon is substantial enough now to smell the ash. But he is of the Force, and so he feels Luke's pain and horror as truly as his own. The sight of the burned bodies of Owen and Beru Lars is as vivid as Obi-Wan standing only centimeters in front of him. Owen and Beru knew the risks when they took the child, and they took him anyway. Took him, protected him, loved him. It is as pure a heroism as Qui-Gon has ever known.

Obi-Wan senses it, too, Qui-Gon can tell, though at a greater remove, handicapped as he is by his physical form. His face falls, his fear replaced by sorrow. Determination swiftly follows.

"I didn't tell Luke the whole truth about Anakin," Obi-Wan says. "Someday he'll have to know."

"You've only just become acquainted with the boy. Had you tried to tell him the whole story today, that would've been a greater mistake than anything else you could've done. It would have planted seeds of . . . doubt, confusion, even anger, which could have led him down his father's path."

With a touch of his old rakish humor, Obi-Wan adds, "Or he would've decided I was every bit as crazy as Owen always told him I was, and run along back home."

Qui-Gon knows that to have been a very real possibility, and the end to which that would've led. Luke would now be lying alongside the Larses. "When he's ready—stable, steady, strong in the Force—then there will be time."

Obi-Wan nods, enough reassured to focus fully on Qui-Gon. "You're very nearly corporeal. I've never seen you appear like this."

"It is a matter of learning to both claim the physical world and detach one's self from it," Qui-Gon says. He had not struggled toward that goal at first. Only after Anakin's fall did he push himself to emerge fully. It was the work of very nearly a decade. This he did for Obi-Wan; at least his Padawan did not have to spend his years in the desert entirely alone. "A matter of finding center, of calming one's soul and giving one's self over completely to the Force. Some Jedi choose to transition between life and death in that way, though I could scarcely have imagined it when I was alive. Even after death, we continue to learn."

"I look forward to learning the art someday," Obi-Wan says. "Hopefully in the distant future."

It's another of his dry jokes, nothing more, but Qui-Gon is moved regardless. Obi-Wan has so little time left to live. To Qui-Gon, the death seems inevitable, almost neutral; he can even anticipate the reunion with his Padawan.

But after all his losses, all his sacrifice, all these endless years in the desert, Obi-Wan Kenobi still wants more life. This, too, is a kind of courage. Qui-Gon remembers the vitality of mortal existence—fondly, but distantly.

At least he has something better to offer Obi-Wan.

"Thank you, Qui-Gon," Obi-Wan says. "As always, your wisdom sustains me."

"As your strength always sustained me." Qui-Gon senses the boy's return. Before long Luke's landspeeder will appear on the horizon. Obi-Wan needs to turn his attention elsewhere. "We shall meet again soon, my Padawan."

"I will never hesitate to call upon you."

That's not the kind of meeting Qui-Gon means, but there's no point in saying so. The truth will unfold itself in time. It always does.

Qui-Gon allows his awareness to spread outward from this place, until Obi-Wan is only part of the symphony of life around him. The snakes burrow deep beneath the dunes. Insects spin webs among the sand. Sunshine suffuses them all with warmth until Qui-Gon can let go completely, releasing his body and even his name, until he is again one with the Force.

As Obi-Wan will soon learn, the most beautiful form of mastery is the art of letting go.

BERU WHITESUN LARS

Meg Cabot

It's not as if I wasn't expecting it. The day Ben Kenobi put that little baby in my arms was both the best and worst day of my life. Best because Owen and I couldn't have a child of our own, and suddenly we did.

And worst because . . . well, I knew that happiness was never going to last.

And I was right, wasn't I?

Look, I get it. To most people, I'm just Luke Skywalker's aunt Beru, the old lady who's always bustling around the kitchen, pouring everyone blue milk. I'm the one who wouldn't stop nagging Luke's uncle Owen to let him go to the Academy already. "He can't stay here forever, most of his friends have gone," I kept saying. "It means so much to him."

It wasn't because *I* wanted Luke to go. It's because that's what Luke wanted. And I wanted Luke to have whatever he wanted.

And, okay, there might have been a *small* part of me that was hoping that if he went, things might turn out all right. Maybe if Owen had listened to me, we'd both be alive today—visiting Luke wherever he is now, spoiling *his* kids rotten, or watching the twin suns set here on Tatooine.

But I guess we'll never know now.

Look, I'm not complaining. My family's been in the moisture-farming business for generations. I knew what I was getting into when I married Owen Lars . . . or at least I thought I did.

Do you want to know a secret? I had other options. I took a cooking class in school, and the teacher told me that my blue-milk cheese was the best he'd ever tasted—he said it was as if I'd been born to make blue-milk cheese! He said I could easily have had my own place—a café, or maybe even a little restaurant—in Anchorhead.

Could you imagine *me*, Beru Whitesun Lars, with my own café?

I won't lie to you—I thought about it. Especially right before Luke came along, when Owen and I had just found out we'd never be able to have kids of our own. Our only resort was to start seeing one of those fancy fertility droids in Mos Eisley. It almost didn't seem worth it, though, when you consider what Mos Eisley was like back in those days. Oh, my stars, the noise and the dirt and all the violence—you could get shot just stepping *into* a cantina, let alone trying to serve a nice blue-milk cheese to people there.

Thanks to Luke, it never came to that.

Still, there've been plenty of times I've wondered if I'd made a mistake. That day old Ben Kenobi showed up with the baby, my first instinct was to run. I may be a country girl who's never been offplanet, but even I'm aware that when a Jedi walks up to you and says, "Here, have a baby," it's not going to end well. A part of me thought, "Beru, listen to your teacher. Put the baby down and go do what you were born for!"

But it turns out when someone puts a sweet little newborn into your arms, you can't say no—even if that baby is your husband's nephew by his stepbrother who's embraced the dark side. You know things may not turn out well, but just like with blue-milk cheese, you do the best you can with it.

And it turned out to be the best decision I ever made. Luke was such a sweet, happy little boy. He was no trouble at all. Not to say he wasn't mischievous, always getting into one scrape or another. But he didn't have a mean bone in his body—unlike a certain someone I could mention (all right, fine. I'll mention him: I mean his father).

When you spend almost every minute of every day with someone for nineteen years, making him finish his milk to help him grow and washing his leggings for him, you get to know that person, and like I told Owen, Luke had too much of his father in him—but I meant all the *best* parts . . . and his mother, too, from what little I knew of her. It was obvious to me from the time Luke was a baby that he was going to grow up to do something amazing, and I'm not just saying that because I was his aunt. I just knew.

91

And I was right.

I'm not trying to take credit for Luke's accomplishments, either, although Owen and I did try to do our best with him. I always thought it was so sad, what happened to Luke's parents, and his grandmother, too. I was there for her funeral. I served blue milk (and cheese) to everyone after. I think my teacher was wrong: making cheese wasn't what I was born to do. I was born to make people feel good when everything around them seemed just awful.

Which, if you think about it, is what all good parents—and café owners—are meant to do.

After Luke came to live with us, I told Owen, "We're going to raise this boy like he was our own. He's never going to know a day of un-happiness, to make up for all the terrible things that happened before he was born."

I really think I succeeded—except for Owen's not allowing Luke to go to the Academy . . .

And of course what happened to Owen and me that day with the stormtroopers. I really wish Luke hadn't seen that.

Then again, if he hadn't, he never would have gone off with old Ben, met the princess, destroyed the Death Star, and saved the galaxy.

So I guess things did turn out all right in the end, didn't they?

Especially now, because up until this moment, no one has ever given me a chance to tell my story.

So thank you for that.

Now go drink your milk. And may the Force be with you.

THE LUCKLESS RODIAN

Renée Ahdieh

Today would be the day. Greedo had known it last night as he'd watched the binary sunset sink along the hazy horizon of Tatooine.

After many long years, justice would finally be served upon Han Solo.

The Rodian bounty hunter sensed something ignite deep within his chest and catch flame. Some long-denied satisfaction. Today Greedo planned to put that arrogant Corellian scum back in the cesspit where he belonged.

His dark eyes narrowed against a gust of billowing sand as he trudged through the winding streets of Mos Eisley, toward a familiar cantina. A smile nearly curled up his green lips when the arched entrance came into view. As luck would have it, his quarry had been sighted just yesterday, seeking business in the very same place Greedo often transacted his own deals. Of course, the two kinds of deals in question differed wildly. The cowardly Corellian was a mere smuggler, whereas Greedo dealt in a variety of death. He'd even begun taking bounties from the greatest crime lord of the Outer Rim, and Jabba the Hutt was known to be particular when it came to his associations. Save for the cowardly Han Solo, of course.

Greedo sneered at the group of hooded Jawas crouched outside the cantina door. He would never understand what Uncelta had found so appealing in Solo all those years ago. The smuggler had always been a worthless excuse for a man, while Uncelta had been everything Greedo had cherished in a woman.

Such a waste.

Kicking aside the nearest Jawa as he passed, Greedo strode through the entrance, careful not to make eye contact with anyone present. His gaze remained fixed on the bar in the dusty center of Chalmun's Cantina. Thankfully the band was playing a less noxious strain of music than usual. There was only so much he could stand from these particular Bith, especially without the solace of several drinks in his stomach.

Even still, it was a fitting backdrop. Figrin D'an and the Modal Nodes' tuneless strains set alongside an occasional brawl. For as long as he could remember, Mos Eisley spaceport had been a beacon for the art of the underworld. It was the same underworld of Greedo's childhood, when he'd been brought from Rodia to live on Tatooine. As luck would have it today, his quarry had chosen to take up temporary residence on one of Greedo's homeworlds.

Today would be the day.

Greedo took a seat at the bar and signaled the sneering bartender for a drink. He watched the silver and brass pipes above gleam dully beneath a fog of swirling hookah smoke.

The tumbler of Corellian red swirled in his hands as he awaited his prey in silence. After he'd downed three of the brews, his attention drifted toward the arrival of a towering Wookiee. Since Chalmun— the purveyor of this establishment—was himself a Wookiee, the sight of these overgrown beasts was far from unusual in these parts. But this particular Wookiee caught Greedo's attention nevertheless. His long green fingers clenched around his tumbler.

From the corner of his eye, Greedo watched the Wookiee begin making his rounds. Watched and waited.

"Hey!" The barkeep pointed over Greedo's shoulder, his already disdainful face contorted with irritation. "We don't serve their kind here!"

Greedo glanced behind him to see a wide-eyed boy with two droids clambering in his shadow. The boy looked like exactly the kind of fool who didn't know any better and would likely die for it before the day was out. Why anyone would bring in droids to take up the spaces of living, breathing patrons, Greedo would never know.

"What?" the boy asked, his ridiculous eyes going even wider.

The barkeep ground out his retort. "Your droids . . . they'll have to wait outside."

His shoulders dropping, the boy muttered something unintelligible to his droids. This fool would be lucky to make it through an entire drink at Chalmun's, never mind another year of his life in general.

Untried bantha fodder.

Snorting to himself, Greedo turned back toward the bar, continuing to tune out the mindless prattle of those seated nearby while the band changed its tune. His gaze settled on a beguiling young creature across the way, with eyes that shone like the barrel of a newly polished blaster.

Eyes just like those of Uncelta.

Curse her for being as big a fool as that boy with the droids.

Greedo would have loved her as she deserved to be loved. Not dallied with her like that Corellian scumbag had chosen to do.

Greedo continued observing Solo's first mate from his periphery, biding his time. If he was patient, the Wookiee would lead Greedo's quarry right into his clutches. Into a justice so long unserved. He was distracted from his musings by raised voices. That same awkward boy was engaged in the beginning of an altercation with exactly the kind of creature who would bring about his inevitable end. What kind of shirt was the boy wearing anyway? What sort of simpleton wore white in a spaceport as dirty as Mos Eisley? Sure enough, the boy flew back into a table at the first sign of a cross word. Further distracted by the ensuing commotion, Greedo twisted around in time to see an old man in a peculiar robe flash a weapon he'd heard of in passing but never seen in person: an ancient saber fashioned from growling blue light. The weapon snarled through the air, and the instigator's severed arm struck the floor in almost the same breath.

Amid the strangled screams, Greedo laughed to himself. With nary a flinch, the Bith resumed playing their tuneless music.

After all, these kinds of disturbances were far from unusual in a place like Chalmun's Cantina. Indeed, if the purveyor of the establishment had been present, he undoubtedly would have relished the spectacle. Wookiees were known to enjoy a good dismemberment as much as any Rodian did.

At the reminder, Greedo craned his neck closer toward the particular Wookiee he'd taken note of earlier. The hulking, fur-covered stranger had loped toward the bar and was now in the midst of a hushed conversation with the old man in possession of the snarling saber.

Greedo remained hunched and alert as the Wookiee signaled to someone hovering in the darkest fringes of the cantina. His stomach tightened into a coil of knots.

Solo was on his way.

A moment later, the smug coward ambled toward a table to the left of the bar and began chatting with the saber-wielding old man and the foolish boy.

The knot in Greedo's stomach became a jumble. Anticipation flared through his center, mingling with that same satisfaction like kindling to a flame.

Today would be the day.

Greedo slunk lower into his barstool, continuing to bide his time. Continuing to wait for his opportunity.

He kept silent and still while a contingent of Imperial troops collected in front of the bar, drawn by the earlier commotion. The barkeep was all too eager to point them in the direction of the fool boy and his elderly bodyguard, who quickly ducked out of sight. Greedo's ire spiked. Worry cut through his earlier blaze of triumph. If the stormtroopers thought to detain Solo, his opportunity would be lost. He thought for a moment about confronting him once and for all, with little concern for the presence of the Empire's lackeys, but the risk was too great. And Greedo could not risk the additional possibility of rousing Jabba's anger.

If Greedo did decide to throw caution to the wind, he might lose the chance to stare his enemy in the face and experience the supreme satisfaction of watching Solo squirm in fear, like the coward he was.

Greedo stood from the bar and moved into the shadows nearest to the alcove where Solo sat with his first mate, smiling as though he had not a care in the galaxy.

A breath of relief past Greedo's lips when the stormtroopers passed the table and continued on their way.

As soon as the Wookiee left and Solo stood from the table, Greedo made his move, yanking his blaster from its holster. He would not waste this opportunity.

Today would be the day.

"Going somewhere, Solo?" he said in Huttese as he shoved the barrel of the blaster into Solo's vest.

"Yes, Greedo, as a matter of fact, I was just going to see your boss." The coward backed away, shoved toward the same alcove, his hands raised at his sides as though to convey a desire for peace. "Tell Jabba that I've got his money." He sat down at the table.

"It's too late," Greedo said as he took the seat opposite Solo, a white lantern glowing before him, bathing the air between them in cool light.

Solo slouched into the back of the bench, an amused half smile beginning to curve up one side of his face.

Fury shot through Greedo's chest. "You should have paid him when you had the chance. Jabba's put a price on your head so large, every bounty hunter in the galaxy will be looking for you. I'm lucky I found you first." He laughed under his breath. Perhaps luck had nothing to do with it. It had been his patience. His intuition. His hatred.

Perhaps if Uncelta could see them now, she would not have made the same mistake she'd made those many years ago.

Hate filled the hollow around Greedo's heart.

The sight of Solo tossing his booted leg onto the tabletop and grinning with casual arrogance only heightened Greedo's growing rage.

The suggestion of a frown fell upon Solo's face. It was gone in almost the same instant. "Yeah, but this time I've got the money." He waved his left hand through the air, once more the picture of supreme arrogance.

"If you give it to me, I might forget I found you." Forget? Greedo could never forget. But he would gladly take the scum's money before delivering him to Jabba.

Or perhaps he'd blast a hole through Solo's chest. Just like Uncelta had done to him.

Solo winced with irritation. "I don't have it with me." He glanced over his shoulder and began circling his fingers across the rough wall at his back, as though he were toying with something only he could see. His head lolled against the gleaming bracer above the bench. "Tell Jabba—"

"Jabba's through with you." Unmistakable irritation laced Greedo's words. "He has no time for smugglers who drop their shipments at the first sign of an Imperial cruiser."

"Even I get boarded sometimes." Solo's retort was curt. "You think I had a choice?"

"You can tell that to Jabba. He may only take your ship." Greedo's finger tightened on the trigger of his blaster.

Solo's left hand fell from the wall. "Over my dead body." Whatever lingering traces of amusement that remained vanished from his eyes as a shadow descended across his features.

"That's the idea." Triumph spread through Greedo as satisfaction began to take root once more. "I've been looking forward to this for a long time." He grinned, peace tinging the air around him with a strange sweetness. At last, vengeance would be his. He would live to see Jabba rob Han Solo of the only thing the coward prized. And it would be glorious.

"Yes, I bet you have." Solo glanced to one side as though in thought. The last thing the luckless Rodian saw was a flash of bright light.

His last memory was that of bitter injustice.

NOT FOR NOTHING

Mur Lafferty

**Excerpt from *The Lady Has a Jocimer: My Life as a Modal Node*,
A Memoir by Ickabel G'ont**

CHAPTER 3: NOT FOR NOTHING

Tatooine was the worst place in the galaxy for Bith.

When your skin is milky white-pink and your eyes are lidless and tearless, a planet with two suns, high heat, and blowing sand is essentially a jail sentence.

When Figrin D'an and the Modal Nodes got a gig on this planet, we all protested.

"Our skin will burn off our skulls!" Tech M'or said.

"What if we get sand in our eyes, D'an?" I demanded. I have the best eyes of the whole band, and even I find myself particularly sensitive to irritants. "How good are we going to play when we are staggering around looking for an eyewash? Do they even have eyewashes on Tatooine?"

Then came Lie #1: "We are invited to play for the ruling lord on Tatooine. I'm sure his palace will have all the accommodations we will need."

He didn't say that the ruling lord was a Hutt, a species that's not really known for hospitable and clean living spaces.

Then came Lie #2: "We are only there for a standard week, tops."

We were there over a year.

Then the best Lie, #3: "The money is incredible."

Now, if I'd been D'an, I would have let the group know the facts this way: "I've got some bad news. I'm in serious debt to a Hutt and have sold all of you into indentured servitude in the sandy armpit of the galaxy. Once we pay off the debt, we will have to find other gigs in order to get enough money to get the hell off the planet. Working for the Hutt will be the worst job you will ever have."

We didn't talk to him for weeks after the truth made itself known. We played for Jabba and his companions within the palace. (Were they companions? Visitors? Prisoners? We were never sure.)

"Palace." Please. I've seen palaces. I've performed for kings. This was no palace.

After a few months we finally accepted that this was our lot in life, and the one bit of good news was we were still the Modal Nodes, which meant we played the best music in the galaxy. Never mind that it was for a crime lord slug and his lackeys and slaves, but it reminded us of our humble beginnings when you took what gigs you got offered.

You also pay attention. You never know what kind of dirt you can get. We watched people wheedle, cajole, and deal with Jabba. One interesting thing about Bith that other species don't really know is how we can separate different sounds around us. It's what makes us such good musicians. We can listen to the different instruments separately or together to make sure everyone is in tune and working well together.

We can also listen to conversations that otherwise would be drowned out in lesser ears. So we were privy to many of Jabba's dealings that happened while we played, and he had no idea. We learned to know and hate many of the residents of this world. One of my least favorite people was Greedo, a Rodian bounty hunter. He is actually the person who found Figrin D'an and delivered him to Jabba.

We hadn't known D'an had a price on his head. The things your bandleader doesn't tell you.

D'an had me keep a close eye on Greedo and find some dirt on him. I pointed out the bucket of sand I had to wash out of my eyes every night and said I got dirt on everyone, it's right there, but he told me to get over it and stop complaining. Brave card to play, as he put us in this situation, but D'an always was a terrible gambler.

So I watched Greedo. He would bring in small-time criminals who owed Jabba, get a pat on the head and a handful of credits, and stalk away, very proud of himself. I kept track of the money he demanded from Jabba, and the money that he got, and the times he would slip keys or blasters to his quarry so they could escape, and then he would bring them back in for another reward. He brought in one poor Jawa *three times.*

When it was time to pay off our debt, Jabba asked for more than twice what he said D'an initially had owed him. We expected this, so D'an counteroffered information instead of more credits. That's when he brought Greedo down. Jabba was furious at the bounty hunter, and actually let us go—

—in the middle of the desert. Naturally. But when a giant slug surrounded by several heavies with weapons sets you free in the middle of the desert, you thank him kindly for the freedom and get moving. We counted our stars that he let us go at night so we could at least avoid the suns. I honestly didn't expect him to let us go at all. So, thanks Jabba. I'll buy you a cup of slime the next time we see you.

[Ed. Note: Since the writing of this memoir, Jabba the Hutt has been murdered by an unknown assassin within his palace. Jabba the Hutt cannot be thanked anymore. Still, the author requested we leave this entreaty in the text.]

We made it to Mos Eisley soon after the suns rose, which was good because my hands were beginning to turn pink, and my eyes were burning. We found a place for the band to stay while D'an, like a good leader, went to get us a gig.

Tech went with him because he wanted to make sure D'an wouldn't go and gamble away our new freedom in pursuit of more credits.

Now is when I suppose I have to answer the question you've been asking yourself. Why in all of the galaxy do we choose to stay with D'an? He put us in slavery to a Hutt. He got us marooned on a planet that is antithetical to Bith. He gambles like a drunken uncle with bad luck.

The reason should be obvious: Figrin D'an is the best composer and bandleader you will ever find this side of the galaxy. We knew that if we left, we'd never be able to find another leader quite like him. When we're getting thrown into shackles or washing sand out of our eyes, it's hard to appreciate him. When we're playing, nothing in all the worlds is better.

We found two cheap rooms to keep all eight of us, and played a game of hiller dice to decide who would be stuck sweeping the filthy place, who had to cover the windows, and who was able to sit and relax from the horrible travel we'd suffered. I was stuck with the window duty, and as I unrolled the black fabric to protect us from the glare, I caught the sight of a slim green snout sticking out from a cloak scurrying down the road.

Uh-oh.

I secured the fabric and then asked if anyone knew where D'an and Tech had gone. The rest of them shrugged, and I grabbed my cloak, left the apartment, and headed back into the Tatooine heat.

Now that we'd had a bit of a rest and some not-so-brackish water to drink, I was able to take a look at the new town we inhabited. It was . . . well it was better than Jabba's palace, but that's not saying much. Hot, sandy, run-down, and no one would look you in the eye.

Also, stormtroopers patrolled the streets. One stopped me with a hand on my shoulder. "We're looking for two droids."

"I haven't seen anything," I said, and then realized I had an opportunity. "Around here, anyway. But I just spent some time at Jabba the Hutt's palace, and I'm pretty sure he brought in at least two new droids recently."

"What did they look like?" he demanded.

"Um, one was green? Or maybe blue," I said, guessing.

He stood back on his heels, and although I couldn't see his face, he exuded a mood of either disbelief or reluctance. A trooper with an orange half sleeve came up to him. "What have you found?" he asked.

"She says she saw a droid like that in the area of the Hutt's domicile," his companion said, as if not wanting to deliver the information.

"Check it out," he said, and left.

The remaining trooper took another look at me, and I could feel the dislike radiating off him.

"Good luck," I said, and scurried away. I had kept an eye on Greedo as he headed with purpose down the street. I wish I'd known where D'an had gone, but I had to think that he was looking for a gig, so he would be searching for bars and dance halls.

Mos Eisley didn't look like a place with many dance halls. But it did look like a place people would need a drink. I inquired of a passing woman where the closest bar was and she pointed me a few doors down. Luckily Greedo had already passed this bar, so I ducked in.

D'an and Tech were inside, speaking with a large Wookiee. A disgruntled Rodian, taller and darker-skinned than Greedo, was packing up a flute and making a big production out of it. He pushed by D'an rudely, shouting that no one fires Doda Bodonawieedo. D'an didn't make things better by shouting after him that Chalmun just had fired Doda Bodonawieedo.

D'an spied me. "Ickabel, this is Chalmun, owner of—"

"—Chalmun's Cantina, I get it," I said. "Can we talk for a second?"

D'an sent Tech to talk to me while he palled around with our new boss.

"What a pit, huh?" Tech asked, looking around the cantina.

"Better than Jabba's," I said. From then on, "better than Jabba's" would be how we would describe anything that was terrible. "And speaking of which, I saw Greedo sniffing around outside. If he finds us in here, we could have a problem."

Tech grinned at me. "The Wookiee says he comes in all the time. But this is the safest place on the planet." He pointed to the signs on the wall listing, in several languages, the rules of the cantina.

I scanned the rules and then read them at a slower pace. I smacked Tech upside the head. "That says *Applaud the band,* not *Do not under any circumstance attack the band,*" I said. "That doesn't guarantee safety!"

"Oh. You're right," he said. He looked back over at D'an, who was signing the contract. I groaned.

"Well," Tech said. "At least he's not selling us into slavery again."

D'an came over all smiles. "We start in an hour. Get the rest of the band over here."

"You do know that Greedo is a regular customer here? And he's not going to be thrilled about you giving him up to Jabba," I said.

"We have a Wookiee on our side! What can go wrong?"

Chalmun's Cantina was better than Jabba's. That's what we could say about it.

When things go wrong, you can try to see how your situation challenges you. We have played in awards ceremonies against the wind, in the middle of a rainstorm, and for lords and ladies whose idea of fun would be to whip prisoners and feed them to rancors. (That last one was Jabba. Did you guess?)

At the cantina, we were shoved onto a small dais on the corner, having to get cozy with one another while we played D'an's furious tunes. The stage was tight and the customers were unenthusiastic, but these kinds of challenges are what I live for. However, I didn't realize what else would happen that afternoon.

First, Chalmun—the super-safe Wookiee that would save us from Greedo—went home. He said he wasn't at the cantina all day and night and he needed a break. He promised Wuher would protect us, but with the sidelong look the bartender shot us, I thought that was unlikely. So I kept my eyes on the door while we played.

As the day went on, the cantina filled up with various unsavory characters. I had to hand it to Wuher, though. When people got pushy or something, he put a stop to it. A bar fight started near us, one patron throwing another one straight at the stage. As there was no free room on stage, we faltered on a song as we scrambled to get out of his way. D'an was furious and stopped the song while he called for Wuher to help out. The bartender threw both brawlers out, but then fixed us with a grungy eye.

"You don't stop playing. Not for nothing. Got it?"

D'an nodded. We got it. We answered by starting the song again at the beat D'an led with.

People at these kinds of places tended to look alike, all of them dirty and shady, with something to hide. Outsiders stood out like—well, like a Bith on Tatooine. So when two humans entered the bar who stood out more than we did, they caught my eye. Wuher grunted at them to keep their droids outside—their gold protocol droid and their blue astromech. I looked from them to D'an and then remembered the rule. Keep playing.

I knew I should tell the Imperials about the droids during our break. There might be a reward that could get us off this hell planet. I begged D'an with my eyes to get us a break, but he ignored me.

These droids were clearly sought after, but why didn't the stormtroopers outside find them? I was curious, but the two men were clearly up to something, as carefully innocent as they acted. It was their innocence that made them stand out, honestly.

108

Ironically, they blended right in once they were challenged by a huge brute, and the hairier of the men brought out a laser sword and cut the arm off their attacker.

The arm smoked slightly on the floor, and its former owner shrieked. We stopped playing, of course. But then Wuher glared at us and we hastily started up again. So we were supposed to just keep on with the music while people were losing limbs? And here I'd thought this place was better than Jabba's. (Say what you will about the slug, he didn't mind if we were startled out of tune when he murdered someone.)

A large Ithorian left his seat and headed for the bar, and I nearly swallowed my jocimer reed when I spotted Greedo. I don't know how long the slimy little guy had been lurking behind him. Greedo looked right at us, and I faltered for a note or two, but we didn't stop. *Not for nothing,* Wuher had said. Not for a severed limb, and definitely not for a bounty hunter with a grudge. Greedo went to the bar and ordered a drink, then watched us, unblinking.

D'an instructed us to start a new song, fast and catchy, and we played it, defiantly ignoring Greedo. He watched, impassively, fingering the blaster at his hip.

We were allowed to quit if our lives were in danger, right? Or did that fall under the *not for nothing* rule? I didn't know. But I was getting into the music when Tech poked me in the back. Greedo had started to move. He was stepping around the bar (I wondered wildly whether someone had cleaned up the arm or if he was going to trip. He didn't.) and heading our way. I tried to get D'an's attention, but he was too into the beat.

In the middle of the song, I felt my double jocimer begin to slip apart at the joints. D'an hadn't given me any chance to properly clean it, and I'd done a messy job oiling it to make up for the ever-present sand. Now I was in trouble.

Everyone has their own version of the next part, and most of them have to do with "look how clumsy Ickabel was!" but here is what really happened: Everything you've heard, I did on purpose. I gave my jocimer a quick turn with both hands, opposite directions, and it fell apart. The valves and tubes went flying, and the circular joints that made up the body and all of the vibrating reeds fell and rolled toward Greedo, who had picked up speed. He stepped on an oily joint and went flying backward.

D'an scowled and pointed at the mess while still playing. *Don't stop not for nothing, right.* I hopped off the stage and got on the floor to grab the discarded pieces of my instrument. Greedo was still down, rubbing his head, and I kept an eye on his blaster. I scurried to the other side of the dais to put my abused instrument together.

The other patrons were giving Greedo a good ribbing, and he finally got up, bright green with anger. He glared at me, and then

109

looked past me. His face changed, slackened, and then he smiled, if you can say his kind can smile. He turned and left us without a backward glance. What had delighted him so?

I saw he was heading toward another white human male who was with a Wookiee conversing with Wuher. Someone he wanted more than us; that must be someone with either a big bounty or with whom Greedo had a bigger grudge. I got back on the dais and started playing an even faster song, one of D'an's favorites. Everyone looked exasperated but gratified that Greedo had been distracted.

They still don't believe I did it on purpose.

I started thinking again about those droids and whether they could get us a good payout. D'an wouldn't give the band a break while the bounty hunter was around, so I wouldn't be able to tell the troopers outside until Greedo was gone.

The human male and Wookiee were speaking with the other two humans, the ones with the droids. Everyone left the table but the human that had caught Greedo's interest. Greedo slipped over and, just as the human stood up, cornered him with a blaster. Greedo calmly encouraged him to sit back down.

The tempo changed and I had to focus on D'an for a moment, and then light flared and Greedo slumped down on the table in front of the human. I don't see a lot of humans, but I thought their facial expressions were more expressive than this man showed. The patrons around them looked over in alarm, and Wuher looked ready to shoot the human himself, but the man tossed him some credits and sauntered out.

Although we wanted to cheer, we kept playing. We didn't stop, not for nothing. We had been saved. Jabba had let us go. Greedo was done for. Our tip jar was filling up, and things might be looking up for the first time in a very long time.

As we played another one of D'an's newest songs (captivity had been strangely inspirational to him, I have to admit), I thought about those droids and the stormtroopers that searched for them. I thought about a possible reward. And then I decided that if that human could do us a favor without us knowing him at all, we could do those other humans a favor and not report them. We were safe now, and could keep playing.

Which is really all we ever wanted to do. Play, and don't stop. Not for nothing.

WE DON'T SERVE THEIR KIND HERE

Chuck Wendig

As if the day wasn't bad enough, the gods-blamed droid detector wasn't working right again. Because who just walked in, but a couple of gods-blamed droids. One was a rickety old protocol droid, tarnished and sand-scoured. The other a blue-topped astromech. Both probably came offa some Jawa sandcrawler—each probably half a circuit shy of a proper droid. A coupla junk-bots that'll just wreck the place, like droids do. They got no hearts. They got no soul. And now they were here in his cantina.

It was bad news in an already crummy day. Like a hawked-up globba spit on top of a poodoo sundae.

Wuher, bartender at the Mos Eisley cantina, started his day the same way as he always did: up before the two suns, weary from a night of ragged dream-worn sleep, breakfasting on salted zucca and pulverized gravel-maggots before stomping upstairs to the cantina. He turned on all the lights. Warmed up the machines. Already the first bad news hit him: They were running low on damn near everything that would calm tempers on this hot, dead world. No gar-slurry, no fistula juice, none of that hooch that the Gamorreans cook up. Wuher pulled out the telescoping arm from underneath the bar top, popping the latches and unfolding his datapad screen with a rackety-clack. Of course, *that* wasn't working either—he had to blow sand-scree off it, then whack it a few times, and all that got him was a glitching screen full of fat, corrupted pixels. That meant he couldn't pull up the delivery schedule.

He was *pretty* sure that his guy, a spacer named Bims Torka, was supposed to deliver a shipment of stuff yesterday. Maybe even the day before. Torka was supposed to bring him the standard stuff, plus maybe a case of Knockback Nectar from Jakku, which was about as nasty a brew as you could get—bubbly, high-octane booster fuel, basically. Got people *too* messed up. Wuher knew that this thing he did, this thing behind the bar, it wasn't art. Any lunk-brained sand-eater could do it. But to do it right, you had to know some things, and one of the things you knew was that you didn't want your drinkers *too* drunk, *too* fast. That happened, and they were out. Stopped buying and starting fighting. Or worse, started puking.

Still, they wanted the stuff, so he charged a premium.

But now he didn't have it. Didn't have *any* of it. What he had was the dregs. Which they'd buy, but they wouldn't like it. And that meant he'd have to hear them *complain,* and the last thing he wanted was to hear them *complain.* What was he, their nursemaid? Soothing the poor little babies?

Animals. Whining, mewling animals.

It was what it was, so he hit the button to open the locks and roll up the gates. That didn't work, either, so he took a pivot wrench to it and gave it three good whacks—*whong, whong, whong!*—which got it open again. The locks hissed. The gate opened with a staccato rattle.

Didn't take long before the joint was full up. Full of spacers and traders, pirates and smugglers. All around were dust-heads, spice-hounds, flesh-peddlers, gear-tinkers. The usual. But no droids. Never droids.

Later in the day, the Modal Nodes were playing, and they were all right guys and girls—at least for Bith, who let's be honest were pretty bizarre—but he hated their music. Just sounded like noise to him.

Then again, everything sounded like noise to Wuher.

Worse than the Nodes was who came in next: that smuggler, Solo, and his walking shag-pile copilot. Wuher didn't know where the hair-stack came from—he thought those Wookiees were a slave species, but this one didn't look like no slave to Wuher. Only other Wookiee he knew was the one that owned this cantina, a fella named Chalmun. Also not a slave. Which was fine by Wuher. Nobody should have to be a slave. It was part of the lifeblood of this planet because of the Hutts, and now thanks to the Empire it was part of the lifeblood of the whole damn galaxy. But *he* wouldn't have a part of it. Sure, he could have help here if he bought a slave or two. Then it wouldn't just be him. Yeah, he's got Ackmena working some nights, but a couple of slaves would take the pressure off him during the day.

But it didn't seem right. It didn't seem right at all.

So then, as Wuher was pumping drinks and ignoring questions, Solo headed over to a dark corner of the cantina. Like he was holding court. Like he was waiting for something or someone. The big hairy sonofagun went to the other side of the joint, which seemed strange to Wuher—you got a bowcaster-sporting tree-trunk bodyguard like *that* fella, you never let him leave your side. That monster looked like he could slap the head right off your shoulders. Solo, yeah, he looked tough enough, but not *Wookiee*-tough.

Plus, last Wuher heard, Solo had debts on his shoulders.

Not just any debts, neither.

A debt to a Hutt. *The* Hutt around these parts. Jabba.

It's practically the kind of wisdom you'd want to hang on your wall: *Never owe Jabba the Hutt anything—ever.*

But there sat Solo, owing Jabba, sitting alone, the Wookiee gone.

That was when one of the freaks on the other side of the bar, a guy named Jerriko, pulled the smoke-stem out of his mouth, blew a few vapor rings, and then said in his undeservedly haughty way:

"Oh my. *Somebody* is in trouble today."

He lifted his chin to indicate who came through the door.

Greedo. The Rodian.

Bounty hunter scum. Wuher didn't care much for bounty hunters and bail-jackers. It went back to the slave thing: people owning other people. But he couldn't close the door to them. (Unless they were droids. He had that droid detector installed for damn good reason.) If word got around he didn't serve the hunters, he'd get a reputation. And on this world, you don't want a reputation if you wanna stay in business.

Greedo walked in, looked around, sat down.

The Rodian saw Solo. Solo pretended not to see the Rodian.

That's when Wuher knew: He was gonna be cleaning up a real farging mess soon enough. This was a trap for Solo. Or maybe, he thought: a trap for Greedo. Wuher figured they'd all find out soon enough.

Then—*then!*—he spied that crazy milk-eye moon-bat sitting down, guy who called himself Roofoo. Roofoo had a friend today, a sad-looking Aqualish who Roofoo introduced in his growly whine of a voice: "Hey. You! This is my friend Sawkee. He drinks for free!"

"Nobody drinks for free," Wuher said.

But Roofoo kept talking like he didn't even hear the answer: "That Rodian you just dragged out of here? I could have taken him. I could have killed him!"

"I'm sure you coulda," Wuher said, scowling. Big boaster, this guy.

"I could kill anyone in here!"

"Uh-huh. You gonna order something?"

Roofoo ordered a couple of black fizzers for him and his brooding Aqualish friend, which Wuher quickly delivered before heading to the other side of the bar to fill a few more requests—

Someone hissed at him. Ugh. The smoker again. Jerriko.

"*What?*" Wuher snapped. The man had a drink already. Wuher always told people: *If you have a drink in your hand, you don't need me for nothing.* And yet they always talked to him. Always had to jabber and yammer.

"That man over there. With the one bad eye and the . . . *face.*"

"Yeah. Roofoo."

"That is *not* his name. He is a killer. A surgeon, or once was, by the name of Dr. Cornelius Evazan. Be wary of him. Be wary of his partner, as well. The Aqualish. Ponda Baba."

"Uh-huh."

Jerriko pursed his lips. The man was an incorrigible know-it-all. "I met him once, at a banquet. Though he surely does not remember. He was different, then. Less . . . mad. Not yet disfigured. But still, a killer." It was then that Jerriko leaned in, conspiratorially. "I could dispatch him for you. Before he causes trouble. Because I assure you: He *will* cause trouble."

"I don't give a hot cup of jerba gall what you do, what he does, what *anybody* does. I just make the drinks and get paid."

Jerriko nodded, a slight smirk on his face. "Ah, yes, I understand you." But the way he said it sounded like he heard Wuher say something he didn't say, and as Jerriko moved to the other side of the bar to be nearer to Evazan, Wuher felt it. Like everything was coming down on his head. Wuher felt hot. Sweaty. And you didn't feel sweaty in a dry place like this, but here he was, feeling slick, woozy, feverish— not with an illness but with a moment of grave indecision about his life and his place in it. Even as he poured a glass of blue spirit for a pilot—a little Chadra-Fan screeching at him—the reality of his situation hit him across the back like a club. Wuher had no one. He had nothing but this bar and these people, these freaks, these spacers and traders, pirates and smugglers. Every day, another body dropped. Every day, protection money paid to the Hutts. Didn't he see a couple Imperial troopers kicking around outside the door? Probably meant he would have to suffer an Imperial inspection soon, too.

And it was then, *right* then, that the gravest indignity hit him.

Those two droids came in the door.

The protocol and the astromech.

They came clanking in with the old hermit who showed up once in a wild moon and this fresh-faced desert kid. Already, Wuher felt heat blistering his forehead: not the heat of the day, which he was used to by now, but the fever of rage flashing across his brow. Droids. *Droids.*

"Hey!" he barked. "We don't serve their kind here!"

The kid, looking flummoxed, asked: "What?"

"Your droids!" he growled. "They'll have to wait outside. We don't want them here."

The kid looked even more flummoxed, and as the droids tottered back out into the desert heat, Wuher had to put his hand out to steady himself against the bar. The memories buffeted him like the winds of a sirocco storm—

—*Wuher, a fresh-faced teen boy, heavy around the belly but spry enough, running down the halls of Arkax Station, the ground shaking, blasterfire lighting the dark behind him*—

—droids, black and gleaming, moving through the station as they killed the power and executed everyone they found—

—his parents, dead, each peppered with blasterfire, the holes in them still smoldering—

—the hiss-and-whisper of pneumatic limbs behind him as droid eyes lit up the black, their blasters leveled at him, ready to fire—

He shuddered, suddenly cold.

Droids.

He *hated* droids. The Clone Wars taught him that. Clankers couldn't be trusted. They were alive as any other, but more powerful: as eternal as their programming would allow, passed from body to body. They were smart. Dangerous. No matter what kind of restraining bolt you put on them. They had no mercy the way a man has mercy. They were cold.

Killers, to the last. Or at least the potential to be.

Wuher did not have long to dwell on this, however.

Because now the fresh-faced kid stood at the bar, tugging on Wuher's sleeve the way a kid does to an elder. Stupid boy, probably just some hick from the sticks. Wuher groused at him, slid a glass of dirty water across the bar—kid wanted clean water, he was welcome to pay a premium for the privilege, just like everyone else.

Near to the bar, the hairball Wookiee was talking to the old hermit. Neither of them was drinking a thing at the moment, of course, just taking up seats.

But out of nowhere, a commotion kicked up. The stupid kid must've bumped into the Aqualish, or maybe the Aqualish bumped into the kid. Didn't matter, because that Sawkee—or Ponda Baba or whatever his name was—became skeeved off something fierce. Worst of all, here came the milk-eye, Evazan. Mad as a sunbaked womp rat.

"He doesn't *like* you," Evazan said to the kid.

The boy, confused, answered simply enough: "I'm sorry."

"*I* don't like you, either!" It's then that the milk-eye goes into

119

boasting mode: "You just watch yourself. We're wanted men! I have the death sentence on *twelve* systems!" Wuher thought: *Who says that? Who announces that they're a gods-blamed criminal with a death sentence? Might as well print your bounty number across your head, make yourself a target to every whackjob with a debt to pay.*

"I'll be careful," the boy said, not being careful at all. Stupid kid.

"You'll be *dead*!" Evazan snarled, grabbing the boy and spinning him around. And that's when the old man, the hermit, got involved.

"This little one's not worth the effort," he said, his voice crisp, regal, not like those in these parts. The old hermit didn't drink much but always paid for clean water. Never caused trouble. Never spoke up much. The old man, in that regal voice of his, offered to buy Evazan something—

Evazan roared, throwing the boy backward and into a table. The kid crashed against it, going down like a sack of rocks. Someone drew a blaster—the Aqualish, maybe. It was like being back on Arkax again, and Wuher thought to get out of the way—

—*their blasters leveled at him, ready to fire*—

A blue spear of light cut through the cantina air, *vwomm, vwomm*—

—*behind the droids, twin spears of light, blue and green*—

Wuher leapt for the ground, panic kicking him in the ribs.

The sound of screams, of a limb hitting the ground.

—*droids screeching, hissing as laser sabers cut them to pieces*—

And then Wuher stood again. The aftermath was plain to see: the Aqualish cradling a stump arm; Evazan collapsed against his stool, his chest rent open; the farmboy staring, eyes wide as the twin suns; and the old man coolly nodding as he led the boy away. And like that, all returned to normal. The music began playing anew. Jerriko harrumphed and turned away, continuing to let vapor rings lazily drift from his puckered lips. Just another day here in a Mos Eisley cantina.

But it wasn't just another day for Wuher.

Not now. Not anymore.

The memory of this day, and that day so long ago, played again and again in his mind, each memory chasing the last. Circles and circles. Round and round.

Blasters up. Droids. Limbs. Sabers of light.

The chaos wasn't over that day, far from it. It wasn't long before a pair of stormtroopers came in, started asking what happened here.

What Wuher thought was this:

I don't much know what happened here today. I know I kicked a couple of dirty droids out, because you can't trust dirty droids. I know that there was a nasty character here who told me his name was Roofoo and that his friend was Sawkee, but he was really someone named Evazan, and his friend was Ponda Baba. I know they messed with the wrong farmboy, because that farmboy had a friend: a hermit who up until now was just that, just a hermit. But I think he was more than a hermit. I think he was a Jedi of old. I thought they were dead and gone, the Jedi. They once saved my life, those Jedi, saved me from a whole battalion of dirty droids. So I'm inclined to give this one a pass. And you should, too.

He didn't say any of that, of course. He knew not to get involved or say the wrong thing to a couple of Imperials. He knew, too, that the old man and the boy were already gone, having seen the troopers come in. He pointed in the direction of the empty tables and shrugged.

Later, a single shot screamed out—and the Rodian Greedo dropped dead on the table as the smuggler, Solo, stood up and walked away, like it was no big thing. He tossed Wuher a couple of credits, said something slick, and then wandered out of the cantina. Wuher had to go over, drag the body out, hastily scrub blood from the table.

But even as he did, those twin memories—

Today in the cantina, and that day, on Arkax Station.

Back and forth, back and forth. Memories chasing memories.

Like two skad-claws chasing each other's tails.

Limbs and sabers. Droids and death.

Eventually the day wound down. Wuher gave the cantina over to the night-shift barkeep, a tough old broad named Ackmena who lived out on the Delkin Ridge with her wife, Sorschi. And Wuher did what he always did: He went, had a glass of blue milk to settle his stomach, and then he went to bed. And he wondered what the next day would bring. He wondered if he would do it all again, or if this was his chance—as it was so many years ago on Arkax Station—to change course, to do something different. That night long ago derailed everything, his parents dead, his life changed. Maybe now it was time to get it back on the rails. Maybe he could change his path, even now. Maybe he could find some place of his own. Some*one* of his own.

Maybe he could change his destiny.

But would he?

THE KLOO HORN CANTINA CAPER

Kelly Sue DeConnick and Matt Fraction

There is a legend, Kabe begins, *in the Bith overworld about the Place That Comes After Death, the Realm of All Light, the Big Sleep—I don't know what they call it. They're Bith. You ever try talking to a Bith? Who knows. Anyway, whatever it is, in Bith Heaven, there's a club, a night-club, and every night the finest Bith musicians who ever lived—well, died—gather there to play. They have a gift for music, the Bith, which you should know in advance so that the contextual arena of the follow-ing anecdote makes sense once I reach its amusing conclusion. Anyway. These dead yet legendary Bith musicians create the sweetest music in the whole quintessence. Onstage, however, sits a simple stool upon which a golden Kloo horn rests that no musician dares play, or even touch.*

Well, if you wait long enough and drink enough of whatever the Bith drink—again I challenge you to talk to one of them and understand a single thing they tell you, and I mean not "understand" as in to know precisely what they are saying, but rather to truly comprehend what the things they are saying actually mean—as the Bith legend goes, in this club, you may see The Stranger when He comes for His horn.

Now you ask, who is this "The Stranger" and why should I care? Well I shall tell you. It is, in fact, the purpose of this delightful parable-slash-joke I have chosen to share with you as an entrée into our business at hand. The Stranger enters this music club in Heaven and approaches the stage. In reverence and respect, everyone watches in silence. The Stranger picks up the horn, plays just one note, and it sounds so beautiful that everyone present weeps in an aesthetic apotheosis. It is revelatory. It is the very sound of light, of love. His single note leaves them all weeping, every time, musician and drinker alike, and then, this Stranger? He leaves, if you can believe it, as quickly and quietly as He came.

One night, The Stranger comes, picks up His horn, rends the hearts of those present in twain, and exits as is His wont. So one regular, rather a newcomer compared with some of the old-timers, turns to another regular, this one an old-timer who will know, unlike the newcomer asking the question, and asks (not without a little incredulity), "Who is that guy? Lirin D'avi?"

And the old-timer says, "No—it is God. He only thinks He is Lirin D'avi!"

Kabe waits for a laugh that never comes.

For you see, in Bith culture, Lirin D'avi was the finest Kloo horn player ever to—

It is a lost cause. The Scrapper opposite gives Kabe *The Look*. It is *The Look* that means "Tiny bat-faced creature, your language sounds like a series of squeaks and chirps to me and I have no idea what you are on about," and Kabe sees it about seventeen times a day. She sighs and places a golden Kloo horn atop the Scrapper's countertop.

Anyway, this is it. Give me fifty-five?

This language, the Scrapper speaks. He haggles Kabe down to forty-eight, which was really three more than Kabe dared hope to get for the tarnished, piece-of-crap sound tube in the first place, and then displays it prominently in the window of his scrapper shop.

Scrapper shops always have a Kloo horn in the window. They are good for business.

The Muftak and Kabe: rulers of the kingdom of the cantina underground, which is a kingdom with a population of two. By night, the Muftak sleeps in the cavernous stone pipeways below the spaceport, below the scorching desert surface of Tatooine, below the view of the twin suns that sear the sky, relishing the lower ambient temperature and the mercy it grants his thick-furred hide. Moisture sometimes collects on the walls, which they reclaim and sell. Kabe sleeps in the tunnels because the darkness feels better on her terrible eyes and because the Muftak sleeps there, too. And where the Muftak goes, safety follows. The Muftak and Kabe, a team, squat there together in the dark, waiting for the impossible: that their luck, or the heat, one day will break.

During business hours, the Muftak and Kabe prowl the dark(er), cool(er) cantina and harvest whatever loot they can from the drunk and damaged denizens staggering around the spaceport, rolling suckers for loose change, their numerous eyes peeled for an easy pickin' or whatever else they might pawn. Casing the tourists and transients, they'll lift from one guy, sell to another, spend the cash on a thing some other third chump somewhere wants but doesn't know how to find. Then they'll mark it up, move it along, and live like lords

125

until the money's gone. And repeat, always, forever, A-B-C, Always Be Certain to hustle, hustle, hustle. Making a living in the Mos Eisley underworld means constant legwork, sketchy math, dubious mark-ups, and always knowing whatever the next thing is gonna be, no matter what, exactly, the next thing is. It is exhausting.

At Mos Eisley, everyone has side hustles, but the Muftak and Kabe? Even their side hustles have side hustles.

Ackmena knows this, and keeps it all on the down-low, because what kind of drinkslinger would she be if she didn't, but at the same time respect must be paid, and by respect, Ackmena means rent. Not a lot, but enough that Ackmena can slip a little something to Chalmun, who owns the whole place, while padding her silk-lined pockets to make the trip underground worth her while.

She clears her throat. The Muftak, sleeping one off, rouses as if waking up from a mild case of light paralysis. Kabe, for her part, chirps. Kabe likes Ackmena, and Ackmena thinks Kabe's voice sounds like music, and so she enjoys listening to her chirp.

"First of the month, my sweet, sweet hairballs," she says, not without some affection, her voice resonating off the cool stone of their lair, echoing into the dark forever.

The Muftak may have drunk their money away last night. Ackmena has a heavy pour for friends. He might have lost the rest of his money—of *their* money—to the Sakiyan over a dubious hand or eleventeen of cards. The Muftak can't be certain (although he is, in fact, Very Certain; let us, for the moment, give him this feint at uncertainty and at least a shred of dignity). One way or the other, Myo was certainly involved in the Muftak's change of fortunes last night. Does Myo owe him money? How does one ask a violence enthusiast like Myo to pay up? The Muftak has many questions.

Kabe chirps.

The Muftak rubs his four eyes, trying to reduce the number of patient Ackmenas waiting for him to pay up. He scratches his head. *Hang on. Where'd I put it,* he clicks, hoping the pantomime buys him time.

Kabe chirps.

The Muftak pats himself for pockets he does not have, as he does not now wear, nor has he ever worn, pants, or any article of clothing for that matter, as he lives his life trapped beneath a thick blanket of fur on an arid planet that may in fact be made, somehow, of actual, real, literal *fire.*

You, the Muftak croaks to Kabe, *with your thunderous cavalcade of nonstop chatterboxing, shall literally murder me if you dare continue such noise. Have mercy, little friend, for inside my head is a violent, angry beast, punishing me for having good luck at the sabacc table last night.*

(The Muftak had very bad luck at the sabacc table last night.)

Yet still Kabe chirps. And what she chirps, what she has chirped the whole time, is this: *I have some money.*

And all four of the Muftak's eyes give Kabe not *The Look* but rather *The Other Look.* The Muftak is the only one who ever gives *The Other Look* to Kabe, probably because the Muftak is the only one who ever understands Kabe, and *The Other Look* means *I know what you are saying, but I do not know what has transpired to compel you to say such a thing. Needless to say as, after all, this is but a silent look we exchange for that most fleeting of moments, we shall talk about it anon in more private company.*

Kabe sighs and digs out forty-five, what she got for the horn (less her handler's fee and early riser's bonus, of course) and waves it at the Muftak. *Dummy.*

Where did you get that? the Muftak clicks. Then he realizes it doesn't matter, and he doesn't really care. The Muftak takes the money from Kabe and hands it to Ackmena. It is one of the only times the

Muftak doesn't extract his customary protectorate surcharge for taking general care of Kabe, but he makes a note to himself to doubly compensate himself in the future.

Ackmena counts it. She *tsk-tsk-tsks*.

"Forty-five? That's more than half light, friends. And with my delivery charge and filing tariffs extracted, you're short sixty at least."

She looks at them. They look at each other. They know she won't kick them out. She knows they know she won't kick them out, and probably physically she couldn't, even if she wanted, which she doesn't; not really. They know that she knows that they know, and she knows, and they know, and on and on, and all any of them really know is, Chalmun, the boss, the landlord, owner of bars, maker of drinks, and breaker of legs, needs his vig or he'll send someone down to the tunnels to extract it the old-fashioned way. If his mood goes particularly sour that day (which, being a Wookiee in the desert, happens with great frequency), he may choose to exterminate the infestation of Muftaks and Chadra-Fans in his pipes, lost income be damned. On this, at least, the Muftak and Chalmun share common ground, but not enough to keep the Muftak alive.

Life gets pretty cheap in Mos Eisley.

I'll get it, the Muftak clicks.

He doesn't know if Ackmena understands his exact words or not. She gets the spirit of the thing, if not the details.

"Tonight, sweethearts. Respect must be paid. You know how it is."

She turns to go, and the sound of her footfalls echoing down the length of the tunnel-pipe makes the Muftak's head throb more.

Small friend, before I die, and I assure you, I shall die, today for certain, tonight if I find luck, but surely, surely my time is now at hand, the Muftak tak-tak-tak'd, *please, Kabe, please tell me where and how you came upon such a small fortune? Because for the life of me, whatever little is left, whatever little it may be worth, I could've sworn you* were in quite the state of financial embarrassment with regard to the liquidity of your resources, and I, myself, am clearly destitute as well, meaning we, my friend, shall continue our streak of very bad luck unless we find some form of windfall today, which, I don't know, seems pretty unlikely.

But a moment ago you said you had good luck, you said you had "very good luck," at the sabacc tables last night, Kabe counters.

Quoth the Muftak, *I may have misspoken.* Blame not the hustler for hustling.

I sold the Kloo horn of Lirin Car'n, Kabe squeaks.

A light—small, dim, but a light all the same—goes off somewhere inside the Muftak's aching skull.

Smallness, forgive me if I am mistaken, but I . . . I seem to have the vaguest recollection that Myo, who owes us both a not-insignificant sum, won said horn last night from Lirin Car'n himself and, in celebration, drank himself to the point of irritability and then left the table and the horn behind when . . . when it was in fact . . . I . . . who then took the instrument in question, the Muftak clicks. *With the intent of converting it into funds later today, in reparation of Myo's aforementioned debt.*

Indeed. And knowing the day and what was due Ackmena, Kabe says, *I relieved you of the horn while you slumbered, as you had relieved him of the horn that he had relieved from Lirin Car'n, and thus made with great haste to a Scrapper I knew who would be in the market for horns, especially for golden horns of Kloo.*

I passed out and you stole it from me, the Muftak counters.

I find that interpretation radiantly unkind, counter-counters the Chadra-Fan.

Blessed suns, the Muftak rages, hangover draining as fear-based adrenaline floods within him and he leaps to his feet, *Myo will eat you for this.*

129

No. Myo will eat you *for this, unless he finds out it was I who actually pawned the thing. But that,* chirps the small one, *is a Tomorrow Problem. Our Today Problem is paying rent.*

Kabe basks in her righteousness. And unless she's stealing his stuff, the Muftak finds that Kabe is usually right.

Lirin Car'n trembles with rage, fear, regret, doubt, anxiety, despair, and whatever the word is for the feeling you get when you drank so much and played so poorly at cards that you lost your father's Kloo horn, which, indeed, is very much a feeling, and a feeling with a name, but it comes from the Bith, who tend to be the only ones who feel it and, as you don't speak Bith anyway, its name does not matter. Trust that this feeling is proper and named and true, albeit rare in its ever being felt, yet it is felt, more than it has ever been felt before, by Lirin Car'n, the Bith, right now, in the Mos Eisley cantina.

"And you want me to find this thing for you?" Djas Puhr asks the Bith.

"You're a bounty hunter, aren't you? Well? I'm putting a bounty on my father's horn. I lost it to Myo. Myo doesn't have it. He believes that while he was in his cups, the thing was stolen from him. His solution to the problem is to scream and growl and look for something to kill. I find that business matters are better handled by businessmen."

"Indeed. In fact, Myo paid me what he swore was his last credit to hunt whoever it was that dared steal from him in the first place. Of course if he finds them first he'll kill them and thus moot the deal, but you understand."

"As far as I am concerned," Car'n says, "the horn stopped belonging to Myo once Myo ceased to actually *have* the thing. It is, as they say, in the wind. And I want it back."

"You're a businessman, you say. You are in the music business.

Without a horn, there is no music, and sans music, you are sans business. How am I to know such a bounty exists?" the Sakiyan asks. As a people, they are nothing if not practical.

"I'm good for it. I'll *make* good for it," Car'n says. "After I can play again. One session, one gig—I'll pay you two hundred."

"So the arrangement is: For two hundred, I find a fifty-credit horn—"

"*Fifty*? How *dare* you! Do you have any idea who my father was? Do you—do—you don't—this horn—the *legend* of this—I—You—" Car'n stammers on like this, but all of his protestations fall on tone-deaf Sakiyan ears. "Your problem, you—you—you—you *Sakiyan*—is you have no appreciation of art!"

"The Bith see the poetry in the mathematics of music; I see the poetry in the mathematics of money. Either way—we both can appreciate the beauty of numbers. So—two hundred, plus expenses. That is, as they say, music to my ears."

"Get my horn. I'll get you your money."

"And allow dear furious Myo to deal with the interlopers?"

"Exactly," says Car'n as his trembling subsides. "Wait—interlopers? Plural?"

"Don't worry about it."

Djas Puhr rises from the dark little alcove table he thinks of as his regular seat and sets about the day's work. He already knows what transpired, and how, and why. He knows, or at least can make an intuitive yet accurate guess, as to how this mess with the Kloo horn began. It isn't terribly difficult, knowing the cohort who frequents his table, but as the only one without a taste for drink, Djas Puhr, bounty hunter, tends to be the one who sees such things first and, if he's stealthy about it, the one who stands to profit. Most people at Mos Eisley think of the place as a port, or a bar, or a bazaar, even. Lirin Car'n thinks of it as a stage.

Djas Puhr knows that, more than anything else, Mos Eisley is a place of business.

The Muftak staggers into the daylight of Tatooine, hating his parents a little bit more for birthing him into a universe where such unreasonable heat could possibly exist. His name isn't "the Muftak" but rather "Muftak." And as for his species: Instead of being "a Muftak" as most people assume (hence the addition of a definite article as a prefix), Muftak is a Talz who came from Orto Plutonia—which is really quite far away from Tatooine and, being full of ice and snow and cold things, could serve as a model of the desert planet's literal polar opposite. How the Muftak—Muftak—how a *Talz* came to Tatooine is another story for another time, but needless to say, neither Muftak nor any of the other regulars has ever seen another like him. At some point Myo, confused as Myo often becomes, decided Muftak the Talz was in fact just "the Muftak" and it kind of stuck after a while, mostly because Muftak got tired of fighting it.

The Muftak does math in his baking, roasting, broiling head: With certain reductions in surcharges, tariffs, consideration taxes, delivery costs, and gratuities, he thinks he can pull together enough to at least live to see the twin suns setting a few more times. First he must find the Smuggler, and then he must find the Pig-Nosed Man—a human, he thinks—or the Walrus-Faced Man—an Aqualish, he knows, and whom he knows will, if the two of them are separate, know where to find the Pig-Nosed probably-human Man.

Nobody likes the Pig-Nosed Man. Except, it would seem, the Walrus-Faced Man. Sooner or later, they'll all end up at the bar. At Mos Eisley, sooner or later everyone ends up at the bar.

So the Muftak trudges to the bar.

Myo, a fight-happy Abyssin with one eye, white muttonchops, and a giant chip on his shoulder, rages at the Scrapper. The Scrapper, secure behind half a meter of what has to at least be Myo-proof shielding, yawns.

"Yell and scream all you like, pal, but business is business. Someone came in and sold me the horn. I put the horn in the window. Someone came in and bought the horn. Kloo horns are good for business, everybody knows that."

"But it was *mine*," Myo yells.

"No," says the Scrapper. "It was mine."

Myo thinks. As this is not his strong suit, it takes awhile.

"Who . . ." He works out the question in his mind, and the Scrapper could swear he hears gears grinding. ". . . who bought it?"

The Scrapper says, "How dare you, sir. The privacy of our clientele and their business is second only to our discretion," but as he says it, the Scrapper curls his first two fingers up and in, two times, *pap-pap*—the intergalactic symbol for "twenty."

Myo slides the money under the razor-thin slit beneath the shielding that separates them. Where he got it is a story for another time and, besides, it isn't his anymore.

"A Sakiyan. Real shiny. Walked in, brought it up like he was looking for it. Didn't even haggle price—three hundred."

"The *hell* you sold that thing for three hundred," Myo says. Nobody's so dumb as to believe a Kloo horn would sell for that much in a scrapper shop like this—not even Myo.

"It was in that neighborhood. Three hundred, two fifty, a hundo, somewhere in there."

Myo narrows his eye.

"And who sold it to you in the first place?"

"Once again, sir, I insist you respect the confidentiality of our customers and blah blah blah," the Scrapper says, again doing the little curl of his two fingers meaning *feed me*.

Another twenty goes under the partition.

"Some little . . . bat weasel? I don't know. Like an Ugnaught with a gland issue or somethin'. I thought he was a really hairy kid at first."

"She," snarls Myo. "Kabe."

Myo mentally adds forty to the price he'll extract from the little Chadra-Fan who sleeps in the tunnels below them—which, again, as thinking is not his strong suit, takes awhile, which only makes Myo more mad, which, as it happens, *is* Myo's strong suit.

A Kloo horn would make a not-ridiculous cane, thinks Djas Puhr, strolling through the spaceport toward the dark(er), cool(er) climes of the cantina. At least a proper cane would have some use, some practical value, instead of this absurd stick that made squeaky sounds that equated to "music." Still, he admits to himself, when the bar was full of music, spirits were raised; and when spirits were raised so, too, were glasses. Full glasses meant drunk patrons, and drunk patrons meant *opportunity.*

Distracted by these thoughts, Djas Puhr does not realize, as he passes inside the saloon's threshold, that the Smuggler and the Wookiee, eyes on the door, have drawn on him.

He let his guard down for half a heartbeat. Half a *heartbeat.* Yet that was all it took for the Smuggler to draw on him.

Han Solo is the fastest draw Djas Puhr has ever seen.

"You wouldn't shoot a man holding a Kloo horn, would you?" asks Djas Puhr.

"That depends," says the Smuggler. "You wouldn't shoot a man wanted by the Hutt, would you?"

"Depends on the Hutt, Han," says Djas Puhr. "Depends on how badly he wants the man."

"You're all heart," Han says. Djas Puhr cannot help but notice Han has yet to lower his blaster.

"'Heart' suggests the warmth and kindness one reserves for friends, yet men like us cannot afford to *have* friends. I consider you a mutually beneficial associate by profession—if I consider you at all."

The Wookiee barks.

"No offense."

Solo answers for Chewbacca. "None taken. I hear talk I might be a marked man. Marked men mean business. That's who we are right now, Puhr—a bounty hunter and a bounty. A businessman and a piece of unfinished business. Unless you convince me otherwise."

"I wouldn't spit on *this* particular Hutt were he burning alive before me and paying for mercy by the pound, let alone the fortune he's offering for your hide. Far be it from me to turn my back on an opportunity, but certain lines even I will not cross." As if to underscore the banality of his intent, he pulls an awkward toot sound from the horn. Han almost laughs, for Djas Puhr has almost made a joke, but he didn't, so he doesn't.

Han considers him. No one knows too much about Djas Puhr. Hunter. Tracker. And they say he clawed his way out of Jabba's slave pits and never looked back. Now, Han Solo doesn't like Jabba, and the feeling at the moment surely is mutual, but even he recoils at the thought of how much hate the Sakiyan must feel toward his former enslaver. Han does a quick equation in his head. Who would Djas Puhr want dead more? Who would Djas Puhr want dead *first*?

Han puts the blaster back in its holster.

"Sorry," he says. Han Solo doesn't really mean it, and Djas Puhr doesn't really care.

"Word is, you were boarded."

Chewbacca growls. A confirmation.

"It was the safe move," Djas Puhr says. "Live to smuggle another day and make repaying the Hutt a tomorrow problem."

Han shrugs. *What else could I have done?*

"I am saddened, though, as, if my memory serves me, among

whatever else you were hauling under your floorboards, you were transferring a certain item on my behalf."

Han nods to the Wookiee. Reaching into his satchel, the Wookiee pulls out the marbled egg of a gwayo bird. He tosses it to Djas Puhr, who catches it with his free hand, then admires the thing.

"Boarded or not, I still know how to take care of my friends," Han says, underlining the word with his tone. Djas Puhr acknowledges it, and/or Han, with a nod.

Solo could have dumped the egg along with the rest of his haul, whatever contraband it was, but chose otherwise. It is a small thing, a tiny kindness, a little law broken here, an import–export regulation flaunted there, and in the face of strict legal penalty, if not actual death. Some chance to take on a mutually beneficial associate by profession, thinks Djas Puhr.

"A taste of home," he says by way of offering a toast, and takes a bite of the egg. "And watch your backs. The Hutt has gone high enough on your bounties that every boy with a blaster and an itch to make his bones will be aiming to make them with yours."

Han nods, a gesture so small, so subtle, it exists on the verge of being visible. Both know what has transpired between them, though.

What a terrible business decision, thinks Djas Puhr, finishing the egg at his usual seat, in his usual alcove, ensconced in the darkness of the bar. For either of them.

Myo shakes Kabe by the neck back and forth and back and forth, inchoate, a font of blackened, sour emotions, all articulated in a guttural rendering of snarls and roars.

Kabe makes the noises one produces while being throttled by a homicidal Abyssin.

"You stole from me!" Myo screams into Kabe's face, and the

Chadra-Fan feels her fur blast back and gather the moisture from Myo's breath.

Kabe squeaks in violent desperation, motioning to Myo's clenched fist around her neck. *I can't tell you anything if you keep crushing my windpipe,* Kabe tries to squeak, but instead she squeaks only "Squeak."

"Speak!" yells Myo, and Kabe motions more frantically to Myo's contact with her throat. Myo realizes what he's doing, and how it may impede upon Kabe answering his question, and lets her go. Kabe falls to the dark, cool stone of the tunnel floor.

Friend, Kabe squeaks, *friend, I never—never—never would I ever steal from a friend. I do not see how one could survive a place such as this without friends. My friend the Muftak, however—*

And in a hot flash, Myo remembers the whiff of the Muftak from the night previous and, with both of his massive fists, pounds the wall over Kabe's head. Bits of rock dust fall on her fur. She covers her head in case anything bigger comes down. It doesn't.

When Myo exhausts himself he says, "I'll kill him," heaving with heavy, angry breath.

Then something happens in his head. Kabe could swear she actually saw it happen.

"Hurmmph," hurmmphs Myo.

Kabe keeps watching.

"Oh," says Myo. Myo then thinks for a moment—which, being Myo, maybe stretches beyond what either of us might reasonably consider a moment. "Oh—no." He trails off. "The drink. Hard to remember sometimes. I think . . ." *Oh boy,* thinks Kabe. ". . . maybe I owed him some money?"

Myo sinks against the wall opposite.

Kabe exhales. Today, she lives.

"Still shouldn't have stolen from me," he says. Then, looking up to Kabe, "We should probably find Djas Puhr before he finds you two

137

and kills you." With that, Myo lumbers off toward daylight. Kabe follows, not so certain she'll survive the day after all.

Somehow, impossible though it may seem, there lives a creature with even worse luck than all the aforementioned combined: a Rodian who considers himself not only a small-time loan shark in the ascendant but also a bounty hunter of great talents and prospects. If he has ever managed to collect a loan or a bounty as of yet—in fact, as if he had ever hunted anything successfully, for that matter—no one quite could tell the tale to you with absolute certainty. What anyone knows about this particular Rodian is—he is an idiot with a gun. A place like the Mos Eisley spaceport bloats with the number of idiots with guns prowling its corridors, so this somehow renders him even more unremarkable unless, for whatever reason, he points it at you, in which case, *Hoo, brother. Good luck.*

His name, Greedo, fits him with an ironic appropriateness suggesting that nurture and nature traipse together, conspiring against us all in a fait accompli, hand in unlovable hand. Greedo's hands are particularly unlovable, with their long, tendril fingers and weird little suckers on the tips. And at this particular moment in our story, he pokes one sad, dangly, puckered protuberance into the chest of Lirin Car'n, the Bith horn player minus one horn, the musician who loves music but hates musicians, the poor sucker who cannot pay off the loan he owes to, of all beings, Greedo.

Lirin Car'n has a secret: He planned on selling the legendary Kloo horn of his father Lirin D'avi that morning anyway. Lirin Car'n hates playing in a band. He hates his bandmates. He hates his bandleader. He hates the endless, restless lifestyle of a professional itinerant where the only constant is discomfort. Never could he ever have imagined anything in the galaxy that could rob the joy of music from him, but it turns out living the life of a musician did the trick. At least that's what he tells himself. That the horn could be converted into money he could use to repay what he owes the shifty Rodian loan shark was only happenstance.

Behind Greedo stands the Pig-Nosed Man and the Walrus-Faced Man, who everyone, save Greedo, knows to avoid. They project a sense of actual menace that the always-this-side-of-desperate Greedo lacks no matter how hard he tries.

"Payday, Bith," Greedo purr-gargles in his native tongue.

"I don't have it. Next week?" asks Lirin Car'n, as if none of this would be remarkable, or create any need for raised tones and physical violence. As far as Lirin Car'n can figure, there is no way around it. Greedo wants a thing he simply does not have. All Lirin Car'n could do would be to, somehow, figure out how to acquire the money he owes that doesn't involve pawning his father's instrument, which he no longer possesses.

Greedo pokes him harder, managing to push Lirin Car'n into the wall. "And why should I provide you clemency? Why should I show you mercy? A debt is a debt. The terms were that I would be paid in full by you today!" he yells.

"I cannot, Greedo. For I literally have no—" He turns his pockets inside out to show the Rodian. "—money at all. I was robbed last night, you see, and—"

Greedo yawlps in frustration. He gets closer.

"I shall only raise your interest rate to thirty-five percent and choose to let you live," he hisses. "You are very lucky."

"I do not feel very lucky," Lirin Car'n says.

"Well, you are, because today is the day Greedo *levels up*, and I don't have the time to chase broke little hustlers like you up and down the spaceport." The Pig-Nosed Man and the Walrus-Faced Man share a smug chuckle, the sound of two bullies about to remove the pocket change from an unknowing, and smaller, child.

Lirin Car'n can't help but laugh at the idea of a hopeless case like

Greedo belonging to the same class of violent criminal as these two, and yet, by association, Lirin Car'n can only assume this is the reputation the Rodian wishes to cultivate. This is the kind of thing to which Greedo aspires; these two chuckling, violent morons radiate Greedo's dream vibe.

Greedo tugs at his blaster, but it catches in its holster, and needing a second hand to extract the thing. The maneuver, so incompetent in its perfect Greedoian absurdity, strikes Lirin Car'n as laughable, and thus he laughs again, rather than doing what any sensible creature would do when an idiot attempts to draw a weapon on them only for the thing to get stuck, which is: run. The laughter only makes things worse.

Before Lirin Car'n knows it, Greedo pushes the unstuck blaster into his chest, keeping the Bith at bay in place against the wall. The gun shivers in Greedo's hand, quivering in anticipation of firing.

"Today I capture or kill the most wanted man on Tatooine. Today I make my name in the court of Jabba the great. Today I collect my first fortune." Every time he says "today" he jabs the pistol harder into Lirin Car'n's already concave chest in a way impossible to consider anything other than *hostile*.

Lirin Car'n cannot stop looking at the gun and snickering. It all feels so remote and surreal.

"Stop it!" Greedo shouts, poking the gun into him one last time for emphasis. Lirin Car'n, actually hurt and actually annoyed now, shoves Greedo's gun hand out of his way as if to say, *Knock it off*, and he slaps it to the side, which sends the lithe little green sylph back into the Pig-Nosed Man. The Walrus-Faced Man chugs like a motor igniting and rams the Bith back into the wall, hard, keeping his massive left arm pressed under Lirin Car'n's chin, and at long last fear ignites inside Lirin Car'n and floods through his body all at once, lightning and fire and panic.

"Orrp-orrp-orrp-orrp," orrps the Walrus-Faced Man.

"*Twelve* systems!" Pig-Nosed Man corrects.

Lirin Car'n feels throttled by genuine, panic-inducing, fight-or-flight fear now. Madness radiates off these two, and Greedo—Greedo wears bad luck around him like a cloud of fart, like ambient surface radiation, like a haunting aura of actual garbage. Mere proximity guaranteed—guaranteed!—his bad luck would contaminate you, too, and closer to now than later. Maybe the Pig-Nosed Man and the Walrus-Faced Man don't know, but Lirin Car'n knows, and Lirin Car'n now, finally, wants to run but cannot.

"All right," says Greedo, touching the Walrus-Faced Man, who frees Lirin Car'n from the wall.

Silence then. Car'n looks from one to the other to the other and they all stare at him. The silence holds. And holds.

"Can I . . . have until next week, then?" asks Lirin Car'n.

Greedo holsters his pistol once more and mutters in the affirmative. Car'n sees, along the length of the barrel of the thing, a little wisp of a prayer Greedo has scratched into its gunmetal surface—the word SOLO.

Desperate. Desperate and crazy.

As far as the Muftak can tell, the Pig-Nosed Man—called *Dr. Evazan* to his pig-nosed face but never in his absence—has no friends, except for the Walrus-Faced Man—called *Ponda Baba* and, same—and even so, they probably don't like each other very much. They have only managed to not kill each other yet because it's fifty–fifty how a fight would go down between them, a pair of psychotically entangled parasites. The Pig-Nosed Man lives life in a constant state of pain and anger. No one quite knew what, exactly, Evazan did to himself or why, but it mangled his face, split his nose, and made him quite impossible to deal with rationally. To mitigate the perpetual agony his wounds cause him, the mad doctor relies on a constant, alternating barrage of narcotics and physical violence, and a man with no friends except for a Walrus-Faced Man has great difficulties finding the first, and far too much ease finding the second. The result of the cycle is this: No one wants to sell Dr. Evazan his drugs, because Dr. Evazan tends toward dumb and dangerous behavior no matter what level of illicit substances flow through him.

This life will not end well for the doctor.

The Muftak hustles too hard to hold his hose shut at such an opportunity. He worked himself into a semi-regular arrangement as an intermediary. Evazan gives the Muftak a cool thousand and, less his danger surcharge and Breaking-the-Law expenditure, the Muftak pays the balance to the Smuggler who, knowing better than to ask why or who-for of his customers, converts the money into the anodyne chemical compounds the good doctor seeks minus his own not-inconsiderable shipping and handling charges, then delivers them to the Muftak, who delivers them to the doctor and hopes this will not be the time their arrangement gets him killed.

"I had to drop my cargo, pal. Sorry," says Han Solo. "Imperial interference." He shrugs. *Nothing could have been done then; nothing can be done now.* The Muftak might as well yell at the sun. Either sun. It won't help.

But-but-but-but, the Muftak panic-tweets, *my client—I took his money. You took his money. Then upon delivery he'd pay me a completion bonus and hazard stipend, as per our agreement. You owe me his money! You owe me my money that he will not pay me now, as I will not provide him with the goods and services he requires! What are we going to do about this, Solo?*

Solo turns to the Wookiee, who barks and growls and snorts a pidgin translation.

"Well," Solo says. "Nothing. Unless you want to take it up with the Empire, we lose this round."

This does not help calm the Muftak.

"Everybody loses sometimes. Even me."

But I lose every time! the Muftak bleats out, banging his big furry fists on the table.

The Wookiee puts his bigger, furrier fists on the table, too, because some things you can say without saying anything sometimes, even if you can't say anything at all. The Muftak inhales. And then exhales. The temperature at the table lowers as quickly as it rose.

The Muftak imagines Evazan doing to his face what was done to his own. He imagines Ponda Baba shoving all of his eyes in, all at once.

He imagines them both coming upon Kabe, helpless and alone without the Muftak's protection, blind in the daylight, dying of heat and then, then, then dying of *them.*

He turns to Chewbacca. *Could I implore you, at least, this: Come with me as I explain to my client our shared predicament in the hope that his fury—and make no mistake, there will be great fury—might find itself diminished by the sheer majesty of your great physical presence?*

The Wookiee snorts. He probably means yes?

143

Stop me if you've heard this one before: A Chadra-Fan, a Bith, a Sakiyan, an Abyssin, an Aqualish, a human, a Rodian, a Wookiee, another human, and a Muftak walk into a bar, all of them trying to rip one another off at best, and kill one another at worst, more or less.

The Muftak freezes. Every head at his usual table turns to him. Some faces look happy; others furious. Only the Sakiyan speaks.

"Come, friend. Join us."

Not the Muftak's first choice. He finds the reception awaiting him at the usual table a complicated array of responses. No one, it would seem, feels terribly happy he has come, except Kabe, of course, who figures her odds of dying in the near future have dropped at least a little bit. Djas Puhr gets up—as does Lirin Car'n—ensuring that the Muftak cannot leave the table with any great ease.

"Quite a day you've had."

I'm doomed, the Muftak says.

"Rightfully so!" shouts Myo.

"Gentlemen, keep your heads," says Djas Puhr.

Myo, I took from you a pawnable thing of value to reimburse what you owed me in losses. It was not mine to take, but I was owed.

Hissing now through gritted teeth, hoping it reduces his volume, Myo leans over. "It was not yours to take."

I just . . . The Muftak looks around to his compatriots. *Did I not just say—yes, Myo, yes. It was not mine to take. In my defense, I collected on a debt.*

"I might have had the money! You don't know!"

The Muftak honestly hadn't considered this. *Did you have the money?*

Myo, a terrible liar, lies. "Maybe."

"Can we address, perhaps, a larger point, Myo," says Lirin Car'n, turning his fury on the furious one, "in that I, in my cups, made a foolish decision and you chose to exploit it?"

"Profit from it, you mean," Myo says, and laughs. He looks to the others to join in, yet they do not. The ugly truth among them all finds its place at the table now, too; the fragility of their civility to one another radiant in the dank alcove of their booth.

I am particularly doomed, the Muftak says. *Today especially.* Sounds of agreement, to varying degrees and with varying levels of enthusiasm, issue forth from his cohort.

"Why today of all days? Why not yesterday? Why not tomorrow?"

Solo wet his pants at the sight of an Imperial garbage barge and dropped cargo. Some of that cargo was mine, owed to someone else, and now they're going to kill me, and if they don't, they're not paying me the balance owed, which means someone else will kill me, as I find myself financially embarrassed at the moment and direly in need of some liquidity, the Muftak squirps, motioning to Myo and Lirin Car'n as he does, the subtext being *to pay these gentles back what they are owed,* even though, strictly speaking, none of them are owed anything, not really. *All of which is to say I have no idea how to resolve the issue of the horn or how to reimburse those who demand and deserve adequate recompense.*

"He dropped your cargo," Djas Puhr says. "And yet he kept mine. Had Solo been searched, and searched thoroughly, by these admirals of the Imperial refuse fleet, possession of the cargo he brought me would have brought him a death sentence. And yet." Djas Puhr lets the notion hang in the space among them.

The Muftak looks to the ceiling, dingy and stained and encrusted with filth generations old, and bleats a noise that sounds, oddly enough, as if it came from the Kloo horn that started this whole mess.

What's your point? Han Solo likes you better than me. You have more friends than me. Fine. Great. You're a beloved figure, Djas Puhr. I'm already dead; I just don't know it yet.

"I am merely intrigued. Solo made a choice. Perhaps not a moral choice, but an ethical one," Djas Puhr says in response. "Perhaps he considers me a threat, so he decided not to drop my contraband. Perhaps he considers you a—well, you are the Muftak."

The Muftak bangs his head on the table.

"You are not a killer, is my point. Maybe the medications you provide Dr. Evazan—"

The Muftak snaps his head up. That . . . arrangement was supposed to be discreet.

"Everybody knows. Sorry."

145

Those at the table agree—demure as they can manage, but agreeing all the same. The Muftak drops his shoulders a little more, thoroughly and totally defeated, as bad a drug dealer as he is a card player, a money-haver, a life-liver.

"One moment," says Lirin Car'n. "You're not giving him narcotics *now*, are you? Today?"

No. Because Solo dropped cargo. I have nothing to give, clicks the Muftak. *Why?*

"Greedo the Rodian is making a play for Solo. Ponda Baba and Evazan are backing it. I thought, for a moment, of an Evazan blitzed to the gills, who would make a violent situation only more violent, and was relieved he shall be without. Though saying it out loud, I'm not so certain. Which Evazan is better? Medicated, or not?"

I need a drink, says Kabe, and she escapes under the table to approach the bar.

I am going to die, the Muftak says.

"Well then, Muftak, on the precipice of death, what sort of creature shall you be? One who values friends? Or profit? By which code have you lived?"

The Muftak wiggles his wee trunk back and forth. He looks around the bar. He sees all sorts: friends, fiends, foes, financial prospects and liabilities. All of whom would just as soon gut him and rob him blind as reach down to help him, he is sure.

And then, as always, he sees the best part of a place like Mos Eisley and is filled with a new hope.

A teenage girl enters, looking around, eyes wide as dying stars, skin radiant with the flush of youth. The Muftak knows she's never been here before because she tries bringing her golden interpreter droid in with her. An old man who should know better follows. The Muftak looks at this girl and tries to imagine how much money she and her ancient father could have between them, how much he could

146

swindle or steal. The prospect of fresh work, of a new project, a new mark, excites him.

The Muftak looks to Lirin Car'n. *Lirin Car'n, I never should have accepted your father's horn from Myo—*

Banging the table in protest, Myo turns. "'Accepted'?"

"Let him finish," Djas Puhr says.

All of us knew that horn meant more than whatever payday it represented. We should have watched out for it, all of us, and for you, and for one another, and we didn't. This . . . I think maybe this is what separates us from the animals.

"Technically, Muftak, I believe your kind may *be* animals," says Djas Puhr.

Nobody likes a pedant, the Muftak says.

"You are not a pendant, you are a know-it-all," Myo says, and snarls. As Myo's intellectual prowess impresses no one, least of all himself, the table finds itself collectively surprised.

147

"We are all just money to one another, that is all. Today or tomorrow, one day, one of us will be a payday to the other and we will pounce. I took your stupid thingy, Lirin Car'n, yes. And I knew you were drunk and I knew you would want it back and I knew I could get money I didn't have for it. Just as the Muftak knew the same and took it from me. And we would both do it again."

"I'm not so sure," says Djas Puhr, looking at the Muftak.

"This is the way the world works," a dejected Lirin Car'n says. "Especially at Mos Eisley. Life is cheap, Kloo horns are cheaper, and money is expensive."

"I propose a wager, friends," says Djas Puhr. "I say Han Solo lives to see the other side of this day, despite unfavorable odds, because he is a man with friends. I say Greedo does not collect his bounty, for Greedo has no friends but for those he pays."

The table considers. The table wonders why.

"Let us wager on the nature of the universe. Who wins? The man with friends, or the man seeking profit at all costs? If I'm right, Lirin Car'n, I will pay your debt to Myo. Myo, I will pay your debt to the Muftak. Muftak, I will pay what you and Kabe owe Ackmena in rent. And if I'm wrong . . . well, Greedo will kill Solo, Evazan will kill the Muftak, or Chalmun will, or, hell, maybe even Myo. Myo will figure out that Kabe took the horn from the Muftak and pawned it and will probably kill her, being robbed of the chance to kill the Muftak, and Lirin, your debt will remain unpaid, so Greedo, confident with a Wookiee pelt across his chest and Solo's scalp nailed to his wall, will inflict great pain, if not actual death, upon you, for he is now a killer and killers can never stop once they've started. He'll drain you like a shallow-dug well, and when you're dry . . ."

He doesn't need to finish the sentence.

"And I . . . I will have to find a new cohort to associate with, which is a shame, as I've quite come to enjoy this table. For all its foibles."

The gathered work through the scenario Djas Puhr has laid out and they realize, one at a time, that he has spoken with unerring accuracy.

The Muftak sighs. *I leave now to see a Pig-Nosed Man about a dropped shipment of illicit narcotics.* He turns, then pauses.

I am sorry, Lirin Car'n. I am sorry, Myo.

Djas Puhr raises his glass to the Muftak.

Wandering through the Mos Eisley crowd, no one feels more friendless in its dim and cool confines than the Muftak. He senses something in his paw.

A drink, handed to him by Kabe.

You look like you need it more than me, friend, she squeaks.

And he does. So he drinks. It is cold and smooth and good. It is relief in a tall blue cup.

Maybe Djas Puhr is right after all.

At the bar, keeping an eye on the door and, one assumes, Djas Puhr, stands Dr. Evazan, and next to him Ponda Baba. Down a piece stands Chewbacca, ready to play backup to the Muftak as promised, but-tressing an expectant space between them being held, the Muftak knows, for the Muftak himself. All he can do is insert himself therein and explain to the psychopaths that he doesn't have their drugs or their money.

He chooses to steady his nerves with the drink before getting probably murdered and, in the time it takes him to start snuffing the thing down his little protuberant gullet, the teenage girl and the old man take that space at the bar in his place.

The Muftak sighs. The only thing worse than waiting is being made to wait when you've resolved to do something after you're fin-ished waiting but now have no control over how long that waiting must last.

He responds in the only sane way possible: He drinks slower.

Before he's gotten even halfway done, the Aqualish lunatic attacks the teenage girl at the bar. And before this registers with anyone in Mos Eisley as anything outside of the positively banal and predict-able, the Old Man ignites the air and slices into Ponda Baba and Dr. Evazan with pure light before they can lay a hand on his daughter's flowing flaxen locks. The chaos lasts half a second longer, until the air stops sizzling and the Old Man and his wee lass head off after Chew-bacca, toward the smuggler's table, away from the downed lunatics.

Chewbacca offers the Muftak a shrug. *Sometimes these things take care of themselves.*

149

Greedo, behind the Old Man and the Wookiee, watching his hired muscle bleed out on the cantina floor, feels his luck shift beneath his feet. Greedo remains too stupid to turn back, and the Muftak knows the feeling.

The Muftak returns to the table where Lirin Car'n seethes, watching the band play, and Djas Puhr looks delighted.

Did you know that was going to happen? he clicks.

"No. Isn't it amazing?" asks Djas Puhr, who is, indeed, genuinely delighted.

Djas Puhr rises to allow the Muftak back into the corner seat, keeping Kabe and the Muftak pinned in between the lamenting Lirin Car'n and the angry Myo.

"I should be up there," the Bith says.

"Where? The bar? You wish to fight as well?" asks Myo, attention going to the mild outbreak of excitement as though the smell of blood holds a tractor beam only Abyssin can feel.

"What? No, the stage, the stage, I should be playing," he says.

I thought you hated music, says the Muftak.

"I hate being a musician," continues Lirin Car'n in a moment of clarity.

Is there a difference?

The Bith leans around to look at the band on what passes for a stage in this dump, playing their jaunty, syncopated, trademark tune.

"One fills your heart. The other breaks it," Lirin Car'n says.

That's insane, says the Muftak. *How could anything so beautiful be a burden? You have a gift. A true gift. Had I any sort of talent, for anything, I—*

A blaster cry breaks the din of Chalmun's Cantina, and Greedo, in a booth with Han Solo, slumps over, smoldering, dead. Everyone turns to stare, except for Djas Puhr, who stares at the Muftak. He smiles.

The Muftak scratches his head. With Greedo, Evazan, and Ponda Baba out of the picture . . .

You are out a fortune, he clicks at Djas Puhr. Djas Puhr shrugs. *Why are you smiling? You've lost the bet and now owe . . . owe . . . owe all of us at least* some*thing. I know you do well as a tracker, but none of us do* that *well.*

Djas Puhr reaches beneath the table and, from behind his legs, brings up the Kloo horn of Lirin D'avi, who gave it to his son Lirin Car'n, who lost it to Myo, who lost it to the Muftak, who lost it to Kabe, who sold it to a Scrapper, who sold it to him. He places it on the table and everyone shuts up for a second.

"Now that," says Myo, "is a funny joke."

Night: The knot of the days' events wound and unwound themselves around the necks of many. Some escaped, some did not, and still yet others wanted only to get home in one piece. The Muftak sits at the bar, drinking, each gulp a relief, each sip sweeter and savored more than the last. He finds himself filled with a romance and sentiment toward everything on this particular night; the Muftak, having found himself in love with the entire world, keeps drinking.

Fortune eventually smiled upon him some, at least a little bit, at the sabacc table with his friends. He's put aside about half of what the Muftak and Kabe owe to Chalmun to stay in the pipes and is imbibing the rest, raising glass after glass to the prospect of living to see another day. Nothing tastes as good as the drink Kabe gave him in the bar that afternoon, but the Muftak intends to keep tasting until he finds its equal.

When he almost falls off the stool, the Muftak gets cut off. As he rises and staggers in the first of many unstable, uncertain steps toward home, he finds himself supported by Lirin Car'n, who escorts him—with great care, with great concern—toward where he'll sleep, in the tunnels below their feet, dreaming endless dreams of all tomorrow's scores, each one more certain than the last to be the one that turns it all around.

It turns out that, sometimes, friends take care of one another, even in a place like Mos Eisley, and that makes all the difference in the world.

ADDED MUSCLE

Paul Dini

Jabba had said to meet him at Docking Bay 94. Told me it was a collection job and he needed some insurance. One look at the duds he dragged along confirmed this. Not a pro in the lot. I'd be lying if I said I didn't enjoy the whispers of surprise when I walked onto the scene. That's right, boys. Fett's here. Do me a favor and fall to the side after you're hit. I really don't want to trip over your idiot corpses once the shooting starts. Sorry, *if* the shooting starts. No reason to get excited yet.

Okay, Wook. There are two ways this is going down. One, we have a nice little chat, Jabba gets his money from Solo, and we all leave happy. Two, someone gets anxious, *zip zip,* Jabba's rid one deadbeat, and I get a new scalp for my collection. No guesses which one I prefer.

Originally, I wasn't supposed to be a part of this. That's what I get, I guess, sticking around Tatooine to snag some Imperial coin. I was supposed to be off this dust ball yesterday, but I picked up trooper buzz that Vader was looking for a couple of runaway droids. Figured I'd collect the bounty and square myself with the headman at the same time. He's still got a mad on over those rebel spies I crisped on Coruscant. Idiots came at me with ion disruptors. What, they thought I wouldn't carry a weapon accelerator? Flash, boom, three tiny ash piles. Tried to collect and Lord "No Disintegrations!" refused to pay without bodies. My word's not good enough, apparently. Reckoned I'd make up the loss by finding his droids and holding out for twice the reward.

No go on that. Trailed one until its footprints were wiped out by a Jawa sandcrawler. Followed those treads a way until I found someone had wiped out the Jawas, too. "Someone" meaning *amateurs* trying to fake a Tusken raid. Probably stormtroopers, judging by the random blast shots. Some might call them precise. Me, I say they can't hit the butt end of a bantha. At least they had brains enough to take out everyone who had seen the droids. Hard luck on the sizzled hicks I found at that torched moisture farm. Had a look-see and discovered there were three settlers living there, not two. Betting the third ran with the droids. I'll hunt around after I'm done here. Vader may triple the bounty if I bring him the fugitive along with the droids. Yeah, I know, intact corpse, "no disintegrations."

Till then, here I stand, adding some credibility to the collection of bums and bugs Jabba calls muscle. Figures he'd want us to shake down Solo, the biggest loser in the galaxy. I could just pop him for target practice, but I never work for free.

Twerp? You're really gonna call me that, Solo? Back it up with your blaster, Wook-hugger. I'll twerp your guts all over that sorry heap of junk you call a ship. Easy, Furball. Paws where I can see them. No one's throwing down just yet. Still, if you want to start something, sure, I can shift my gun a little, move the braids where you can see them . . . there you go. You like that? Take a good look. Friends of yours, maybe? Family? Smart critter. No reaction. Play it cool.

Meanwhile Solo plays for time. Same old song and dance. "I'll pay you tomorrow for a charter I'm taking today." Garbage. He'll run at the first chance, and I'll chase him down. Fine by me. The more I work, the more I'll make Jabba pay for the pirate's head.

Not that I really have anything against the big slug—his money is just as good as anyone's, and better than most. But business is business, and we both know to press the advantage when we have it. Mama Fett didn't raise any fools. Strictly speaking, my mama was a birthing pod, but you get the point.

Still, I can't help but think Jabba considers me the closest thing he has to a friend. Well, closer anyway than that creepy suck-up Fortuna and that shrieking varmint he keeps for a pet. Some nights when the lights are down in the palace and his scum buddies are snoozing, Jabba pulls out a bottle of his really prime gardulla, kicks Rebo awake, orders him to play something low and sad, and invites me to have a few. So I take off my helmet (but never my gun) and drink as he pours. And the Hutt talks. A lot. Personal stuff, things no one else ever hears. Stories of loves lost, enemies crushed, deals brokered then broken, regrets, possibly, things that eat at his soul, if he's got one. 'Course I don't understand a word he says, but the drink is good and the company, considering what Jabba pays, is tolerable.

What, we're done? Jabba actually gave Solo an extension. Unbelievable. And after Solo fried Greedo and tromped on the slug's tail to boot. Jabba's getting soft. Either that, or he figures Solo's got ties to people with deeper pockets. Must be that. The Hutt can smell money, and he never misses a trick. You lead a charmed life, Solo, and I'd very much like to change that. You, too, Wook. That auburn scalp of yours will make a fine trophy. Someday. Right now Jabba just said *"Boska,"* and when the boss says *boska,* we *boska.* As long as he's in a generous mood, I'll hit him up for a mug of that fine brew. After today I could use one.

YOU OWE ME A RIDE

Zoraida Córdova

Brea Tonnika couldn't remember where she was. Not at first.

The stale stench of wine and lingering haliat perfume on her skin helped her focus on the cracked bedroom walls smeared with stains, the origins of which she didn't want to try to guess. Still hungover, she recoiled from the noonday rays filtering through her window and let herself sink back into the hard mattress. Try as she might, she couldn't keep out the cacophony of merchant chatter and hissing transports. Over the years, Brea and her sister had stayed in some funky places, but the best room for rent in Mos Eisley's dusty port was only a fraction better than pitching a tent on one of Tatooine's vast sand dunes.

The door opened, and Brea reached for the blaster on the nightstand.

"You're finally up," Senni Tonnika said.

Brea and Senni Tonnika were alike in so many ways. They shared the same lean, muscular legs and braided dark hair. The same wide expressive eyes and that roguish smirk when they set their sights on a mark. But the resemblance stopped there. Sometimes, Brea wished she could charm strangers the way Senni could with just a turn of her lovely head. Senni was tall, and her hair made her appear even taller. She found power in being able to look down at nearly anyone when negotiating contracts—contracts that lately were few and far between, and fulfilling them not made easier with the arrival of Imperial troops snooping around.

Brea sat up and grabbed a robe from the floor. "Please tell me it's not more flatbread and beans."

Senni kicked off her boots and hooked her cloak on the back of the door. She threw the fiber bag across the small room. Two beds, a shower, and a table for their weapons. That's all they needed.

"It's *not* more beans?" Senni said, trying to keep a straight face as her twin ripped open the bag of food to find fresh loaves of flatbread.

Brea ripped off a piece and shoved it between her lips, still smeared with her favorite metallic lipstick.

"I hate this place," she said, finally getting out of bed. She sat at the table covered with blasters and rifles. She picked up her favorite pistol—the metal was the blue of Ithorian roses.

"We *could* stay at the palace," Senni said. "You know Jabba has always taken a liking to you."

"*Us,*" Brea said, chewing rudely to make her sister cringe. "And simply because the word *palace* is in its description does not a palace make."

"Speaking of overstuffed snot, His Royal Slug has a job."

"What is it?"

"If I knew, I wouldn't be sitting here watching you nurse your hangover."

"I feel perfect."

Senni threw her head back and cackled. "If it weren't for me, you would've made out with a Rodian pirate last night."

Brea grimaced, trying to recall the night. But there was only darkness. Darkness was better than the memories that threatened to push their way to the forefront of her thoughts. Blood, and guns, and jobs gone so south she wasn't sure she'd ever recover. Memories like that didn't have place in the present. So she did as her sister asked and showered, the water tepid and smelling of chemicals she couldn't name.

When she was ready, she stood in front of Senni, who without speaking zipped up the back of her bodysuit. Each sister carried a pistol at her hip and a knife in her boot. They put on their cloaks and headed out into the dry, suffocating street, where it was nearly impossible not to inhale dust.

They hopped on a speeder and zoomed toward Jabba's palace.

159

Brea and Senni watched the suns set from atop a rock formation. Tatooine might be a desert wasteland lacking in any culinary delicacies, but few things in the galaxy compared to the brilliance of its sunsets.

The Tonnika sisters stalked down the cavernous corridor that led to the dank hall where Jabba held court. The Royal Slug's body odor was impossible to miss. Brea always pinched the bridge of her nose until she was able to stand the smells, but Senni wasn't fazed by things like comfort. She wanted to get on with the next job, mainly because their accounts were nearly depleted and their faces were in every criminal database in the galaxy. So Senni Tonnika held her head high, her braids swishing around her broad shoulders like fringe as she walked in.

They wore different-colored suits, Brea's blue and Senni's acid-green, and waded through the crowds, returning the cordial nods that were thrown in their direction. Jabba was still hidden under shadow, slumbering the way he did no matter how loudly the court bustled around him.

Brea ordered two Tatooine sunsets from a waitress, ignoring her sister's glare, and they picked an empty spot against a wall where they could watch.

"Ugh," Brea muttered under her breath. Since they were little, they'd developed a way of speaking without many words. Brea's dark eyes flitted across the room where Bib Fortuna stalked around the band. His bright-red eyes sent shivers down Brea's spine.

Senni touched her sister's shoulder but steeled her features. "Not long."

But it *was* a long time before Jabba deigned to wake up, despite having been the one to call the gathering. No one questioned him. No one complained that they'd been waiting and waiting, or that the band was recycling songs it had played when they first arrived. Brea drank another tall orange-and-pink drink, smiled at a Wookiee with a great scar across his face, and watched the Twi'lek girl twirl her delicate wrists to the rhythm of the horns. It wasn't the music that woke Jabba, but the growl of the rancor that lived in the cage beneath his throne.

Senni and Brea glanced at each other, then at the other bounty hunters in attendance. There was a moment of stillness. The Max Rebo Band was dead silent. A deep grumble echoed in the bowels of the palace, and Brea felt her heart quicken because she knew what would happen when Jabba moved his throne back and opened the hatch. She'd seen hunters and slaves of any and all species plunge into the deep dark beneath and never come out.

Instead of feeding his pet, Jabba opened the wide slit of his drooling mouth and laughed.

"*Gather around, my friends,*" Jabba ordered in Huttese. He turned his serpent eyes on the band and said, "*Did I ask you to stop playing?*"

Max set his fat blue digits to pressing the keys of his organ, and an upbeat tune played in the background as every bounty hunter present stepped closer to Jabba's throne.

Senni stood in front of her sister, as if she could shield her with her body. She looked from side to side at the others in attendance. Among her peers, she wasn't someone's sister and she wasn't some orphan. No, she was a hunter and a thief and a smuggler. She was capable of many things, even if Brea was the one whose mugshot was listed in the criminal database for murder.

Whatever this job was, Senni would do it because they needed to get far away where they wouldn't be recognized and their names wouldn't be flagged on scans. They could get off this world and have what *passed* as a normal life. For that, they needed credits. Lots of them, and only Jabba offered that kind of currency.

"*As many of you know,*" Jabba began in his guttural voice, "*Han Solo lost my cargo. He has ignored my summons. I want him brought to me. My sources tell me he is seeking to get offplanet as soon as he can. Whoever brings Solo to me, alive, will be rewarded.*"

There was a bevy of murmurs. A dark-haired hunter wearing a black jacket looked at Brea and then at Senni. But the sisters kept quiet and waited. The scar-faced Wookiee stepped forward. The sisters didn't understand his wailing speech, but whatever he said made Jabba laugh again.

Brea watched the Royal Slug throw his slimy head back, his tail wiggling happily, and she wondered if he ever stopped laughing. She shifted beneath the nervous ripple in the crowd, because she knew what would come next.

Senni grabbed her sister's hand and they took a step back. The latch opened beneath the Wookiee's feet, and his scream was the flat note of a horn.

"*Bring me Solo,*" Jabba said when the Wookiee's cry died down, and then there were only the jingling tunes of the band, and the crunching of bone between the rancor's teeth.

Brea and Senni discussed the job over and over again through the night and into the next morning.

"I say he won't come with us," Brea said.

"He can't still be mad about the Lando ordeal. It was *his* idea."

Brea wanted to correct her sister. There were many things that had happened between them and the cocky smuggler. Maybe not friendship, but there was history. When Jabba put out a prize like that, he was pitting a whole lot of rancors against one another. Why shouldn't the sisters be the ones to come out triumphant?

"It doesn't matter," Brea said. "Solo is going to take one look at us and bolt. He won't come willingly."

"Then we won't take him willingly." Senni licked her lips coquettishly.

"Have you forgotten his Wookiee bodyguard? Senni, it's *Han.* If he's got any brains in that thick skull of his, he's already fixing to run. We'll find another job."

Senni crossed her arms and scoffed stubbornly. "Oh, yeah? When?"

"I don't know, but—"

"*But nothing.* When did you go soft for Solo, anyway? You've been cursing his name across the galaxy for years. We need a fast ship and to get that we need credits. *Someone* is going to bring him in. Why shouldn't it be us?"

"I get it," Brea said, her brow furrowed. She was surprised at Senni. "I have a debt to pay Solo, but I've never been brave enough to go through with it. After all, he was responsible for my greatest humiliation, and that I'll never, ever forget."

Senni was startled by her own thoughtless. How could she have mistaken her sister's hesitation for concern? "It's your call. This could be our chance to have what we've always wanted."

In their cramped room in the heart of Mos Eisley, Brea and Senni Tonnika faced each other from the edges of their twin beds. *What we've always wanted.* Freedom. Peace. Life. Everyone knew how people like them ended up—blown up, in prison, or on the wrong end of a blaster.

Then Brea made that face she always made when she was up to no good. Because they *could* have it all. The freedom and the peace of mind. All of it.

"I have a better idea," she told Senni who quirked a single brow.

"This isn't like the time we broke into House Organa's palace to lift the royal jewels and had to hide in a dumpster for two nights, is it?"

Brea rolled her eyes. "For the last time, I got a bad tip. How was I supposed to know the housemaids don't wear orange?"

"Or the time—"

"Enough," Brea said, and this time her sister listened. "We can have it all—the ship, the credits, and we won't get our limbs ripped off in the process."

"How?"

"Let's steal the *Falcon*."

When Brea Tonnika stepped into Chalmun's Cantina, she felt just as she had during her first con back on Kiffex. Her palms were sweating and her heart was racing out of her chest. Back then, she and Senni had been trying to break a friend out of a detention center. Back then,

163

no credits had been involved, just duty. Everything had gone smoothly, until a guard came back to his post early and caught them. Brea stayed behind to give them cover, and her sweaty, nervous hands shot to kill. It was only her on the footage.

After that they had no choice but to go offworld. To run and keep running until there came a day when they would have a place to call home that wasn't a dank rented room or a freighter ship.

"It's the fastest ship in the galaxy," Brea pleaded with her sister.

"That's what *Han* says, and everyone's too scared to challenge him. Besides, Jabba's reward could buy a dozen fast ships."

They looked down at the same time, as if they were sharing the same thought—the rancor devouring the Wookiee at Jabba's palace. It wasn't the first time they'd seen the creature in action, but every time they hoped it would be the last. Brea wondered if she could really leave Solo to that fate. She steeled her heart because taking care of Senni would always come first.

Senni sighed and said, "I don't know. Solo would probably rather take his chances with the entire Empire than give up his ship."

"He's a rat roach," Brea said, and chuckled. "I know he's somewhere on this dirtball trying to find a new soul to swindle. But we've got to act now, Sen. We have to beat Jabba's men to the ship. The place is crawling with stormtroopers. If it goes south, there is no way I'm taking work from the Empire. Not after what they've done to our kind."

"You're a *hunter*," Senni reminded her. "You don't get to choose where your job comes from."

"If this is our last job, then yes, we can choose."

So they chose. Brea cut a path through the tightly packed dark aisles of the tavern and settled at the bar. Wuher, the bartender, barely looked in their direction before he pulled on a draft handle and set two tall glasses in front of them. Not one for pleasantries, he grumbled his "hello" and stalked off to take another order.

"There he is," Senni whispered into her sister's ear.

A couple of regulars cozied up beside them, already in their cups, tapping their feet to the jumping rhythm of the band. Senni smiled and delighted two locals with stories of a job they had worked in the Canto Bight Casino. Meanwhile, Brea watched the crowd. A man in a brown robe walked in and struck up a conversation with a pilot. Beside her, Senni laughed and was her usual charming self.

"I tell you, I can't get anything done with those helmet-heads parading about," one of the locals told Brea, his thick bottom lip drooping.

"Never seen anything like it," another one said.

That piqued Senni's interest and she joined the conversation. From farmers to merchants, no one on Tatooine was pleased with the recent arrival of stormtroopers.

"What are they after?" she asked.

"Droids, sounds like," the man said. "I've got a mess of them piled up in my shed if they want droids."

Brea glanced at her sister and shared a frown for a moment before recommencing her careful scan of the cantina. She noticed a young farmer walk in. His hair was the shade of beaten gold, and even in the dark of the room she could see how bright his eyes were. There was an innocence about him as he *asked* his droids to wait outside, then walked up to the bar beside the old man in the brown robe.

Brea liked him, for some inexplicable reason. He had the kind of innocence she and Senni never could.

Then Brea grabbed her sister's arm. "Docking Bay Ninety-Four."

"Something strange is happening," Senni told her twin as they raced through the crowded Mos Eisley streets. Each sandstone building looked exactly like the next; every person wore a cloak to protect

165

themselves from the sand and the dust. It was the perfect port to get lost in, if one truly wanted to.

"Something strange is always happening," Brea said. "First, there's so much heat on this speck of rock—"

"It's a desert, of course there's heat."

"You know what I mean. I think something terrible is going to happen."

Brea sidestepped a kid racing on a hover bike. She would've yelled at him if she didn't have somewhere to be. "Listen to me," she said to Senni. "Terrible things will always happen. They happened on Kiffex and they happen on Naboo and they happen on Tatooine. There will always be a war, and there will always be someone who wants us locked up. But the only thing we can do is survive, Sen. Survive until they won't let us."

They got to Docking Bay 94, and there she was—the *Millennium Falcon*. Dirty and in need of a shine, but the Tonnika sisters knew how fast she could go. In that moment they had the same memory of seemingly endless nights aboard the most magnificent hunk of junk in the galaxy. But that was the past. Memories.

"Do you remember how to work the control panels?" Senni asked Brea.

Brea shrugged, but a quirk at her lip betrayed her thoughts. "Lando taught me a thing or two."

They took a step toward the *Falcon,* but a familiar laugh stopped them cold. *Jabba.* Brea yanked her sister to the side and hid around a stack of crates.

"Blast!" Senni hissed.

"How many?" Brea asked.

Senni shook her head. She propped herself up and stole a glance from over the top of the crates. There were Jabba and a handful of bounty hunters, guarding the *Falcon* like a pack of womp rats. There were too many of them, all concentrated around the entrance to the ship. There was no way they could get on board now. Stealing the *Falcon* while there was a price on Solo's head would be like stealing from Jabba himself, but it would've been worth it. Brea cursed herself for not acting faster, for letting her hesitation drag her down. They were too late.

"Why send hunters out for Solo if he knew where he was the whole time?" Brea wondered.

"I told you. Something strange is happening. We *have* to get off-world!"

"Our ride is a little off limits," Brea whisper-hissed.

"We'll find another way. We always do."

Brea thought back to the time they stowed away on a ship belonging to the Ohnaka Gang or the time they were stranded in Wild Space or the time they trashed their room on Coruscant just to get back at Lando . . . Senni was right; they always found another way.

Brea smiled at her sister and waited for the coast to be clear. As soon as Jabba and his men weren't looking in their direction, they slipped back out the door and onto the crowded street.

Brea and Senni Tonnika needed to regroup. Find another way to break free. It seemed as if that life they wanted was as distant as the outermost ring of the galaxy. But for now, as they ducked into a nearby alleyway, they had each other.

"You owe me a ride," Senni told her sister after a long silence.

Brea wanted to say that she owed her more than that.

They waited to see Jabba's next move but a scuffle broke out on the streets. Brea lifted her hood back up to see what the commotion was about. She kept close to the wall and saw a group of stormtroopers march by with rifles at the ready. Their presence ignited a wave of chatter among the street dwellers and locals, who watched them run into Docking Bay 94.

In the flurry of the moment, dozens of bodies were clamoring to see the stormtroopers in action. Their distraction brought a spark to Brea's eyes.

The docking bays nearby were left unmanned. Any ship in Jabba's position would sell handsomely, and if this was their last score, they were going out in style.

"What is it?" Senni whispered into her sister's ear, craning her neck like so many others.

"We're getting off this rock."

Brea smirked as she grabbed her sister's hand and led her back into the street, knowing quite well they couldn't stop running until they were surrounded by the stars.

THE SECRETS OF LONG SNOOT

Delilah S. Dawson

"**D**'you know what your problem is, Long Snoot?"

The human elbows me as if unsure he has my attention, and I allow it.

"What's that?" I say. His language is difficult for me to speak, inelegantly forced through two sets of teeth and out of my sensitive snout, an organ that can express a thousand emotions in my own language with a mere twitch.

"You're a stuck-up spy. Immoral and arrogant at the same time. See, you can be one or the other, but you can't be both." He swigs the acid he considers a beverage. The fumes make my snout wrinkle. "Think you're better than us. Pretend you're not rich. Sit around the cantina like you fit in. But you're just another alien, sticking your ugly mug where it don't belong."

My snout wrinkles, an elegant poem he can't read. "I will take that into consideration."

The human snorts and stands. "Sheesh. Don't even know when you're being insulted. Not even smart enough to take offense." He wobbles off to another table filled with raucous humans. They're laughing at me now, at the strange creature with the long snoot who hides behind robes and goggles. Their species grates on my nerves. Noisy, rude, unsubtle, uneducated, especially in the rougher corners of a planet like Tatooine. Their sweat stinks of fear and desperation. They're as trapped here as I am, although they tell themselves they chose this life.

"Know what your problem is?" I say in my own language, quietly and to myself. "Your problem is that your entire species thinks itself a sun around which the petty planets and moons spin, but really you're just another rock, doomed to ever orbit something grander but remain ignorant of your own insignificance."

He wouldn't understand that, even if I said it in his language.

Soon, he'll discover that his leather bag of credits is gone.

That, at least, is a language he understands.

He was wrong about the rich part, you see.

When I first came here, they called me Long Snoot. No one asked my name or species, which I at first considered the height of discourtesy. Soon I learned that it was a protective measure among thieves and felons, all hiding out here on a planet that's not worth searching. Did I tell them my name is Garindan ezz Zavor, and that I come from a respectable hive on Kubindi? Or that my clan is known for breeding and farming a sought-after strain of succulent picolet beetle? Did I tell them my children are well-known senators, orators, and artists, that my grandchildren fill the crèches and academies to bring future glory to our hive?

No, I did not.

For one, because no one asked. For another, because their petty thoughts don't matter. They are merely scavengers run to ground by a bigger predator. Fate chased us all here, but it won't keep me here much longer.

I look down at my datapad, checking my accounts. Yesterday I was wealthy by any standard. Then a robed spy offered me a garbled comm message from Kubindi. I haven't heard my own language in years, and I was more than willing to pay the substantial amount she demanded.

"Father, come home," my daughter said, her pain thrumming in every tone. "Mother is dead, and the family is in trouble. We—"

The message cut off. The stranger disappeared. My account dipped to nearly nothing.

I didn't care.

After that, my entire focus changed.

Before, I was quietly building my account to return home with riches at a time of my leisure. Then I could begin the process of freeing Kubindi from the control of the lying Empire. Now I have about three standard days to scrape together enough intel and creds to get me off this planet and back home, where I must bury my mate with full honors and regain control of my clan.

But my network is large, and I've already arranged for an informant to supply the codes I need to get home. The time is nigh, so I adjust my hood and goggles and slip out of the cantina, leaving half a credit out for the bartender, Wuher, one of the least offensive humans I know.

It's a pleasure to be outside, free from the stench of drunken, poorly washed fools. The light on this planet would blind me if I took off my goggles, but the scent of the night air is pleasurable. The sand scours the wind clean, and I always curl my snout with joy at the clear, mineral freshness of it. Moments later, I'll adjust, and the odor of dewbacks and rontos will hit me, big and warm, plus the smaller notes of fusty Jawas and the oily clank of metal. It's like a symphony, the way the scents flow anew with each breeze. But it only makes me long all the more for Kubindi, for the odors that speak of home. I haven't tasted dainty leevil pâté or robust beesh legs in ages. The only thing sweeter will be rubbing snouts with my children and meeting the new grandchildren, of which I'm sure there will be many.

I snatch a night moth from the air and try to swallow it before the vile taste hits me. Me, reduced to eating moths.

The air grows stale as I hurry through alleys and under billowing fabric tents. The humans narrow their eyes at me, their flesh radiating the scent of distrust and anxiety. They see me as a monster from their nightmares, a hideous, dishonest creature that lives to swindle and degrade them. If only they could understand that I see them exactly the same way, but with the added bonus of slavery and oppression. I am here only because their people brought me here and abandoned me. They are here by choice.

I reach the meeting place first and put my back against the rough clay dwelling. Sending my senses out into the night, I smell thieves counting creds, murderers with blood still on their hands, enforcers with smoking blasters, females drenched in hopelessness, starving children, and a hundred different species sleeping fretfully behind locked doors. This is normal in the slums of a place like Tatooine. All the honorable life happens farther out, on respectable moisture farms. Things I never smell here include the tang of fresh oil paint, the resin flaking off an instrument's plucked strings, the nutty zing of ink, or the powdery cosmetics painted on actors waiting behind dusty curtains. Of all the places for a cultured Kubaz to end up, it's ironic that it's on a planet bereft of arts, decorum, and education.

Not that it matters. I'll be gone soon.

I smell my informant before I see him. He's human, because of course he is. Nervous, sweating, his flesh still redolent of the armor he's worn all day while tromping around, cajoling and intimidating and killing his own kind on an order he doesn't fully understand and never questions. I was never that naïve. It's the nature of my species to question. It just so happens that I didn't question the right things, and that's how I came to be here.

He's jumpy, and he's still wearing a blaster. The less I speak, the more comfortable he will feel, so I simply hold out the worn purse of dewback leather I snatched from my unkind neighbor in the cantina, jingling it slightly in my glove.

That noise propels him forward. "Turn it out so I can see," he whispers.

It's a foolish demand. There are too many credits here, more than I can hold in my hands, but I pour out enough to satisfy him. Even through the goggles, I can see his bulbous eyes gleaming. Just as I want something, so does he. We are both willing to do underhanded things to make it happen. I wonder what purpose this money will serve. Perhaps a crime boss has stolen the dancing girl he thinks he loves, or maybe his child is sitting in irons in the market. Maybe he, too, just wants to escape the lies of the Empire. It doesn't matter. I tuck the coins back into the bag, and he snatches it without touching my glove and hands me a slip of paper with several codes scribbled in Basic.

"These will get me past the blockade?" I ask.

He jerks back when he hears my voice. I've been told it reminds humans of the whine of insects, which makes sense, as I am descended from insects. They never question that I have gone to the

173

trouble to learn their entire language, while not a single one has bothered to learn my name. If I told him his voice reminds me of the hooting complaints of a Kowakian monkey-lizard, he'd probably shoot me where I stand.

"The codes are good, at least for a few days. It would be best if you were on a ship with no guns, some sort of trader. Nothing the rebels would fly."

When he says the word *rebels,* he spits in the sand, and I can smell his moisture soaking up the dust. So this one—he still thinks his people are the good guys.

"Your friend is about to get jumped," I observe, and he pulls his hood down and spins. A soft thump and cry around the corner send him running toward the compatriot who watched his back during our exchange. My work is done, and I melt into the night.

The scent of their blood follows me. Even for villains, this place is dangerous.

I live here, but I would not call this place a home. My people build beautifully complex hives, each person curling in their own tight cell at night to dream the dreams of grubs. My hovel on Tatooine feels both too small to be a home and too big to be a sleeping cell. Someone stored beasts here once, but I prefer their lingering odor to that of humans and the other sentient creatures who surround me. Beasts have honest interests, most of them pertaining to the physical drives dictated by their body chemistry. Their odors are predictable, harmless, dependable.

But people emit thousands of pheromones in their secretions, their thoughts and feelings laid down like the whispered conversations that mar a concert. Tatooine is no place for a thinking being who relies on unspoken communication, especially when the communicators are unaware of how they lie to themselves. It is unfortunate that my business keeps me waiting for hours in cantinas, the air thick with lust and greed and fear. Perhaps this is why they hate me: Somewhere, deep down, they know someone is listening.

I lock my door as everyone else does. My blue light is calming, and I buzz a sigh as I finally remove my hood and goggles. I worry that when I return to Kubindi, my family and friends will focus on the unattractive ridges worn into my flesh by this disguise, the lines of tight leather pressing around my snout and drawing circles around my eyes. My hair will stand up straight, but parts of me will feel as if they droop. Among the Kubaz, little can be hidden, and I will be out of practice.

My datapad pings, alerting me to a new bounty. I must be choosy. For all of my strengths, I have many weaknesses, and I only select jobs that keep them hidden. No hand-to-hand combat. No kidnapping. No killing. No guarding. I rarely use my blaster but make a point of letting everyone see it. Information is my currency, and fortunately, that's exactly what's currently desired. The Empire has placed a high bounty on any information leading it to two droids. One is golden, one squat. Tomorrow morning, I'll find them. My snout wiggles with glee. The high price on this last job will pay for my passage off the planet and back to Kubindi. It means that the very Empire that lured me from my home with false promises is effectively paying to return me to my planet.

In the crèche, our instructors taught us of our history with the Empire and the Rebellion. The Empire was our friend, but the rebels had long sabotaged our technological advances to keep us offplanet. If we helped them, the Empire promised to help us gain a foothold in galactic trade and politics. The cunning protocol droids who spoke for the Empire on Kubindi were carefully bathed in hot oil before doddering down the ships' ramps to meet with our elders and proudly

175

lead us into the belly of their grand vessel as our people buzzed a cheer. We could not detect their lies.

I was one of the chosen students picked from the academy to study under the Empire as a diplomat and return to my mate and hive with new accolades. At least, that's what they told us. Instead I was indentured and trained as a spy. My ability to read body language, smell pheromones and weapons, and hear from long distances was to become a mere tool in the hand of galaxy-wide tyranny. My fifty companions and I were put in manacles and forced to withstand propaganda, indoctrination, and reprogramming.

Mine, as might be guessed, did not take.

I slipped away on a job and attempted to return to Kubindi, only to find its orbit guarded by Imperial firepower. Since then, I've been working quietly and steadily to create my current reality.

After this job, I will have enough credits to hire a ship.

I now have Imperial codes to get me past the blockade.

And I have a datapad crammed with the most current information, diagrams, and manuals on advanced technology and hyperspace travel. When I return to Kubindi, my people will finally learn that the Empire holds them hostage, keeping them from a much wider universe and sabotaging their every effort to get offplanet. I also have the intel necessary to build weapons that can shoot their buzzing TIE fighters out of the sky.

Tomorrow I will find the droids. I will collect the bounty.

And then I will leave.

My day begins in Chalmun's Cantina. Labria the Devaronian is already here, hiding his pointy smile and tapping his fingers to music no one else can hear. I take my place in a shadowy booth and order the only thing I can, a single shot of fermented mead from Geonosis.

It has taken me months to drink the whole bottle, but I tip Wuher for keeping it around. There are only a few shots left, worms sloshing around at the bottom of the green liquid. I dip in my snout and take a dainty sip, tasting hundreds of other mouths on the dirty glass.

I can hear almost everything said in this cantina, and by afternoon I've heard nothing of the droids. I slurp up the worm at the bottom of my glass and leave, just another hooded figure disappearing through Wuher's door. Outside, I do something I rarely do and take a full breath through my snout, drawing in every scent for blocks. Pain throbs behind my eyes; it's too much. This place is too crowded, too filthy, too full of flesh. I follow the scent of hot metal, but it's just another Jawa selling his wares. The next whiff of droid takes me to a pile of parts outside a mobster's apartment. I hurry from droid to droid, hunting for the gold one and the squat one. My hope begins to run out. If they're in the desert, I will have trouble finding them. Even with my goggles, that much yellow light quickly leaves me drained and hurting.

Then: I smell it. Something new.

An old speeder's exhaust, and with it the bright odor of droids left too long in the sun. They're not as close as I'd like, and by the time I get to the scent, they're gone, probably hiding in one of the myriad labyrinthine buildings. I stalk the area outside Wuher's cantina and hear a fight within. Ponda Baba and Evazan again, harassing outsiders. I hide in the shade as they lurch outside, Ponda's arm held in Evazan's hands like he's in the middle of one of his disgusting surgeries. The odor of charred flesh makes my snout wrinkle in revulsion, and foul red blood still drips from the wounds. I slip in the door once they're gone and lean against the wall, my hood pulled down. A strange scent rides the air, something I've never smelled before, like burning rock and cooked meat, like lightning given life. I trace it to three humans and a Wookiee. It's that disreputable Han Solo. The new humans need passage to Alderaan for themselves and two droids.

I almost laugh. Do these men even know what secrecy is? They're wanted, this town is being patrolled by stormtroopers, but they announce their intentions in plain sight. It's almost too easy. But the droids aren't with them, so I hurry out of the bar and squat in a dark corner between the cantina and Han's junker ship. If their deal works out, and it will, because I know Han needs money and a reason to get off Tatooine, they will come this way.

Soon I'm rewarded for my efforts. The men walk by with two droids, one golden and one squat, as they hurry to the *Millennium Falcon*. My snout crinkles with delight, and I find a quiet place to comm my contact within the Empire. Thanks to the protocol droids that answer this channel, I'm able to speak in Kubazian, and it's a small delight to taste the words of home . . .

"I've found the droids," I say. "Mos Eisley spaceport. Docking Bay Ninety-Four."

A mechanized voice answers, "Roger. Will credit account after collection."

How I hate droids. My people communicate what they wish you to know, and humans communicate everything, but droids communicate nothing.

I follow my quarry to make sure they're headed in the direction I've reported. They linger outside the ramp instead of hurrying onto the ship. I lean nonchalantly against the wall as the troopers appear to claim the droids.

"Is this Docking Bay Ninety-Four?" one asks me.

"Yes, that way! That way!" I say. Even though, in my excitement, I've forgotten to speak Basic, he understands well enough and hurries on.

As blasterfire erupts, I run away. The scent burns the hairs in my snout, and the lights give me a headache. I am not made for this place. It is pleasant, letting someone else do the dirty work. Back at the cantina, I order another drink at the bar. There's something fitting about finishing the bottle before I leave, as if giving myself concrete evidence that no Kubaz remain on this dratted planet.

"Two in a day?" Wuher asks, but I know he's not expecting an answer.

He moves on, and I take a sip and consider my datapad. The credits should appear at any time, and then I will look around this cantina and select the least terrible smuggler to escort me home. The bulk of my savings paid for my daughter's message, so collecting this bounty is imperative.

"The band is good, eh?" Labria comments, giving me the full benefit of his real smile, showing only his pointed teeth against his red skin.

For once, I respond honestly. "Functional but lacking in higher tones," I say in Basic.

The Devaronian shakes his head, ears going up in annoyance. "You know nothing," he grumbles.

Little does he know. A band on Kubindi has at least three times as many players as this simple Bith grouping, and the intricacies of our music would soar over his horns. I was once an accomplished percussionist myself.

"Perhaps you are correct," I offer.

I check my datapad, but still the credits aren't there. As I stare at the balance, a new message pings in.

"Droids avoided capture. Bounty not awarded," it says.

And that's it.

My snout deflates and sags with disappointment. I have a day or two, maybe mere hours to secure enough credits to buy my way off this planet while the Imperial codes are still good. I scroll through the boards, looking for some new or previously hidden bounty I can pick up, some easy little job to drop just enough credits into my account. It is not lost on me that, back home on Kubindi, my clan is wealthy enough to buy this cantina and everyone in it. But my daughter's message cost everything I had, and they can't get off Kubindi, and I can't get a message to them, and so I sit here, surrounded by dross, so close and yet so far from saying goodbye to my mate and seeing my grandchildren and children again.

"Bad news, Long Snoot?" Labria asks.

I shake my head. If he understood me, if he could read a tiny fraction of what I'm expressing, he wouldn't have to ask. But he looks at me and sees a hood, goggles, and a long snoot. Nothing more, nothing less.

There are no good bounties, no simple requests for information. Nothing that can be accomplished with only my senses and my cleverness.

"I need a job," I say to Labria. "Something quick. Today."

He looks at me with renewed interest, and I hear his teeth sliding in and out of place as he thinks. "Do you know Derrida, the Ketton?" he asks.

I nod.

"She needs a number two for a job. Tonight."

"Why don't you take it, then?"

Labria barks a laugh and sips his golden drink, considering. "Too much work."

"Why has no one else taken the job?"

He glances at the bar in an assumptive way, and I produce a half cred. I've watched him enough in my time here to know that nothing is free.

"It's against the Alliance. No one likes taking sides." He sneers as he looks around the room. "The humans don't, I mean. One master is much the same as another."

He's wrong. That very assumption is what landed me here, my people lured by the Empire into thinking that the Alliance was our enemy. Alone in space, we could only believe what we were told. How wrong we were. Yet even knowing that the Empire has enslaved my planet and tried to turn me into a brainless drone, I need those credits. I need them more than I need righteousness. And besides, from my understanding of intergalactic history, a small assassination on a backward planet never did change the world.

"Tell her I'll do it," I say.

Labria dashes off a message on his datapad. "It's done. She'll send you coordinates." He sips his drink and considers me as if seeing me for the first time. "You know, some say you're the greatest spy in Mos Eisley spaceport. Some say you're wildly wealthy. Some say you're greedy, unprincipled, and dirty, that you do what you do for the pure joy of destroying so many well-laid plans. So tell me, Long Snoot. What are you really?"

I stare at the bar for a moment before realizing that he can't see my eyes through the goggles. Slowly and with emphasis, I tap the bar with my finger. Labria chuckles and replaces my half cred.

"I am very far from home," I say.

Whisking away the half cred, I hurry outside to prepare for my last bounty.

BORN IN THE STORM

Daniel José Older

STORMTROOPER CORPS OF THE IMPERIAL ARMY DIVISION OF THE IMPERIAL MILITARY, GALACTIC EMPIRE

OFFICIAL IMPERIAL INCIDENT REPORT FORM

INSTRUCTIONS:

Please fill out fully and completely. Details help! Sometimes seemingly small elements can change the whole story. As such, please don't leave anything out. Be thorough! Follow the instructions carefully and answer the questions asked in each section. Paint a picture! And remem-

ber, failure to comply with proper Imperial military protocol can result in disciplinary action including docked pay, loss of equipment, expulsion, and/or summary execution. Remember also that this is an official imperial document and any discrepancy between what you write and what actually occurred is an infraction of the Imperial military protocol. Thank you for your service!

Name: Sardis Ramsin   *Operating Number:* TD-7556

Corps: Stormtrooper   *Division:* Sandtrooper

Unit: Foot Patrol 7   *Commanding Officer:*
Commander TD-110

Location of Incident (Settlement, Planet, Region): Mos Eisley, Tatooine, Outer Rim

Were any other members of your detachment involved in this incident? Oh yes. Very much so.

Which ones? (Be specific!) Literally all of them.

Were any officers injured during this incident? One can only hope.

Please list all officers injured during this incident: I'd really rather not, actually.

Are you an officer? (If no, skip the following question): No.

Were you injured in this incident: . . .

Are all participants in the incident accounted for currently? Absolutely the krizz not.

What were the initial events that led up to the incident in question? (Be specific!)

Right, well, I guess it starts in the Mos Eisley barracks then, right? We were sent as a specific designated detachment regiment by Grand Moff Tarkin to this armpit of a planet in the literal butt of the galaxy to recover some missing droids. At least, that's what I heard. They don't really tell us much, you know. Well, I guess you *do* know, don't you, since they = you, but I digress and whatnot. There we were, bunked up in just our underskivvies, which by the way, since we're on the subject, are all well and good when you're freezing your balls off on Faz or Rhen Var or something but in the double-sunned deserts of Tatooine serve only to bake you thoroughly to a crisp and lodge sand in the most unmentionable and unreachable places. So thanks for that. Also the temp regulators in those helmets you gave us are an absolute sham; like, not even remotely functional. So, you know . . . you might want to get on that or something.

Anyway, there we were, shlanging about and waiting for run orders from 110.

Commander TD-4445 had moved into the city proper with his mounted squad (according to their melodramatic outbursts on the comms). I really don't know what the mounties are so fussy about. They have it made, if you ask me. While we futz around like holograms on the dejarik board, these lucky moes get to roll nobly across the desert on dewbacks. And look, those animals, I can't explain it. There's something graceful about them. They just move like every particle of 'em is perfectly aligned and entirely free. They'll take you

185

through a storm, over a river, into a building. They'll maul the kriff out of anyone that gets in your way. They're basically a stormtrooper's best friend. Before you say anything else, yes, I put in to be in the mounties, and no, I wasn't accepted. No, I don't know why, but I'm still pretty miffed.

Anyway, I was actually sitting there pondering that—why I didn't get positioned in the mounties instead of with this inept pile of foot-patrol trash. And Tintop was being a nuisance again, as I recall. He'd slipped TD-787 something that made him gassy and TD-787 was about to wreck him (again!) when Old Crag spoke up, and the whole of Unit 7 knows that when Crag has something to say, you listen. Even though, if we're being honest, 99 percent of what that relic spews is unadulterated bantha piss. But whatever; it breaks the monotony, I guess.

"Do you blokes know where we get our name from?" Crag says all mysterious like. TD-787 is stopped mid-lurch, like absolutely about to choke the useless life out of Tintop, but instead TD-787 turns and goes, "Because our helmets are shaped like buckets, I always figured."

Everyone scoffed, because that would've actually been funny if he'd meant it as a joke, but TD-787 was born bereft of even the remotest sense of humor, so . . . well, it actually makes it even funnier that he was serious, honestly. Either way, we all had a good chuckle, except Crag, who scowled—the old clone's permanent expression augmented—and said, "Not that name, you cog!"

"It's because we were born in the storm," Commander 110 said from the doorway. And then, because 110 always gotta say everything twice, the second time wistfully: "Born in the storm." I can't lie, though: He looked impressive standing there in his full body armor, helmet off, backlit by the twin Tatooine suns, his shadow thrown long across the barracks floor.

"Ay," Crag said. "The storm of history. As the galaxy transitioned from chaos to order, our regiment was created to maintain that order."

"That's one version anyway," Commander 110 said. Even backlit, I could tell he was smiling some. Could hear it in his voice. He was having one of those patriotic sway type moments, when the whole Galactic Empire seemed to sparkle in his eyes and whatever ridiculous mission was ahead appeared infinitely manageable—all part of the grand design. And that's all well and good, but there was sand in my butt crack and the day wasn't getting any cooler, so quite frankly I wished he'd hurry up and get to the point. Which he then did: "Run orders, boys."

Everyone groaned.

110 ignored us, wisely. "We're moving into Mos Eisley proper." (The barracks are on the outskirts of town, apparently to discourage too much fraternizing with the locals, but like . . . fat chance, if you know what I mean. Also, outside of town = closer to the endless barren infinity of a wasteland festering with Sand People, banthas, and a million other ways to die. Also: sand. All the sand. All the sand ever.)

So, Mos Eisley proper didn't seem like so terrible a thing, by comparison. If those droids had been wandering around the deep desert, they wouldn't have made it back to base in one piece, let's just put it that way. Bad enough you run off to some stinking banthahole planet with secret plans or whatever on board. Don't add insult to injury by making me deal with even more sand. You know? And anyway, the dewbacks were there. And maybe . . . well, a stormtrooper can dream.

So we geared up, put on our inefficient, technically archaic, and altogether butt-scratchingly uncomfortable armor, put on our absolute garbage-dump helmets that don't let us see a dang thing, and loaded up these E-11s you've given us, which require one to aim as far as possible away from what one's shooting at in order to have half a chance of hitting it. So thanks for all that!

What actions did you take based on the initial events leading up to the incident in question?

Nothing, we just sat there.

Like, really, my dear interrogative application system, what kind of kriffing question is that? 110 gave us the order to move, so we moved. If we didn't we'd be summarily executed, remember? Or long-distance choke-smashed by your beloved archwizard woo-woo-in-chief. Hard pass on that option, thanks! So we geared up, rolled out, and there we were in the heart of Mos Eisley, getting crispy beneath all those layers of armor and this giant black bodysock, and quite frankly craving a thirst quencher, and I don't mean the kind that actually quenches thirst. I mean the kind that dehydrates, in fact. A beverage, specifically one that frizzles, to be precise. Jawa juice, in case I wasn't clear. I wanted a damn drink.

And look: We had no leads really, so what's one direction or another in that rotting scumrat basin? "I think they may have headed for the cantina," I said, sounding authoritative and not leaving any room for debate.

But of course, TD-787 wouldn't be TD-787 if he didn't play the contrarian at any given opportunity, so he chimes in with, "What makes you think that, Sar?" and I was about to snap back at him when 110—Commander 110, I guess—holds up one hand, all serious like.

Look, I don't know if you've ever been to Mos Eisley but it's crammed with about eight million hard-up, squirming, slimy, writhing, multilimbed, sometimes tentacled, seething, heaving, bleeding (literally), frothing demented useless wastes of skin and bone and sometimes gear and data. Yes, it's a spaceport, but if you're looking for the dead end of the galaxy and its denizens, look no further. So there are plenty of suspicious-looking droids. They hobble past, zip along on their rusty little wheels, stumble by through the sand-

crusted streets. They wait outside of junk shops and currency ex-
changes, bleeping and burping and being their little self-righteous
selves.

I don't like droids, in case you weren't sure. They annoy me.

Anyway, that's what made it remarkable that Commander 110
seemed to have such a strong feeling about this speeder coming our
way with two droids, an old guy, and a kid driving. They were unremarkable to me in every way, really, but 110 gets his feelings about
stuff and runs with it, and he's the one with the orange pauldron, not
me, so . . . whatever he says, I guess.

We surround the speeder looking all heavy and serious, even
though we're the ones with the blasters. However useless, they still
woulda made quick work of the kid and his obviously somewhat-off-
the-deep-end grandpa.

110 asks how long they've had the droids and they say something.
I wasn't really paying attention, to be honest, because we weren't that
far from the cantina, and I figured if we could wrap this up quick and
head over there I could be slurping Jawa juice within the hour, blam!
But ol' 110 has other plans, of course, because the Rebel Alliance is
really going to rely on an ancient freak and a teenager who needs a
haircut to ferry their top-secret cargo around.

189

The esteemed Commander 110 demands their IDs. If you could
see through these stupid buckets we wear, you would've seen my eyes
roll so hard. All our eyes, probably, except TD-787 because: annoying.

Then the Old Guy's like, "You don't need to see his identification,"
and the first thing I thought was, whoa—is this geezer an Imperial?
He just had that way about him, like he was one of us somehow, but
busted and goofy and strung out. Maybe it was the accent. That
thought really didn't last long though, because the next thing that
happened was that I was absolutely, 100 percent sure that we did not
need to see his identification. I mean, to be fair, it didn't seem that

necessary in the first place, but listen: You would've had to hold me down and shove his scan docs in my face (and probably take my helmet off if you really wanted me to see anything) if you wanted me to look at 'em. It was imperative that I *not* see them, right at that moment. In fact, all I wanted was to get the krizz out of there. And not just to get sizzled on some Jawa juice, either.

Seems Commander 110 finally came to his senses, too, because then he says: "We don't need to see his identification."

Bless! I almost yelled, but I kept it contained.

"These are not the droids you're looking for," Old Guy says.

And he was right. He was so right. It was like, of course they're not!

110 agreed and then Old Guy says that he can go about his business, and I'm like *Yes! Yes, Old Guy! Say that!* And 110 agrees again! Word for word in fact!

"Move along," this remarkable little geezer says.

Commander 110 nods. "Move along." And then, because he's 110 and he can't help himself, he repeats it for good measure.

What further actions did you take following the initial events surrounding the incident in question?

Well, we went and got sizzled on some Jawa juice, my guy! What do you think? At that point we were already fed up.

Of course we finally get to the cantina and there they are. No, not the droids we were looking for. Dewbacks. Two beautiful, shining dewbacks. Females, I think; just standing there, breathing in and out and reflecting on their dewback lives, taking in the suns. At that moment, to be honest, I didn't care about the droids or the Galactic Empire or even the Jawa juice. I just wanted to go up and lay my hand on that snout and close my eyes and just be still, you know?

But the dewbacks being there also meant TD-4445's guys were

around somewhere, so we had to go in and see what we could, lest another unit get the drop on us and deliver the droids instead.

"Look lively, boys," Commander 110 said, and Crag just chuckled. Then we go in that ruthless dingepot and are instantly surrounded by various forms of star scum and asteroid excrement, the never-ending stench of cheap milk and bodies that have been cramped into spaceships with no showers for far too long.

First thing I see is an Ithorian, and he's looking jumpy, to be honest. I'm not even trying to smash heads like that, but this Ithorian seems downright shook when we walk in. I send him a scowl, which of course he can't see, but it doesn't matter; he'll be moving along soon enough anyway. The whole joint seems to tingle with the murmur of some mess that must've just gone down. One of those little eager-faced freaks with the beady eyes is mopping someone's blood off the floor, and I hear whispers and grunts about a lightsaber. A lightsaber! I'm tired, man. I'm just tired. The bartender points TD-787 and 110 toward a corner table where some cats involved in the mess were supposed to have been, and I try to take the opportunity to signal that I want a drink. The bartender's a surly scrug, though; he just scoffs and looks away. And then I noticed Tintop has actually managed to get one. The damn fool's lifting up his bucket to steal a few sips and I'm about to curse him out when I hear a polite little "ahem" from the seat next to me. There's a Talz sitting there—you know, one of those little gray hairy things that looks like an Ewok that got punched in the face. It's sitting at the bar next to me, scratching its icky little proboscis and looking, I think, at me. Then it burbles something. I can't be bothered with languages I don't know, so I just shake my head, and then the bartender (speaking of faces that have been punched too many times) goes: "He says the droids you're looking for headed into the desert with some Sand People."

Then, as if to seal the deal, he puts a drink down in front of me. I glance over at Tintop, who's just guzzling at this point, and then

191

across the room to where 110, Crag, and TD-787 are hassling the band. I shrug. Then I look at the drink and the waiting Talz with its beady little eyes. Information recon, right?

"Does he know how long ago they left?" I ask as I lift up the ol' 'met and take a nice long chug.

The gray guy squabbles some, and then the bartender says, "They just went before you lot walked in. Said they had a bantha with them."

"A bantha!" Tintop yells in a way that makes it clear he's well sizzled already. Then he gets a little too close to my ear and mutters, "But can we trust the little fuzz bugger? You know this cantina ain't exactly Imperial friendly, Ram."

I shrug. At this point, I'm not sure how Imperial friendly I am myself, if we're being honest. Which we are, apparently. I hate my unit; I hate my uniform. I hate that I can be hauled out to any ol' galactic wastebin on a moment's notice just to annihilate some random one-celled troglodyte. It's the constant feeling that the world may be very, very beautiful somehow if only one could remove the crap-stained glasses that come with being a member of this ridiculous army.

Tintop shrugs, too, because whether he agrees with all my deep inner sentiments about the Empire or not, Tintop generally just can't be bothered. Especially when he's toe up on the juice.

Crag and 110 come back around to let us know there was no one over there but some smug-looking tool and his Wookiee, and that the band interrogation came up empty. We tell 'em the new info.

"Bugger," 110 says as we shove our way through the crowd and out of the cantina. "Kriff!"

Describe the incident in question. Be specific!

Ha. Well, about that . . . Once we left the cantina, everything started happening fast. First of all, those dewbacks were still there, just grazing and smiling even, maybe. Can a dewback smile? I think so. They certainly seemed to see us, nod a little. Immediately, TD-4445 comes up on the comm to be all, "We're pursuing a lead that some rebels have commissioned a ship and are trying to get off Tatooine with the droids."

"Our intel says they're desert-bound with some Tusken Raiders," 110 says. "Who's your source?"

"Garindan" comes the gurgled response.

"Garindan the Kubaz?" 110 asks.

"Affirmative. He is following the suspects. Will advise."

Look, I'm not bigoted or nothing, but the Kubaz are a trash species. Period, point blank, no exceptions. So, like, okay, a long-snouted goggled armpit gave you some information. Are you gonna believe it? I rather think not, frankly. I'm not anyway. I say as much to 110.

"Regardless," TD-787 blurts out, being punchable as always, "that's a confirmed Imperial source. We have to follow up his lead first. Right, Commander?"

Maybe it's the juice, but I almost just deck TD-787 right then and there. I'm pretty sure I'd have been acting on behalf of the whole squad if I had, not for nothing. I mean, those dewbacks were *right there* and as far we knew, the rebels were getting away as we spoke, just vanishing into the never-ending sands of Tatooine.

Commander 110 shakes his head, then nods, unhelpful as always. "The Imperial lead," he mutters.

"We have confirmation," TD-4445 suddenly garbles over the comm. "The rebels are heading for the hangar! All units, converge on Docking Bay Ninety-Four!"

"There's your answer," Commander 110 grunts, and then we're off, before I even have time to object, tearing through the cluttered streets, pushing through a crowd of stinky Jawas. I know this is wrong; I can feel its wrongness all over my body. It's inescapable. But I'm a solider. A stormtrooper. I'm the faceless enforcement fist of the Galactic Empire. What can I do about it? I shove along with my unit, trying to ignore the deep-down ache that tugs on me like a tractor beam back through the crowd to the front of the cantina where those dewbacks wait.

"This way!" Crag yells, because he always has to be the one that knows everything. And then we're somewhere we had definitely just been; the winding dusty walls and sandy alleyways and leering stares seem somehow familiar, but this whole place looks like that, so who's to say? "Now over here," Crag insists, and we follow, because what else are we to do? We follow orders. It's the sum and extent of our existence. Say kill, and we will. Say die, and our arms fly up and take the blasterfire full on. Watch our pointless existence extinguished on command. This romp through these crumbling backstreets? Sums up our entire sad lives pretty ruthlessly. It's clear now none of us have any sense of where the hangar is and it doesn't matter anyway, because the rebels are probably almost to the far edge of the city by now and about to breach out into the infinite sands.

194

"Over there," Crag says, and it seems like he's running out of steam, or maybe we're getting close. Then I realize we're definitely getting close, because a growl of engines erupts all around us and I hear blasterfire from not too far away. Then some hunk of absolute junk hurls up above the buildings around us and launches out into the sky. The comm is thick with static and units yelling for backup, but I'm a hundred klicks away: As soon as the junkship took off, something in me let go and I knew what I had to do. I don't know how, but I did. It wasn't even a conscious decision, to be honest with you. Before I realized I had made a move, I was tearing back through the streets. I don't even know how I made any sense of that dungheap of a city; I just plowed forward like some invisible thread was yanking me along, and then there I was and there they were, still outside the cantina just where we'd left them, the two dewbacks, looking polite and slightly impatient, to tell you the truth.

I was running, I must've been, because the closer one reared up a little and snarled as I got close, but then I wrapped one hand on the saddle and I was up on it and I pulled the restraining cord free and we were off!

What were your actions in response to the incident in question?

We charged through the streets of Mos Eisley, me and the dewback. We were one at that moment, an unstoppable wave of man and muscle, teeth and saddle. Smugglers and local denizens dived out of our path. Up ahead, the desert loomed, unfathomable and immense. There was something I was supposed to be doing, I vaguely recalled. Something urgent, supposedly. It didn't seem to matter, though. All that mattered then was the whisper of desert wind against my helmet, the thundering beast beneath me, the yawning maw of desert ahead.

Rebels. Droids. That's right. At the edge of town, I slowed the beast down and lifted my macrobinoculars. Sand and emptiness stretched for klicks and klicks ahead of me, interrupted only by an occasional hovel or comm tower.

The beast stirred impatiently beneath me. It wanted the thrill of movement again. So did I. And then, there! On the horizon, the dim shape of a bantha shimmered against the bright sky. A few Sand People stood scattered around it. They were moving over the crest of a dune, would soon be out of sight. I kicked my heels against the dewback and together we launched out into the desert.

What were the initial results of your actions during the incident? Paint a picture!

It's funny you should ask that. The whole galaxy condensed around me, became the sand and dunes. The world became one, a singular scope of life as it stretched toward an emptiness in a never-ending cycle. The beast heaved beneath me, plunging forward toward that emptiness, too. I took out my datapad, and I've used it to transmit this report, which is probably the last you'll hear from me. At some point, I wasn't wearing my gear anymore, and then the suns sent their soothing emissaries of light to dance across my skin, and the sand kicked up in a ferocious hellwind that swept out of nowhere and lit the world on fire with screaming and the brittle dust of the desert, and it was like a gentle, terrible whisper that this world I once thought to be dead is so alive, just like me: so alive, and born and reborn in the storm, and absolutely free.

LAINA

Wil Wheaton

Ryland climbed into the lookout and scanned the sky. The fighters were already in the air, ahead of the transport they were escorting out of the system. He knew he was doing the right thing. He knew Eron and Rhee would take good care of Laina, be good mothers to her, and raise her as their own until they could be reunited. He knew it was too dangerous to keep her with him on Yavin, which was a legitimate military target, should the Empire ever discover its existence. He knew that he could have gone with her, that nobody from his wing would have held it against him, that he could be holding his young daughter right now as they climbed the edge of the atmosphere toward relative peace and safety.

Ryland knew that he was not the only person on the base—hell, he wasn't the only one on duty at this moment—who had lost something, given up something, made some sacrifice in service of the Rebellion against the Empire. Knowing all of these facts did not make the moment any easier, or any less painful.

He wiped away tears, held his scanner to his eyes, and said goodbye to his daughter as he watched her transport kiss the top of the atmosphere and vanish into the darkness of space.

"This is Gold Tower to transport Echo Delta One," he said into his comm. "You have cleared atmosphere and are a go for hyperspace. May the Force be with you." He didn't believe in the Force, but today, he would make an exception. He took his thumb off the button. "Take good care of my little girl," he said, softly. He sat down and wept.

Eighteen hours earlier

Ryland adjusted the camera and softly cleared his throat. He looked at Laina, sleeping restlessly in her crib. She'd thrown the covers halfway off her and had turned almost entirely sideways across the mattress. Her legs kicked gently and her eyes flicked side to side. Whatever she was dreaming about, he hoped it was something joyful. Maybe Fiona was there, with her, maybe the three of them were together again. He would be careful that he didn't wake her.

He turned his attention to the camera's lens and began recording.

"Hello, Laina. I'm recording this message to you a few hours before you get on a transport to go to your new home with your aunts. I don't know how long it's going to be until I get to see you again, and it's important to me that you don't have to wait until then to know who you are, where you came from, and who your parents were.

"By the time you are old enough to see this, and understand it, I hope that we're watching it together, and I hope that we're laughing about how silly I look right now. But since I joined the Rebel Alliance, I've said goodbye to a lot of friends, and I haven't been able to say goodbye to a lot more . . ." He took a deep breath to steady himself. Living under Imperial occupation was terrible, and the Rebellion was not just right but *necessary*. A lot of good people had given their lives—or, worse, their freedom—in service of the struggle.

"So," he said with a smile he hoped wasn't too forced, "if this is how you're meeting me . . . Hi, sweetheart. I'm your dad. I'm thirty-eight standard years old right now, and you're almost two. I can't give you a lot of specific information, because if the Empire ever sees this, it could put us all in danger, but right now, we are on a rebel base, and you are sleeping right over there." He grabbed the camera and pointed it at her. "That's you! You're so little right now!" He looked at her, listened to her soft breaths. He could feel that he was about to lose his nerve, keep her with him at a place that he knew wasn't safe, but would at least keep them together, but if the reports about the Empire's battle station were true . . . He refocused his courage, and turned the camera back on himself. "You and I came here when you were just six months old, right after your mother died. I'll tell you about her in a second, but first I want you to know where you're from.

"You were born in an underground mining colony on a moon, in a place called the Outer Rim. There's no atmosphere on the moon, so some folks who live there now have never even been above the surface, and they'll never see the stars. But where you're going, you'll get to see the stars every night. Your mother and I aren't from there, and it probably isn't safe to tell you where we both came from (if we're watching this together, I'll tell you right now. Pause this and ask me!) but we were both mechanics—I still am, I work on Y-wings instead of extractors now—and we met there when we worked in the same sector."

He held up a holo of Fiona and showed it to the camera. "This is

199

your mom. Her name was Fiona, and she was my favorite human in the whole galaxy, until you came along. She was clever and kind. She understood how machines worked better than the people who designed them, and she could fix them faster than anyone I've ever met. I loved her as much as she loved you, and she loved you more than anything."

"You have your mother's beautiful eyes, but it looks like you got my big dumb ears. Sorry about that." He chuckled. "Your mom loved math and music, and when you were a tiny, tiny baby, she sang 'Mama Moon' to you every single day." His voice caught in his throat and his eyes watered. He missed Fiona so much.

"Okay. So. The Empire came to our colony a few months before you were born. An Imperial officer assembled us in the core and told us that the company we worked for had been taken over by the Empire. He said it was because the company wasn't meeting safety regulations, but that was a lie. He knew it and we knew it. The Empire needed doonium, and we had a lot of it. And if there's one thing you need to know and understand about the Empire it is that it will take whatever it wants, whenever it wants it. The Empire will take everything you care about, everything and everyone you love, if you let them."

He realized that he had clenched his fists and tightened up his shoulders. He willed himself to relax, looked down and opened his hands. He touched the ring he still wore on his left hand as blood pumped back into his fingers.

"The Empire took your mom away from us, honey. An Imperial officer named Duggan killed her, just because he could. I want you to know this, so you never forget what we are fighting against, and why I'm sending you away.

"I also want you to know that not everyone is courageous enough to stand up to the Empire, and those people, who we call *collaborators,* are just as bad as the Empire is. They may even be worse, because they should know better. It's because of a collaborator that your mom isn't here. His name was Corbin, and he had been our friend for years, until the Empire arrived. It happens so fast, Laina, you don't even realize it's happening. One day, your friends are eating breakfast with you in the canteen, and when it's time for dinner, they're wearing an Imperial uniform."

Outside their room, a muffled voice announced the duty change. He would have to wake her up soon, dress her for travel. Say good-bye.

"Corbin's new uniform fit him too well. It was like he'd always wanted to wear one, because it was how he could feel important. But he wasn't important. He wasn't any more important than the blaster Duggan used to kill your mom. I know I'm talking about him a lot, but I need you to know that the Empire exists because of people like Corbin, who are too weak or ambitious to stand up to people like Duggan, and the Rebellion exists because of people like your mom, who are willing to risk their freedom and their lives to stand up to them both.

"Corbin didn't have a family before the Empire came, and when he saw how happy your mom and I were to have you, it made him jealous. He started doing little things to bother us, like making me work extra shifts, and yelling at your mom that she couldn't have you with her in the canteen, even though everyone on our crew loved it when you were around.

"This went on until one day your mom just ran out of patience with him and she told him to stop being a bully. Well, later that night, Corbin showed up at our quarters with Duggan, the Imperial officer in charge. Corbin had told Duggan that your mom and I were se-cretly rebel spies. We weren't rebels then, and Corbin knew it. We were just parents trying to take care of our family, who were tired of being pushed around by someone with a little bit of power.

"I still don't know if Duggan believed Corbin, or if he just wanted

201

to use your mom and me to frighten and intimidate the rest of our crew. But he and his Loyalty Officers ordered your mom and me to confess to being rebel spies in front of everyone, and when we didn't have anything to confess to, Duggan killed her. He just shot her, right in front of me, as casually as turning off a light."

Ryland reached out and stopped recording. Did Laina really need to know all of that? If this was the only recording of him she would ever have, if she was going to watch this as she grew up, did he want to make her relive the death of her mother the way he did, night after night? He played the recording back, watched himself say *the Rebellion exists because of people like your mom, who are willing to risk their freedom and their lives to stand up to them both*, and tapped Record again.

"All of us who joined the Rebel Alliance have lost something, or someone, or someplace we loved. I've lost all three, and it isn't easy for me to say goodbye to you today. But I have to send you someplace where you'll be safe, where you'll get to grow up and have a family, if you want one. I hope that we don't need the Rebel Alliance by the time you're old enough to join it, but if we do, I want you to know that it's in your blood to fight back. You are your mother's daughter.

"I will miss you every day, but I know that you'll be safe with your Aunt Rhee and Aunt Eron. They helped our family escape from the Empire, and they introduced me to the rebels. I don't have time to tell you that part of the story, but you can ask them to tell it to you, when you're ready to know. They love you very much, and they're going to take you to a planet called Alderaan, which is far away from any fighting. You'll be safe there. You can grow up and make friends, and have the kind of life I always wanted you to have. I'll fight for you as long as I have to, and I'll see you soon.

"I love you so much, Laina, and I miss you already."

He stopped recording, and saved the file.

202

LAINA

Ryland walked over to his daughter's bed and put his hand on her shoulder.

"Sweetheart," he said gently, "it's time to wake up."

Eighteen hours later

When his watch was over, Ryland declined an invitation to join some of the pilots from Blue Squadron in the canteen and took a transport back to his quarters. He lingered at the door, his hand heavy as he lifted it to key the entry code. For the first time since they had arrived from Burnin Konn a year ago, he would open it to find an empty room on the other side.

He'd been standing there for several minutes when Mol Hastur, their neighbor, walked by. She paused and put her hand on his shoulder. "You did the right thing, Ry," she said.

"I know," he answered.

"The Force is with her," Mol said. "It's with us all."

"Thanks, Mol. I hope you're right." He typed in his code and went inside. The door hissed closed heavily behind him.

FULLY OPERATIONAL

Beth Revis

A weapon was meant to be fired.

Every military man could tell you that. Treat all weapons as charged; never assume a blaster was set simply to stun and not kill.

General Cassio Tagge, Chief of the Imperial Army, knew that. As he walked the corridors of the greatest battle station ever built in this or any galaxy, he was deeply aware that he walked through the heart of a weapon. Power simmered beneath the doonium.

He had not been aboard the Death Star when it had gone through its initial test firing on Jedha, but he'd joined soon after and witnessed Scarif. He paused now, a hand on the sleek metal wall, remembering the rumble of power as the Death Star charged and fired. It had been a subtle vibration, something he might not have noticed had he not been looking for it. That was a mark of how big the battle station was—it could kill off half a planet, and most of the people who resided within the station wouldn't even notice.

A credit to Director Orson Krennic, to be sure. Even when the Joint Chiefs had questioned the validity of such an enormous—and expensive—weapon, Krennic had insisted it was both possible and needed. Tagge had never really liked Krennic. He'd found the man obsessive, but perhaps it took a man obsessed with firepower to make something like the Death Star.

And a man such as Grand Moff Tarkin to take it.

Tagge paused now, his hand still brushing the metal wall of the corridor. He straightened. Without meaning to, he'd arrived at the meeting room early. His thoughts, lingering on Krennic, recalled the last Joint Chiefs meeting in this room, the one where Krennic had insisted the Death Star could do more than destroy a small city like Jedha. Krennic had shoved his chair aside, standing up and beating a fist on the table. Tagge, two seats down, had both admired the man's passion for the battle station and been disgusted by the childish way in which he presented it.

In the end, Krennic got what he'd wanted. Another test fire, a larger one. Now the seat two chairs down from Tagge's was empty.

A weapon was meant to be fired. You just had to make sure you were on the correct end of it.

Tagge continued past the meeting room door with purpose in his strides. He had a private office that branched off the tactical room, and there he brought up the reports and footage of Scarif.

Krennic had ever been a man too mercurial for a leadership position. He had guts, true, but he'd relied too heavily on them. Tagge was a man of graphs, of data, of facts and information. They were cold, but they were true.

And the truth of the matter was that the Empire had a problem.

The surveillance droids had been able to transmit some of the rebel activity on the surface of Scarif prior to being destroyed, and Tagge had carefully compiled the data. Unlike the little partisan units scattered throughout the galaxy that caused middling annoyance at best, Scarif showed a concentrated effort. It showed *communication*. Take ten black hive ants and put them in separate jars, and they could do nothing. But put them in the same jar and they vibrated in harmony until the glass shattered. Hive ants weren't sentient, exactly, but they were destructive.

The same could be said of the rebels.

Tagge waved his hand, dismissing the Scarif footage. He turned his attention to the list of names in the Imperial Senate that he had compiled. Some were obvious—Mon Mothma had a price on her head for being too blatantly treasonous, and Bail Organa would soon as well, if he did not curb his rebellious tendencies. The man slipped through the political world like oil over water, skimming close to insurgency and relying on legalese and luck. Malicious compliance was still compliance, but it wouldn't be long before the senator slipped on his own sharp edge. But there were others. Lingering opinions, doubts against the Emperor . . . they were separated in their little jars now, but Mon Mothma's dramatic escape from the Senate had opened the lids.

The Senate was abuzz.

And then there was Scarif. Tagge kept coming back to it. The transmission that had leaked. The Death Star plans. The stolen data somewhere out there in the galaxy, a threat hidden in the vast emptiness of space.

It was hard to think that the very battle station he now stood in, so solid, so powerful, could have any weakness. But Tagge forced himself to look at his data, not the solid walls around him. A restless Senate *here,* a group of targeted, communicating rebels *there,* and that damn data tape . . . it wasn't hard to connect the pieces.

207

Tagge stared at the data, sorting it in his mind. He debated whether or not he dared ask the Emperor for access to the plans stolen on Scarif. All other copies had been sealed under the highest security—security so high that even he, as Chief of the Imperial Army, was denied access. He understood the concern but knew if he could examine the data there, he might find something before the rebels did . . .

"General Tagge?" A junior officer's voice sounded through the intercom.

"Yes?" Tagge replied impatiently.

"Admiral Motti to see you."

Tagge grunted his affirmation, and the door to his office slid open.

"Thought I'd find you here," Admiral Conan Antonio Motti said. His gaze swung over the room. He took in the screens Tagge had been examining and, although he said nothing, the sneer on his face indicated his dismissal of Tagge's concerns.

"Let's go," Tagge said gruffly. The two men didn't talk as they strode down the corridor to the Joint Chiefs' meeting room. A few of the senior officers were already seated, chatting among themselves. Idle conversations. Meaningless words. Tagge took his seat without speaking, a scowl growing on his face. These men were old. They'd had their war, and they believed they'd ended all war with the finality of it. They leaned in their chairs, comfortable, firm in the safety of the battle station around them.

Tagge swore to himself that he would never slip into passivity like that. He would inevitably grow old and gray like the senior chiefs, he would have his wars behind him as they did, but he would never lean back in his chair and sip his caf and ignore the looming threat merely because he didn't want to believe it to be there.

"Is something wrong?" one of the senior advisers asked at Tagge's scowl.

Before he could answer, Motti burst in. "He's being paranoid," he said in a dismissive tone.

Tagge swallowed down his anger, but he couldn't help but insist on the truth. "Until this battle station is *fully* operational, we are vulnerable." He caught a glimpse of Motti's gleam of triumph for having successfully baited him, but he continued anyway. "The Rebel Alliance is too well equipped. They're more dangerous than you realize!"

"Dangerous to your starfleet, Commander. *Not* to this battle station."

Motti was so quick to respond that Tagge was certain he'd been crafting this comeback since he stopped by the tactical room.

Tagge cast a surreptitious look around the room. The senior advisers clearly agreed with Motti. They were *comfortable*, Tagge realized. Made lenient by the protection they felt inside the doonium walls. Soft. Weak.

Unwilling to see that the large round laser at the heart of the Death Star was just as easily a target as a weapon.

An image of Director Orson Krennic flashed in Tagge's mind, and he had to resist the urge to look at the seat the man had once occupied in this very room. He thought of the enraged way the director had insisted the Death Star was ready, that it would revolutionize the galaxy and quell even the most fleeting thought of rebellion.

Would it take the veins popping out of my neck, spittle flying from my lips, a crazed look in my eye before these men would listen? Tagge thought.

And then he remembered Krennic's fate, and thought, *Was that what happened to men who argued in this room?*

Still. He needed them to see. To understand.

"The Rebellion will continue to gain support in the Imperial Senate until—"

Grand Moff Wilhuff Tarkin strode into the room, and Tagge's words died in his throat. "The Imperial Senate will no longer be of any concern to us. I have just received word that the Emperor has dissolved the council permanently. The last remnants of the Republic have been swept away."

A sliver of ice ran down Tagge's back. *No Senate?* he thought. He imagined the hive ants, each in individual jars, and then he imagined the lids on each of them disappearing, and the swarm rising up.

"That's impossible!" Tagge exclaimed. "How will the Emperor maintain control without the bureaucracy?"

He caught a disapproving look from one of the senior advisers, but he disregarded it. It wasn't weapons that kept people obedient, despite what Motti, what Krennic, what Tarkin himself believed. Weapons riled people up, reminded them that they could fight. It was bureaucratic mediocrity that made them accept their fate. Show a man a blaster, and he looked for a way to take it for himself and turn it on you. Tell a man he can fight in court, and nine times out of ten he'll disappear just to avoid the tediousness.

"The regional governors now have direct control over their territories," Tarkin continued, his voice almost idle. "Fear will keep the systems in line." He shot a quick glance at Tagge. "Fear of this battle station," he continued, speaking to the rest of the group.

Tagge ignored the subtle dig and the way Motti reveled in it. "And what of the Rebellion?" he insisted. "If the rebels have obtained a complete technical readout of this station, it is possible—however unlikely—that they might find a weakness and exploit it."

Tagge had intended Tarkin to answer him. Instead the gravelly, deep voice of Lord Vader filled the room. "The plans you refer to will soon be back in our hands."

Tagge thought for a moment that he heard the sounds of distant screams and shouting, the clatter of a battle in a small area, the swish of a weapon he didn't recognize. But before his brain could fully process the phantom sounds, they were gone.

When he looked up, Lord Vader faced him. Not for the first time,

Tagge wondered what was behind the mask, and then he questioned whether he truly wanted to know. He ground his teeth, unwilling to show the way Lord Vader's gaze intimidated him.

He didn't breathe until the black-suited lord shifted his attention to Motti. He watched dispassionately as they exchanged words, as Vader strolled from behind Tarkin toward Motti. The tension crackled as Motti's anger flared.

Vader raised his hand.

Motti's words stuttered to nothing but gasping breaths, desperate for air.

Motti had called Vader's beliefs ancient and sorcerous, and Tagge couldn't help but agree. Nothing but wizardry could have made Motti choke while Vader, meters away, merely raised his hands and *squeezed*.

Tagge couldn't help but bring his own hand to his mouth, but he knew better than to speak. The men around the table watched as Motti struggled to breathe until Tarkin, seemingly bored, ordered his release.

Tagge glanced at the chair two down from his, then his eyes met Motti's. A thin sheen of sweat dotted Motti's brow, his eyes still bulging slightly from the choking. But he didn't say anything further. And neither did Tagge.

His data had been wrong, he knew that now. Tagge had looked at the angles incorrectly, surmised the outcomes based on incomplete data. He had assumed the Empire's greatest weapon was the Death Star.

But he was beginning to realize that it might just be Lord Vader himself.

AN INCIDENT REPORT

Mallory Ortberg

It didn't make him *right*, you know. It made him *angry*, it made him *violent*, but it didn't make him *right*. You may or may not have already reviewed the footage—it's my opinion that attempted murder at a meeting of the Joint Chiefs of the Galactic Empire merits a thorough, personal investigation by the members of High Command, but you gentlemen will of course act as you see fit. The point is, whatever conclusions you ultimately draw about the incident taking place between myself and Lord Vader during yesterday morning's briefing, he was wrong, and trying to crush someone else's windpipe doesn't make you any less wrong, if you're wrong to begin with. Which he was. I do not concede the argument.

I submit myself willingly to discipline if I am in error, but I believe I am correct in saying that I have been appointed the Chief of the Imperial Navy. I believe I am also correct in stating that the Imperial Navy is a military organization, that its goals and aims are martial in nature, that we seek to both engage in armed hostilities and ultimately win them, and that therefore we have every *right* to place the majority of our hopes on the technological marvel that is this battle station, and that I was not out of line to suggest that said battle station is both a technological marvel and the pride of the Imperial Navy, and that we would be well served to put it to use as quickly and as often as necessary, if not as possible.

I wish to take this opportunity to point out that I have no objection to the gentleman's religious beliefs, nor do I object to the prospect of working with Lord Vader again in future, assuming the Empire is willing to take all necessary precautions to ensure public safety, and with Lord Vader's personal guarantee that he will confine himself to using words to win arguments in future, as befits a ranking member of the Imperial Council, and save acts of out-and-out violence for members of the Rebel Alliance. I can assure you, gentlemen, that I have no interest in holding grudges, nor in re-creating the type of petty feuds of all too recent memory that characterized the day-to-day operations of the Imperial Senate.

Moreover, I am not a bigot; it is a point of pride with me that in my native sector of Seswenna there are over three hundred distinct religious traditions with active practitioners, all officially recognized by their Imperial administrator. I myself am a man of faith, as it happens, and believe that Imperial unity can only be strengthened through cooperative and constructive dialogue among citizens following diverse spiritual traditions. I would welcome, under more appropriate circumstances, the opportunity to learn more about Lord Vader's understanding of the Force, and how it enriches his daily life.

I do not welcome Lord Vader quite literally attempting to shove his religious beliefs down my throat. This was a *military* meeting at a *military* installation attended exclusively by *military* personnel; I will not apologize for asking Lord Vader to refrain from commandeering the conversation into a referendum on his religious devotion, nor will I apologize for attempting to give credit to the hardworking men, women, and neutrois whose years of dedication made this day possible by praising the capabilities of the Death Star station. It is my belief that effective managers should offer at least as much praise as they do criticism.

At any rate, if you've reviewed the footage, which I strongly encourage you to do, you'll notice two things. The first, and most critical to my argument, is that Lord Vader expressed open contempt for the Death Star project in front of his subordinates, many of whom have dedicated their lives to seeing the station completed. It was, to put it mildly, a speech that undermined public faith in both the Galactic Empire's vision and its competency. The Empire has invested over twenty years, countless man-hours, and over one trillion credits in the development of the Death Star. I need hardly remind you gentlemen that it cannot possibly serve any of our aims to have a member of the Joint Chiefs blatantly disparaging the most ambitious and expensive military venture in recent history. He has had more than two decades to express any relevant concerns to our engineering and development teams, and has always been free to make whatever suggestions he deems necessary about the creation of a Force-sensitive unit to either Grand Moff Tarkin or the Emperor himself. The day we are set to launch the most ambitious military project in Imperial history is not the time; in front of the first joint meeting of Imperial governors and rear admirals is not the place.

I quote directly from Lord Vader moments before he assaulted me: "Don't be too proud of this technological terror you've constructed. The ability to destroy a planet is insignificant next to the power of the Force."

(It should go without saying, gentlemen, that I am perfectly accustomed to a little briefing room brawling every now and again. I am a military man. I am not asking for pity. I am perfectly well. I am not asking for special treatment.)

I mean to say: "Don't be too proud" of the Death Star? Of the battle station we are currently holding a meeting in, upon which the Emperor himself has pinned his greatest hopes? Is this how the Imperial leadership hopes to inspire our troops? Ask them to dedicate their careers and lives to technological innovation, only to tell them not to be "too proud" when their labors finally come to fruition? Have I missed an official change in policy? I will not apologize for taking pride in my work, nor for encouraging my employees to take pride in theirs. If the Empire wishes to reprimand me for this, so be it.

This felt, frankly, like an act of workplace proselytization. Again, I have no objection whatever to Lord Vader's private faith. It must, however, be pointed out that at present the number of planets destroyed solely by the unaided power of the Force is *zero*. The number of planets destroyed by the power of the Death Star is one. The number of days the Death Star has been fully operational is also one.

The *second* thing you will notice, gentlemen, while watching the tape, is that Lord Vader is forced to take *several steps in my direction* before—to use a colloquialism, and for lack of a more accurate term—Force-choking me. For all his claims that the power of the Force is greater than the destructive capabilities of this Death Star, it strikes me as more than a little disingenuous if he cannot even remotely choke a single individual from across the room. I imagine Lord Vader would have had to stand very close to the planet Alderaan indeed today if he had wanted to demonstrate how thoroughly his Force-wielding abilities outmatch the Death Star.

AN INCIDENT REPORT

But I digress. I am here to give an account of the events that transpired in yesterday's briefing and to submit myself for possible correction, nothing more. We were in the main conference room on the officer's deck—Vice Admiral Tallatz, Rear Admiral Tiaan Jerjerrod, Kendal Ozzel, Commander Cassio Tagge, Admiral Nils Tenant, and myself—discussing the relative threat levels facing our respective commands. Commander Tagge was, in my opinion, distressingly myopic on the subject of the Rebel Alliance. Although I commend him for his concern for the well-being of his own troops, the threat posed by a patchwork fleet of secondhand X- and Y-wing starfighters led by a complement of informally trained pilots is in my opinion minimal. That is not to say there is not a time or a place for discussing the rebel threat—no one ever won a war through overconfidence—merely that Tagge's concerns are not universal. The dog nipping at his heels in the street is no threat to my locked and guarded house, so to speak.

At this point we were joined by Grand Moff Tarkin and Lord Vader, who informed us that the Imperial Senate had been formally and permanently dissolved by the Emperor. May I take this opportunity to say I think this action was a long time in coming and can only benefit us as an organization moving forward. Tagge, who only moments before had feared that rebel support within the Senate would destroy us, now feared the opposite: namely, that without the apparatus of the state bureaucracy, the Emperor would be unable to maintain order. I would like to say, personally, that I do not believe the Emperor requires any such assistance, and that Tagge's repeated questioning of the Emperor's actions, if not outright treasonous, at the very least bespeaks a lack of fitness for command. Perhaps once the High Command is finished investigating Lord Vader's outburst it will turn its attention to Tagge's competence, loyalty, and overall value to our organization.

It was then that I dismissed Tagge and Vader's line of argument (namely, that the Rebellion, if in possession of the Death Star blueprints, might pose an immediate threat to our safety) by pointing out that merely obtaining technical data was not the same thing as an imminent assault. There are blueprints of every single Star Destroyer, governor's mansion, Imperial palace, and naval shipyard in the Empire, and most of them have backups kept in various data storage facilities throughout the galaxy. Does Tagge mean to suggest that the mere *existence* of the artifacts necessary to the architectural process poses an existential threat?

We have, I might add, an entire military intelligence unit whose sole job it is to evaluate the credibility of possible threats. I then encouraged the other admirals that, having invested so much time and energy into building the Death Star, it might perhaps behoove us to use it. I need hardly to say to *you,* gentlemen, that this was merely restating the official Tarkin Doctrine; it is scarcely in dispute. If the rebels launch an attack, we will defend ourselves. In the meantime, I believe we should continue to employ every method at our disposal to ending the war.

The rest you know. Lord Vader for some reason took issue with my idea that we use the weapon we had only recently finished building, suggested that we take less pride in our military achievements as an organization, and once again loudly evangelized his specific religious beliefs. I may have been heated in my response, but I merely spoke the truth: Lord Vader's devotion to a nearly extinct faith has *not* resulted in the recovery of the stolen data tapes, *nor* has it given him insight into the rebels' secret base, nor has he ever destroyed a planet. His response was showy and attention grabbing, certainly, but he could not refute a single one of my arguments. *He* found *my* lack of faith disturbing? I have never claimed to be an adherent to his sect. I found *his* lack of faith in this military installation disturbing. I do

not attend Lord Vader's religious ceremonies and demand he vener-
ate the Death Star's architectural staff; I ask him to refrain from interrupting my meetings and insisting I kowtow before this Force of his.

I also, as I stated before, object to his choking me. I concede nothing. I maintain, as I always have, that if we were going to build the
Death Star we might as well use it. It should please the members of
High Command to note that I am at the present moment able to confirm that this battle station is in fact fully operational and has thus far
exceeded every hope we have ever placed in its construction. I have
no doubt the Emperor will be gratified to hear this. I myself initiated
the firing sequence upon Grand Moff Tarkin's command; Lord Vader
himself can confirm this, if you care to ask him. I might add that the
planet Alderaan was selected, targeted, and destroyed, all without the
aid of Lord Vader's precious Force—thanks entirely to the competence, diligence, and efficiency of the Death Star operations team. I
have no further comment on the matter.

CHANGE OF HEART

Elizabeth Wein

The hardest part of the work was keeping your feelings under control. You couldn't afford to show discomfort, even if the light was too bright. You were trained to mask your physical response to pain, to fear, to surprise, to *anything*. Not just in your face, but in your entire body. You took pride in it, too. On guard, you had to be as smooth-faced and immobile as a droid. And Lord Vader would always know if you faltered, if you twitched a finger or even an eyebrow—even if he wasn't looking at you.

It was easier being in the faceless armored ranks of the storm-troopers, where no one could see your twitching eyebrow beneath the hard white mask.

Being here, at Vader's side, flanking him, a meter ahead of him or a meter behind in pace with the partner whose name you didn't know and with whom you'd never exchanged a spoken word, was an honor and a privilege. Your face was uncovered. Your mask was invisible. You were in the inner circle.

Everyone knew you were ambitious; you wouldn't be here otherwise. But you couldn't ever show it. You couldn't show anything. You saw things, you learned things, you *knew* things that no one but Lord Vader himself knew.

This was why you joined; this was what you'd come for, what you'd thirsted for: to be here on the cutting edge of military technology, to be among the first watch to witness the galaxy yielding up its treasures and its secrets to the ever-expanding Galactic Empire. And here you were, aboard the mightiest battle station the galaxy had ever seen, at the side of the Emperor's most feared and powerful strategist—

222

—And yet sometimes it still took all your concentration to keep your mouth set and your brow straight.

You walked ahead of Vader, on his right, as he strode through the sterile corridors of the detention block. You and your silent counterpart had to set the pace for him, while keeping in perfect step with each other, a challenging and often daunting game of skill. On this occasion, though, after Vader had keyed in the codes to open the door to the unlucky prisoner he was about to interrogate, he stepped into the cell ahead of you.

There was no invitation to follow, but of course you did it automatically.

This was exactly the kind of moment you *hated*. No matter how hard you'd trained for it, you never stopped *hating* being taken by surprise.

The prisoner was a young girl.

CHANGE OF HEART

It came as a shock. You'd known Princess Leia Organa of Alderaan was a member of the Galactic Senate. But you hadn't realized she would be so young, and never in a million years had it occurred to you to expect such winning beauty.

Small-boned, neat, round-faced, still wearing the formal white gown of a diplomat and with her long dark hair still smoothly rolled around her head in formal elegance, she sat straight and defiant against the smooth cold wall of her cell. But this work had made you good at reading faces, and it took only a glance for you to see that she was terrified. She was controlling it, but not well. Her dark eyes were wide and frightened, and she was cringing backward into the corner of the cell, bracing herself as Vader approached.

All this hit you in the second it took to enter the small room. Lord Vader loomed tall and menacing over the cowering girl. But you kept your face still. You were better at it than she was.

Don't look at her, you reminded yourself; *don't catch her eye.*

The single unit that you made with your counterpart was split as you stepped aside, one of you on each side of the door, so that the menacing black globe of the interrogator droid could drift in.

You didn't blink as it hovered less than an arm's length from your head, the mind probe hypodermic poised dangerously close to your own eye. It wasn't here for you.

The girl's dark eyes widened when she saw it. She gave a little gasp of apprehension.

Vader said to her: "And now, Your Highness, we will discuss the location of your hidden rebel base."

And the cell door glided smoothly shut behind you, sealing all four of you in together.

The crowded cell was never designed to hold so many. You stood rigid and passive and thought of the command you'd someday have. You had to watch. There was no choice but to watch. But you weren't going to let yourself think of anything else but your own bright future—

It didn't work.

You were undone with shock at how much of yourself you recognized in this fragile, fearful, defiant young rebel with a backbone of steel.

You could see, as surely as Vader himself could, that the girl knew more than she was revealing. She resisted and battled against the intrusion into her mind, but showed none of the confusion or outrage you'd expect from someone who had nothing to hide. She knew why she was here and, *just like you,* she was focused on endurance, on holding herself in. Her entire being was centered on not letting Darth Vader see what was going on in her head.

She was exactly like you.

When the heavy door slid open again and the exhausting session had come to its temporary close, the girl was left on her own again, wrung out in a quivering heap of emotional and physical collapse.

But unlike her, you weren't allowed the luxury of either emotion or collapse.

She'd still given up nothing when Governor Tarkin sent for her.

Her hands were manacled as you marched her through the Death Star's labyrinthine corridors. She was composed again, though. It wasn't obvious that she was scurrying to keep up; the pace Vader set was hard for her small frame to match. She still looked the part of a young ambassador on a diplomatic mission, and she was still playing that role with steely composure, just as you were playing your own role.

You felt it as a shock in the pit of your stomach when you realized that she was matching *your* stride.

You were shorter than your counterpart by a couple of fingers, and she was measuring her steps against yours to help her maintain her dignity.

You stared straight ahead, expressionless as always.

You were not helping her.

You felt your composure slipping even though your expression didn't change. If Vader weren't so focused on the prisoner, would he look at you and guess?

Focus, you told yourself fiercely. *Focus!* You forced your hard soles to strike the shining decking of the corridor in perfect time with those of your counterpart. You pretended you couldn't hear the pattering footfalls of the girl's soft white boots exactly matching your own steps.

Governor Tarkin was waiting in the Overbridge with Admiral Motti. Beyond the plating of the broad curved viewport was a black canvas of starlight and the blue glow of the planet Alderaan, floating serenely against its backdrop.

You and your counterpart fell back to take your expected positions in deference to the commanders present, and Vader halted, but the undaunted girl swept forward majestically to take on Tarkin herself. She was formal and snide. She told him he stank.

Vader stepped behind her, looming over her with all the menace of his full height. The top of her head came only to his breastplate. He laid one heavy, gloved hand in warning against her back, reminding her she was still his prisoner—as if it were possible for her to forget, here in the control room of the Death Star, surrounded by enemies and guards with her hands bound.

From where you stood behind the girl and Vader, you couldn't see her face. But you could see Tarkin's wry grin as he took her chin in his hand and told her he had signed the order for her execution.

Again, for a moment, your stomach plummeted in cold shock. But you didn't swallow; you didn't even blink.

She didn't flinch, either. She answered Tarkin, still icily formal:

225

"I'm surprised you had the courage to take the responsibility your-self."

Tarkin didn't rise to her highbrow baiting. Instead he stepped away from her. Coolly, he invited her to watch the first ceremonial demonstration of the Death Star's capabilities. "No star system will dare oppose the Emperor now," he taunted her.

You were now so invested in her defiance that you'd forgotten you weren't supposed to be listening. Your feigned indifference was trained; it came automatically.

But the girl had no such training. She didn't realize how Tarkin was playing her. She was unaware he'd taken over her interrogation, and already he was succeeding at stripping information out of her that neither Lord Vader nor the interrogator droid had been able to. Tarkin was forcing her into declaring her loyalty.

She was so angry and defiant and scared that she didn't even realize she was doing it. Her speech was tight and clipped as she gave herself away, her voice full of pride and hatred: "The more you tighten your grip, Tarkin, the more star systems will slip through your fingers."

He was sure of her now. She'd as much as admitted her loyalty to the Rebellion.

He turned away from her and stared out at the blue glowing orb of the planet in the near distance. He said, "I have chosen to test this station's destructive power on your home planet of Alderaan."

And she broke.

You did not, but she did.

"*No!*" She leapt forward, entreating him, no longer taking care with how she shaped her words. "Alderaan is peaceful, we have no weapons—"

He turned around abruptly. She was still crying out in protest, "*You can't possibly—*"

He cut her short, speaking over her exclamation. "You will provide another target, a military target? Then *name the system!*"

This was, in its way, more painful to witness than the physical torment the young princess had borne with such fierce determination, as Vader had probed her mind beneath the hungry needles of the interrogator droid.

Tarkin had unmasked her. The steel was gone. She was frightened and desperate. But still she hesitated, still unwilling to answer his question.

And now Tarkin, too, was on the edge of coming unmasked.

There was cold anger in his voice as he confronted her. "I grow tired of asking this—" The girl recoiled from his fury and backed straight into Lord Vader. "—so it'll be the last time." She flinched at last. She bent her head away from Tarkin's, then forced herself to look directly at him again as he demanded, *"Where is the rebel base?"*

Her small body was trapped between Governor Tarkin and Lord Vader. All you could see was the back of her elegant, shining head. But you could tell she wasn't looking at Tarkin now. She was staring over his shoulder at the beautiful blue planet floating beyond the wide viewing panel, the planet that was her home.

There was a strange, quiet moment in which time seemed to stand still, a pause in which the young girl thought hard and fast about who she was going to betray.

"Dantooine," she said in defeat, still staring over Tarkin's shoulder.

You saw Tarkin's grim, triumphant smile.

After another moment the girl looked up at him. And then almost immediately, as if she couldn't bear the victory in his eyes, she lowered her head. You still couldn't see her face, and now neither could Tarkin. She repeated unsteadily, "They're on Dantooine."

She was lying through her teeth.

227

Governor Tarkin spoke to Lord Vader over the smooth crown of the princess's lowered head. "There."

Tarkin stepped away from his menacing position in front of the bound and cowering girl, and for just a split second he came toward you, standing motionless behind Lord Vader. In that fraction of a second you thought that he knew it, too, that he'd seen her lie, and that he was looking to you for confirmation.

But he wasn't seeing you as anything other than the silent fixture that you always were in his presence, and in another fraction of a second he'd stepped away and added, "You see, Lord Vader. She can be reasonable."

You stood unbroken, not moving, not blinking.

But your entire inner being was quivering in disbelief.

He didn't see it.

She was lying through her teeth and her interrogator *didn't see it.*

Vader didn't see it.

No one saw it but you.

The training held you still. The training controlled your body, but your mind raced with turmoil.

Should you say something? Is it a trick to test your own loyalty? Has someone seen through your soaring ambition, guessed at the hierarchy you'd like to penetrate, the command post you thirst for? What will you gain by speaking out against her? Will it show keen perception, your ability to know a prisoner's thoughts, your own untapped potential as an interrogator—?

No. Through the storm of uncertainty, you knew you were no latent interrogator. You didn't have Tarkin's skill or Vader's power.

You weren't reading the girl's mind. It was simpler than that.

You knew she was lying because it was exactly what you would do.

"Continue with the operation." Tarkin gave the order offhandedly to Admiral Motti. "You may fire when ready."

"*What?*" the princess cried out.

There was a scuffle. Tarkin, reverting to his dry and formal self, told her, "You're far too trusting." The princess leapt forward as if she could somehow stop him or attack him, bound as she was, but Lord Vader seized her by the shoulder and pulled her back against the hard casing of his hulking breastplate. He held her helpless there and forced her to watch.

No one forced you.

But you and your silent counterpart stood facing the view of the doomed blue world, and just as in the prison cell earlier, you had no choice but to watch.

You're far too trusting.

She wasn't trusting, you realized. She might be broken and she might be under threat of execution, but she still hadn't given anything away.

Even to save her world.

The destruction of Alderaan was blinding. There was no noise in the control room of the Death Star; all the company watched, hushed, as the terrible brightness flared around them.

You could have betrayed her now.

Whenever they inevitably sent their scouts and probes to Dantooine, you knew for certain they would find nothing there. You could have spared them the effort, the expense, the wasted power. You could have been rewarded for it.

But doubt bloomed in your heart, and you hesitated.

You're far too trusting.

There was no reason Governor Tarkin would ever reward you.

Why not betray her, though? Why not call out her falseness, just because you were a loyal Imperial guard?

The brightness burned your eyes. You dared not blink.

You stood still and said nothing, momentarily blinded.

You would not betray her. Your spirit was shaken, and your loyalty changed. Your silence made you her ally. You were now as doomed as she was. You would never betray her.

You had joined her rebellion.

ECLIPSE

Madeleine Roux

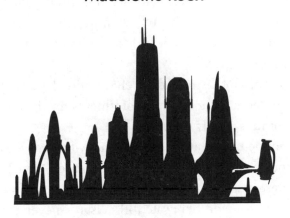

Breha Organa watched the slanted sunbeam behind Visaiya's shoulder. The light in the gallery above the palace's grand entrance hall grew gold, and then orange, signaling the end of the afternoon. Another day without her husband and daughter was coming to a close, but it had passed as slowly as a lifetime.

Visaiya spoke just as slowly, methodically reminding the queen of her schedule for the remainder of the day. With each word, each "then," followed by another chore, another meeting, another duty, Breha became wearier and wearier. A tight wrinkle formed between her eyes as she watched that one solitary sunbeam. It had sneaked in through one of the high windows above them, a single splash of gold amid the silvery-blue splendor of the palace. Even when she was a child, the hall had reminded her of the inside of a seashell, smooth and lustrous, always slightly cool even at the height of summer.

"Then, you are expected to found a school for underprivileged nerfs who just want to follow their dreams and become dancers . . ."

Breha snapped her gaze away from the sunbeam, looking in startled bemusement at the middle-aged woman beside her. As an adviser, Visaiya was so important to her that Breha often joked that losing her would be like cutting off a hand. She had even had matching rings made for them, simple little silver bands they each wore on their right index fingers.

"Perhaps I am a bit distracted," Breha admitted, passing a soothing hand over her face. "Cancel my appointments for the rest of the day, please; my mind is simply elsewhere."

Visaiya nodded, consulting her datapad with renewed determination. "Of course. Easily done." Then she paused, and Breha might have lost interest again and let her mind wander, but something in the woman's face made her watchful. Visaiya never demonstrated concern, always maintaining a mask of relaxed confidence. But now . . . Now her dark brows were drawn in, furrowed, her foot tapping under her gown, rippling the silk.

"There is still no word," Breha told her, reaching out to touch the woman's wrist. It was an overly familiar gesture, perhaps, but these were unusual times. "Captain Anderam has asked me to stop raising him in the spaceport. He swears I will be the first to know when his shuttle lands."

Visaiya did not look at all relieved. "I could go and keep watch. I don't mind."

Breha smiled gently. "Captain Anderam insisted. He is not to be bothered again today."

"Oh, but he only requested that *you* stop asking for him. I was issued no such warning."

And this was why Visaiya was her right hand. Breha was not above admitting to herself that without help she would not have weathered the recent storm—the dissolution of the Senate had come as such a blow, turning every incoming piece of news into possible calamity. The Empire was far beyond subtle politicking now; they were desperate to crush the Rebellion, and desperate animals were always the most dangerous. Breha pressed her lips together briefly and then nodded once. "Be discreet, and thank you. Now I think I will retire. I never knew I could be this exhausted."

Visaiya made her curtsey and bustled away, silk skirts trailing in her wake like a silver shadow. Unburdened but still preoccupied, Breha turned and made her way down the gallery. Normally, nothing short of a planetwide catastrophe could make her neglect her queenly duties, but she felt tired, tired down to her bones. And normally she would welcome a hectic day to keep her mind off her husband's and daughter's absences, but day after worrying day had ground her down. She had never felt old until recently, never found it difficult to get out of bed refreshed and energetic, but now she felt her advancing years keenly.

"Your Majesty? A minute of your time, if you could—"

Her daughter's attendant droid, WA-2V, approached from seemingly out of nowhere, the overhead light glinting off her bluish chassis as she darted out from behind a plant in the corridor leading toward the royal apartments. The droid rolled along quickly behind Breha, just a handsbreadth from the train of her gown.

"It's just . . ." The droid hurried on, gears whirring as she struggled to keep up. "Well, the gala for the equinox is in just three weeks and the draper really must know if the princess can attend and, if so, if she might prefer silk or satin."

"Later, TooVee," Breha said softly. Ambushed. And here she had hoped to arrive at her chambers alone, granted—at last—a moment's peace. "My appointments are being rescheduled. I'm not to be disturbed."

"Majesty?" And now the minister of finance, running to catch up with them.

Peace. It was not to be.

Fast on the minister's heels came another shiny chrome head, her daughter's old tutor droid CZ-7OB, clickity-clacking after them on metal feet. That droid was the only one of them that actually had an appointment, and it was probably far too late to cancel that one. Breha did not slow her pace, shrugging off the minister's questions as rapidly as they came. Soon they approached the tall, arched doors leading to the royal apartments, and the two armored sentinels that stood on either side.

Through the slits in one enameled helmet, she found the sentinel's eyes and gave the slightest shake of her head.

"But Your Majesty! The gown!" 2V sounded ready to pop a servo with frustration.

"Step aside, droid, there's hardly a credit in the budget to spare on such ridiculous—"

The doors to the royal apartments opened, and with them came a rush of clean, linen-scented air, the sweet sound of her youngest attendant practicing at her lute, and the even more welcoming clank as the halberds of her guards went down behind her, barring entry.

Breha stopped just inside the apartment and turned, opening her hands to them as if in surrender. Minister Lintreyst and 2V stopped short, the tutor droid bumping softly into the girl's back with a muttered apology.

Finances. Galas. Silks. Budgets. Would Leia return in time for the equinox? It seemed unlikely, and yet in a small, private corner of her heart that had nothing to do with rebellions or politics, Breha hoped it would be so. Would it mean her success or her failure if she returned that soon? What outcome did she dare wish for?

She winced and closed her eyes tightly. It was a mother's duty to worry, but a queen's responsibility to endure.

"That is enough for today," Breha told them in her firmest voice. She hated the feeling that she was being chased, and hated even more the sense that this was somehow a retreat. "Resources for the gala were allocated months ago, Lintreyst, which I'm certain you already know. TooVee, the draper can pull one of my gowns from storage; the princess may not attend the gala at all, and it would be a waste to begin a new garment from scratch."

The droid hummed with satisfaction, even giving a little turn on her rolling lower half, as if she could not contain her excitement. "Could . . . Could he at least add a few embellishments here and there? A crystal or two? Perhaps embroidery along the hem?"

Walking backward into her apartments, Breha closed her eyes again and suppressed a grin. "Why, yes, TooVee, that's an excellent idea. I'm certain Leia will be pleased."

Lintreyst, by contrast, was not an excitable or easily satisfied attendant. He grimaced and turned with a flounce, his cape swirling behind him as he stalked back down the corridor and away from them. Well, that was one problem taken care of and dispatched, at least.

"SeeZee-Seven? You may follow," Breha said, gesturing the droid forward.

Then she entered her apartments in earnest, breathing deeply as she stepped through first the antechamber, lush with plants and flowers, then the greeting salon, where her attendant Falena remained bent over her practice, and then through a short, curved corridor that led to their private balcony.

Mountain air. There was simply nothing like it for the nerves.

Breha closed her eyes against the setting sun. Pink tufts of clouds stretched across the sky, joined by a cascading sunset of orange and deep, dark blue. The melting snow off the Juran Mountains shimmered, a promise of warmer months to come, great migrating groups of thrantas swooping up from the mountains and toward those pink clouds. She smiled and fought the unease in her heart, enjoying as always the sight of those beautiful beasts, gray wings flapping, beating the air as their mournful cries filled the valley.

Behind her, her daughter's tutor droid clacked to a stop, and she could hear the soft whir as the droid shifted from foot to foot, waiting.

"Your Majesty," the droid began in his clear, automated voice. "I regret to inform you that I have discovered a grave discrepancy in your daughter's diplomatic records. Ordinarily, this would be simple enough to correct, but with the princess already departed, the error could affect her mission."

Ah yes, her *mission*. Nobody in the palace, of course, save a few key spies and officials, knew exactly where Leia had gone or why. It was crucial to keep the true reason for her trip a secret. Breha nodded, watching a little iridescent beetle make its way across the balcony banister. It pushed along a tiny tuft of balled-up grass, material for some growing nest.

"What is the discrepancy?"

CZ-7OB shuffled forward, joining her at the banister. If it was possible for a protocol droid to look nervous, this one accomplished it nearly constantly. Its glowing mechanical eyes darted from side to side, then up and down, and its answer came after a long hesitation. She could all but hear the circuits firing rapidly in the thing's head.

"According to her diplomatic profile, Princess Leia speaks both Huttese and Shyriiwook fluently. Regretfully, and as Your Majesty is keenly aware, the princess is merely proficient in Shyriiwook. This is, naturally, a failure of mine and not the princess, but I worry that such an error might cause her embarrassment. Oh, it is too, too humiliating."

Breha allowed herself a smile and turned, putting a motherly hand on the droid's shoulder. "It's hardly your fault that Leia did not apply herself more rigorously. I wouldn't worry. I'm struggling to imagine a scenario in which fluent Shyriiwook would benefit her." The droid's eyes flickered, brighter, as if in shock. "On this particular mission, of course," the queen quickly added.

Nodding, CZ-7OB glanced down at its hands. "That is perhaps true, Your Majesty, and a relief to hear, but more alarming still is my discovery that . . . that . . ." And here the droid leaned forward, whispering, "I hesitate to even make this accusation, but the princess altered the record *herself*."

From behind them came a soft chuckle. "That *does* sound like our daughter."

Both Breha and the droid startled in surprise, but it was the queen who gasped and let her royal demeanor slip for a moment. Her husband had returned, worn, perhaps, but as handsome as ever in a well-worn brown cape. She rushed to him, hurling herself gratefully into his open arms. The mountain air of her home was a balm, certainly, but the embrace of her beloved was bliss itself. The war, the Rebellion, their daughter's absence . . . All fled from her mind for one single moment.

"So long," she whispered, pulling back from him and touching his cheek. "So long."

"And here again," Bail replied, craning down from his height to kiss her. "SeeZee," he said absently, never taking his eyes off Breha's face, "go now and fix the record, and know that we are all of us grateful for your . . . particular brand of diligence."

The droid teetered by them, regarding them with wide, bright eyes as it went. "I only hope my correction does not come too late. It is dreadfully easy to insult a Wookiee."

"But Visaiya should have told me!" Breha's mind reeled. "You must have just crossed paths with her, and that damn Anderam! I told him to alert me at once . . ."

Bail held her at arm's length as the droid departed, but the smile he gave didn't reach his eyes. Something was deeply wrong. She noticed new lines at his eyes and longer swipes of gray at his temples, and her heart twisted at the thought of all the dangers he had survived to return to that very balcony. She held him tightly again and then allowed him to lead her to the railing, their hands entwined on the cool marble. A second herd of thrantas soared overhead, their cries echoing off the perimeter of the valley and the heights of the palace.

"Don't be cross with either of them, heart. I told them I wanted the surprise to be mine. Stars, but I missed you and this place," he whispered, tilting his head up toward the sky.

Breha wanted desperately to allow herself more time to feel relieved, but her grip on his hand tightened. "Scarif . . . Are the rumors true? They couldn't possibly be true . . ."

Her husband glanced away from her as he lowered his chin and sighed. He seemed to turn paler, a distant, haunted look coming into his eyes. "You must not think of that now," he assured her. Their eyes met and he forced half of a smile. "I had so hoped to make this reunion a happier one, but the news I have . . ." He trailed off, and for a moment he looked as if he might be sick.

"The Senate has been disbanded," she said. "We heard days ago, Bail. It's monstrous. I knew the Emperor was bold, but I expected at least a measure of subtlety."

"The Senate." Bail shook his head, his grip on her tightening. "That's not what I must tell you. I thought I knew what I would say, and it's only right that I'm the one to bear the news but now that it comes to it . . ."

Breha was silent, terrified that if she said another word he would only falter again. On the railing, she watched the little beetle succumb to a sudden wind, toppling over, all of his hard work lost and scattered.

Bail took in a deep breath, and she watched him grow steadier but still sickly pale. They had known each other for so long, survived so much, but in all their private mythology never had she seen him look this way. Her husband, a man of unshakeable courage and faith, now shaken to his core.

"The *Tantive* is lost," he whispered. "Destroyed."

For a moment, Breha couldn't hear a single thing. Panic. She knew the feeling well, had known it when news of the Senate's dissolution came, but this was something else. This wasn't just panic, it was a perfect, hollow place carving itself out in her chest. A high whine in her head made her deaf to anything but the blood pounding in her ears. She blinked, looking through the face of her husband, through the railing, through the mountains . . . Then her eyes finally fixed on that little beetle rolling his way across the banister. Bail had fallen to his knees, what little of his strength remained had only lasted until he could deliver that message.

It falls to you now.

That void in her chest had to be filled with something or she would collapse inward, a helpless pulsar. Purpose could fill the void. For now, at least. Breha folded her hands together, clasping them tighter and tighter, as if that single point of pressure could somehow keep her upright and together.

"We must know more than that. Send another scouting party at once. Escape pods could have been jettisoned. Our daughter is not so easily killed; she will have made every attempt to survive. We need a chart of all planets near that asteroid field. That's where we will begin looking for survivors. And who reported this? Can they be trusted?" she demanded, hearing her voice rise until she could control it again.

"I will not accept any report until I have seen the wreckage with my own eyes."

She nearly demanded to know what exactly the Senate was doing about it but remembered that they were alone in this, lost in an unfamiliar wilderness.

Nodding, Bail reached for her and with shaking hands she helped him from the ground.

"I've asked for all that and more," he assured her. "We may no longer have the Senate, but we are not without allies. Breha, there is a squadron looking, but we are at war now. You know I would use every possible resource, but our personal loss must be balanced against the needs of the Rebellion."

The tears were coming unbidden, and Breha was powerless against them. *Our personal loss.* She leaned into her husband, shrugging deep into his embrace, hiding the twitch in her chin that signaled her moment of steely political resolve was crumbling.

240

"Not loss," she said. "Not yet. I won't give up. But Bail, we should never have agreed to this, to let her go . . ."

He rested his chin heavily on her head, and Breha felt suddenly ancient and afraid, frail, battered on all sides by a war she could not stop and evil she could not understand.

"This war is just beginning, and we must make what preparations we can here. Even if we do nothing but look for her, even if we do nothing but hope, the war *is* here," he said softly. "It *will* be fought by Leia when we find her. We could try to keep her hidden and safe here on Alderaan if—when—she's recovered, but we both know she would find a way to leave."

"Yes, I know." She pulled away, scrubbing her eyes with both hands. "We should be out there looking, too. Captain Anderam can prepare a transport for us, we should raise him."

"I'm sorry," he said. "You know as well as I do that it's simply too dangerous. If the *Tantive* can be taken then so can we."

Breha shook her head and hugged herself, rubbing warmth into already warm arms. Her anger subsided into sadness, and she returned to her husband, letting him fold her into a tight embrace as the last comforting touch of the sun fell on their faces.

"Of course . . . Of course that's true. But I can't do nothing, love. I refuse to do nothing."

She pulled a small holo device from the pockets in her voluminous skirts, finding that even that simple task required full focus. Even standing and breathing felt like unfairly cruel tasks. But she steeled herself, prepared to be a queen for a moment longer and a mother the moment the call went through.

The blue image of Captain Anderam flickered to life on the holo as he accepted the transmission.

"Perhaps we must indeed stay here," Breha said quietly. "But we have able pilots and agents, and they will search where we cannot."

Knowing there would be no sleep did not make its absence any easier. A constant tremor began in her hands, one Breha felt echoed in her brain. There was no word of her daughter yet, not in the direction of life or death, and the possibility that they would never really discover Leia's fate was becoming likelier by the day. That possibility hung over her like a blind spot, and at certain moments, exhausted to the point of delusion, she swore an actual black void was beginning to obscure her vision permanently.

Every blip on every communication device sent her into another paroxysm of expectant fear. She let nobody but Bail see it, or at least, she did her best to hide the weariness darkening under her eyes and the shaking of her hands.

Two days. Two days had passed since her husband's return and it felt like a lifetime, the lack of sleep blurring the hours together until she could no more rest than divine the hour or day. The long, vaulted chamber at the north end of the palace had once hosted dignitaries and been the place of sober, serious political discussion, but now it had become the hub of information while their best-trained agents searched quietly for Leia. Breha spent too much time there. She ate there, when she could stomach it. And she watched Bail from across the vastness of the meeting table, their eyes ricocheting off each other's. Any lingering glance and Breha would feel herself hurtling toward tears.

There would be no tears in front of their generals.

She saw a page cross from the high-arched door to the table and stand at Bail's elbow. Their whispered exchange was lost over the constant chatter of the men and women around them and the steady stream of incoming and outgoing holo calls. But Breha observed closely, every new piece of information bringing a surge of hope. Leads, most of them empty, seemed to circle endlessly back to the same conclusion: The *Tantive* had been annihilated, and with it, every soul on board.

Bail shook his head, and she noticed the same telling tremor in his hands as he pinched the bridge of his nose in frustration. "Someone must know something. Do you hear me? Go back," he said, his voice rising in irritation. *"Go back and check again, and then check once more."*

The page swept the blue cap off his head and bowed his way out of the hall, stricken, his sweet young face turning bright crimson.

Breha joined her husband, finding his hand under the table and taking it. He did not look at her, but he leaned almost imperceptibly into her shoulder.

"They are worried, too, Bail. Don't forget that."

"I shouldn't have snapped at him."

She had only tired smiles left in her, so she gave him one. "He will forgive you."

"Oh, Your Majesties!" WA-2V wheeled into the chaos of the room, deftly weaving through the concerned crowd to where Bail and Breha stood. Her slender arms were laden with a gown, one Breha recognized at once as her own. It had been changed slightly, the length taken up for Leia's petite size, a glittering spray of gems added to the hem. The droid stopped just short of them and Breha had to put up a hand to keep the dress from tumbling out of 2V's grasp. Her fingers brushed the familiar silk and a new wave of grief crested.

"You were right, it was a much better idea to freshen up one of your old gowns," the droid said, fussing with the sleeves of the dress. "This one is just so special, and it would be a shame to leave it in storage. It will suit the princess just perfectly!"

"This is not the time," Bail interrupted, turning toward the attendant. "There are . . . other considerations worthy of our attention."

But the droid continued to look to Breha, holding out the empty gown. The queen forced herself to put her hand on the rich fabric, numbing herself to the fresh pain.

"It's lovely," she assured the attendant. "When Leia returns she will be very pleased."

2V wheeled back and forth, fidgeting, then replied with a chirp, "I think so, too, Majesty, and she will be home soon to see it."

A blue man shimmered to life to their left, an incoming holo from Captain Anderam making him glow in miniature as he shouted frantically from his offices in the spaceport.

"What now?" Bail stalked toward the end of the long table, wedging himself between two ministers huddling over the holo.

Breha was there an instant later, leaning forward to speak clearly into the recording device. "Anderam? Can you hear me? Is there news?"

"Above!" The captain sounded panicked. "Can you see? Something is moving into position in orbit, we had no warning . . ."

243

"What are you saying? You aren't making any sense," Breha replied, watching the call begin to fail. Something was interfering with the transmission. "Captain—"

But Bail grabbed her by the wrist, turning to her slowly, his eyes searching the floor between them. "Come," he whispered. "Outside. Transfer the captain to my personal line!"

She let him lead her out of the hall and down the corridor at a run, and Breha picked up her skirts to keep pace, breath catching in her throat as he brought them sprinting through the palace and to the nearest balcony, the familiar outdoor haven off their chambers. They both skidded to a stop, Anderam springing to life in Bail's hand as they stared up at the darkening sky.

"Get . . . safety . . ." The captain's voice was just a crackle now.

"Think, Bail. The *Tantive* goes down, our communications blocked . . ." She sighed and watched as the image of the captain cut out entirely. "They must know it was Leia. This is a retaliation."

Her husband began to pace, sweat beading at his temples as he threw down the comm in frustration. Most of what he muttered to himself was too soft to be heard. "Impossible. They wouldn't dare!"

Maybe this was all a distraction, some Imperial plot to keep them from searching for their daughter. Nothing was certain, she reminded herself, nothing was to be believed until they had absolute confirmation. And if the Empire's attention had turned to Alderaan, then all the better—let them be distracted here, it might allow her daughter to escape the wreck. As long as she survived, there was hope; no matter what far-flung planet Leia landed on, she would find a way to deliver the data and complete her task.

A shadow fell across the balcony, draping them both in cold and sudden darkness. She reached for Bail instinctively, looping her arm in his as they both turned in unison to face the valley. Breha shielded her eyes with the flat of her hand, gazing up at the sky and the mas-

244

sive object that moved slowly across the sun. In an instant, the thing had obscured the sun completely.

"What could be so large?" Breha murmured. Fear knotted tightly in her stomach, and she clung harder to her husband. What was she seeing? She had witnessed an eclipse once on Coruscant, but this was so much faster. So *unnatural.*

Beside her, Bail gasped and then seemed to go limp. He turned to her, eyes empty, mouth moving but silent. At last, he found his voice and searched the ground at her feet.

"The planet killer."

She fought back the surge of nausea that slammed into her like a breaking wave and placed her hands on his face, forcing Bail to look at her. It couldn't be true. Not Alderaan. They were in the heart of the galaxy, a major planet, a bastion of tradition and peace and prosperity . . .

The perfect symbol to destroy. The perfect message to send. No planet was too sacred, too populous . . . No planet was safe.

"My love, they wouldn't," she said, even as she knew they would.

Bail smoothed his hands over hers and touched their foreheads together. "At least we will be together."

"No!" She refused to believe it. How could such evil exist? "There . . . There must be time. The spaceport is too far, but we could reach our private shuttle. We . . . We could evacuate as many as possible! There must be something, anything, that we can—"

The sound was incredible. They turned toward it in awe and dread, a deadening of air that pulled all noise from around them before a tremendous blast like lightning rent the air. Bail yanked her into his arms, squeezing her as light blinded them, a ring of white that grew from the horizon, spreading fast, bringing trees, beasts, and rocks with it.

"She made it out," Breha whispered, trembling hands balled in his cloak, her disbelieving eyes watching as the planet itself burst with a thousand bright, terrible geysers. "I would know if she was gone, Bail."

"She lives." He kissed her forehead, leaving his lips there as the palace shook under them and the beams holding the balcony aloft screamed and gave. The attendants inside their apartments gave a wail of fright, and the castle sagged with no ground left beneath it.

Her bones hurt. It felt like they were being shaken apart.

"She lives," Bail said once more.

Breha closed her eyes. "I know."

The mountains rose up, folding toward them, swallowing them whole. She felt her husband's warmth, his breath on her neck, then the scent of ash and smoke, and in the next moment, oblivion.

VERGE OF GREATNESS

Pablo Hidalgo

THEN:

You may fire when ready.

Wilhuff Tarkin was not the type to have rehearsed words. He was not given to standing before a mirror and imagining his moments of triumph, mouthing or whispering statements that would become cemented in history.

But these words were different. He had waited over two decades to say them. These words would begin an unfathomable frenzy of actions and reactions deep within the enormous weapon he stood in control of, and unleash a torrent of primordial fire that would erase the enemies of the Empire in a searing instant.

It pricked him that Director Krennic had already given the order to fire a test shot that had vaporized Jedha City, but such precautions were necessary. *What if it had failed?* Better such embarrassment lie at the feet of Orson Krennic than Grand Moff Tarkin. Krennic's test proved spectacular, but the good director was destined to receive only a footnote mention in the annals of the Empire, as being tangentially connected to a mining disaster on the ancient moon.

Tarkin had carefully modulated his own distance from the project over the years—hovering ever closer when signs pointed to success, floating farther away when delays gnawed at the Emperor's patience. In that moment over Jedha, the Death Star had moved from concept to proof, and Tarkin had stepped from distant backer to chief architect.

Krennic had tried to steal that moment. What was it he had said? That they stood there amid *his* achievement? *Nonsense.* Such claims were as absurd as a bricklayer taking pride in a parapet built at the behest of a king. It is *the king's* castle. Glory ascends ever skyward.

Now Tarkin stood atop the sky, looking down at Scarif, a world violated by rebel intruders. A world *infested,* its secrets—*Imperial* secrets—exposed to rebel vermin. These secrets were not irreplaceable; there were duplicates of the military development records on Coruscant and, knowing the Emperor, elsewhere. That was beside the point; the rebel threat was *here* and *now.* The matter called for an executive decision.

The rebels could not leave Scarif. The information needed to be purged as a limb needed to be amputated before the infection spread elsewhere.

And Krennic was down there, wasn't he? Returned to the Citadel on Scarif to clean up the mess he'd started. Well, Tarkin could do him a favor and sterilize that mess far more effectively from his current vantage point, inside the Death Star, orbiting high above the tropical planet.

Scarif turned below, bringing the Citadel to the horizon.

"You may fire when ready," Tarkin said at long last. And he allowed himself the briefest of smiles.

NOW:

Tarkin stood on the Overbridge of the Death Star, surrounded by luminescent instrumentation and humming machinery. General Tagge waited nearby, as did Admiral Motti, examining a readout display, though a glance that failed to notice these officers could be forgiven, what with the other presence on the floor: the imposing form of Darth Vader, Dark Lord of the Sith.

"Her resistance to the mind probe is considerable. It'll be some time before we can extract any information from her," rumbled Vader, describing the tenacity of their prisoner, Princess Leia Organa of Alderaan.

Time. The word echoed in Tarkin's mind, bringing up thoughts of the past again. *You have made time an ally of the Rebellion.* Tarkin had scolded that idiot Krennic over such matters.

249

"The final checkout is completed." Motti beamed. The admiral took care to ensure that Tarkin stood directly between him and the capricious Dark Lord. Motti and Vader had had a recent *disagreement* on matters of spirituality and procedure. "All systems are operational. What course shall we set?"

An operational Death Star and the entire galaxy within reach, a moment two decades in the making—and yet Tarkin could not savor it. The questions buzzed at him like a gnat in a bedroom: Where were these rebels? Where were they operating from? Where was their base?

And the most stinging question: What good was having the most powerful weapon in the universe if this girl could defy them?

"Perhaps she would respond to an alternative form of persuasion," he proposed. The Senate and its appeals to the populace were no more; the Emperor had seen to that with the long-overdue dissolution of that quarrelsome body. Planets that brooked treason but were afforded some protection by invoking the sympathies of the Empire's citizens would have no voice to appeal to the people. These worlds needed a reminder of what ultimate power looked like.

"What do you mean?" asked Vader, though no doubt the Dark Lord already suspected the eventual destination of Tarkin's train of thought.

"I think it is time we demonstrated the full power of this station," said Tarkin. He turned to the young admiral. "Set your course for Alderaan."

Motti grinned. "With pleasure."

250

The Death Star's jump to hyperspace occurred with little incident. It was, literally, no small matter to propel such a massive object at superluminal velocities, but the marvel of engineering that was this battle station performed to expectation. Only slight shudders could be felt in Tarkin's spacious office, where they resonated in rings in a cup of water on the gleaming surface of his desk.

Tarkin sat looking over engineering reports scrolling across his desk monitor. Per Krennic's standards, each hyperspace jump was accompanied by an exhaustive list chronicling the performance of every system and subsystem involved in the process. Tarkin's bony fingers flicked a scroll of information, but he soon grew disinterested. The station worked; he didn't need an autopsy on every mechanical event. Let the engineers pore through it.

He shuffled this technical data feed out of view and pulled up the news coming out of the capital. The disbanding of the Senate demanded the attention of the media, and the holonews outlets were obediently repeating the narrative that the Empire's advisers had prepared. Rebel traitors had infiltrated the Senate. Such infiltration resulted in a devastating terrorist strike on a major Imperial military installation on Scarif. For the duration of the emergency, the Emperor needed absolute control to bring a swift end to this threat and root out insurgents who had access to the heart of the Imperial bureaucracy.

Tarkin saw a dramatic display of the Death Star's prime weapon as the perfect way to punctuate that decree with an undeniable example of Imperial power. Tarkin had the authority to make such decisions. Surely he need not seek permission from Coruscant to do what he planned.

The door chime rang, interrupting Tarkin's reading. From his desk, he unsealed the door and invited his visitor to enter. Motti stepped forward. "I wish to congratulate you, Governor, on a more personal level than formality would ordinarily allow. You have achieved what many nonbelievers deemed would be impossible," he said. Motti's nostrils flared as he breathed deeply. "The Death Star is ready and is yours."

"Your sentiment is noted and appreciated, Motti, but I'm not one to have time wasted on overly emotional displays," said Tarkin, watching the admiral closely. "You did not come here just to share such words."

Motti swallowed, then spoke. "Sir, if I may. This station can destroy any planet you care to select. The entire starfleet, in pitched battle, couldn't stop us. Couldn't stop *you*. You now have in your hand the power of life and death over every living thing in the galaxy."

Tarkin waited, saying nothing. Motti continued, "Ultimate power. It rests with you now."

"And with the Emperor, of course," said Tarkin, spearing Motti with his gaze.

251

"To be sure, Governor," Motti quickly replied. "That's what I meant. But the Emperor is far from here, and you are in actual command."

Tarkin reached for his water, but still watched Motti closely. "This isn't the first time you've spoken in this fashion, Motti." He took a brief sip. "Say what is on your mind."

"If you order so." Motti's pause was almost imperceptible. "The battle station has become the very source of the Empire's power. All that power lies at your command. And your command alone."

"You are close to treason, Motti," Tarkin warned. He had known that the conversation would arrive at this mark when Motti had shown himself in.

"Is it treason to point out that you could demand a position of authority second only to that of the Emperor?" asked Motti.

"I would not care to have the Emperor as my enemy," Tarkin said, breaking eye contact with Motti to glance down at the reports from Coruscant. With a flick of a button, he collapsed that data feed.

"But command of the Death Star makes you his equal," said Motti. "You could share dominion of the galaxy."

The slight emphasis on *share* painted a clear picture of motivation in Tarkin's mind. He looked back up at Motti and grinned his lipless grin. "With you at my right hand?"

"I'm your willing servant, Governor Tarkin."

Tarkin stood. Motti took an expectant half step forward, but Tarkin stayed behind his desk. "Thank you for the sentiment regarding this station's operation, Admiral. But we shall now return to the formality of procedure and record, and continue our mission that the Emperor has decreed."

Motti nodded, regaining his more rigid posture and the degree of circumspection that Imperial protocols dictated. But the gleam was still in his eye. It had been a gamble, but Motti had successfully launched the first volley in an ambitious bid for power and still stood possessed of his rank and his life. Tarkin dismissed him with a nod, and Motti turned on his heels and stepped out of the office.

Politics, thought Tarkin, was where Krennic failed. The loud-mouthed engineer knew the intricacies of hyperdrives and energy conversion ratios, but he had failed to see the pitfalls of the Imperial court. Krennic had wanted to ascend but was at a loss as to how to climb. Tarkin had blocked his every path, and not even a Death Star had allowed Krennic to rise.

Krennic had been a builder pretending to be a leader. In the end, it was his undoing.

Tarkin stood on the Overbridge. Admiral Motti had informed him of the safe reversion from hyperspace and that the Death Star now loomed closer to Alderaan.

Tarkin had visited the world on many occasions. It was steeped in history, its royal family having launched many of the ancient expeditions that had first opened up the galaxy. Such a pedigree elevated it to untouchable heights of import, and a cloud of arrogance surrounded it. The Organas had thought they could act with impunity in defying the Emperor's decrees, because history had afforded them a *special* place in the hearts and minds of the people.

Alderaan and its royals were overdue for a lesson.

"Governor Tarkin," said a haughty voice cloaked in an affected accent. "I should have expected to find you holding Vader's leash. I recognized your foul stench when I was brought on board."

Despite her small frame, entirely overshadowed by the oppressive black form of Darth Vader, Princess Leia Organa stood straight and proud. She was a fraction of Tarkin's height and age, but she stood her ground well as they exchanged barbs dressed as pleasantries. But Tarkin soon grew weary of the interchange.

"Princess Leia," he said, "before your execution, I would like you to be my guest at a ceremony that will make this battle station operational." Tarkin spread his arms, taking in the sweep of the Death Star. "No star system will dare oppose the Emperor now."

Leia faced him and spoke evenly. "The more you tighten your grip, Tarkin, the more star systems will slip through your fingers."

"Not after we demonstrate the power of this station. In a way, you have determined the choice of the planet that will be destroyed first," Tarkin said. He turned to the Overbridge monitor that displayed the image of blue-green Alderaan. So very much like Scarif, when he last stood in control of the Death Star's prime weapon. Except now, there would be no half measures in the battle station's operation.

"Since you are reluctant to provide us with the location of the rebel base, I have chosen to test this station's destructive power on your home planet of Alderaan," he said.

Leia gasped. There it was. The crack in the façade. The crumbling of hope. The death of that rebellious spark. Leia pleaded. Tarkin savored it.

Vader was as impassive and unreadable as ever.

It was different, this time, the blast that emanated from the battle station's superlaser. The eight tributary beams funneled into a single ray that reduced Alderaan into fiery rubble. Tens of thousands of years of history were wiped out in an instant.

Tarkin saw his future in the bright shock wave of fire that radiated into the cosmos. He thought of the distant Emperor, and how little Palpatine's reaction would matter. He thought of the girl, sobbing at the destruction of her treasonous world. He thought of Motti's words. And in this moment of triumph, Tarkin couldn't help but think of Krennic, and all he had taken from the unworthy man.

THEN:

His shoulder burned. Charred flesh cracked with every move.

Orson Krennic's consciousness swam up from pain-induced darkness. His senses focused the blurry sunlight into a comprehensible image. He was on Scarif, in the grip of what could only be described as a nightmare. But it was no dream; it was all true, and had just gotten worse.

Krennic looked skyward and saw his creation: the Death Star, looming beyond the clouds, revolving slowly.

Tarkin, Krennic fumed. Tarkin was now in control of his battle station. Or so Tarkin thought.

You do not know the power you stand upon, Tarkin. You don't know how to tame this.

If the rebels had succeeded in stealing the technical readouts of the battle station, then Krennic's immediate course of action would have been to order a complete review of the schematics. Now aware of Galen Erso's treachery, Krennic would have combed through the data to find anything, any aberration, no matter how insignificant. He would plug any gap that Erso might have made in the Death Star's armor.

Krennic would do so, even though some would scoff that the Death Star was a proven success. Krennic would pull the station offline to examine every bolt. Krennic would have weathered the political fallout of depriving the Emperor of his new weapon to ensure it worked flawlessly.

Because Krennic was an engineer. Tarkin was not. Tarkin could not fathom the complexity of this creation. Tarkin would instead be consumed by impatience.

Tarkin was a politician pretending to be an architect. In the end, Krennic knew, it would be his undoing.

My creation will be your destruction.

And with a flash of green energy, funneled through an array of composite kyber crystals engineered by Galen Erso, whose daughter just moments ago he had caught trespassing in the very heart of Imperial secrets, Orson Krennic became dust.

FAR TOO REMOTE

Jeffrey Brown

THE TRIGGER

Kieron Gillen

Maybe Aphra didn't look like a rebel. Maybe she wasn't going to get shot.

As she tumbled through the undergrowth, the vicious Dantooine thorns tearing at her, she realized that all she had were her prejudices of what rebels actually looked like. She pictured them having jutting chins, chests swollen with pride, and heads slightly creaking with a surfeit of misplaced idealism. That wasn't Aphra. That said, with dual blasters at the hip, goggles perched on her tatty pilot's helmet, and a wiry build, she looked more like a successful scavenger or an unsuccessful criminal than a doctor of archaeology. It'd be best to keep her head down, get back to the *Ark Angel,* and get the hell off this dumb green planet before she crossed paths with one of the Imperial patrols.

It didn't matter what she looked like. If they found her near this rebel base, they'd be suspicious, inevitably in that murderously suspicious way the Empire was so fond of.

Aphra's life alternated between finding interesting ancient artifacts and reactivating interesting ancient artifacts, with brief interstitial periods of selling the interesting ancient artifacts. She liked to describe herself as a rogue archaeologist. Others tended to describe her as a weapons dealer. After spending the best years of her twenties doing so, she couldn't in good faith argue that hard against that.

She had been holed up in Dantoo Town, trying to reactivate and upgrade some war-surplus droidekas. Having the deflection fields integrate with the newly added rocket pods was nightmarish—her first experiment led to the payload detonating on the inside of the field. Cue Aphra spending two weeks rebuilding the droids from scratch. She could solve the problem easily enough . . . if she had a 3.23 colicoidic pulse field modulator.

None of her usual contacts had one, so she looked for salvage. She thought she had a lead. This base on the far side of Dantooine had been secret enough not to draw attention to itself, but big enough that it couldn't be hidden from anyone actually looking. Aphra hacked into an orbital station's feeds, which let her track the regular, secretive movement of snubfighters into orbit and back. She presumed it was criminals or criminals with delusions of altruism—as in, rebels. But it had been quiet for a while now. Probably abandoned. Possibly salvage-rich.

The base itself was elegantly integrated with Dantooine's endless tree canopy. From orbit, you'd likely think it was a larger example of one of the planet's many sap farms. It'd take an expert eye to notice the snubfighter bays in a circle around a low, main bunker. In her time picking over the sprawl, Aphra had learned a couple of things. Firstly, it was definitely a rebel base. Secondly, rebels were worryingly efficient in cleaning up after themselves. She felt sure actual criminals would have left more of a useful mess. Curse the Rebellion.

Aphra had . . . complicated feelings toward the Rebellion. Their instincts were good, but good wasn't good enough. People like the rebels, all bighearted and high-minded, led to the Galactic Civil War. As far as Aphra had an ethical orientation, it had been formed by growing up in the shadow of the war. Most people needed order. Better the Empire when the alternative was *that*. Weak people died in their billions in that alternative.

Not that Aphra needed anyone, of course.

She was working her way through what she was pretty sure was the central comm before it had been stripped when the *Ark Angel* sent her an alert. A fly-by of TIE fighters had triggered her alerts. She had just enough time to run from the compound and throw herself into the wild undergrowth. Then the drop pods crashed down, gleaming stormtrooper kill teams spreading across the base like insects.

Aphra decided she didn't really need the 3.23 colicoidic pulse field modulator that badly and ran back to her ship through a purgatory of thorns, viscous sap, and all-permeating forest damp.

She almost burst through the undergrowth into the open when she saw the camouflaged curve of her pocket cruiser's unusually towering curved nose peaking beneath the holo-webbing she'd left to conceal it.

Aphra had made it to safety.

A second later, she realized that she hadn't.

Working their way unknowingly toward the *Ark Angel* were three stormtroopers, making a perimeter sweep. It was an obvious problem for her. It was also a problem for them, in that they were about to hit the layer of micromines she'd left to cover the approach. A moral dilemma. Or, as Aphra preferred to think of them, dilemmas. "Moral" never really came into it.

Option one: She lets them hit the mines. She finishes anyone left with her blasters. She gets the *Ark Angel* into orbit, trying to dodge the inevitable Star Destroyer that brought all these troopers here. She almost certainly has to abandon the droideka hulls she's left in Dantoo Town, and has to burn through another transponder identity on the *Ark Angel*. Oh, and she murders a bunch of people, too.

Alternatively . . .

Aphra sighed, holstered her blaster, and stepped forward, hands raised, smile wide.

"Hey, guys!" she shouted. "How can I help you fine gentlemen of the Imperial Army?"

Plus, those mines were *expensive*. She wasn't going to waste them on stormtroopers.

The stormtroopers questioned her, searched her, and escorted-*cum*-dragged her toward the compound. They found both blasters and the knife, but they'd left her with her tools, which was probably a mistake. If they'd scanned her, they'd have found the explosive putty in the lining of her hat, stored safely in two inert packages. If she could work out an excuse to remove her hat and play with the putty for the better part of a minute, that'd be useful. Maybe she could offer to show them clay animals?

She was pushed into what was once the rebels' HQ, and was now the Imperials'. Support staff milled around, but Aphra knew they were irrelevant. The only man who mattered in the room stood, dressed in an Imperial uniform, looking at the holomaps of the area with a displeased expression. Aphra didn't read too much into that.

Aphra suspected that good news or bad, that expression would sit there, glowering, perpetually disappointed. He was a gray cloud in a gray uniform.

He was a general. Aphra couldn't interpret the string of colored buttons on his lapel, but he fulfilled every prejudice Aphra had of Imperial High Command.

She felt the gun still in the small of her back as the stormtrooper reported.

"Found her skulking around the outer perimeter, General Tagge," said the stormtrooper in a surprisingly thin voice. "She says she's from Dantoo Town. Her speeder bike is hidden east of the base. We're trying to locate it."

The speeder didn't exist, but Aphra was damned if she was going to let anyone go poking around the *Ark Angel*. Aphra beamed, both to try to make a good first impression, and because she'd correctly identified this Tagge as a general. Her knowledge of military ranks at any time past the Republic was foggy at best.

"Er . . . I surrendered. And handed over my weapons. I just want to help," she said with all the sincerity she could muster. Tagge looked her over. He grunted, unconvinced, and turned back to the map.

"Why are you here?"

"I'm stealing stuff. Well . . . salvaging, but I think I should get bonus marks for honesty, right?" Aphra said. "The base cleared out months ago, so I figured if there was anything left here, it was mine."

Tagge glanced back, analyzing her as if she were a spreadsheet and he wanted to check if the columns tallied or not.

"I find you in the middle of an abandoned rebel base, and you claim you know nothing?" he said.

Aphra gave her best attempt at an innocent gasp. It perhaps reached the level of "faux innocent."

"Surely not *rebels*!" she said. "The rebels are small and disorganized, barely more than bandits. This place could have held dozens of spaceships. Surely the rebels couldn't support a base like this?"

Tagge's face was as motionless as the stormtroopers' masks.

"I think you're mistaking being clever for being smart," said Tagge.

Aphra winced a little. Getting shot for that would be dumb, even for her.

"I'm sorry. No one had any idea this was a rebel base. It'd been abandoned for months by the time I got here. And . . ." She paused, searching for an angle that would allow her to continue her blessed non-blaster-wounded life. ". . . this is the biggest military force Dantooine has ever seen. Dantooine is quiet. Indoor lighting is a novelty. A show of force like this and everyone from around here will know that no one could dream of resisting the Empire."

Tagge snorted, a single sharp noise. A laugh, or Tagge's equivalent.

"I do not think there is any danger of the Empire's seriousness being underestimated," he said, "Today, scavenger, the Empire destroyed Alderaan."

The room was silent. Tagge let the fact hang in the air, expecting silence to rule. It was immediately overthrown.

"How?" said Aphra. "Surface bombing? Even with a fleet of Star Destroyers that'd take weeks. Or a bioplague, like on Genosha? Is this Tarkin Initiative technology? I've loved the work I've seen coming from the labs. Is it like a cities-flattened thing, or a leave-the-buildings-standing thing? Are we talking about just sentients, or a full flora/fauna extinction event? Seriously, *how*? Atmosphere ignition? I've seen plans for that. Ooh—mantle fissure. Magma core exposure can make a mess out of a civilization. Or . . . oh, I'm torturing myself. What do you mean *exactly*?"

Tagge stared at her. "I mean the planet is dust," he said.

Aphra was faintly aware that this was not the response Tagge was expecting, but her excitement had its own momentum.

"Like . . . *dust* dust? Like, bits of asteroid and people floating in space? *That?*"

"The Death Star destroyed Alderaan," said Tagge, somehow being dragged along in the wake of Aphra's enthusiasm.

"Wow," said Aphra, "that's amazing."

She was aware that she was being stared at.

"Er . . . well done, Empire?" Aphra said.

The awkward silence was broken when the other stormtroopers entered the room, saluting.

"Sir," said the first. "We've looked for her speeder and can't find it."

"Of course," said Aphra. "I hid it. That's what *hidden* means."

The silence returned. Aphra's Aphra routine had gone down better.

Tagge walked slowly up to her, arms behind his back, and considered her. Once more, Aphra's spreadsheet was tallied as Tagge made his final analysis.

"I don't think you're a rebel," he said.

Aphra tried not to laugh. She was going to live.

265

"I do think you're trouble," he said, "and I suspect the world would be better off without you."

Oh no. She wasn't going to live. She was going to do the opposite of that.

When Tagge ordered the trooper to take her to the trees, execute her, and return to the search, Aphra had to fight every urge in her body not to run and kick and lash out. Her head screamed. Her face twisted. If she ran now, she would be shot. If she fought, she'd be dragged out by a mob. Instead she complied, and the stormtrooper guided her. Every step, she looked for her opening. There had to be something. Her luck got her into this kind of situation. Her luck got her out of it. That was how it worked.

A voice inside her added a taunting, *That's how it works until it doesn't.*

She winced. She knew it would eventually be It. Maybe this would be It.

"So, is this the first time you've executed someone?" she asked, voice breaking.

"Don't speak, prisoner," said the trooper. His voice was unsteady, too.

Okay. Aphra could work with that.

Aphra laughed nervously, glancing slowly over her shoulder, and winked. "Or what are you going to do? Shoot me?"

They carried on toward the tree line, Aphra a model of compliance.

"Were you aboard the Death Star?" she asked.

After a pause, he replied: "You are very interested in planetary destruction."

"Er . . . who wouldn't be?" she said, stepping over a log while considering whether she could make a break for the cover of the next trunk. No, she couldn't. Not unless she wanted to do it with a five-centimeter hole in her back.

"It's a weapon like that, and you're *excited* by it?" he said.

"It just makes you think. How do you even design something like that?" she said, before glancing back to check the distance. Could she rush him? Unlikely going on No. Even if she did, he had about half a meter on her.

"I mean . . . do you think the Death Star had a trigger?" she said, "Someone ordered it to be fired, but that's easy. Did someone actually have to pull the trigger?"

She carried on into the wood. He followed, the two deadly steps behind her.

"I'll bet there wasn't. I bet it's a bunch of people, so everyone can have some deniability of responsibility. Six engineers, all charging up firing chambers, and it's only when they're all powered-up the weapon engages. That's how I'd do it. Because if someone has the weight of knowing they killed a whole planet on them . . . that could break them. They could just not press the button.

"That's how they do firing squads on some worlds," she went on, glancing back. "There's someone who's gun isn't firing for real, so they can always think, *Hey—maybe I didn't do it*. It's those little illusions that get us through. It's hardest when you've got no way to self-deceive.

"You're doing this solo. You're as unlucky as I am," she continued. "Well, nearly as unlucky."

Aphra turned around and stopped.

"You ever shot anyone in cold blood?"

"Turn around," he ordered.

"Hey, I'm trying to help. I want to make this easy for you. This is going to sit inside you forever . . . and if I'm going to die, I want to really think about this. Imagine actually killing Alderaan. Alderaan of all places! Alderaan is nice. Who'd blow up Alderaan? Hell of a place. Incredible history. Good party town. Hell, even had great sunsets. Now it doesn't even have a sky."

Aphra took a slow step toward him, holding his gaze.

"And you're here, with a gun pointing at some chatty lady, and you're always going to remember this day . . ."

And half a step, pulling the tool from her waistband, trying to remember the code she needed . . .

"People are going to ask us all where we were today. Where were you when Alderaan died? And you're going to say, *That's the day I went for a walk into some beautiful woods on Dantooine and shot that weird innocent scavenger lady*."

Aphra almost dropped the tool, and tried not to twist her face in anger. *Don't mess up now, Aphra.*

"If you're feeling philosophical, you'll say add something like . . ."

She smiles. ". . . *All innocence died that day,* and people will nod, and know that just because you did this really bad thing, it doesn't make you a bad person."

Aphra reached out with her hand, activating the tool. Lights on, but silent. Her hand touched his, holding that eye contact, knowing if he looked down and saw her tool near his blaster, it would all be over . . .

"It's okay," she said. "I forgive you."

He pulled the trigger. A click.

Aphra's knee went toward a not-nearly-armored-enough groin. As he reeled, she pulled the blaster from his hand.

"You can always induce a jam with the Imperial-model blasters if you've got the right frequency. Which I do." She pointed his own gun at him. "Reboots after a couple of seconds."

There was a low hum as the gun reactivated.

"You've never shot someone in cold blood," she said, gesturing the barrel at him. "Guess who has?"

The stormtrooper stumbled, backing off, falling over a log and then freezing, hands raised. He did all he could think of to do.

"No. Please," he begged.

Aphra shook her head. "They train you to shoot. They train you to follow orders. They train you in . . . well, other things. Marching, I guess. But they don't train you how to beg for your life," she said. "Take your helmet off."

Aphra was expecting to have to repeat herself, but he pulled the helmet off instantly. They did have the following-orders thing nailed down. He was about a decade younger than Aphra, not out of his teens yet. Nose too big, eyes blue and scared. She sighed.

"See, now you're a human. If you're begging for your life, you want people to know you're a living breathing thing and not some weird enamel droid. It's easy to kill stormtroopers.

"Because all that stuff about triggers I just told you?" she said. "I don't think any of it's true. I think that the Death Star has a trigger, because I think it's easy to kill a planet. It's all so abstract. It's why guys like Tagge are fine with sending armies to their death, while they order their troopers to take me out of sight to put a blast through my chest.

"A planet doesn't have a face," she said. "It'd take a real monster to pull the trigger if Alderaan had a face."

His eyes moved between Aphra and the black of the gun barrel.

Aphra had always defended the Empire as the best available choice—better than anarchy. Today the Empire had destroyed a planet, worse than a war's cost in an afternoon. She had no idea what to do with these feelings. Maybe when they had chilled, she could justify it—*what's one planet if it cements a real peace?* That sounds like the sort of logic she'd turn to. The needs justify the ends and all that.

But right now, she just wished there could be a better Empire and wished there was someone who could *do* that.

The boy was crying. Aphra felt shame and anger mix inside her. Her excitement was real. Her anger was real. It was all real.

But it was clouded by the shame, shame that she was right. She could have shot a stormtrooper. She wasn't going to shoot this boy with a wet face and terrified eyes.

"Okay," she said, starting to back away. "This is the deal. Put your helmet back on. Tell them you shot me. If they ask, tell them I begged, but they won't ask. Another death today isn't exactly going to rate, right?"

She shot the blaster at the ground. He jumped back.

"That's your people thinking you've done your job," she said. "Alderaan's dead, and scavenger and stormtrooper both live. Sound good?"

269

He nodded. She winked and then she turned and ran, dropping the blaster where he could find it.

Within one hundred meters she heard shouts.

Within two hundred, she heard the scream of the alarm.

Within five minutes, she was punching the *Ark Angel* into orbit, TIE fighters on her aft, engines screaming, seeing the white dagger of a Star Destroyer loom into view ahead of her. As she fumbled with the navigation computer, looking for a route to the safe blue of hyperspace, she cursed herself for another moment of weakness in a universe that has none. One day, she'd learn.

OF MSE-6 AND MEN

Glen Weldon

08:00.01 . . . EXIT SLEEP MODE
08:01.03 . . . SYNC WITH DS-1OBS Network
08:02.00 . . . RUN SELF-DIAGNOSTIC:

DESIGNATION: MSE-6-G735Y
FUNCTION: Delivery/Repair
ASSIGNED TO: Maintenance Unit, Sector AA-345, DS-1
Orbital Battle Station
SYSTEMS CHECK:
Modular Circuit Matrix Processor: Optimal
Proximity Sensors: Optimal

Internal Bay Sensors: Optimal
Dorsal Doors: Optimal
Holorecorder: Optimal
Dynadrive 9-ES Motors: Optimal
Wheels: Left front tread depth SUBOPTIMAL; will require replacement in 30 cycles

08:04.12 . . . STANDBY MODE ENTERED

08:15.37 . . . PROXIMITY SENSORS: Bioform detected.

08:15.38 . . . IDENTIFY BIOFORM: Designation TK-421. Security Level: Lambda.

"Morning, G7."

08:15.40 . . . BIOFORM VOICE COMMAND "morning G7" LOGGED. RESPONSE REQUIRED, AFFIRMATIVE: Beepbeep.

"Open up for me."

08:15.45 . . . BIOFORM VOICE COMMAND "open up for me" LOGGED. RESPONSE REQUIRED: DISENGAGE LOCK, OPEN DORSAL DOORS

"Great. Get this scanner servo to TK-450 at Docking Bay 228. You know the drill."

08:15.55 . . . BIOFORM VOICE COMMAND "get this scanner servo to TK-450 at docking bay 228" LOGGED. RESPONSE REQUIRED: CARGO DELIVERY/RECEIPT SUBROUTINE

08:16.23 . . . CARGO RECEIVED FROM BIOFORM TK-421

08:16.33 . . . CLOSE DORSAL DOORS, ENGAGE LOCK

08:16.36 . . . ENGAGE INTERNAL BAY SENSORS

08:16.45 . . . ONBOARD CARGO IDENTIFIED: Servo, Imperial Scanner 97-DX-8

08:16.52 . . . AUTONAV ROUTE; ENGAGE MOTORS

08:44.33 . . . ARRIVE DESTINATION: DB-228

08:45.04 . . . PROXIMITY SENSORS: Recipient detected.

08:45.10 . . . IDENTIFY RECIPIENT: Designation TK-450. Security Level: Rho.

08:45.33 . . . ALERT RECIPIENT OF PRESENCE: Beepbeep.

"Oh! Didn't see you down there, buddy."

08:45.48 . . . DISENGAGE LOCK, OPEN DORSAL DOORS

"*There* it is. Finally. Been waiting 6 cycles for this."

08:45.55 . . . ENGAGE HOLORECORDER FOR RECEIPT AC-KNOWLEDGMENT

"Ah. Right. 'TK-450, acknowledging receipt of cargo.' There you go. Anyway, it took you guys down there long enough. We're backed up; I've got 12 ships waiting on scanner crews. General Tagge was up here yesterday. That vein in his forehead pounding away. You guys have really got to start—"

08:46.39 . . . DISENGAGE HOLORECORDER

"Wow, okay you know, I hadn't finished. No, you know what, fine. That's just typical. I can tell TK-421 programmed you. You're *just* like him, ignore the stuff you don't want to hear. Fine, little guy. Whatever."

08:46.46 . . . CLOSE DORSAL DOORS, ENGAGE LOCK

"You know what: 421 wouldn't last a minute up here, I tell you that much. And he knows it. Never had to deal with people. Just spends every cycle down there talking to droids who got barely two synaptic processors to rub together. He's never had officers like Tagge breathing down his neck. Or Tarkin. Or Tarkin's pet, the iron lung in a cape. I'd like to see 421 try to look *that* guy in the transparisteel holoplates. He'd faint dead awa—"

08:46.59 . . . INPUT IRRELEVANT TO DELIVERY/RECEIPT SUBROUTINE MISSION PARAMETERS

08:47:00 . . . AUTONAV ROUTE; ENGAGE MOTORS

09:12.07 . . . ARRIVE DESTINATION: MAINTENANCE UNIT SECTOR AA-345

09:12.10 . . . PROXIMITY SENSORS: Bioform detected.

09:12.12 . . . IDENTIFY BIOFORM: Designation TK-421. Security Level: Lambda.

"That was *quick*, G7. Fastest mouse droid in the fleet. It's those new rotors I put in, I'm telling you. You know what: We should get you on a racing circuit. Would you like that?"

09:12.15 . . . BIOFORM QUERY "would you like that" LOGGED. RESPONSE REQUIRED, AFFIRMATIVE: Beepbeep.

"That transfer comes through, G7, I'll take you with me. That's a promise. Me to you. We get ourselves set up on Coruscant, paint some racing stripes on you, and we start raking in the credits. You just wait, buddy. You'll see."

09:13.33 . . . BIOFORM VOICE COMMAND "you just wait buddy you'll see" LOGGED. SYNTACTICAL ANALYSIS: RHETORICAL. NO RESPONSE REQUIRED

"We're *trapped* on this station, G7. That's the truth of it. Oh, don't get me wrong: sure, aesthetically? It's great here. Clean lines, nice soothing gray color palette, and the lighting's, like, *seriously* flattering. When I was stationed on Lasan, they were all about overhead lighting. Ucch. Can you imagine?"

09:14.00 . . . BIOFORM QUERY "can you imagine" LOGGED. SYNTACTICAL ANALYSIS: RHETORICAL. NO RESPONSE REQUIRED

"We went around all the time looking so . . . *sallow*. It was depressing. But this, here? Lighting the walls, not the ceilings? That's *smart*. That's Imperial engineering at work. If I get us that place on Coruscant, G7, I'm definitely gonna go with this . . . this whole . . . lighting scheme. You know, these long . . . thin, uh, vertical . . . wall-ovals, I guess you'd call them? Absolutely.

"And yeah: moon-sized planet vaporizer. I get it. I'm not saying that it's not sexy, living on a giant orbital death machine. But there's no downtime, is the thing. You're always *on*. All these drills, these last-minute inspections. I hate having to wear this helmet all the time. I mean, it's so so so *so* bad for the skin, G7, you have no idea. Just *look* at this."

09:15.02 . . . BIOFORM VOICE COMMAND "just look at this" LOGGED. SYNTACTICAL ANALYSIS: IMPERATIVE. RESPONSE REQUIRED: ENGAGE HOLORECORDER

"I mean I could get in trouble just for taking this stupid bucket off, but this is what I'm talking about. I mean, this zit here on my chin? It's the size of a Kowakian monkey-lizard, honestly. Ugh, I feel so gross. Don't look at me!"

09:15.56 . . . BIOFORM VOICE COMMAND "don't look at me" LOGGED. RESPONSE REQUIRED: DISENGAGE HOLORE-CORDER

"Anyway. I'm rambling. Log delivery of cargo. Enter standby mode."

09:16.43 . . . MULTIPLE BIOFORM VOICE COMMANDS LOGGED. RESPONSE REQUIRED: LOG DELIVERY OF CARGO WITH DS-1OBS DATABASE. STANDBY MODE ENTERED

13:31.04 . . . PROXIMITY SENSORS: Bioform detected.

13:31.05 . . . IDENTIFY BIOFORM: Designation TK-421. Security Level: Lambda.

"Wake up, G7."

13:31.09 . . . BIOFORM VOICE COMMAND "wake up G7" LOGGED. EXIT STANDBY MODE. RESPONSE REQUIRED, AF-FIRMATIVE: Beepbeep.

"Open."

13:35.45 . . . BIOFORM VOICE COMMAND "open" LOGGED. RESPONSE REQUIRED: DISENGAGE LOCK, OPEN DORSAL DOORS

"Deliver to the Detention Level."

13:44.09 . . . BIOFORM VOICE COMMAND "deliver to the detention level" LOGGED. RESPONSE REQUIRED: CARGO DELIVERY/ RECEIPT SUBROUTINE

13:44.15 . . . CARGO RECEIVED FROM BIOFORM TK-421

13:44.18 . . . CLOSE DORSAL DOORS, ENGAGE LOCK

13:44.28 . . . ENGAGE INTERNAL SENSORS

13:44.35 . . . CARGO IDENTIFIED: Replacement IT-O Interrogator Droid HypnoHypodermal Injector Needle C-7R

13:44.39 . . . AUTONAV ROUTE; ENGAGE MOTORS

14:59.04 . . . ARRIVE DESTINATION: Detention Block AA-23

14:59.35 . . . PROXIMITY SENSORS: Recipient detected. IT-O interrogator droid also detected.

14:59.40 . . . IDENTIFY RECIPIENT: Designation unknown. Security Level: Gamma.

"*There you are.* You had better be carrying my infuser needle, rat-droid. I put in that order two subcycles ago. Such delays are unforgivable! He's on his way now! Well? *Open up, open up.*"

14:59.49 . . . RECIPIENT VOICE COMMAND "open up open up" LOGGED. RESPONSE REQUIRED: DISENGAGE LOCK, OPEN DORSAL DOORS

"Finally! You're lucky. I'll have just enough time to install it before he gets here. Because of you, I have to hurry. If I'd had to delay this interrogation because of your rank incompetence—"

15:00.00 . . . PROXIMITY SENSORS: Bioform approaching from south corridor turbolift. Arrival in 00:00.10.

"That's him! Go! Get out! Quickly!"

15:00.03 . . . PROTOCOL CONFLICT. PROTOCOL CONFLICT. 1. CARGO/DELIVERY SUBROUTINE EXPRESSLY REQUIRES HOLORECORDED ACKNOWLEDGMENT OF RECEIPT OF CARGO BY RECIPIENT. 2. BIOFORM VOICE COMMAND "go get out quickly" LOGGED. REQUIRES RESPONSE

RESOLUTION OF CONFLICT: BIOFORM ISSUING VOICE COMMAND "go get out quickly" HOLDS GAMMA-LEVEL CLEARANCE; SUPERSEDES LAMBDA-LEVEL CARGO/DELIVERY SUBROUTINE

RESPONSE REQUIRED: IMMEDIATE RETURN TO MAINTE-NANCE UNIT, SECTOR AA-345, TOP SPEED

15:00.05 . . . AUTONAV ROUTE; ENGAGE MOTORS, FULL THROTTLE

"Uuulp!"

15:00.09 . . . ALERT INCIDENT REPORT: COLLISION EN ROUTE . . . ALERT INCIDENT REPORT: COLLISION EN ROUTE . . . ALERT DAMAGE TO MSE-6 UNIT INCURRED

"Sir! Are you hurt?"

15:00.15 . . . COLLISION OBJECT: Previously detected approach-ing bioform.

15:00.17 . . . IDENTIFY BIOFORM: Designation unknown. SE-CURITY LEVEL: Alpha One. STATUS: Prone.

15:00.18 . . . ALERT: CATASTROPHIC DAMAGE TO HOLO-RECORDER MATRIX DETECTED

15:00.19 . . . RUN DAMAGE ASSESSMENT SELF-DIAGNOSTIC:

DESIGNATION: MSE-6-G735Y
FUNCTION: Delivery/Repair

ASSIGNED TO: Maintenance Unit, Sector AA-345, DS-1
Orbital Battle Station
SYSTEMS CHECK:
Modular Circuit Matrix Processor: Optimal
Proximity Sensors: SUBOPTIMAL
Internal Bay Sensors: Optimal
Dorsal Doors: Optimal
Holorecorder: SUBOPTIMAL: CATASTROPHIC MAL-
FUNCTION IMMINENT
Dynadrive 9-ES Motors: Optimal
Wheels: Left front tread depth SUBOPTIMAL; will require re-
placement in 30 cycles

"What—what happened?"

"I'm sorry, sir. That MSE-6 unit just . . . it ran straight into you. At top speed. No idea why. Must have a bad motivator. I'm very sorry, sir."

"Uch. Beastly things, mouse droids. Always scuttering underfoot. Why did it—"

"I'll have it melted down for scrap, sir, and the trooper who dispatched it in this sorry condition punished most severely."

". . . Yes. Yes, do that. Gross incompetence."

"Let me help you up, sir."

"And at such a crucial time for the Empire, when so much depends upon our collective *rigor* and *discipline* and *aaaah*! Ahhh. Blagg, I . . . I seem—I seem to have bruised my hip, Blagg."

"I'm sorry, sir."

"*Stop saying you're sorry and do something about* wait what's going on—"

15:00.19 . . . FAULT IN HOLORECORDER SYSTEM DE-
TECTED. PLAYBACK ENGAGED

15:00.20 . . . ABORT PLAYBACK. OVERRIDE

"What's happening to it, Blagg."

15:00.22 . . . CANNOT ABORT PLAYBACK . . . OVERRIDE UNSUCCESSFUL . . . CANNOT ABORT PLAYBACK . . . OVER-RIDE UNSUCCESSFUL

"It's . . . trying to play a holorecording, I think, sir."

"A . . . recording? What sort of recor—"

15:00.26 . . . FAILURE TO SHUT DOWN HOLORECORDER PLAYBACK

"I mean I could get in trouble just for taking this stupid bucket off, but this is what I'm talking about. I mean, this zit here on my chin? It's the size of a Kowakian monkey-lizard, honestly. Ugh, I feel so gross. Don't look at me!"

". . . What?"

"Ugh, I feel so gross. Don't look at me!"

"I'll try to shut it down, sir."

"Ugh, I feel so gross. Don't look at me!"

". . . Who is he? He's . . . *beautiful!*"

15:01.33 . . . EMERGENCY SHUTDOWN OF HOLORE-CORDER SYSTEM ACHIEVED

"What? No! Bring him back! Play back the entire message!"

15:01.40 . . . BIOFORM VOICE COMMAND "play back the en-tire message" LOGGED. REQUIRES RESPONSE. CONFLICT: 1. BIOFORM ISSUING VOICE COMMAND HOLDS ALPHA-ONE-LEVEL CLEARANCE, SUPERSEDES ALL KNOWN COMMANDS AND SUBROUTINES. 2. HOLORECORDER IN UNRECOVER-ABLE FAILURE. REQUIRES COMPLETE SYSTEM REBOOT AND MAINTENANCE

RESOLUTION OF CONFLICT: RESPONSE REQUIRED, NEG-ATIVE: Beepboop.

"I . . . don't think it can comply, sir. Not without a systems over-haul."

". . . I see."

279

"Shall we proceed to her cell and begin the interrogation, sir? I just need to install the hypodermic on the torture droid—"

"*Interrogator* droid, Blagg."

"Yes, of course, sir. Sorry, sir. On the . . . interrogator droid. And then we can proceed."

"Oh no, Blagg, I shan't be doing the interrogation, and neither shall you. That's Vader's work. He does so . . . relish it. I just came down to ensure you were on schedule. I've had reports."

"I assure you, sir, that I'm working as fast as possible. I'm keeping to the timetable, but it's taken longer than necessary to secure the required equipment, and—"

"Excuses, Blagg, do not interest me. But I'll tell you what does. That trooper, in the holorecording."

". . . Yes, sir?"

"I take it he's the one who dispatched this appallingly willful droid? And the one who, if I'm not mistaken, you were about to blame for your section's woeful lack of readiness?"

"Sir, I . . . Yes, sir."

"I'm going back to my quarters, Blagg, and I'm taking this horrid little droid with me."

". . . Sir?"

"I'm going to put some ice on my hip, Blagg, and I will deal *personally* with the trooper whose incompetence is responsible for the painful inconvenience I have suffered. As for your prisoner, Vader will be down to interrogate her presently . . . but of course . . . only once you've had adequate time to prepare the interrogator droid. I shouldn't wish to *rush* you."

". . . No, sir, of course. I assure you all will be ready, sir."

"Your assurances, Blagg, are meaningless in the extreme. Results, Lieutenant. That's what matters at this juncture. A great day is dawning for the Empire, Blagg, if arrant witlessness like yours can be kept at bay. She must tell us what she knows; that is your only priority. Leave the handling of that trooper . . . to me. Dismissed."

"Sir, yes sir."

"Now. You there: droid."

15:04.44 . . . BIOFORM VOICE COMMAND "you there droid" PRIORITY ALPHA ONE LOGGED. RESPONSE REQUIRED, AF-FIRMATIVE: Beepbeep.

"Your holorecorder is rather spectacularly offline, but I trust your other systems are functioning, howsoever crudely? You can follow basic commands, yes? Your rather enthusiastic tryst with my left ankle just now hasn't catastrophically disabled your central matrix processor?"

15:04.50 . . . BIOFORM VOICE QUERY "you can follow basic commands yes" PRIORITY ALPHA ONE LOGGED. RESPONSE REQUIRED, AFFIRMATIVE: Beepbeep.

"And your motor functions? If I turn you back upright, onto those filthy, grimy little wheels of yours, like . . . so? You can still find your way around, ideally without barreling into passersby and causing them undue mental and physical anguish, as you have me?"

15:50.43 . . . BIOFORM VOICE QUERY "you can still find your way around, ideally without barreling into passersby and causing them undue mental and physical anguish as you have me" PRIOR-ITY ALPHA ONE LOGGED. SYNTACTICAL ANALYSIS: SAR-CASTIC BUT NOT RHETORICAL. RESPONSE REQUIRED, AFFIRMATIVE: Beepbeep.

"Excellent. Go to my quarters immediately, and close down."

15:50.43 . . . BIOFORM VOICE COMMAND "go to my quarters immediately and close down" PRIORITY ALPHA ONE LOGGED. RESPONSE REQUIRED: AUTONAV ROUTE; ENGAGE MOTORS

281

———

17:37.22 . . . ARRIVE DESTINATION: OFFICER'S QUARTERS—
SECTOR GM1-A

17:37.23 . . . ENTER SLEEP MODE

"There we are. Wake, MSE-6-G735Y."

XX:XX.XX . . . EXIT SLEEP MODE

XX:XX.XX . . . SYNC WITH DS-1OBS Network; ALERT: LOG
PASSAGE OF 2.52 CYCLES IN SLEEP MODE; SYNC INTERNAL
CHRONO

09:44.03 . . . RUN SELF-DIAGNOSTIC:

DESIGNATION: MSE-6-G735Y
FUNCTION: Delivery/Repair
ASSIGNED TO: Maintenance Unit, Sector AA-345, DS-1
Orbital Battle Station
SYSTEMS CHECK:
Modular Circuit Matrix Processor: Optimal
Proximity Sensors: Optimal
Internal Bay Sensors: Optimal
Dorsal Doors: Optimal
Holorecorder: Optimal
Dynadrive 9-ES Motors: Optimal
Wheels: Optimal

"Yes. I've repaired your systems, inasmuch as an old man remembers basic droid mechanics from his Academy days."

09:44.36 . . . PROXIMITY SENSORS: Bioform detected.

09:44.38 . . . IDENITIFY BIOFORM: Designation unknown. SECURITY LEVEL: Alpha One.

09:44.55 . . . LOCATION GEOSYNC ALERT: OFFICER'S
QUARTERS—SECTOR GM1-A

"Fortunately your circuit maps are about as simple as they come. It's taken me a few cycles to get your holorecorder back online. I have also procured you a new set of wheel treads, as I didn't want those nasty grotty ones you arrived with tracking gun grease and garbage water and who knows what else onto my carpet. My lovely new carpet, which—not that your rudimentary sensors would be sensitive enough to register it—is Coruscant fiberweave. A single square centimeter of which is worth more than 100 vermin-droids like yourself, put together.

"Now. To business! I am now going to record a message for your master, the stormtrooper designated TK-421. And I'm going to place an item inside your cargo bay, which you will deliver to him, along with the holomessage I am about to record, as is your purpose. And one more thing, please do pay attention:

"I hereby invoke Imperial Protocol Alpha One. Acknowledge."

09:46.02 . . . ALERT ALERT BIOFORM VOICE COMMAND OVERRIDES ALL PREVIOUS DIRECTIVES. RESET. INCOMING VOICE COMMAND "i hereby invoke imperial protocol alpha one acknowledge" ASSUMES PRIORITY PROTOCOL. RESPONSE REQUIRED, AFFIRMATIVE: Beepbeep.

"Yes, very good. Of those instructions I have just issued, there will exist no holorecord. No geosync data. No routine uplink to the Imperial network. Instead you will shunt those instructions, and all ensuing related subroutines, to my personal ephemeradata-neurocloud, where they will be hosted until such time as you carry them out, when they will be summarily scrambled and expunged from your memory. Acknowledge."

09:46.33 . . . BIOFORM VOICE COMMAND "acknowledge" PRIORITY ALPHA ONE LOGGED. REPSONSE REQUIRED, AFFIRMATIVE: Beepbeep.

"Very well, then. Engage holorecorder."

09:46.40 . . . BIOFORM VOICE COMMAND "engage holore-

corder" PRIORITY ALHPA ONE LOGGED. RESPONSE RE-
QUIRED: ENGAGE HOLORECORDER
[MEMORY MISSING]

[MEMORY MISSING]
XX:XX.XX . . . DISENGAGE HOLORECORDER PLAYBACK.
"Well. Well, well, well. Isn't that . . . isn't that just *something*, G7."
XX:XX.XX . . . SYNC WITH DS-1OBS Network; SYNC INTER-
NAL CHRONO
10:38.16 . . . ALERT: MEMORY MISSING
10:38.16 . . . ALERT: LOCATION UNKNOWN; GEOSYNC RE-
QUIRED
10:38.17 . . . ALERT: DORSAL DOORS OPEN. INTERIOR BAY
EMPTY.
10:38.19 . . . RUN SELF-DIAGNOSTIC:

DESIGNATION: MSE-6-G735Y
FUNCTION: Delivery/Repair
ASSIGNED TO: Maintenance Unit, Sector AA-345, DS-1
Orbital Battle Station
SYSTEMS CHECK:
Modular Circuit Matrix Processor: Optimal
Proximity Sensors: Optimal
Internal Bay Sensors: Optimal
Dorsal Doors: Optimal; ALERT: OPEN
Holorecorder: Optimal
Dynadrive 9-ES Motors: Optimal
Wheels: Optimal

10:38.51 . . . LOCATION GEOSYNC: Maintenance Unit, Sector
AA-345, DS-1 Orbital Battle Station

10:38.52 . . . PROXIMITY SENSORS: Bioform detected.

10:38.53 . . . IDENTIFY BIOFORM: Designation TK-421. Security Level: Lambda.

"I mean you don't receive a holomessage like *that* every day. Looks like I caught someone's eye, G7. Which is always flattering, I'm not gonna lie. Still got it! Don't know how it happened, but I have a feeling you had something to do with it.

"Huh . . . Okay. This . . . this could be good, G7. Very good, for both of us. I play this right, I could get us that transfer to Coruscant.

". . . And if I play this *very* right, I could get us . . . anything.

"*How* to play it, though, that's the question. My next move is crucial, G7. I can't come on too strong, because he wants to be in control, that much is clear. And he's certainly not being coy about his intentions. So. Direct, but not aggressive, not tradey . . . Still. I should probably . . . butch it up a *bit,* though, right?"

10:39.44 . . . BIOFORM VOICE QUERY "i should probably butch it up a bit though right" LOGGED. SYNTACTICAL ANALYSIS: INCONCLUSIVE. INSUFFICIENT DATA

"No, yeah, I should. He's a graysuit, he went through the Academy. They always want the whole 'backwater, rough-around-the-edges military grunt' thing. You know: 'Oh my, sir, I never . . . I ain't never done *this* before.' Trust me, I know his type.

"All right. Engage holoreco— Wait!"

10:40.23 . . . BIOFORM VOICE COMMAND "engage holoreco-wait" LOGGED. SYNTACTICAL ANALYSIS: ENGAGE HOLORECORDER; HALT RECORDING

"Helmet . . . *off,* I think, for this, G7. Give him something to get him started . . . There. Okay. Engage holorecorder."

10:40.39 . . . BIOFORM VOICE COMMAND "engage holorecorder" LOGGED. ENGAGE HOLORECORDER

"Sir! TK-421, acknowledging your order. I will report to your quarters at once, sir! Just as soon as I . . . shower with this here . . . this antibacterial nanofoam ya sent. Awful thoughtful of you, sir. It will be an honor for me to repair your aqualeisure unit, sir. And may I say, sir, thank ya kindly for sendin' my little MSE-6 droid back to me all fixed up so good! Ya got a gift, if that's not too forward of me, sir. TK-421 out! . . . Disengage holorecorder."

10:41.40 . . . BIOFORM VOICE COMMAND "disengage holorecorder" LOGGED. DISENGAGE HOLORECORDER

"Always leave them with a little flattery at the end there, G7. A little tag like that, so it's the last thing they hear before they hang up, and it'll be the first thing they think of the next time you see them. Never hurts. Okay, now go on up to his quarters, deliver the message, and put yourself in standby mode."

10:41.45 . . . MULTIPLE BIOFORM VOICE COMMANDS LOGGED

"I'll be up in a few minutes. Just got to . . . make myself presentable. Do some push-ups."

10:41.55 . . . AUTONAV ROUTE; ENGAGE MOTORS

11:35.33 . . . ARRIVE DESTINATION: OFFICER'S QUARTERS—SECTOR GM1-A

11:35.33 . . . PROXIMITY SENSORS: Bioform detected.

11:35.34 . . . IDENITIFY BIOFORM: Designation unknown. SECURITY LEVEL: Alpha One.

"Yes? Well? What did he say? Is he coming?"

11:35.34 . . . BIOFORM VOICE QUERY "what did he say" LOGGED. ENGAGE HOLORECORDER PLAYBACK

I say, sir, thank ya kindly for sendin' my little MSE-6 droid back to me all fixed up so good! Ya got a gift, if that's not too forward of me, sir. TK-421 out!

".. . My, but *he's* laying it on a bit thick . . . Ah well. The games we play."

11:36.48 . . . ENTER STANDBY MODE

12:03.48 . . . PROMIXIMITY SENSOR: Two bioforms detected.

12:03.49 . . . IDENTIFY BIOFORMS: 1. Designation unknown. SECURITY LEVEL: Alpha One. 2. Designation TK-421. SECURITY LEVEL: Lambda.

12:03.55 . . . EXIT STANDBY MODE

"Sir! TK-421 reporting!"

"I know who you are, trooper. Come inside."

"Yes, sir—"

"But first, remove your armor."

". . . Sir?"

"Your *armor.* I don't want you tracking grease and blaster carbon and who knows what else into my chambers; I've just had new carpet put in, and—"

"I see that, sir. It's lovely. Coruscant fiberweave, isn't it?"

". . . It is indeed. I see there's more to you than meets the eye, trooper."

"Ooh, it feels so nice between my toes! That's quality, you can tell, that's *craftsmanship*! . . . Uh. Um. Where kin ah set down mah armor, sir? While ah work?"

"On the chair next to the bed, trooper. . . . That's veermok hide, by the way. Nasty creatures."

"Golly! Very impressive, sir!"

". . . Indeed. Well, the aqualesiure unit is through here. You go about your business. I've got to . . . prepare for a meeting with the Joint Chiefs. I'll just be . . . right over . . . here."

"Yes, sir!"

287

"Psst! Droid. Execute Imperial Protocol Alpha One. Acknowledge."
[MEMORY MISSING]

[MEMORY MISSING]
    XX:XX.XX . . . EXIT SLEEP MODE
    XX:XX.XX . . . SYNC WITH DS-1OBS Network; ALERT: LOG
PASSAGE OF 7.52 CYCLES; SYNC INTERNAL CHRONO
    08:33.06 . . . ALERT: MEMORY MISSING
    08:33.07 . . . ALERT: LOCATION UNKNOWN; GEOSYNC RE-
QUIRED
    08:33.10 . . . RUN SELF-DIAGNOSTIC:

DESIGNATION: MSE-6-G735Y
FUNCTION: Delivery/Repair
ASSIGNED TO: Maintenance Unit, Sector AA-345, DS-1
Orbital Battle Station
SYSTEMS CHECK:
Modular Circuit Matrix Processor: Optimal
Proximity Sensors: Optimal
Internal Bay Sensors: Optimal
Dorsal Doors: Optimal
Holorecorder: Optimal
Dynadrive 9-ES Motors: Optimal
Wheels: Optimal

    08:33.15 . . . LOCATION GEOSYNC: Maintenance Unit, Sector
AA-345, DS-1 Orbital Battle Station
    "Welcome back to the world, G7."
    08:33.16 . . . PROXIMITY SENSORS: Bioform detected.
    08:33.20 . . . IDENTIFY BIOFORM: Designation TK-421. Secu-
rity Level: Beta [NOTE: UPGRADE]

"Yeah, I know, I know. Your memory's . . . choppy. Don't worry. You're not malfunctioning, it's . . . well, he's just being careful. 'An abundance of caution,' he says. He talks like that. In the long run, it's for the best. Don't take it personally, okay? He's . . . got a lot on him. Lot going on. He's *very* stressed."

08:33.42 . . . BIOFORM VOICE QUERY "don't take it personally okay" LOGGED. SYNTACTICAL ANALYSIS: INCONCLUSIVE. INSUFFICIENT DATA

"He's got this shell, you know. This icy exterior. He has to, everything's riding on him. But with me, he can drop it, and just be himself. We talk about the silliest stuff, G7. Afterward. During, sometimes. He says I'm the only one who can make him laugh. It's . . . sweet.

"What I'm saying, G7, is if you can hang in there just a bit longer, we'll be out of here.

"And between you and me . . . look, G7, you're just gonna have to trust me on this . . . there's some stuff that you . . . don't need to see, frankly. Human-being stuff. Complicated.

". . . Messy.

"Anyway, good news: I got us that transfer. Now, it's not Coruscant—not yet, but we're getting closer. I'm station security now. Up on the 300 level. It's not sexy—mostly guard duty, I gather—but it's a pretty cushy gig, he says. And I get to carry a blaster rifle, and order people around. It's all *very* butch.

"We'll let a little time pass, see, then he taps me to be on his personal detail. And then, G7: Coruscant. You on the droid racing circuit. Me set up in his penthouse—which he says has overhead lighting, okay, but I mean—that's fixable. It's got a balcony that faces the Imperial Palace ruins so, you know. Pret-tee sweet.

"Wait, hold on. I'm getting a helmet . . . transmission . . . thingy.

". . . *TK-421 here. Yes, sir.*

"My first assignment's coming down, G7! Guard duty—told you!

289

Guarding a . . . *Commander, please repeat* . . . guarding a captured light freighter. *Roger, Commander. TK-421 out.*

"Well, there you are. Standing around with a blaster for who knows how many subcycles. Still, it's just for now, G7.

"Okay, head up to his quarters. He's going to require your . . . services, when I get up there."

08:35.22 . . . BIOFORM VOICE COMMAND "head up to his quarters" LOGGED. RESPONSE REQUIRED: AUTONAV ROUTE; ENGAGE MOTORS

09:08.26 . . . ARRIVE DESTINATION: OFFICER'S QUARTERS—SECTOR GM1-A

09:08.27 . . . PROXIMITY SENSORS: Bioform detected.

09:08.28 . . . IDENITIFY BIOFORM: Designation unknown. SECURITY LEVEL: Alpha One.

"What are *you* doing here? Has . . . has he sent me something? A message? Or . . . something else?"

09:08.30 . . . BIOFORM VOICE QUERY "has he sent me something a message or something else" PRIORITY ALPHA ONE LOGGED. RESPONSE REQUIRED, NEGATIVE: Beepboop.

"Then what are you—you know what, never mind. Doesn't matter. I've had a terribly, terribly exciting day at work—gave a presentation that went just *exceedingly* well—*explosively* well, heh heh heh heh—and now I'm quite, I'm quite *keyed up.*

"Find him. Bring him here. Immediately."

09:09.13 . . . BIOFORM VOICE COMMANDS "find him bring him here immediately" PRIORITY ALPHA ONE LOGGED. RESPONSE REQUIRED: TRACKING/GEOLOCATION SUBROUTINE. EXECUTE

09:09.15 . . . UPLINK TO DS-1OBS NETWORK. SCAN FOR UNIT TK-421 HELMET ID GEOSYNC BEACON

09:09.48 . . . UNIT TK-421 HELMET ID GEOSYNC BEACON LOCATED: DOCKING BAY 327

09:09.50 . . . AUTONAV ROUTE; ENGAGE MOTORS, TOP SPEED

09:52.21 . . . ALERT: ROUTE UPDATE REQUIRED: UNIT TK-421 HELMET ID GEOSYNC BEACON IN MOTION DEPARTING DOCKING BAY 327. MOVING ALONG CORRIDOR 327E-6

09:52.30 . . . UPDATE ROUTE TO INTERCEPT AT TURBO-LIFT BANK L301-E. ENGAGE MOTORS, TOP SPEED

09:59.02 . . . APPROACHING TURBOLIFT BANK L301-E

09:59.04 . . . PROXIMITY SENSORS: 3 bioforms detected.

09:59.07 . . . IDENTIFY BIOFORMS: 1. Wookiee, designation unknown. Security Level: N/A. Threat Level: Unknown. 2. Designation TK-710. Security Level: Zeta. 3. Designation TK-421. Security Level: Beta [Updated]. EXECUTE "find him bring him here immediately" PRIORITY ALPHA ONE VOICE COMMAND RETRIEVAL SUBROUT—

09:59.08 . . . ALERT

09:59.09 . . . ALERT: TK-421 BIOMETRIC ANAMOLY DE-TECTED. ALERT: TK-421 BIOMETRIC ANAMOLY DETECTED

09:59.10 . . . TK-421 BIODATA IN CONFLICT WITH STORED IMPERIAL NETWORK BIODATA. HEIGHT VARIANCE: -12.7 cm. ATTEMPTING TO RECONCILE

09:59.11 . . . RUN SELF-DIAGNOSTo2j390rtqhwp9

09:59.12 . . . ALERT ALERT WOOKIEE AGGRESSION DIS-PLAY INITIATED ALERT ALERT ALERT THREAT LEVEL: RED. CANCEL SELF-DIAGNOSTIC ALERT ALERT

09:59.13 . . . ALERT ALERT EXECUTE SELF-PRESERVATION/FLIGHT SUBROUTINE. SHUTDOWN HIGHER FUNCTIONS. ENGAGE MOTORS, TOP SPEED ALERT ALERT

09:59.14 . . . ALERT ALERT ALERT ALERT ALERT ALERT ALERT ALERT ALERT

10:05.22 . . . ALERT ALERT ALERT ALERT ALERT ALERT ALERT

10:06.23 . . . THREAT LEVEL: GREEN. DISENGAGE SELF-PRESERVATION/FLIGHT SUBROUTINE. RESTORE HIGHER FUNCTIONS

10:06.38 . . . RUN SELF-DIAGNOSTIC:

DESIGNATION: MSE-6-G735Y
FUNCTION: Delivery/Repair
ASSIGNED TO: Maintenance Unit, Sector AA-345, DS-1 Orbital Battle Station
SYSTEMS CHECK:
Modular Circuit Matrix Processor: SUBOPTIMAL. MULTI-PLE INSTANCES OF MISSING MEMORY DETECTED
Proximity Sensors: Optimal
Internal Bay Sensors: Optimal
Dorsal Doors: Optimal
Holorecorder: Optimal
Dynadrive 9-ES Motors: Optimal
Wheels: Optimal

10:07.41 . . . LOCATION GEOSYNC: Maintenance Unit, Sector AA-345, DS-1 Orbital Battle Station.

10:47.45 . . . ENTER SLEEP MODE
[MEMORY MISSING]

[MEMORY MISSING]
XX:XX.XX . . . EXIT SLEEP MODE

XX:XX.XX ... SYNC WITH DS-1OBS Network; ALERT: LOG PASSAGE OF 3.73 CYCLES IN STANDBY MODE; SYNC INTERNAL CHRONO

08:33.03 ... ALERT: MEMORY MISSING

08:33.07 ... ALERT: LOCATION UNKNOWN; GEOSYNC REQUIRED

08:33.10 ... RUN SELF-DIAGNOSTIC:

DESIGNATION: MSE-6-G735Y

FUNCTION: Delivery/Repair

ASSIGNED TO: Maintenance Unit, Sector AA-345, DS-1 Orbital Battle Station

SYSTEMS CHECK:

Modular Circuit Matrix Processor: SUBOPTIMAL. MULTIPLE INSTANCES OF MISSING MEMORY DETECTED

Proximity Sensors: Optimal

Internal Bay Sensors: Optimal

Dorsal Doors: Optimal

Holorecorder: Optimal

Dynadrive 9-ES Motors: Optimal

Wheels: Optimal

293

08:33.15 ... LOCATION GEOSYNC: OFFICER'S QUARTERS— SECTOR GM1-A

08:33.16 ... ALERT: PROXIMITY SENSORS: Bioform detected.

"Your master, little droid. He's dead."

08:33.17 ... IDENITIFY BIOFORM: Designation unknown. SECURITY LEVEL: Alpha One.

"Murdered. By rebel scum. Stole his armor, and stuffed that rather ... remarkable body of his in a crawl space.

"I want you to know they will ... they will pay. In mere seconds, this station will annihilate the last pitiful dregs of the Rebellion, and your master will be avenged.

"He was . . . cleverer than he let on. He thought I didn't notice, but . . . ah well. I had . . . such plans for him, you know. For . . . for us. Such plans."

08:34.05 . . . ALERT: PROXIMITY SENSORS: EXPLOSION DE-TECTED ON 100 Level, Sector GM1-B, Corridor L104E. MINOR FLUCTUATION IN BATTLE STATION MAGNETIC SHIELD. EX-ECUTE REPAIR SUBROUTINE. AUTONAV ROUTE; ENGAGE MOTORS

"Where do you think *you're* going? Stay here!"

08:34.011 . . . BIOFORM VOICE COMMAND "stay here" PRI-ORITY ALPHA ONE LOGGED. DISENGAGE MOTORS

"This rebel attack on the station is inconsequential. They are pests, mynocks, vaporizing themselves against our outermost defenses. Ig-nore them, and whatever minor damage they manage to incur before snuffing themselves out.

"Because today, little one, today you are no lowly repair and maintenance droid. Today and today only, for your master's sake, you shall stand witness to the awesome destructive power of this battle station."

08:34.49 . . . ALERT: PROXIMITY SENSORS: EXPLOSION DE-TECTED ON 200 Level, Sector XR-8, Corridor R383E. MICRO-BREACH IN ION CONTAINMENT CASING. DO NOT EXECUTE REPAIR SUBROUTINE, PRIORITY ALPHA ONE

"The feckless fools! Let them come! Now. I am headed to the command bridge. Wait thirty seconds, and follow me there. Find a good spot to view the destruction, but stay out of sight, and keep out from underfoot, and do *not* acknowledge me in the room. Un-derstood?"

08:35.45 . . . MULTIPLE VOICE COMMANDS LOGGED, PRI-ORITY ALPHA ONE. RESPONSE REQUIRED, AFFIRMATIVE: Beepbeep.

294

08:35.50 . . . PROXIMITY SENSORS: Bioform departed.

08:36.20 . . . AUTONAV ROUTE; ENGAGE MOTORS

08:36.36 . . . ALERT ALERT

08:36.37 . . . ALERT INCIDENT REPORT: EXPLOSION EN ROUTE . . . ALERT INCIDENT REPORT: EXPLOSION EN ROUTE . . . ALERT DAMAGE TO MSE-6 UNIT INCURRED

08:36.38 . . . EXPLOSION SOURCE: Corridor wall.

08:36.43 . . . ALERT: CATASTROPHIC DAMAGE TO MSE-6 UNIT DETECTED. SEVERAL SYSTEMS IN SHUTDOWN

15:00.19 . . . RUN DAMAGE ASSESSMENT SELF-DIAGNO2xx19h0p

DESIGNATION: MSE-6 hu95rxxseaq45

FUNCTION: Delivery/Rep28h3t8940h

ASSIGNED TO: Maintenance Uni5 y7j778j90yu89p

SYSTEMS CHECK:

Modular Circuit Matrix Processor: SUBOPTIM-j29034th1uht94h

Proximity Sensors: SUBOPT29428t7180jg390

Internal Bay Sensors: OFFLINE

Dorsal Doors: OFFLINsquw932jirj

Holorecorder: OFFLINE

Dynadrive 9-ES Motors: SUBOPTIn29j—[ifj92gj

Wheels: LF, LR OFFLIN0i09iE

15:00.26 . . . EXTENSIVE BLAST DAMAGE DETECTED. INTERNAL BAY BREACHED. DORSAL DOORS FUSED SHUT, ADVANCED CARBON SCORING ACROSS ENTIRE CHASSIS

"Hey. Look at you, little guy. You're pretty worse for wear, hunh?"

15:00.54 . . . PROXIMITY SENSORS: Bioform detected.

15:00.58 . . . IDENTIFY BIOFORM: . . . working . . . working . . .

"That wall panel fried you good when it blew. Saw the whole thing. Figured you were a goner for sure. But no, you'll be okay. Man, you're a sturdy thing."

15:01.13 . . . IDENTIFY BIOFORM: . . . working . . . working . . .

"Rebel base, 30 seconds and closing."

"I gotta get to my station. I'll come back for you, afterward, and patch you up."

15:01.23 . . . IDENTIFY BIOFORM: . . . working . . . working . . .

"Not *too* good, though, right? You'll wanna keep *some* battle scars. Make you look tough. Like, I'd definitely keep those badass streaks of carbon scoring, if I were you."

15:01.33 . . . IDENTIFY BIOFORM: . . . working . . . working . . .

"Rebel base, in range."

15:01.43 . . . IDENTIFY BIOFORM: Stormtrooper, designation . . . working . . .

"Funny, but in this lighting, you know what those streaks look like? Is racing str—"

BUMP

Ben Acker and Ben Blacker

I'm back on the Death Star for about two seconds before the alarm sounds. I'm sore and tired, my head is killing me; all I'm trying to do is end my shift. My sidearm is racked at the depot, my black-and-whites are in detox, I've entered my helm feed into the log station, and I'm all set to shower off the sour desert stink of Tatooine when I hear it. Which alarm is this? Short, short, long. Short, short, long. Short, short, long. Pause. Short, short, long, and on and on. Intruder alert. Great. If this is a drill, I swear to the ancients I will lead the revolt myself. My head is throbbing now, in time with the alarm. Short, short, long. *Ow, ow, owww.*

The hygiene chamber is ten meters in front of me, calling me like an oasis on that awful desert planet, if it had had the good sense to have an oasis. I'm so close that I can smell the solvents, but I can feel the moff descending on me. If I sprint, will I make it? My calves clench. My quadriceps dare me to run. Short, short, long. Short, short, long. *Clack clack clack.* The moff's boots freeze me where I am. I stand at attention in nothing but my towel. The moff is here, standing between me and the hygiene chamber door. He sneers at my towel as if it had something nasty printed on it about the Emperor.

"That alarm." The moff points above his head to the sound that comes from everywhere. "Do you think it's for other people?"

The alarm is for exactly other people. Troopers starting their shift, their armor crisp and clean. My shift is over. I did a triple. I'm fried from two suns competing to see which one would take me down. I can still taste the sand. I'm lucky it didn't fritz my armor like it did TD-422's and TD-909's. TD-328's helmet cracked in a sandstorm and we were sped here on the hurry-up instead of continuing with the *Devastator* to Alderaan. He's in the infirmary and I can't claim to feel much better. My head is throbbing. I feel like I'm coming down with something. I'm completely spent. If the order were given, I could go to sleep right here, standing up like a tauntaun. I would give anything to get that order. But no one ever gives the order to sleep.

"Sir, no sir," I say. "I hear it."

"Hear this, TD-110," he cautions. "There are intruders upon my base." As moffs always seem to do, he's telling me something I already know. "No stormtrooper will be granted reprieve until this situation is rectified."

Reprieve. Rectified. Moffs are so clever with words. They read more than we grunts get the chance to, because we're busy fighting their battles for them. Must be nice. Someday, I hope I'll get to deploy wit in the direction of the strong, armed, and armored without fear of being blasted the second my back is turned.

BUMP

As always, I forget the class struggle the moment I suit up. Maybe it's the sense memory and adrenaline of being in the line of fire, or maybe it's the cool temperature and pure oxygen, but I'm no longer exhausted. My head feels clear; the once throbbing pain is just a dull pull behind my ears, as if I'm straining to hear something. I feel strong. I've got my sidearm in my hand and my unit by my side. Anyone idiot enough to sneak onto a weaponized stronghold with *Death* right in its name will die today, and hopefully we'll get to help kill them.

This has always been the life. I have nearly entirely forgotten my time growing up on the wilds of Parsh, for I may as well have been feral. The same could be said of everyone on Parsh back then. It was, in its eon-spanning infancy, wild. Clannish, starving, and wild. My time as a helpling was pathetic. I needed the protection of my clan's Alphon most often, and therefore I most often aroused his ire. This time is thin in my recall as it is so far behind me as to have happened to someone else. When the Empire found us, they yoked the Alphoni and put them to work building mines. I was mostly ignored, for I was still frail, a useless helpling. My Alphon still saw me fed, for he found a new purpose for me. He used my invisibility to have me pass messages to the other yoked Alphoni. His intent was revolution. It was then that I found a new purpose for my Alphon. I reported on him to the Empire. I was no longer useless or invisible. I neutralized my Alphon myself with a sidearm they gave me for that purpose. Size and strength are nothing to a blaster. That was the day I was born. The burning blood of my Alphon was my baptism. New Parsh, now a sophisticated labyrinth of cloud cities, shines like a jewel in the crown of the Empire, just as I, with my will and my training, am an armored glove on its fist.

The intruders, rebel scum, we now hear, are down in Detention Block AA-23. Were it up to TD-787, we would jettison the whole of the block into space. That wouldn't be my call. I'd rather look the rebels in the eyes as we blast them into atoms. I would rewatch the logged record of it for a month. I've done it before. It's important to see what you do right. The recordings that we download to the information banks allow for that. I see a look in the eyes of my victims that satisfies me, as if every one of them finally realizes that they should not have refused the succor of the Empire, but now it is too late. Resistance to aid from your betters makes you, as my Alphon was, too stupid to enjoy the gift of life. I wish I had a record of my Alphon from when I sent him to congregate with the ancients of Parsh. I would watch it forever.

As the moff gives us our orders, I feel a tickle in my skull. The headache had receded nearly entirely but now plants itself firmly into a ridiculous itch. Did I catch something on Tatooine? The mission brief didn't mention brain parasites, but it looked like the kind of planet to have plenty, and since when are mission briefs perfect? I'll have to visit the infirmary once I send the targets in AA-23 to meet the ancients of whichever planet they're stupid enough to be from. Or I would, if that were where we were being dispatched. We're being sent to a docking station. Control Room 327 has been compromised. We receive orders to investigate the security breach and get comms back online. I hope the insurgents that compromised it are still there. My unit will take them offline.

I make TD-787 the point man for this assault. This itch, this tickle, is nagging at me, and I'll be cursed if I let some head flu or parasite from planet Podunk hink the mission. It feels like I'm about to sneeze, but from the back of my head. If I could just go ahead and sneeze already, I'd feel better. For want of that, TD-787 is on point. It won't be a complex mission. He can handle it.

He needs to start handling it.

If he doesn't call us into formation in five seconds, I'm taking him off point.

BUMP

TD-787 calls us into formation. Finally.

We cross other units on their way to the detention block. MG-26 gives me a nod as he passes. His unit backed ours on Lothal. He's a conscript but loyal. We take mess together from time to time. We're due another meal. The moffs can't tell one of us troopers from another, which is by design. I don't know if they know that we can tell who's who, but I'm sure they wouldn't approve. We recognize one another by how we move. When we run, we may as well be yelling our call signs. There's SS-922, maybe the laziest stormtrooper, bringing up the rear of his unit, to no one's surprise. There's TA-519, the first stormtrooper I ever met, devoted and wise. PD-528 and I came up in the ranks together. He owes me thirty-five credits. He nearly trips on a mouse droid, then he nearly shoots it. On our way to the control room, I see units I've fought beside. Units alongside which I'm proud to serve. Units that will exterminate the rebels so completely and so quickly that we'll all be back in our bunks in no time, watching the feed of whoever is lucky enough to have killed the trespassers.

We run past that zealot Darth Vader as he exits the office of our boss's bosses' boss. I don't think Vader is a good manager of people. I'm constantly surprised to see him fail upward, but that, more than anything, is the way it goes. There are so many qualified military minds on this base, and they all defer to him. There are so many rumors about what his relationship with the Emperor must be to have such sway. I know better than to care too much about what might be true. As we take the stairs toward the control room, I think a sarcastic *May the Force be with you* at him with all my might, knowing that there has never been, nor ever will be, such a thing as "the Force." He swivels his thick helmet to look at me, and my mind races—*Oh my ancients, the Force is—The Force is—The Force is a coincidence is what the Force is.*

That's when, and how, the dam bursts. That itch, the tickle in my brain, floods my skull and crashes into memory. Our mission on Ta-tooine was to locate and detain a pair of droids, and *I saw those droids!* An old man fanned his fingers at me and I—I can't believe this—I let them pass. I didn't even check his papers. I just sent them through. I have never disobeyed a single order and now I—

Ow! I crack my head on the threshold on my way into the control room. It snaps me back into the moment. There are dead men all over the place. TK-421 is dead. I didn't know TK-421 well, but he was strong. He didn't deserve this. None of them did. Our soldiers are dead, and there is no sign of anyone to punish for it.

Punishment.

I will be punished for what I did on Tatooine. I deserve to be. Why would I let them through? Why wouldn't I check their identification? My own voice echoes in my ears. *Move along.* I must have a parasite. Maybe I have twin-sun poisoning.

Panic is unfamiliar. I remember it poorly from when I was a helpling, but it comes back now. Separated from my clan, lost in the woods as the moon set and true darkness set in. It would be hours before the first sun would come, and there was no certainty I would see it. I lose focus and the room goes dark, like the woods. I snap back to attention; these helmets require focus or it can be hard to see in them. TD-787 is doing the job, even if I'm not. He's flushed a pair of droids from the supply closet. I give them a cursory glance; they are not the droids I'm looking for. They direct us to the prison level, which is where we'd all rather be. It's all the excuse TD-787 needs to lead the unit to action.

He leaves me to stand guard, alone with my thoughts. Is there something, anything, I can do about my infraction on Tatooine? Should I report to the moff now? In the middle of a mission? Do I leave my post? There's no telling how urgent the report could be. Those droids were important enough to dispatch a contingent to Tatooine, the most useless planet in the sector. For all I know those droids hold the key to another millennium of Empire rule. For all I know, those were the most important droids in history. The protocol droid—the one I'm meant to be minding—interrupts my thoughts, bringing me back from Mos Eisley to the control room. He excuses himself and his counterpart. They have to go to maintenance. *You and me both,* I think bitterly, and wave the droids on their way.

Again.

I waved the droids on their way *again.*

Recognition smacks me across the helmet. Those were the same droids! Tall, officious goldy and stubby blue. The old man on Tatooine must have spiked my intake unit somehow. There will be time for blame later. For now, I have to catch those droids!

Before I can report that I'm in pursuit, my comm crackles to life and I'm told to report to command. I no longer feel the tickle in my head. I feel warm, despite my suit's cooling system. I know with utter certainty that they've reviewed my feed. They know what I've done.

My only hope is to redeem myself right now. There! The blue astromech rolls with purpose while goldy struggles to keep up. I raise my firearm. Two shots is all it will take. My call sign rings out in my comm again. I shake it off and take aim. I'll put a hole through the blue one first . . .

"TD-110, lower your weapon," the moff sighs urbanely, "and do report to command. Are you awaiting an engraved invitation? Consider this that"—he looks at me from the corner of his eye—"and go."

"But . . ." I say, and he stops me with a look. I'm torn. I want to defend myself. I know my future hangs on this moment. I may grumble and grouse when I'm spent and tired, but all I possess in this life is the need to serve the Empire.

"Further comment is not required, TD-110. All that is required is compliance."

I lower my weapon, bite my lip, and watch the two droids leave the docking station.

PB-106 relieves me of my weapon. He and his unit escort me to command. I know better than to speak unless spoken to, and they know better than to speak to me. I cannot read anything in PB-106's gait. Not sympathy, not duty, not anger. I'll never be able to ask, because the moffs have seen the feed, and now they'll expel me from the Death Star. Probably to some floating ice chunk like Ottinger 7 to spend the remainder of my days shivering and dodging woolly long-tailed tawds.

I take in the hallways one last time. I love this place. More than anywhere I've been, it was home. I swear to the ancients of Parsh and the elders of the Empire, if I have to fight for one hundred years, I will prove myself. I'll return to the Death Star. I swear I will fight my way back home.

END OF WATCH

Adam Christopher

Commander Pamel Poul rolled her neck and stood from the command chair, lifting the datapad in her hand to check the time.

Just ten minutes to go. Ten long, *long* minutes, until the end of another twelve-hour shift of . . . well, of almost nothing at all. Twelve hours of routine, of protocol, of answering simple queries, giving simple orders. Twelve hours of supervising a skeleton crew as they monitored the largely autonomous, redundant systems of the largest battle station in the history of the galaxy.

And that suited Commander Poul *perfectly*. She may have been a career officer, one dedicated more to the Imperial Navy than to the Emperor it served, but she was no warrior. Unlike many of her childhood friends who grew up in a more affluent sector of the Coruscant ecumenopolis, Poul had never had any desire to be a pilot or a field officer. She never had any desire to serve on the front lines—never had any desire to be a hero. Because the business of the Imperial Navy was one of war, and in war, being a hero got you killed. And with the Empire's struggle against the rebel insurgency feeling like it was about to reach a flashpoint, dying in battle was the last thing Pamel Poul intended to do.

No. Commander Poul was an *administrator*. She reveled in the functions of an executive officer: logistics, management, supervision. Yes, it was dull. It could be boring. But she enjoyed her work and, more important, she was good at it—good enough to earn a quick promotion, good enough to be assigned to the Empire's greatest technological achievement, the DS-1 Orbital Battle Station, as a station commander.

That the Death Star didn't require much actual *command* was irrelevant. The battle station was so vast—160 kilometers in diameter, with a full crew rumored to number more than a million, although the exact number remained classified—that it would be impossible for it to be run from a single control room or command center. What the Death Star had instead was a multitude of command posts, communications posts, and supervisor stations, scattered at various levels across the station sectors, all of which fell under the watch of one of the four control rooms, each positioned mid-level in one of the station's hemispheres. Commander Poul was assigned to Station Control West, and while it was possible for her to take direct control of the Death Star's systems if absolutely required, Poul was proud of the fact that hundreds of thousands of station crew in her hemisphere depended on her constant vigilance.

As she put her datapad to sleep, Poul glanced around the room. Station Control West—like its three counterparts—was a circular chamber, the circumference lined with monitor consoles, at which sat two dozen ensigns and junior officers, patiently staring at monitors, checking readings, the room filled with the constant sound of their murmuring as they quietly spoke into their headsets. Above the ring of consoles, four huge, trapezoidal display screens shone, one at each of the compass points, providing a continuous stream of status information. The data was almost too much to taken in, but Poul appreciated the at-a-glance updates for various systems she was responsible for.

One of which had been causing something of a minor headache for the last thirty minutes. Poul stepped down from the command dais and folded her arms as she glanced up at the screen directly ahead. On it, a swarm of ever-moving, multicolored indicators representing traffic control for hangars 250 to 350 crawled like zess-flies, but Poul ignored the confusing mess, focusing instead on a red block that pulsed on the left-hand side.

Docking Bay 327 was on lockdown, all traffic diverted to Bays 328 and 329.

Flight delays were not uncommon, an unavoidable consequence of the sheer volume of traffic and coordination this required—both automated and manually supervised—between the five hundred different hangars and docking bays that were buried all over the skin of the battle station. Having Docking Bay 327 out of action was, in reality, nothing more than a minor inconvenience, but it would remain an annoying status alert sullying her otherwise perfect shift report unless she could get the diversions cleared in the next—

She checked the time on her datapad again.

—*seven* minutes.

Poul frowned and headed over to the monitor station beneath the display. Two crew were positioned at their control consoles, one— Ensign Toos—hunched across the controls as he stared at a small square display in front of him, while his companion, Sublieutenant Slallen, leaned back in her seat, arms folded, shaking her head. As Poul approached, neither seemed aware of her presence.

"Remind me again," said Slallen. "What am I looking at here?"

Toos clicked his tongue and tapped the screen with an index finger. "Come on, you're telling me you don't recognize a classic when you see one?" He whistled softly between his teeth. "Just wait until I tell your brother when he gets back from Scarif."

Slallen cocked her head. "What I do recognize, *Ensign,* is a piece of junk when I see one. I'm amazed it didn't break up as soon as the tractor beam got a lock."

"Piece of junk? Sublieutenant Slallen, I despair, I really do. That piece of junk, as you call it, is—"

"A YT-1300 light freighter," said Poul, resting one hand on the back of Slallen's chair, "that is currently disrupting the docking bay schedule."

Slallen and Toos immediately straightened up, their backs ramrod-straight. Toos cleared his throat.

"Yes, ma'am. Sorry, ma'am."

"Don't apologize, Ensign," said Poul. "Just get the docking bay cleared, *now.*"

"Ma'am," said Slallen. "Captain Khurgee still has a scanning crew aboard the vessel. We need an all-clear from the hangar deck before we can lift the lockdown."

"The scan still isn't finished? What are they *doing* down there?"

Toos and Slallen said nothing, both junior officers just looking up at their commander. Poul sighed. "Fine," she said. "Continue monitoring and let me know when Captain Khurgee is done."

On the other side of the control room, the turbolift hissed open. Poul turned and saw her shift replacement step out.

"Actually, no," said Poul. "You can let Commander Sheard know."

Poul turned and gave Sheard a casual salute, which he returned before heading around the arc of the room toward her. Poul handed the datapad to her fellow officer and briefed him on the events of the last shift—in particular, on the status of the mystery freighter currently holding up the schedule down in Docking Bay 327.

Sheard nodded as he listened, brushing one index finger along the underside of his thick mustache, then he tapped the back of Toos's chair.

"Show me the ship, main screen."

"Sir."

Ensign Toos swung back around to his console. He snapped a switch, and the view of the freighter in the docking bay shown on his console's screen flashed up onto the main wall display. Toos and Slallen sat back and looked up at the image, while Poul took a step back and tapped a finger on the edge of her datapad.

"I didn't even know these things were still flying," said Commander Sheard.

Poul nodded. He was right—the YT-1300 was an old ship, virtually a relic. And the example down in Docking Bay 327 was no exception, she thought as she gazed up at the screen. The vessel was battered, the hull carbon-scored in several places, the vector thrust plates that cradled the main drive ports in serious need of not just cleaning but replacing altogether.

But . . . there was something else about the ship. Poul had seen a couple of YT-series freighters in her time—both long past their service and certainly not operational—and while she couldn't remember the exact models, this one looked . . . different. Wasn't the sensor dish larger than standard? And the dorsal armament . . . it was a quad laser cannon. The YT-1300 had weapons, certainly, but a gun like that just *had* to be unlicensed.

Poul didn't know why the ship had been captured and dragged

into the docking bay, but there was more than a fair chance it was smugglers, or pirates. That made sense. The ship was modified, customized, far beyond factory specs.

Although quite what the Death Star was doing policing the hyperspace lanes was another question entirely.

Poul cocked her head as she looked at the display. "Ensign Toos said you have a brother on Scarif, Slallen? Ship designer?"

Sublieutenant Slallen turned in her chair. "Naval architect, ma'am. We took starship design together as an elective at the Academy, but he was the one with the talent." She turned and pointed back at the main display. "You don't see many working examples of this older kind of ship. I'll have to send him a data tape, once he's out of operations."

"What's his assignment?" asked Commander Sheard.

Slallen gave a shrug. "I don't know, sir. The operation on Scarif is classified. I haven't heard from him in four weeks." She slumped, just a little, in her chair. "We were due to meet for shore leave, but I haven't heard from him yet. I guess his operation has been extended."

"Quite possibly," said Poul, and she left it at that. Because she knew something the sublieutenant clearly didn't—that the Death Star itself had *been* at Scarif, and had left the system just three days ago. Slallen was right—the operation on the planet *was* classified. Commander Poul had been on duty, and was of a senior-enough rank to have been informed of their destination, but even she hadn't known what the station's mission there was. There was talk in her mess that it was another shakedown run—something about a second test, following the first one over the moon of Jedha. Although a test of what, Poul didn't know.

But that was the thing about the Death Star. The battle station was so big that, short of a Star Destroyer crashing into it, most of the crew would have no idea about what was going on at any given time. Only essential mission personnel had the required clearance. Poul understood that. It was a matter not just of security, but also of pure logistics.

Poul nodded at Commander Sheard. Her watch was over and it was time to go.

"Station Control West is—"

An alarm chimed from the console in front of Ensign Toos—Poul saw a red light flashing by his hand, quickly joined by another. Next to the ensign, Slallen glanced over her own console, checking systems, while Toos began cycling through a series of switches, peering at his monitor as he did so, a frown firmly etched on his face.

Poul and Sheard exchanged a glance, then Poul leaned over the console between her two junior officers.

"Something wrong?"

"Ah . . . yes, ma'am . . . ah, maybe." Toos flicked some more switches, then twisted a dial as he began cycling through a series of surveillance frequencies patched into the station's security system. On his small display, the view of the docking bay was replaced by screen after screen of roaring static as he flicked through the channels.

At her console, Slallen had one hand on her earpiece as she listened, then she acknowledged the message and turned to the two commanders.

"There's an alarm from level five, Detention Block AA-Twenty-Three. Subcontrol reports all sensors in the block have gone down."

"Confirmed," said Toos, pointing to his display of rolling static. "All cams are out."

Poul glanced at Commander Sheard, who folded his arms and stepped back. "All yours, Commander."

"Thank you," she said, before turning back to the ensign. "Put me through to the detention block."

Toos cycled his comm again and opened the channel, but the light beside the switch changed not from red to green as expected, but from red to *blue*.

"They have their comm in secure mode." The ensign looked up at Commander Poul. "We'll have to wait for them to answer."

Poul lifted her datapad and quickly swiped through to the station directory. Her eyes flicked over the data, then she nodded.

"Detention block AA-Twenty-Three is reserved for political prisoners," she said. "So secure comm is standard. Okay, let's just hope they answer quickly."

That was when the comm deck chimed. Poul moved closer to the console as Toos opened the channel. The ensign opened his mouth to speak, only for the operator on the other end to cut in first.

"Ah, everything's under control, situation normal."

Poul glanced up at Sheard, who frowned. Toos and Slallen looked at each other. Then Toos pressed the comm switch again.

"What happened?"

"Ah, had a slight weapons malfunction, but, ah, everything's perfectly all right now, we're fine, we're all fine here now, thank you."

Poul didn't recognize the voice, but whoever it was, they sounded almost breathless. She glanced down at her datapad to check, but then looked up in surprise as the voice spoke again.

"How are you?"

Toos looked back at Slallen, who nodded. He leaned back over the comm. "We're sending a squad in."

The channel clicked back into life. "Ah, ah, negative, negative, we have, ah, a reactor leak here, ah, now, give us a few minutes to lock it down. Ah . . . large leak, very dangerous."

"Who's the duty officer down there?" asked Commander Sheard.

Poul checked her datapad. "Lieutenant Childsen."

Toos shook his head. "Ma'am, that doesn't sound like Lieutenant Childsen." He pressed the comm button. "Who is this? What's your operating number?"

"Ah—"

Then the comm popped, and the control room was filled with a roar of white noise. Toos winced and killed the volume, then tried the comm again. "Detention Block AA-Twenty-Three, what is your status? Report please."

He was answered by static. He tried a few more times, then gave up. "Nothing. Comm down."

Slallen looked up at Commander Poul. "We should send a squad. I have a security team ready and waiting."

Poul held up a hand. "Keep them on standby." She turned to Toos. "Ensign, systems report. If there's a reactor leak, it could be serious. We'll need to get engineering in."

Toos brought up data feeds at his console, then sat back and shook his head. He tapped a button, and the main screen changed from the docking bay view to a schematic of the power grid for this hemisphere of the station.

"Power systems at normal status. Output is steady. No variables detected."

"No reactor leak then," said Slallen. "Ma'am, the squad is ready to go."

Poul nodded. "Send them in. But we need to report this. Get me Grand Moff Tarkin."

Slallen nodded and turned to her own comm deck, selecting the channel before calling it up.

"Overbridge ready room," came a female voice from the desk.

"Grand Moff Tarkin, please."

"Grand Moff Tarkin is currently in conference."

Commander Sheard shook his head and strode over to the com-

313

mand dais. He stepped up to the chair and pulled it around, then cut into Slallen's comm channel from the panel on the armrest.

"This is Station Control West, Commander Sheard. This is a priority red request. Put us through to the grand moff immediately."

"One moment, sir."

The comm chimed again.

"Yes."

It wasn't a question, it was just a statement, spoken by an old man with a clipped accent. Poul ground her teeth—she had only met Grand Moff Tarkin twice, and that was two times too many. Already she could imagine the cloying scent of lavallel, the rich, purple-flowering herb, that seemed to hang around the battle station's chief commanding officer like a cloud. She met Commander Sheard's gaze as he made his report to their superior. "We have an emergency alert in Detention Block AA-Twenty-Three."

"The princess? Put all sections on alert."

Poul felt the breath catch in her throat. Princess? What princess?

And then she heard the voice of the man Tarkin was in conference with, the deep, resonant bass voice echoing down the open comm channel.

Well, perhaps *man* was the wrong word. Because who knew what was inside that suit.

"Obi-Wan is here. The Force is with him."

The comm clicked off.

Lord Vader. Tarkin's adviser—his *enforcer*. Poul knew he was aboard the station, but even so, hearing him speak sent a chill down her spine. She looked at Sheard and saw his throat bob as he gulped. It seemed that Vader had that effect on a lot of people.

Then Poul realized that the control room had gone quiet, the constant murmuring of the crew absent as they all watched the two commanders.

Now it was Poul's turn to swallow. Over at the console, Slallen sat with her back rigid, her hands hovering over her console, ready to accept the next order. Beside her, Toos mimicked her posture, but he looked pale, his own hands curled tightly in his lap.

Commander Poul gestured to the sublieutenant. "Send in the squad. Let's get this situation under control." Then she walked up to the command dais as, behind her, Slallen gave the order.

"You're welcome to stay, Commander," said Sheard as he stood by the empty dais chair. But Poul rolled her neck, took a deep breath, and gave her colleague a smile.

"No thanks, my watch is done. Good luck, Commander."

As she headed to the turbolift, ready for a shower, something to eat, something to drink—something quite strong, perhaps—Commander Pamel Poul tried to ignore the growing sense of unease and the rolling ball of cold that seemed to have taken the place of her stomach.

She didn't know what was going on—with the old freighter, with the detention block . . . and Tarkin had said *princess*, hadn't he? What was that about?—but it wasn't her problem, not anymore. Let Sheard handle it, and she could read his report in the next shift.

A shift that, Poul hoped, would be another twelve hours of glorious, routine boredom.

Now, *that* would be perfect.

THE BAPTIST

Nnedi Okorafor

There's something alive in here.

—Luke Skywalker

When they came, she wasn't ready. She was asleep, so her guard was down. Vodrans didn't usually come this deep into the swamps. They surrounded her before she could have known they were there.

Still, Omi had the spirit of a warrior and so she was fighting as she woke. Rough leathery Vodran hands grasped each of Omi's tentacles, their thick, hard nails pressing into Omi's soft flesh, hauling her out of the water. They shouted instructions to one another in their oily language that always reminded her of the thin scum on the surface of the water when too much light came through the trees. She thrashed and rippled her flesh transparent, but she wasn't much bigger than each of them was. She twisted her body, attempting to bite at limbs or torsos, but she was caught. Then something stabbed into her and she felt cold flood into the sensitive spot between two of her tentacles. Her strength left her.

Through an awful haze, she was powerless to stop her capture. They rolled each of her tentacles into a large ball and shackled them all with thick shiny magnetized metal bands. She was fading, losing consciousness, as she held up her eyestalk, taking in all the Vodran faces, hard, knobbed, expressionless. She fell into the darkness as several of them hauled her into the spherical tank that was like a body-sized bubble that would not pop. She should have looked around at the swamp, her home, one last time. But instead, she was unconscious before her body settled on the bottom of the tank. She dreamed of home . . .

318

Soft lands she could travel over. Warm rich waters, squelching mud, blasts of swamp gas, spindly trees. Here there was music, there was play, and there was plenty to eat and watch. Omi moved about the swamp knowing that she belonged, her eyestalk swiveling as she traveled, seeing so much of the world. When she settled in for a deep night's sleep, she was safe and warm, her mind not on survival, but on where she planned to go next . . .

Omi woke, instantly remembering that she'd been captured, and instinctively pulled her tentacles in. When she was sure nothing was grabbing her, she took inventory. One, two, three, four, five, six, seven tentacles. All intact. And so Omi settled some, glancing around.

She was in a thick, clear crystal sphere, its lid screwed on tightly, the better to preserve the gases in the swamp water. The sphere was positioned against a window, among various other cargo. As far as she could tell, she was the only living thing in this place. Large and small white containers were stacked to the high ceiling; a narrow pathway led to an open doorway. Omi could see the swamplands right out her window, just beyond a flat, hard-looking plane of land. She'd seen these flying metal beasts before, passing across the sky, far above the trees, so large that one could be inside them and live. They flew here and there. She'd never imagined she'd be swallowed by one, contained in a crystal bowl. She pressed herself against her transparent prison, trying to get as close to home as possible.

Everything began to rumble, the cargo stacks shaking but not falling. The water in her tank sloshed her this way and that. She turned her eyestalk to the window and realized her home was retreating. At first slowly, then faster than she could imagine. Something seemed to be pulling it down. What would happen to the swamplands if it was pressed into the ground? She shut her eye. Had this large beast just destroyed her home? And it was in this way Omi experienced her first sense of antigravity. She began to float about in her tank, losing her sense of location. *None of this is possible,* was all she kept thinking. *None of this is possible. But it is happening.*

It was as if she were everywhere all at once. Where she had pressed herself to the sphere trying to stay close to home, suddenly she felt her body wanted to be all over the sphere. She pulsated with terror and after experiencing this intense emotion for several minutes, she felt something deep in her being click and let go. She floated upward and then turned to what her eye told her was upside down—but her other senses, like the feeling in her tentacles, the feel of the water, the heft of her body, told her differently.

As she floated, she turned her eye back to the large window and stared for the first time deep into outer space. Her hearts' beats quickened. This was a place she was not supposed to ever see. She was meant to travel the swamp, not into this . . . into this *beyond.* She felt herself pulled forcibly toward space. She pressed against the round

319

glass of the sphere and suddenly all the rushing and flushing and flowing and stress in her seven tentacles and head stopped. Everything stopped.

Quiet.

Nothing.

But everything.

There was purpose.

Omi twitched. Then involuntarily, her body shifted to being transparent, and then the black color with pricks of starlight. *Home will stay home, but you must go,* she understood, more than heard. And she knew deep in her hearts that she would not die. No, she was in the right place. In the right moment.

Stay your path. This time she heard the words in the deep complex humming language that her people often spoke in when they weren't feeding. To speak this language was to scare away all nearby food, the reverberations carried so completely in the water. To hear it now was like feeling a final breeze from home. Though she was gazing into space, she heard the voice humming from her flesh: Maybe it came from within the tiny links that her people said chained with one another to form her flesh.

There was a great flash and Omi instantly knew. She was positive, at least in that moment, that this place she was in was going to burn. Then the moment passed and she was no longer sure of anything, except that feeling of oneness. What did that feeling even mean, though? She was no longer so sure. Maybe it was just her fear of death.

Not so long ago, she'd been similarly forgetful when she'd gotten into a battle with another of her clan. She remembered that this one had identified as male, and they'd met while crossing over a piece of land, going in opposite directions. His name had been Iduna and she'd been intrigued by his male identity. Her people could choose the gender they wanted. They were physically hermaphroditic, so one's choice said much about one as an individual. In her years, she'd met several females and even more who were diangous (the most common gender), but she'd never met a male until this moment.

He had wanted to exchange a few eggs. She had refused, and that was when he grew angry. They'd fought a violent bloody battle, and during this battle, she'd fought with great focus and precision. To her, the battle had been like an argument that she controlled and eventually won. Iduna soon realized that if he didn't flee, she'd kill him. Thankfully, Iduna chose not to die.

Omi may have surprised herself with her incredible combat skills, but as she fought, the terror of the experience, the fear of death left her so forgetful that she couldn't remember from which direction she'd come. This was how she'd wound up in the southern part of the land instead of the western, napping in the perfect place to be kidnapped and taken into space.

321

What must have been days passed and Omi was still wondering if the vision of this place going up in flames had been inspired by her intense fear. Obsessing over the fiery vision was all that kept her restlessness and anger over being kidnapped at bay. Her sense of up and down had returned, and Omi felt she could think clearly. Twice a Vodran had come and sprinkled some smelly but somehow bland dried fish through a small hole in the lid.

It was the taste of this fish that stoked Omi's already heated anger enough to make her escape attempt. Back home, everything had flavor, juices, salt, the spice of food the fish had eaten in their bellies. But these people kidnapped her and then fed her food that was an insult. And her only view was of star-filled outer space and the white cargo on the other side of her sphere. She had to get out of here.

She felt around the lid of her prison with her tentacles, gently touching every gap, even the tiniest ones, testing the pressure. The lid was made of a smooth, hard substance she had never felt before, and it smelled tangy and smoky; the material it was made of was weak. She pushed and felt some give. She pushed again, using her suckers to grip and turn. The lid clicked and began to easily slide in a circle. Around and around it went until it fell to the floor with a dull thud. She waited and then extended her eyestalk from her swamp-water prison. She hauled herself out.

Back in the swamp, she'd moved freely over the damp land from one body of water to the next. Leaving the sphere was not much different. Instead of trees, she skirted hard containers made of the same smoky-tangy-smelling weak material. And instead of moist fragrant air caressing her skin, the atmosphere was dry and crackling and sucked at her flesh. But the ground was flat and she moved easily enough over it. Smooth and black. When she slithered into the hallway, she paused. All angles, dead, everything smooth and hard and blacker. The insides of this space-traveling beast were either rotten or dead.

Never in her life had she seen such a place. But she was still rather young, so there was always more to see. For a second, she returned to that epic moment when she'd looked out into space and become one with it. And with it came her vision that this place was going to go up in flames. Would that be because this beast was going to fly into a sun?

She couldn't think about that now. Her front tentacle twitched. Something was coming. She felt it arriving before she saw it, the vibration buzzing across the floor. And so she pressed herself against the wall, turning herself black and shiny, blending in perfectly.

The creature rolled up the hall like a large black mouse or, more accurately to Omi, an insect. Black and podlike in body, swift in motion; something about it was not right. Omi pressed herself flatter against and up the wall. Like the giant beast they were all traveling in, this large insect was not alive, Omi was sure of it. It zipped by without even noticing how the wall bulged, despite being the same color and sheen. Omi stayed this way for several minutes as other similar dead creatures zipped and walked up and down the hall, some tiny as swamp turtles, others tall as Vodrans, and one as large as a Hutt. Then Omi *did* see one of the Hutts pass by with what could have been a Vodran in white hard casing.

When the hallway finally grew quiet again, Omi knew this had to be her chance for escape. She smelled moisture nearby. It was beyond the hard walls, and she had to find it before she completely dried out. She rolled into the middle of the hallway, her flesh aching from the lack of moisture. Dropping her black coloring to her usual mature deep purple, she slithered toward the smell of water. She'd reached the end of the hall when two Vodran-like individuals encased in white nearly stepped on her.

One exclaimed in a language that was not Vodran. The other pointed something black and long at her. Somehow she knew to move before it blasted fire. A smoking crater appeared beside her. She only had seconds. Back. Toward the one closest to her, instead of away. She was in a hurricane of terror again, just as she had been during the fight with the male member of her tribe. When she'd been fighting for her life.

With her terror came that sweet clarity. She shot her two front tentacles toward him, moving like a zip fish. She had to be impossible. She could not miss the parts of its body she needed to grasp. Milliseconds. She could not miss. Or she was going to die. She was not meant to die here in this cold, dead place. She was entitled to so much more. She couldn't miss.

There was that voice again. Reverberating through the space between the milliseconds. Through the space in her flesh. Telling her to trust. Submit.

She grasped his legs and was on him in seconds with the spur in her left tentacle. And in this way, she stung. She could not see the other; this was the weakness of having only one eyestalk. Her blind spots were many. But she could see in other ways sometimes. Yes. The one was stumbling back, turning toward the other, raising its weapon. She could smell the smoke from the burned ground.

She leapt. And as she spun in the air toward the second one, all her tentacles flew out and, for a moment, she was a huge seven-point star in space. Her back tentacle slapped him first, then her other three. The fifth and sixth grasped him, and the seventh dug her poison spur right through its white helmet into the meaty soft flesh beneath. It felt similar to smashing through the shell of a large crab.

Omi slapped wetly on the floor, her body now screaming with pain. She stared at what she'd done. She swiveled her eyestalk to look up the hallway in one direction and then the other. Her suckers could taste the ground. There *was* water nearby. But could she make it there without being discovered again? And was the water just another container? For the first time she wondered where she could even go in here. Within this beast that would eventually burn.

Omi decided to return the way she'd come. Quickly. Moving and hiding. Slowly. Gradually. Even as chaos erupted behind her when the bodies were discovered, she stayed her course and eventually made it back to the transparent bowl, lifting the large lid and pulling it over her. She'd twisted it firmly back in place and settled on the bottom of the bowl in a scrunched ball just as the guards burst in. She shut her eyes, feeling their scrutiny as they approached her. From underwater, she heard their garbled voices as they stepped up to the glass and tapped on it. She lazily opened her eye and closed it.

After a few seconds, she cracked her eye open a bit and watched one of them test the bowl lid's tightness. After walking around her bowl and searching the storage room, the two of them left and Omi found herself alone again. She stared out into space. Her painful skin recovered to its hydrated self in the swamp water. At least there was that.

After a while, Omi stopped caring about how much time had passed. They came and fed her smelly fish, sometimes chopped up, sometimes whole. Disgusting fish that didn't taste like anything from her home, and when she ate, she missed home that much more. They placed two solid metal bars over the top of her bowl, but only she knew that doing this was a waste of time. She had no intention of escaping. There was nowhere to escape to on this doomed vessel—living or dead animal, it didn't matter to her.

All she could do was wait. Eventually, who knew, maybe there would be another chance to escape somewhere, on some planet.

And then she saw it, first from a distance in space and then closer and closer and closer. It looked like a fruit of the dead. Suspended there in space. The size of a moon. Soon it filled the view in the window and Omi could not see above, around, or below it. It became the world. And into it they flew.

For a second time, Omi felt the disorientation of adjusting to another type of gravity, that of this huge dead moon. She was nowhere; then she knew the bottom of her bowl and she settled down in it. When they came, again, she was asleep. The bowl shook as it was hauled away on what looked like a large flat insect.

She was taken down the sterile corridors, this time far past the place where she'd killed the two individuals in her aborted quest for freedom. The spot where it had all happened was clear, unoccupied. And then they were moving through the biggest inside place Omi had ever seen. The ceiling looked high as the sky, but it was a ceiling. She could see that. At the top were more bars, and a network of metal tubes. In this place, she saw more metal birds and insects and Vodran-like people in white casing. Hundreds of them. The ground was smooth, like the tops of ancient dead swamp trees that had been blasted by the winds. She'd climbed one of those trees once, out of curiosity. Its surface was so dry, the winds near the top so biting. She'd probably never do that again.

They entered a narrow, dim black tunnel where the ground became porous, red light shining through perfect tiny square holes. Not land, a sort of rigid grate that could hold all of their weight. The sound of the feet of those escorting her tapped on the hard surface as they walked. They stopped at a large hole in the wall with the squiggles 3263827 etched above the entrance, and that was when she was sure she was going to die. The symbols looked like images of what her body would look like if they tore her apart.

Was this where they were going to eat her? She could smell organic matter, strong and pungent in a way that reminded her of home. The insect beneath her rose, somehow lifting the large water-filled bowl. It dumped her and her swamp water into the hole and then Omi was tumbling down a black tunnel, throwing out her tentacles but unable to gain purchase. Her head bumped the side, her mouth of sharp teeth clattering together. She pulled her tentacles and eye-stalk in and tucked her head as close to herself as possible.

Plash! She plunged into a soup of water, metal parts, pieces that were not metal but were just as dead, excrement from the Vodran-like people who ran the ship, and other organic matter. As bits and pieces bumped and pressed against her body, she let herself sink, still in a protective ball, until she softly bounced onto the bottom.

She waited. Some of the floating things around her were hard, some of them soft, none of them alive. She smelled things she could eat that were better than the smelly alien fish. Slowly, she reached out a tentacle and suckered the ground beneath her. Metal, and not all smooth. She knotted herself up again and stayed like this for hours. What she learned in that time was that this place was dimly lit by dirty lights on the ceiling, the water was tepid, and every so often garbage would fall into it, giving Omi something new to eat. It wasn't home, but it was as close to it as she could come in the middle of space.

Over time, Omi grew to understand that she was on a dead planet that had never been alive. A planet that was small and made of materials that would never know life. But things she could consume were dumped into the false swamp, and she supposed this was why she was captured and dumped there. She grew strong and large. She missed home and wished she could find a clear tank with no lid beside a window where she could see the vastness of space. But she also never forgot that she had a purpose, though she didn't know what it was.

Omi survived the false swamp by memorizing the routine of the walls. Twice a "day" the thick metal walls would rumble once, quietly, and then rumble again and slowly march toward each other. The first time this had happened, Omi had not panicked. She'd spent hours exploring the false swamp, learning its shallows and depth, its perimeter, searching for an escape.

There was a large pipe near the bottom whose opening was protected by an invisible barrier until that moment when it flushed out much of the old water during these wall marches. However, there was also a large indenture near the bottom where something too impossibly hard had made a deep dent in the left wall. When the walls marched, she pressed herself here, protected even when the walls had pressed all the debris that she did not consume into a thick sheet. The sheet was ejected through a long slot below.

327

On that fateful day, an hour before it happened, Omi saw outer space again. When she was inside with no window. It was impossible. She was in her spot just as the sheet of compressed metals and dead materials was ejected. In that moment, everything seemed to burst from her mind. Suddenly, after so much time being by herself here, she was not alone. And what was with her was vast and beautiful. Again, she involuntarily shifted her flesh to the black of space with speckles of distant stars. And whatever was with her told her again through her skin that she had a mission and it would be in this false swamp. It told Omi that she was in the right place at the right time.

By the time the walls marched themselves apart, she was alone again. The walls were moving away, but they simultaneously seemed to close in on her because again she had the vision of everything going up in flames and again she wanted to escape her prison. But she had her mission first. More garbage was dumped into the false swamp, and soon she found a large hunk of rotting meat, consumed it, and settled in the corner as the fresh garbage soaked up the water.

Five minutes later, the four fell into her prison.

Omi's tentacles twitched as she immediately recognized something in the smaller male. Yes, that one was male, not just by choice but by physical design. However, there was something about him that was like her; she could smell it on him. He had just left home, too, as she had so long ago. There was that, but there was something else, as well, if she relaxed and focused completely on him. There was something sparkly and electric that she felt in every part of her flesh. She did not understand their languages and she wished she could. The first thing she'd have demanded of this one was to know why he could submit to It, too. Because if he had not already, she knew he would eventually. Just as she had back when she had faced and killed those two white-shelled individuals when she was trying to escape.

She climbed out of the water, changing to its dirty-gray color beneath the dingy pink lighting, suctioning her tentacles to the wall so that she could get a better look. There she stayed, her tentacles spread, like a giant spider on the wall. One was a hairless female and three were larger males, one of them protected by fur. Omi would beware of the female, despite her lack of hair. The female would be most savage and cunning. If any of them could kill Omi, it would be that one. Omi dropped into the water with a soft splash.

She flattened herself and moved stealthily around their feet. When she brushed the small male's leg, she heard It speak to her again, her tentacles tingling with Its demand. She didn't want to; she had plenty of food down here, meat, bones, thick green stalks she'd come to especially enjoy. And all she sensed from these four who could not see her was fear. Omi had no reason to harm any of them.

She knew when she did it. It was her choice. Despite the fact that it felt as if she'd made the choice while part of something greater. Yes. She rolled smoothly beneath the surface, then tumbled and stretched four tentacles before her. She opened her mouth and could not resist letting out a roar from deep in her body, the rumble of her speech reverberating beneath the false swamp and along the metal walls to the ceiling. The individuals shuddered, spoke among themselves, freezing and looking around. She poked her eyestalk up, needing to see his face.

Then she wrapped a tentacle around him and pulled him under. He was screaming and thrashing, then choking. Back home, sometimes the sky would swirl and fight itself and light would crash down into the water. If this happened close to where Omi was hiding, she'd feel her entire body tense up, becoming hard as stone, and she'd feel the light traveling through her. Touching him was like this: Everything in her body was aware of everything in him. She wondered if everything in him was aware of everything in her. She wondered if this creature could be her mate, not for procreating but for adventure. It was *his* destiny to leave home, too.

She was sure of her mission, but now she was also *unsure*. What if

329

he died? Something blasted past her, red and hot. The others were attacking. *Pain* exploded in one of her tentacles and the water around her turned blue with her blood. She let go and flung him back to the surface.

Her back tentacle hung limply, a gaping hole in its center. She pulled it close to her body and a second, even more powerful explosion of pain vibrated through her so intensely that for a moment she lost consciousness. But the energy in her, around her, through her was stronger. She had a mission and it was right now. She pulled him down again.

He fought her, but she was stronger. She held him still, wrapping her three other thick tentacles around him. She heard a brilliant humming and it vibrated through her body. For the third time, she saw that this place, along with the small beast she'd arrived in, would all go up in flames.

What was happening to him now, though? As he struggled, pulled at her tentacles, kicking his legs, bubbles of air escaping from his mouth, he was shedding. No, not the protective material he wore over his flesh. With her sharp eyes, she saw it: A shade of him sloughed off, the flesh of this shade pale and delicate looking, naked. It shook off him, the face of this dim version of him wide-eyed, the mouth open, shocked. Then the shade dissolved in the water. Omi's mission was complete. She was so preoccupied with what she'd seen that she nearly forgot to release him. Nearly. When she did, he swam frantically to the surface. The walls rumbled.

As she fled to her space in the wall, she knew he would be okay. And when the walls stopped their usual march forward to press all the remaining metal and waste into a sheet, she was not surprised. Even when one of the larger males spat one more ball of fire into the false swamp after they'd gotten out, she wasn't afraid.

Soon, the four were gone and Omi never again saw the one who was so much like her. But she trusted that he went on to do great things, for she'd been chosen to baptize him through a sort of death. To her people, water was where life was given. Water was the Great Cleanser When It Was Time to Be Cleansed. And this was also true for those who could not live in it.

Omi's injured tentacle fell off and grew back. She went on living in the false swamp, swimming about, eating its garbage, hiding in her safe space. Days, months, she did not know. There was no dim sun with which she could mark time. There were no other people of her tribe to tell her the time. However, once in a while that which she could feel in her flesh and beyond spoke to her and told her stories of the universe. It told her of peoples, places, wars, and deep lessons. It taught her how to spin her body in ways she did not think were possible until she did them. In that dim place, she learned how to make a large twisted hunk of metal and two pieces of waterlogged insulation lift into the air like great birds. Or maybe Omi was just talking to and teaching herself, and all her knowledge came from within her very cells.

When the fire came that consumed every part of the great beast she'd been swallowed by, Omi submitted to her destiny. And her last thought was *Who will I be the next time around?*

TIME OF DEATH

Cavan Scott

My name is Obi-Wan Kenobi, and I am dead.

I know how that sounds. Crazy old Ben with his crazy old stories. But this isn't crazy. This is happening.

At least, I think it is.

One minute I am standing in the heart of the Empire's new battle station, facing the man who, for good or ill, has defined the last thirty years of my life. I close my eyes, and wait; hearing the sweep of his lightsaber and . . .

And *what*?

What happens next?

If you strike me down, I shall become more powerful than you can ever imagine.

Did I say those words? Did I *believe* them?

I have no idea. Not anymore.

It happens over and over again. I close my eyes, waiting for the inevitable. I hear the rasp of Vader's breath, the creak of his armor, the scream of the lightsaber.

I feel the searing pain in my side.

Eyes. Scream. Saber. Pain.

Eyes. Scream. Saber. Pain.

Eyes. Scream. Saber—

I sit up, crying out in the stillness of the room. I'm not where I was. The battle station, the troopers, even Vader . . . they're all gone, as if they never existed.

I am home, perched on the pourstone slab that has served as a bed for nearly twenty years. Where is my mattress? I glance around the cramped room. Everything is as it should be, although some of the more recent additions are missing. The wooden chair that I built from japor wood. The set of clay bowls scavenged from a deserted Jawa caravan. The humidifier purchased from Watto, at a highly inflated price, I should add.

Have I been robbed? No, this is how the hut looked in the early days of my exile, when I still etched a calendar of sorts into the wall above my bed to mark the passage of time. I run my hand across the pitted surface. Three years scored into the stone.

I'd found the old prospector's hut perched high on a windswept bluff, it was empty, long since abandoned, but I knew immediately that it would serve me well. The walls were solid, the roof sound, and the caves beneath the cellar an ideal place for meditation and training. Most important, it was remote, surrounded by a vast sea of dunes. I would be left alone.

I swing my legs onto the rough stone floor. That's when I realize. I don't ache. For the first time in years, my body doesn't complain when I push myself from the bed. I look down at my hands. They're

the hands of a much younger man. They don't shake, they don't tremble. The skin is supple, tanned but not yet discolored by the twin
suns' constant glare. I flex my fingers, expecting to hear the creak of
rheumatic joints. Nothing. The fingers are strong. One might even
suggest, dexterous.

I run them through my beard, a thought occurring to me. I rush
through to the back of the modest dwelling, past the stove and pan-
try, to the tarnished mirror hanging on the far wall. The face in the
glass is largely free of lines, the skin smooth. The tousled shock of
hair is thick, only the beard betraying a smattering of gray.

The world lurches. I throw a hand against the wall to steady myself. This is the past. The mattress, the chair, the bowls, and the humidifier; they're not missing. They just haven't arrived yet.

I pitch forward, falling into the swirling cycle of my death.

Eyes. Scream. Saber. Pain.

Eyes. Scream. Saber. Pain.

Eyes. Scream. Saber. Pain.

But this time, there's more. So much more.

A newborn baby, cradled in my arms, wailing as his mother
breathes her last.

Qui-Gon sinking to his knees, smoke rising from the jagged hole
in his gut.

Eyes that once looked on me as a brother corrupted by the dark
side, burning yellow with hate.

Maul's pyre raging beneath the desert sky.

A severed arm twitching by the light of my saber.

Empty robes tumbling to the floor.

A voice calling my name.

Eyes. Scream. Saber. Pain.

Eyes. Scream. Saber—

I sit up, gasping for air. I'm back on the bed, dust motes dancing in
the light that streams through the hut's narrow windows.

My vision blurs and I am in the Temple on Coruscant, the way it was, long before Palpatine made a mockery of those hallowed halls. Yoda stares at me across the chamber, a wry smile creasing that ancient face.

"For everything, a reason there is."

"But why here?" I yell as I slide back to the sun-beaten hut. "Why now?"

There is no answer.

I sit on the edge of the bed, trying to remember what happened when I first lived this morning.

I look down, seeing a ghost of my younger self twisting and turning on the slab, caught in a nightmare. He moans, he whimpers, he sits bolt-upright, a single word on his lips as he wakes.

A single name.

"Luke!"

And then I am alone again.

I know what day this is. I recognize the knot in the pit of my stomach, the sense of foreboding that makes my skin crawl. Luke is in danger. Something is about to happen that will change everything.

"Go to him," urges a voice inside my head.

"Yes, Master," I reply, shielding my eyes as I barrel out into the sunlight. Neda is waiting for me, lounging beneath a makeshift shelter, animal skins stretched taut across a rickety frame. The structure will remain long after the poor thing dies of old age, the tattered cover keeping me awake at night as it flaps incessantly in the wind. Then one morning it will be gone, ripped from the side of the house by a desert storm.

But that hasn't happened yet. My trusty, if cantankerous, eopie is alive and well, snuffling around in the dirt, foraging for roots in the scorched ground. I have an overwhelming urge to throw my arms around her, but Neda regards me with her usual disdain, a surly snort her only greeting before she resumes the fruitless search for sustenance.

Quite right. Just as it should be; but for now, her breakfast needs to wait.

She doesn't complain as I tighten the cracked leather straps around her middle, ignoring me completely as I hoist myself onto the saddle.

"Come on, old girl. Let's go."

I pull on the reins, gently jabbing my heels into her flank when she still doesn't respond. Finally, she grunts and begrudgingly obliges, picking up the pace as we trot down the winding path to the valley beneath.

Soon, we are charging across the salt flats, Neda snorting as I push her harder than ever before. Her broad feet pound the sand, rushing past bone-white skeletons picked clean by the claw-condors. I imagine a cavalcade of scenarios, each more terrible than the last.

Is it the Sand People? Owen can handle Tusken Raiders as well as anyone on the wastes, but the nomads have a special reason to hate his family, a grudge still not forgotten and far from forgiven. Have they finally taken their revenge? The sins of the father visited upon the son.

I tighten my grip on Neda's reins, urging her on. Of course, there are other terrors on Tatooine; the loathsome clump of blubber that is Jabba the Hutt for one. Owen is a proud man. He's likely to fight rather than pay the protection money Jabba demands of his neighbors. Surely Owen wouldn't be that stupid, after what he's promised?

No, Owen knows when to fight his battles. But what if the threat comes not from Tatooine at all, but from the stars above? Gangsters and raiders are one thing, but the Empire is another. Owen wouldn't stand a chance against a crack squad of Imperial troopers. Is a drop ship already plummeting through Tatooine's thin atmosphere? Are my worst fears about to be realized?

I imagine sand crunching beneath heavy black boots, a dark cape billowing in a desert squall, the mechanical wheeze of a respirator.

And then I am back on the battle station. Vader is waiting for me in the corridor ahead, standing in silence, his lightsaber already pulsing red. He knew I was coming, that I was on board his engine of destruction. Does he know what I've done? Have all my efforts been for naught?

Why won't he say anything, as motionless as a statue? Nineteen years. Nineteen years since I left him to die. Nineteen years of reliving his corruption every night in my dreams.

What does he look like under that mask? What does he see through those ruby lenses?

A friend? An enemy?

A relic?

He appears so calm, so controlled, but I can feel his rage, seething like the perdition nebula beneath that heartless faceplate. His fury threatens to overwhelm him, just as it always did, but he keeps it in check. I can't help but be impressed. The Emperor has taught my former Padawan well. I can only imagine the poison that has spilled from Palpatine's lips since Mustafar.

Savor your hatred, my apprentice. Nurture it. Let it empower you. Let it bring you strength.

I always knew this day would come. I just didn't know where, or when. I certainly never imagined it would be in a place like this, on a planet killer the like of which the galaxy has never seen.

A million voices cry out as one, washing over me, their pain my own.

Finally, Vader steps forward to meet me. My lightsaber ignites, the vibration of the power cell rising up my arm.

"I've been waiting for you, Obi-Wan. We meet again, at last."

The voice is unrecognizable. How little of my friend is left?

Another memory assaults me. A woman lying on a bed, her breath shallow. *"There's good in him..."* Did she really believe that, after everything he had done? If she did, wouldn't she still be here? Wouldn't she have lived? What would she think of him now?

No. My friend is dead, of that I am certain. The thing is front of me is not Anakin Skywalker.

"The circle is now complete," the usurper declares, his arrogance the final betrayal. "When I left you, I was but the learner."

When I left you.

Every word is a trigger, dragging me back and forth through the years. I'm standing on loose scree, a river of molten lava churning below. Is this where you left me, Darth? Or was it even earlier: when you leapt onto a speeder bike and raced into the night, or when you held Padmé by the throat?

I feel my own anger rising, my years of training, of discipline, ebbing away. I barely hear what he's saying.

"Now *I* am the Master."

His image flickers, like a disrupted holofeed. One second, he is the armored giant I see before me, the next a charred husk reaching out on a carbonized shore. One face impassive and angular, the other blackened and screaming in agony. Then there are more, joining the fluctuating cycle. A fresh-faced teen, eager to take up the mantle of a Jedi. A spirited slave boy, pulling grime-ridden goggles over innocent eyes. A limbless wreck hanging in a bacta tank, necrotic skin pallid and scarred. I see them all at once, everything he was and everything he has become.

"Only a master of evil, Darth."

I cannot use his real name. It would undo me, even after all this time, catching in my throat. The time for talk is at an end. This must be decided once and for all.

I strike first, our lightsabers flaring as they clash. The sudden il-

339

lumination draws another shadow of Coruscant, Anakin railing against the wooden sticks I force him to use rather than energy weapons.

"I am not a child anymore, Obi-Wan. Why must we use toys?"

"You must be patient, my young Padawan. This is but the first step. We have time."

Not anymore. I sweep down and he blocks, anticipating the attack. Our blades hold, energy fields discharging as they grind against each other. I see my face distorted in the reflective surface of his helmet. Old. Tired. Nearing the end.

He's holding back, testing my limits. He wants to know how time has diminished my abilities. I'm doing the same with him, exploring whether cybernetic joints move as smoothly as muscle honed from years of training. Perhaps we are more alike than I care to think.

Now he takes control, the blows coming faster and harder. I'm forced to duck, his lightsaber tracing a gleaming line down the metal wall.

Sparks rain down and I blink, long enough for the torment to begin anew. *Eyes. Scream. Saber. Pain. Anakin. Padmé. Qui-Gon. Maul.*

I'm back on Tatooine, Neda wheezing after her exertion. It's taken so long to cross the flats, the suns now high in the sky. Not for the first time, I curse my decision to settle so far from the moisture farm. What was I thinking?

Another shift, another memory: standing at Owen's door, explaining what has happened, asking for the strangers' help.

He makes his terms abundantly clear: "We'll take him in, but you'll play no part in his upbringing. If you *have* to stay on Tatooine, you keep your distance, do you hear? You neither see the boy nor speak to him. He must know *nothing* about his father."

Neda grunts as I pull her to a stop. The farm is ahead, its dome the only landmark for kilometers around. All is as it should be. There is no evidence of blasterfire, no dark plumes of smoke billowing into the air. I allow my shoulders to relax. Perhaps I was mistaken. Perhaps Luke isn't in danger at all.

Neda grumbles, tossing her head to dislodge the sandflies that have settled in her long eyelashes. I pat her neck, calming her, scanning my eyes along the ring of environmental sensors and motion detectors that form a protective border around the boy's adopted home.

There he is, sitting cross-legged next to a moisture vaporator. He's hunched over in the sand, playing with a toy that I can't quite make out at this distance. I smile. I can guess what it is: the latest in a long line of model spaceships. I wonder if Owen knows where they come from, who it is that leaves them next to Shmi's sandblasted tombstone, for Beru to find. As I sit here, watching Luke sweep the wooden fighter through the air, I think of the toy corvette I am building in my workshop. It is almost complete. I am particularly pleased with the ion engines. My finest work yet.

Even now, at just three years old, it is obvious that Luke longs to fly. It is like seeing Anakin all over again. The mop of unruly blond hair, the bright-blue eyes, the hands permanently tinkering. Luke isn't content to just play with his toys. He's constantly at work modifying them, making improvements.

So much like his father.

"Your powers are weak, old man."

Our lightsabers clash. I try to push forward, only to be thrust violently back. It's like striking iron. There's no give in Vader's arms, and far too much in mine.

"You can't win, Darth." He barely reacts to the jibe, knowing all too well that I am aiming to provoke him, to turn his anger against himself. "If you strike me down, I shall become more powerful than you can possibly imagine."

Eyes. Scream. Saber. Pain.

341

Eyes. Scream. Saber. Pain.

Eyes. Scream. Saber. Pain.

Is this power? This torture? I am like a leaf tossed in a storm. The present and the past crashing together. I can no longer tell what is real, and what is a distant memory brought into sharp relief.

Luke is safe.

Luke is in danger.

I am on Tatooine.

I am on the battle station.

It shouldn't be like this. This is not what Yoda promised me. I am being overwhelmed. The past, the present, even the future. I see things that are not yet to be. Leia slumped beside a console, her heart breaking, Captain Solo falling so very far. Evil triumphant, and then vanquished, and then rising again.

And worst of all, Luke, as I am now, an old man, his face creased, his eyes haunted. He's cut off from those who love him, consumed by regret and sorrow. It is too much to bear, a future I never want to see.

The raucous wail of a siren snaps me back to the past. My eyes dart from Luke to the invaders who have tripped the motion detectors. They wear a hodgepodge of body armor and animal skins, their band comprising at least half a dozen different species. There has been talk of bandits operating from Mos Eisley, plundering farms and settlements in the area, leaving only devastation and grief. Why hadn't I listened to the rumors? Why didn't I intervene before it was too late?

I am a Jedi. Was a Jedi. Will be again.

Beru calls for her nephew, but there is nowhere for Luke to run. If he tries to return to the dome, he will die. If he makes for the caverns across the flats, he will die.

My other lives are forgotten in an instant; the betrayal of the past, the fight that is to come. All that matters is the here and now. Neda charges forward, my hand snatching for the lightsaber on my belt.

The blade ignites even as I launch myself from Neda's back, flipping over to land between the startled child and a towering brute wearing rancor hide.

"Run, Luke! Run!"

I can't tell if the boy heeds my words. The brute in front of me raises his blaster and I swing, easily deflecting the bolt. The farm is overrun in seconds, the marauders taking up positions both left and right. I spin, blocking blasterfire from all directions. At least I'm not alone in the defense of the farm. Owen joins the fray, battered rifle in hand. There is no time to think, only react.

A sinewy hand grabs my shoulder. I whirl, relieving my would-be attacker of his life. My lightsaber dances through the air, my surroundings changing, flickering back and forth as Vader's form shifted before. Is sand beneath my feet or the metallic deck of the battle station? The bandits advance, and Vader gains ground. I am young and I am old, I am here and I am there. I block and parry, attack and retreat. Vader is too strong, the bandits too numerous. The fight is against me twice over.

Vader feints to the left, and I turn, only to receive a vibro-mace to my chest. I skid along the sand as a gigantic Gamorrean boar lumbers toward me, his blunt weapon raised and ready to strike.

Before I can even respond, something small and fragile smacks against the Gamorrean's flattened snout. The bemused thug hesitates, long enough for my blade to separate his feet from his ankles. I roll out of the way as the squealing boar crashes down where I lay, something sharp jabbing into my side. It is the fragments of the toy starfighter that had been tossed at the Gamorrean's head. Luke grabs my hand, attempting to haul me up. He has saved my life, this remarkable child.

"Luke!" Owen yells from across the settlement. "Get away!"

I leap back to my feet, rejoining the fight, which is now ours to win. The tide has turned and the bandits are diminished one by one, decimated by blasterfire and plasma blade. As my last opponent cools at my feet, Luke cries out a warning. A Devaronian has reared up behind Owen, ready to bring the butt of his blaster down on the unsuspecting farmer's head. I pull back my arm and throw my lightsaber with all my might. The blade pinwheels through the air, finding its mark. The Devaronian drops, his body split in two. I reach out with the Force, extinguishing the lightsaber before drawing the hilt back to my open palm.

Luke cheers, running full pelt toward me, arms as wide as his smile. There is a crunch behind me and I turn, Owen's fist burying itself in my nose. I slam down hard onto the ground, the lightsaber skittering from my hand. All my training, all my experience, and a humble moisture farmer has achieved what neither battle droid nor Sith has achieved, knocking me flat on my back.

"Uncle Owen!" Luke cries in confusion as his uncle manhandles the boy toward his aunt before turning to glower at me.

"Go," he all but spits, an accusatory finger punctuating the furious decree. "Get away from here. Haven't you people done enough to this family?"

"Done enough?" I splutter, gingerly inspecting my throbbing nose for signs of blood. "I'm not sure if you noticed, but I was *trying* to protect you."

"We don't need your protection. We don't need you at all. I could have handled this alone. I always have, and I always will."

"Owen, please . . ."

And I'm staring down the barrel of his rifle. I have no idea how much energy remains in the power pack, and have no urge to find out.

"I saw him," Owen hisses through gritted teeth. "He tried to save you."

My eyes flick to Luke, now safe in Beru's arms. "He's a brave boy."

"He could have been killed!"

I open my mouth, but no words come.

Breathing heavily, Owens lowers his blaster and turns his back on me. "I will protect him," he tells me as he walks away. "*I* will keep him safe."

I look past Owen's back. Beru catches my eye and shakes her head sadly. She ushers Luke back to the dome, Owen stalking after them. Luke glances back for a moment, before all three vanish from sight. I'm left alone with the dead, the twin suns beating down on me.

Eyes. Scream. Saber. Pain.

Eyes. Scream. Saber. Pain.

I know why I'm here, why I'm reliving this moment time and time again. This was when I failed Luke, just as I failed his father. I'd always believed—always hoped—that Owen's anger would cool toward me, that one day I would be allowed to train young Luke in the ways of the Force. The events of this fateful morning meant that Owen never let me near the boy again. He hadn't just been angry. He'd been scared; scared of the look we'd both seen in his nephew's eyes. The bravery. The *defiance*.

We'd seen that look before, in other eyes.

"You should not have come back," Vader tells me.

My resources are depleted, my body screaming with pain. I have no hope of winning this fight. He lunges at me; slash and counter-slash, stab and riposte. The air is thick with plasma discharge, lights dancing on the edge of my vision. I'm forced back, muscles burning, breath ragged. The grip of my lightsaber is slick in my hands, my ears ringing.

Luke is near. I can feel him, and pray that Vader cannot. I have so much to teach the boy. So much to share. *Why* did I listen to Owen? *Why* did I wait too long?

Haven't you people done enough to this family?

Now it's too late. There's no way to prepare Luke for what is to come. I'm leaving him with who? A smuggler and a Wookiee? Even if by some miracle they've found Leia, what can they do? They're barely more than children. The Rebellion isn't prepared for a weapon of this magnitude. No one is. And it's all my fault.

I have failed Luke again. I can't hold on. It is over.

Unless . . .

"Ben?"

Luke's cry echoes across the landing bay. There he is, watching us fight, the open hatch of the freighter behind him. He knows full well that I cannot win. He is frozen with shock, unsure what to do, but that won't last long. Soon, the spell will be broken and he will come running. Those brave, defiant eyes will be cut down in a blaze of trooper fire. He needs more than a toy fighter this time. He needs to escape; to save himself, not me.

Go to him.

The voice in my head is louder than it has been for years.

Yes, Master.

I am an old man. Even if I tried, I couldn't outrun a blaster shot, not anymore. I'll never make it to Luke's side in time to save him.

This is where we came in.

I am Obi-Wan Kenobi, and I am dead.

I glance back at Vader and smile. I can't even begin to imagine what he makes of that. It doesn't matter anymore. All that matters is Luke.

I straighten my back, closing my eyes as I raise my saber in front of me. I don't see the blade sweeping through the air, barely even hear its whine. I imagine Luke, cross-legged in the sand, playing with a wooden corvette.

Eyes. Scream. Saber. Pain.

Eyes. Scream. Saber. Pain.

Eyes. Scream. Saber. Pain.

"Ben! No!"

Luke cries out again, consumed with grief. I see everything at once. The blaster in his hand. Solo taking out stormtroopers. Leia calling his name. The troopers advance, guns raised. If Luke stays, he will die. If he fights, he will die.

I didn't let that happen before, and I won't let it happen now. I whisper the words I spoke when he was a child, words I know that only he will hear.

Run, Luke! Run!

And he does. Luke Skywalker runs and doesn't stop. And I am at his side. From this moment, he will never be alone. He will learn, and he will grow, and I will guide him every step of the way.

We have all the time we need.

THERE IS ANOTHER

Gary D. Schmidt

Yoda stood at the door of his hut, watching the straight streaks of sunlight tear apart the gathered gray of the sky.

He turned and looked inside.

Then back to the sky.

It was time. Probably past time. The rains had ended more than half an orbit before. Soon the sun would bear down upon Dagobah and the uplands would be too hot for even a small one like himself to bear. He had maybe a few days. Maybe less.

He sighed. Of the two seasons on Dagobah, the dry was the one he preferred. The view from the uplands reminded him of . . . a time and place from long ago. But by now the lower lands would have drained some, and the trees would have begun to emerge from their watery covering. It would soon be time to plant in the soggy reaches.

Planting was a bother, but even a Jedi Master needs to eat.

He looked back inside his hut again. *Age,* he thought, *has its advantages. More and more want the young, but less and less need the old.* He had felt this lessening over the last two centuries. He had sloughed off almost everything now—except those things dearest to him.

His cane, begun as a joke really, to convince the young Padawans that he was only an old and feeble Jedi. He would hobble to the class and they would make way for their limping Master. Then he would cast his cane aside and slice open the air with his lightsaber and they would gasp to see such an old and tired Master ripple with the strength and quickness of the Force. And when his lesson was over, he would take up his cane again and stump away—but they were not sure what to believe. Did he need the cane or not?

Now they would believe it.

350

And the blanket on his bed, made from his old friend's cloak. How long had it been since Qui-Gon Jinn had become one with the Force? He went back inside and fingered the hem. Sometimes, one strong in the Force might leave a hint of himself in what he had owned, but now, so many years had gone by. If Yoda had felt the hint once, he felt it no longer.

And on the shelf above the bed, Obi-Wan's small pot, rounded by his own hands. Yoda reached up and called the pot to him. Its handle was cold.

That was all, really. Once he had treasured his lightsaber, but that was lost in the ruins of the Senate chamber. He regretted that. It would have pleased him to have put the weapon into young Skywalker's hands. He imagined her feeling its weight, and then suddenly she would be surprised at the beam that leapt out.

But she knew nothing of the Force and its ways. She had had no one to teach her.

That, thought Yoda, was possibly a mistake.

Still, he smiled. If the old needed less and less in this physical world, perhaps it was because they dwelled so much in the world of memory and the world of what might have been. There was little he loved to dwell upon more than the thought of young Skywalker coming into herself, learning of the powers that lay deep within her, and perhaps bringing to the galaxy a new age that she could not even hope to imagine.

But how could she? Who she was, she did not know!

It had been so many orbits since he had been a Master to a Padawan. But sometimes, he wished . . .

The hut was growing warm. It was time to pack what little there was to pack, and to move downward and away from the sun's hot breath.

It did not take long. He stuffed what he had into a sack: a pouch of seeds gathered over the years, then the blanket, then the pot on top of that. He picked up his cane and stood at the door a moment, looking one last time at the hut he would not see for eight orbits, and then he closed his eyes and reached out to check for the droids that had once searched so pitilessly for him. He still checked whenever he left the hut, but it had been a long, very long, time since the last droid had swept past. Perhaps the Empire thought he was long dead and had ceased searching. Or, more likely, the Empire did not even care, so unimportant one ancient Jedi Master had become.

He sighed again. Maybe the Empire was right. About how unimportant he had become, that was.

He started down toward the lowlands. Already many of the trees had leafed out, even though some still stood with their feet in the green and thick water. But they wouldn't be standing in water for long. Yoda could see the water receding under the sun's glare like something afraid of the light. Soon, the lowlands would all be marshy swamp again, and he would plant last season's seeds. Then, before the sun began its long journey away, they would sprout. The gray clouds would come back and hold in the planet's humid air, and the sprouts would grow and flower and yield their fruit before a quarter orbit had passed. And by then the sun would be far enough away that the rains would plunge down again, and the floods begin their inundation, and Yoda would trudge back to the uplands, carting behind him the food for the long season.

He could hear the voices of his Padawans from long ago: "What is it like to live the life of a Jedi Master?" they would ask.

If only they could see him now, he thought.

He brushed his hand across his eyes.

If only they could.

But there are worse things than Dagobah.

For much of the day, he trudged down toward the lowlands, the sand and rock beneath him growing warmer and warmer until he came to the edge of the planetary floods, where the water had barely sunk beneath the surface.

Then, he felt something on the very edge of his reach.

And he was out in the open.

This is what comes of not keeping your mind on where you are and what you are doing!

Thumping along with his cane, he headed toward the shelter of three upended rocks that might survive a blast, maybe two.

Nearly nine hundred years, and still he wanted more time. Foolish, Yoda thought.

But if he had more time, he would wish that he could have trained one more Padawan. If only he'd had the time to train *her*.

He reached the rocks, and then he stopped.

He felt it again.

It wasn't a droid. Nor was it one of the Empire's ships.

He reached out again.

It wasn't even for him.

And then it shifted, and it *was* for him. That old and familiar thrum the Force carried on its back, a steady vibration, calm—not the calm of a still night, but the calm of the sea that rose and fell with sureness and ease.

It was Obi-Wan.

Yoda leaned against the stones and smiled. Their exile had been too long and too lonely. But had the two of them remained together, the Empire would surely have found them. And there was the other Skywalker to watch over—impetuous, headstrong, unruly, inattentive. He needed Obi-Wan's eye on him. Unlike the other, whose strength and will and clarity showed all the markings of a great Jedi.

Still, as the vibration pulsed against him, Yoda felt loneliness grow. It was at least something to feel Obi-Wan's place in the Force, but how good it would be to sit down and talk together, to walk under the stars, perhaps to spar once again—that would be a delight he almost could not bear thinking about.

And then, another vibration came—and this one, too, was familiar. This one was hard and strong, and it pulsed fiercely. In its rhythm it carried . . . arrogance. In its rhythm, it carried darkness.

And in its rhythm, it carried—this was the first that Yoda had ever noticed it—a terrible, angry, despairing loneliness.

Loneliness!

It was Anakin . . . or what had become of him. And he was in pain. And the remedy he used to soothe himself was pain—the pain of both others and himself. Yoda brought his hand to the center of his chest.

Then the two vibrations met, and their pulses fought across the back of the Force.

And that was when the searching droid suddenly came up from the lowlands, hovering over the sand, moving quickly above the flood line.

How could he not have sensed it?

Automatically Yoda's hand dropped the cane and went to his belt, but no lightsaber had hung there for a very long time. The bulbous eye of the droid was still turned away, but it would not be so for long. Its thermal sensors would pick up even his small body, especially as its heat reflected off the rock. Slowly he let down his sack and rummaged inside. Obi-Wan's small pot, cool to the touch. He rubbed his hand across its side and sensed his Padawan—one last time. Then he slowly set the pot on the ground.

The thermal sensor of the droid flashed from blue to red. Its bulbous eye began to swivel his way.

Yoda closed his eyes and felt the Force flowing beside him, flowing into the rock, flowing around Obi-Wan's small pot, and flowing into the sand beneath his feet—the sand, which rose up as Yoda raised his arms, and then flung itself at the droid as if in a fierce wind, and swirled around it in a blinding storm.

And then Yoda raised his right arm even higher. He paused for a moment, then lowered his arm toward the droid, and Obi-Wan's pot flew through the swirl of sand and into the bulbous eye, shattering it in a rush of sparks.

The explosion that came next was expected. These droids always had a self-destruct mechanism to use once damaged.

The cries from the swamps below were loud and long. Explosions were unusual in the Dagobah system. Even from this far away, Yoda could hear the scurrying of small feet and the fluty flutterings of reptilian wings, and they lasted longer than it took the pieces of the droid, large and small, to fall from the sky.

Yoda picked up his cane and went to what remained. The pot was gone—disintegrated, no doubt.

And it was right at that moment—at that exact moment—that Yoda felt Obi-Wan grow suddenly stronger, and stronger, and stronger, and then move in a quick burst into the netherworld of the Force.

And Yoda felt Anakin fall even more deeply into painful loneliness—a loneliness so terrible that Yoda almost felt pity for him. He almost wished he could speak to him, to tell him that he needn't be lonely after all. There were . . .

Yoda looked down at the ground, and there was the handle of the shattered pot; somehow it had survived. But Obi-Wan was gone from this world. Yoda felt himself lower to the ground.

Obi-Wan.

And Anakin. If only what had happened to Anakin had not been shadowed and hidden from them all . . . No. That was not true. If only he had perceived the paths that Anakin was beginning to follow. It was his own failing. That was why it would have been so important for him to train the young Skywalker. What might she have done to bring her father back?

And to this disappointment, now, Obi-Wan gone from this world. What did this mean for that other Skywalker, whose impatience and anger were terrible weaknesses?

Obi-Wan.

For Yoda, the galaxy was so rapidly becoming emptier and emptier.

Perhaps that was why he did not sense the two new droids until they were almost upon him, drawn by the obliteration of their comrade.

Again he reached automatically for his lightsaber, and almost smiled when his hand touched nothing. For just a moment he felt how good it once was to fight with another Jedi at his back, to feel the Force binding them together, to feel their wills in one accord.

Then, Yoda looked at the two droids rushing upon him, their eyes upon him, their sensors trained toward him, their devices whirring with the robotic pleasure of fulfilling a mission.

He was old.

He raised his hand to . . .

A shot, and lightning ripped the air over his shoulder, struck the rock behind him, and bounced back into the sack, which burst into immediate flame.

His blanket! Qui-Gon's cloak!

Yoda reached to the air around the two droids and pulled it closed like a curtain.

The glass of their eyes burst, the old metal bodies crumpled into each other, the droids fell into a smoking heap—and Yoda quickly stamped out the flames and pulled the blanket from the sack.

Singed, but not too badly.

He reached in again. The pouch of seeds was unharmed.

He felt Qui-Gon laughing at him, all the way from the nether-world of the Force.

He would have to keep his mind on where he was—and that is what he did the rest of that day.

He buried the droids. He probably did not need to, but it was best to be safe.

356

He wrapped the seeds in the blanket and tied the ends tightly together.

He reached out carefully—this time very, very carefully—and felt the atmosphere around the planet. No more droids.

He held back the loneliness. He held back a galaxy without Obi-Wan.

Down, down the hills and into the lowlands he went, the ground becoming wetter and wetter, spongy under his feet—which, he had to admit, felt cool and soothing after all the orbits of sand and rock. He came into the trees, the weeds still draining from their branches, and he heard the voices of all those who had spent the wet season hibernating beneath the waters, now coughing open their lungs to allow air in again, and stretching their wings and flapping them to dry. He would have to be sure to bury his seeds deeply and cover their scent with the springy moss.

He found his lowland house easily. It, too, had survived its hibernation beneath the water, and it looked, for the most part, undamaged. Dripping and green with mold, as always—but, he laughed, so was he. And the walls he could clean. Inside, the floors had drained; they would be dry within a day or two. The bunk was soaked through, of course, but a fire would soon set things right. It would not take long at all to resume life in the lowlands.

And he was right; it did not.

Five days later, the house was dry and tight, a fire burning brightly in its hearth. He had trimmed the blanket; he was getting smaller and smaller anyway. But the shelf where he had always set the pot was empty, and every time he looked at it, he felt a stillness where he had once felt vibration, and he remembered.

And he whispered to himself, "Mourn them do not. Miss them do not. Rejoice for those who transform into the Force."

But he was lonely.

"Train yourself to let go of everything you fear to lose."

But he was lonely, and old.

And he had failed.

He had not seen the paths the young Padawan Anakin had begun to take.

He had missed his chance with the young Skywalker.

And what would happen with this other, reckless Skywalker? The one who was as angry as his father had been?

The next few days, when he planted the seeds, he planted them deeply, thrusting them into the damp and soft ground with his cane, so deep they might not come up again. But he gathered the moss from the branches and covered the plot, and when he had finished, it looked as if nothing at all had been planted there, as if nothing would come up from all that effort.

Nothing at all.

Nothing at all.

Nothing at all.

The night he finished, Yoda sat in front of his fire, and he was lonely.

And he missed, more than he could say, old friends now gone.

So he reached out across the netherworld of the Force for Qui-Gon, but he could not sense him. He reached again, and again, but there was no reply.

"Qui-Gon is occupied, Master Yoda," said Obi-Wan.

Yoda looked up, though he hardly needed to. He suddenly felt the hut so full of . . . life. So full of Obi-Wan, who sat cross-legged inside the doorway, shimmering.

"Never before so quietly have you come into a room, Master Kenobi."

Obi-Wan nodded his shining head. "I find I have developed several new . . . skills, of late."

"An entry into the world of the Force it would take for you to develop this one."

"As you say, Master."

Yoda crossed the room and sat down on his bunk. It was no longer as damp as it had been. "I am old, Master Kenobi."

"Nine hundred years is old," he agreed.

"And worn out."

"Not so worn out as you might think, Master. Where is my pot?"

Yoda looked up at the empty shelf. "There was an encounter," he said.

"An encounter? Not so difficult an encounter that you were unable to preserve Qui-Gon's cloak, I see."

"Always with you it has to be both. Difficult choices must we sometimes make in this world."

"As now, Master."

"Here you are for that?"

"Master, I want you to take on a new Padawan."

"You do, do you?"

"I want you to train young Skywalker."

Yoda felt his heart thrill. He had not imagined it could have happened, but here it was. "Yes."

"You agree so quickly?"

"Long have I wanted to train her."

"Master, I want you to train Luke."

Yoda looked at the shimmering face. "No," he said. He stamped his cane on the floor. "That is not the one. Not ready is he."

"Who is ever ready?"

"Not that one. A Jedi must have the deepest commitment. That one looks from one cloud to another. A Jedi must have the most serious mind. That one cannot keep his mind from his speeder. Not him. Her."

"Master."

"He will not finish what he begins. He is reckless."

"Master."

"And well we know the path a reckless one will set his foot."

The shimmering Obi-Wan sat down on the bunk beside his old Master.

"This is damp," said Obi-Wan.

"Bother you does dampness still, Master Kenobi?"

"You will be surprised, Master."

"For one nine hundred years old, no more surprises are there."

Obi-Wan smiled. "I promise you, Master, you will be surprised."

"Humph," said Yoda. He lay down on his bed and pulled the blanket up around him. "Already come the time is to be with you. Already come the time is to become one with the Force."

Obi-Wan shook his head. "Not yet," he said.

"And to tell me this, you are the one?"

Obi-Wan spread his arms wide, almost as if he would embrace his old Master. "I am the one to tell you this," he said.

"Impertinent still."

"Yes, Master."

A long silence.

"The other Skywalker I would train. She is ready."

Obi-Wan shook his head again.

"Oh, demanding now we have become, have we?" said Yoda.

"Forgive me, Master."

"And if I try to teach this rash, this impatient, this mindless boy the ways of the Force and fail, what then?"

Obi-Wan smiled. "I seem to remember an old Master of mine who liked to say something about trying."

"Humph," said Yoda, and drew the blanket up closer. He closed his eyes, and Obi-Wan waited.

"Send him to me then," said Yoda, in a voice quiet as a whisper.

Obi-Wan tucked the blanket under Yoda's chin.

"And Obi-Wan?"

"Yes, Master."

"Sorry about the pot, I am."

"It was old and ugly."

Yoda opened his eyes. "So am I."

"No, Master."

"Look, Master Kenobi. Look. Old and ugly. What see you?"

Obi-Wan leaned down close. "A luminous being," he said.

"Humph," said Yoda, and closed his eyes again. "Annoying, one's own words to use against him. A bad feeling I have about that."

But Obi-Wan was already gone.

Yoda nestled deeply into Qui-Gon Jinn's cloak. He would sleep now. At least, he would try to sleep.

His eyes opened.

He probably would not sleep.

It was not what he had wished for. Not at all. Still, for the first time in a long time, he was eager for the next day.

PALPATINE

Ian Doescher

*Enter EMPEROR PALPATINE, having received news from DARTH
VADER of OBI-WAN KENOBI's death.*

PALPATINE

Communication hath just been receiv'd,

E'en better than my fantasies conceiv'd.

Darth Vader—my apprentice and my tool,

Th'intimidating fist by which I rule—

Hath told me of Kenobi's swift demise,

Which news hath struck me with profound surprise.

Upon the Death Star, th'Empire's latest threat,

The battle was borne out, the old foes met:

Kenobi—feeble, elderly, and weak—

Hath dar'd his former Padawan to seek.

The two men met, and clash'd like fire and ice,

Darth Vader, though, hath triumph'd in a trice.

A few quick parries of his saber red,

And old Kenobi fell—now air, now dead.

Our troopers now report 'twas Tatooine

Whereon Kenobi hid unfound, unseen,

And lo these years hath liv'd in mystery,

Whilst I, the Emperor, made history.

Why Tatooine? And wherefore there so long?

What are the notes that form'd Kenobi's song?

What melody was it whereat he play'd?

Why in those measures hath he so long stay'd?

Was he designing his own instrument?

And wherefore were his rests so prominent?

His death should fill an Emperor with glee,

Forsooth, my heart should soar inside of me,

Yet there is that which plagueth still my mind—

Yea, questions to these answers I would find.

For instance, there is this that still perplexes—

A riddle that, with obfuscation, vexes.

Darth Vader saith that at the very time—

The second when he hath perform'd the crime,

When his lightsaber struck Kenobi's robe—

The Jedi's body vanish'd from the globe.

Not slain, precisely, nay, but disappear'd,

Which is enough to make e'en me afeard.

Then, too, there are the final words of his,

Which Vader hath convey'd as 'twere a quiz:

"If thou dost strike me down, e'en now, e'en here,

I shall more great and powerful appear

Than e'er thou hast imagin'd possible"—

These words are each like needles in my skull.

Is this a simple lie, or Jedi trick?

Is this the Force's might? Have I been thick?

Is there aught that can make Kenobi live?

Is there relief that logic yet can give?

And even if Kenobi's dead and gone,

Another worry still comes hard upon:

Although this wretched Jedi is destroy'd,

By Yoda is mine intellect annoy'd:

Where hath the errant, verdant coward fled?

Somewhere within the galaxy his head

Doth wait to meet an Emperor's dark rage—

Unless the weakling hath expir'd from age.

If Yoda and Kenobi were alive,

And somehow did our Jedi purge survive,

What else exists of which we're unaware?
What threat shall come, by land or sea or air?
I would be certain of our dominance,
I would have proof of mine own prominence.
For surety I'd give the universe,
Yet questions dog me, like a witch's curse.
The answers to these things are still unknown,
And doubts within my brain make endless drone
With mocking voice that speaketh, "Palpatine,
Couldst thou not wipe thy rivals from the scene?"
Kenobi's death, then, gives but poor release,
Since worries do pursue me sans surcease.
These matters shake me, though I should rejoice,
Thus, hear the proclamation of my voice:
This moment marks a time that I shall savor—
From now, the Empire's power ne'er shall waver,
Today begins an era of resolve,
As fully unto darkness we evolve.
No slip of our foul purpose shall we know,
No misstep shall e'er threaten to o'erthrow,
No hidden Jedi plot shall give us pause,
No vile uncertainty shall stay our cause,
No mercy tolerated in our ranks,
No weakness found within our data banks:
Henceforth the Empire shall not be assail'd,

PALPATINE

Impervious we'll be, no fault unveil'd.

A vulnerable realm's a dying breed;

This shall not be the Empire's fate, indeed.

I shall have full control, whatever come,

And strike mine enemies both deaf and dumb.

It starteth with the end of the Rebellion,

Wherein I am the reaper, Darth my hellion.

The Death Star, fully operational,

Shall wallop with a might sensational.

Lord Vader's cunning found the rebel base;

Anon he'll bring destruction on the place.

By th'Death Star shall the rogues be apprehended,

Its list of massacres shall be extended:

'Twas Jedha, Scarif, and then Alderaan,

Next Yavin 4, with rebels found thereon.

This triumph cannot happen soon enow—

Brought to its knees, the galaxy shall bow.

Come, Death, and let the rebels know thy might:

Thou ever wert our ally in a fight,

Thou art the rider, th'Empire is thy horse,

Thou showest all the dark side of the Force,

Thou art our strength, our talisman, our sign,

Thou art supreme, and thy full strength is mine.

I'll wield thee swiftly on the rebel gang,

And bring on them their life-concluding pang.

This news of Vader's spurs me onward still:

Kenobi first, and by my iron will

The rebels and the galaxy entire

Shall call me Emperor or see their pyre.

Go, Palpatine, release thine awful dread,

Until each filthy rebel knave is dead.

Exit.

SPARKS

Paul S. Kemp

Dex sat on the side of his bunk, elbows on his knees, staring at nothing, but thinking about everything. His past stretched out behind him, a line of events much longer than the future he saw remaining before him.

The Empire was coming, its power projected by way of a moon-sized battle station that had already destroyed more than one planet and murdered billions. Billions. Everyone knew someone who knew someone who'd been on Alderaan, or Scarif, or Jedha. Dex had even been to Alderaan once with his parents, years before the Republic had transformed into the Empire.

Thinking of the people there, their lives obliterated in an instant of fire and pain, at once enraged and afflicted him. It was an atrocity, and he wanted the Empire to answer for it.

But he wasn't naïve. Whatever answer the Rebel Alliance would force from the Empire in just a few hours would be . . . likely futile. He knew how things would probably end. Seemed to him their choices were to run from Yavin's moon and live—maybe—or to stay and fight and die.

And no one was running.

Not one person. Not anymore.

Alderaan had put a fierce resolve in everyone, from support troops to pilots. They were done running.

True, rumors swirled among the flight crews that Princess Organa had returned with some kind of secret intelligence about the Empire, but Dex didn't see how mere intelligence could help. The battle with the Death Star would come down to a test of flesh and metal. And the Empire had much more of both. The remaining Alliance forces on Yavin 4 were a ragtag collection of starfighters and light cruisers—almost no capital ships had survived the battle at Scarif. Together, all their soldiers couldn't even operate a fraction of the Death Star.

But even so, no one was running. Not one person.

You fly your run and hit what you can—that was Gold Squadron's credo. Dex had internalized it long ago. He'd fly his damn run, come what may.

And he had his own credo, too, one based on something his mother had often said. "Small sparks can start big fires."

Thinking of his mom chased his inner darkness and made him smile. In his mind's eye, he could see her in one of the simple dresses she favored, gray hair in a bun, her crooked front teeth exposed in a smile.

He took a deep breath, blew it out, fiddled with his flight suit, and tried to square away his mental state. He checked the chrono. They had hours, a bit less, and then he'd fly his Y-wing at an enormous sphere of steel and weapons and do what he could.

You fly your run.

Small sparks.

An interrogatory chirp brought him back to the present. He smiled at the battle-scarred R5 unit that had been with him since his run over Corellia. He'd nicknamed the droid Sparks.

"I was just thinking, Sparks. That's all."

A sympathetic purr from Sparks. More beeps with a question mark at the end.

"Oh, about lots of things. Mostly about my mom and dad and Onderon. I haven't seen them in . . . a long time. And my little sister, she'd be twelve now. Twelve." He shook his head. Time had passed so quickly, and now he had so little left.

Sparks wheeled closer, hummed in sympathy.

"Did I ever tell you what my mom used to say about small sparks? That's why I named you Sparks. Well, that and the fire you started on Utapau's moon. Remember?"

An embarrassed moan and shudder from Sparks.

Dex smiled, patted the droid on his head, and lied. "Listen, things are gonna be fine."

Spark's ambivalent beeps suggested that he saw through the words to the truth.

"We'll do what we can, right? We make our run."

Sparks perked up, beeped enthusiastically.

"And hit what we can," Dex said. "Right."

In hindsight, he realized that his mother's phrase was the through-line of his life. It had played through his mind when he'd joined the Rebellion, had sustained him through dark times. He'd joined knowing that things looked bleak, but he'd always fancied himself a spark, always imagined himself starting the big fire.

But it appeared not. Instead it looked like things would end on a backwater moon.

A voice carried over the station's intercom.

"The Imperial space station has entered the system. Report to your stations. Flight crews to the—"

A long pause. The usual end to that sentence would have been . . . *to the launch bay.* After all, they'd already had their mission briefing.

A crackle on the intercom. "All flight crews report immediately to the main briefing room."

Sparks whirred an observation.

Dex stood. "Agreed that it's odd. I'll go see what's what. See you at the ship."

The briefing room, filled with pilots and flight crew, fell silent as General Dodonna spoke, his tone as somber as a eulogist's.

370

Dex leaned in closer as the schematics of the Death Star appeared on the briefing room screen. General Dodonna explained its weakness—a tiny exhaust port at the end of a narrow trench. Someone would have to put a proton torpedo directly in it at precisely the right angle of approach.

A few audible gasps answered the declaration, several head shakes, a pervading sense of despondency. Someone across the room said the shot couldn't be made. Someone else—a voice Dex did not recognize—responded by saying something about shooting womp rats on Tatooine.

Dex filtered it out. He'd already committed the details of the briefing to memory. He knew the shot could be made. And he figured he was just the pilot to make it.

He could see the exhaust in his mind, as vivid as a picture. Dodonna's words hadn't increased his despondency; they'd dispelled it. He felt hopeful for the first time in several days.

Small sparks, he thought. And big fires.

They filed out of the briefing room and hustled for the flight deck, where ground crew and droids readied the fleet of X-wings and Y-wings. Dex hurried to his fighter. Sparks was already being lifted toward his socket. The droid chirped and whirred a melody as Dex climbed into his cockpit and started a system check. He felt like he was floating, already flying, already dropping a torpedo down the bunghole of that Imperial station and saving the Rebellion.

Davish called up from the flight deck. He was in his flight suit, his helmet in his right hand, the standard grin pasted on his timeworn face. "You gonna be a hero today, Dex?"

Dex smiled down. "Gotta be someone, Davish."

"I suppose it does," Davish said.

"I'll see you up there."

"Right behind you," Davish said and hurried toward his ship.

Dex went through his preflight checklist quickly, saw that all was in order. Sparks beeped the okay. The ground crew signaled that he was clear to go. He engaged the antigrav and lifted off the pad.

"Let's get up there, Sparks," he said.

The droid whistled eager agreement.

371

Dex broke atmo and the blue gave way to the black. Sparks ran through a quick instrument and weapons check, beeped that all was in order. He followed that with a whirred query about Dex's vital signs.

"No, I'm fine," Dex told the droid. He was just giddy. He'd gone from hopeless to hopeful so quickly he was still spinning from it. He took a few deep, calming breaths, brought himself down and found his focus.

"On me, Gold Squadron," said Gold Leader over the comm.

Affirmatives around.

The squad fell into attack formation, Dex on the starboard end of the V-pattern. Through the cockpit glass, he saw Red and Green squadrons' X-wings in formation to his right, slightly lagging Gold's lead. They sped around and away from the moon, the usual banter carrying across the comms.

As the Death Star came into view, the comm chatter fell silent, quieted by the enormity of the station. Even from a distance, Dex could see the differentiated structures all over the station's surface, the huge convex disk that he knew served to focus the station's planet-busting weapon. He went over the broad strokes of the attack in his mind: first the turbolasers, then the deflector stations, then Gold and Red would take the trench by turn.

"No support craft," he said.

"Not yet," said Davish. "We get to eat some turbolasers first."

Gold Leader's stern voice crackled through the comm. "Less chatter and more focus. You know your jobs. Do them."

"We fly our run," Dex said.

"And hit what we can," Davish answered.

The station grew in size as they sped toward it, until it filled Dex's field of view. Sparks scanned the station, fed pertinent information to Dex's heads-up display. Dex noted the location of the turbolasers.

"Accelerate to attack speed," said Gold Leader.

Dex fired his engines. "Deflectors at full, Sparks. Here we go."

As they closed on the Death Star, turbolasers swung toward them and painted red lines across space. Dex pulled hard on the stick, rose, spun a circle, shoved it down, and opened up with his weapons. The Y-wing's cannons sprayed the surface of the Death Star and birthed plumes of flame. He jerked hard right, locked on to a turbolaser turret, fired, and watched it explode. Pulling back on the stick, he shot high over the surface of the battle station, chased by laserfire. He glanced down, saw the rest of Gold and Red squadrons darting over the surface of the station. The turbolasers—designed as they were to defend the station against capital ships rather than fighters—had trouble tracking the elusive X- and Y-wings.

"Find me something else to blow up, Sparks," he said, and the droid fed him the coordinates for a deflector tower.

He slammed the stick down and closed on the tower, flying straight into a spray of fire from a turbolaser. He spun the ship, dancing between the ionized lines, while Sparks whooped. He sprayed the turbolaser with his cannons, took it out, and turned hard at the deflector tower. He locked on, fired, and watched it blossom into flame.

"Nice shot, Gold Two," said Davish.

"Someone's gotta be a hero," Dex answered.

He pulled up, went high, and noticed that the turbolasers had stopped firing. They could not have destroyed them all so fast, so that could mean only one thing.

Gold Leader's voice affirmed his thinking. "Fighters incoming. Gold Two and Five on me for the trench. The rest of the squad, engage the TIEs. Hold them off."

"Active scan, Sparks," Dex said, wheeling his Y-wing in beside Gold Leader and Davish. "Let me know if we get any attention from the TIEs."

Sparks beeped agreement. Below them, elements of Red squadron engaged with the TIEs that had poured out of the station's launch bays.

"It'll be tight in the trench," Gold Leader said. "Hold formation whatever comes. I lead. You two lagging on my nacelles. Copy?"

"Copy," Davish and Dex said in sequence.

A few moments of quiet, then Gold Leader said, "We go."

The three Y-wings streaked toward the trench. Dex's vision distilled down to the dark line of it, a gash crosscutting the battle station. In his mind, he pictured the exhaust port at its end. They needed to fly in the trench to allow their targeting computers to properly calculate the shot.

"All systems square, Sparks?"

The droid beeped an affirmative.

The three Y-wings swooped down into the shadowed trench, Dex and Davish right behind Gold Leader's engine nacelles. The flying felt claustrophobic. The sides of the trench were a blur, whipping past at a dizzying speed. Dex kept his eyes forward and on his instruments so as not to get disoriented.

The distance to the exhaust port showed as a countdown on his heads-up. They were getting close.

Small sparks, he thought. Small sparks.

Sparks beeped a warning a moment before Gold Leader said, "They're coming in! Three marks at two ten."

The scanner showed TIEs in the trench behind them, closing fast. Dex compared their closing speed with the remaining distance to the exhaust port.

It would be close.

"Engines at full," Gold Leader said. "And hold formation, damn it."

Sparks adjusted power settings, increasing the engine's output, and the Y-wing accelerated.

"Rear deflectors at full," Dex said, and Sparks redirected power. Dex was sweating under his flight suit, his breath coming fast, white-knuckling the stick. The narrowness of the trench gave him no room to maneuver. He stared at the display that showed the approaching exhaust port. He was just waiting for his targeting computer to affirm a lock.

Almost there. Almost.

Come on. Come on.

A shot from one of the TIEs struck the side of the trench, exploded, and the blast wave wobbled Dex's Y-wing. He scraped the side of the trench wall but straightened up.

"I'm good," he said. "I'm good."

374

The TIEs had closed faster than expected. He checked the heads-up again. So close.

"Hold formation," Gold Leader said, his normally emotionless voice tight with tension. "Wobble as best you can but do not break off."

There was no real room to wobble the craft, though, not without risking a collision. They'd just have to rely on their deflectors. They were nearly to the port.

"Everything we have to the rear deflectors, Sparks."

More shots from the TIEs put red lines over his cockpit.

Almost there.

His ship shook with a sudden impact, as if kicked from behind. Sirens screamed, the depressurization warning. Sparks beeped in alarm.

"I'm hit," Dex said, calmer than he would have expected. "Deflector down. I'm holding formation. I'm holding."

Smoke leaked from his control panel, sparks sizzling from an electrical short somewhere deep in the electronics. The stick felt heavy in his hand, unresponsive. He found it hard to breathe.

The ship lurched again and the pressure wave from an explosion in the rear caused him to see sparks. Sparks let out an alarmed squeal that cut short.

Dex flashed on his mom, her smile, his dad and his mustache, his sister's giggle.

Someone had to be the hero. Someone had to be—

A flash of orange, a brief moment of searing heat, a roar in his ears, as much felt as heard, then nothing more.

375

DUTY ROSTER

Jason Fry

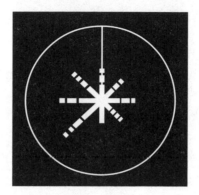

"**Y**ou know I hate that nickname," Col said.

He knew immediately that he'd made another mistake—Puck Naeco was immune to fear and disinclined to mercy, whether behind the stick of a T-65 starfighter or killing time in the ready room deep within Yavin 4's Massassi temple.

A corner of Puck's mouth twitched upward. As had happened too many times in simulations, Col had let the older pilot maneuver him into position for the kill shot.

Two other pilots, John D. Branon and Theron Nett, exchanged an amused glance.

"What have I told you about taking the bait?" Puck asked Col.

Col sighed. "Not to."

"And what did you just do?"

"Took the bait. Can't you think of something else, though? I mean, we don't even look alike."

"You do to me," rumbled the Mon Calamari ground tech Kelemah, one lamplike eye swiveling up from patching a leaking oxygen hose. "But then you all do."

"Very helpful, Kel," Col muttered.

"And you *sound* exactly alike. It's uncanny, really. I'd swear you were the same person."

Puck grinned. "He's got you there, Fa—"

"Don't," Col said, his voice loud enough that the other pilots looked over.

"I mean it, Puck," he said more quietly. "Don't. Today of all days, don't."

Somehow that succeeded where previous efforts hadn't. Puck nodded and raised his hands peaceably.

"So what exactly did the kid say that set you off, Col?" asked John D. "In all the excitement I missed that."

"Well, I'd just said that it's impossible to hit a two-meter target with a proton torpedo, even with a computer."

A glance passed between Puck and John D.

"What? Don't tell me you weren't thinking the same thing while Dodonna was showing us those schematics."

"Maybe," John D. said. "I'm guessing the kid thought it was possible. What did he say?"

The door opened and other pilots began entering the room in twos and threes. Col spotted Biggs Darklighter, a newcomer whose carefully groomed mustache was another of Puck's favorite targets; grim, gravel-voiced Elyhek Rue; the talented, volatile Bren Quersey; and cool, analytically minded Wenton Chan.

378

And trailing behind them, the last person Col wanted to see: Wedge Antilles, the young pilot he was sure had been sent to Yavin 4 solely to bedevil him.

"Look, it was nothing," Col told John D. "Forget it."

"Really?" Puck asked. "A minute ago, you were having one of your fits."

Rue, at the end of the line for the caf dispenser, looked up absently. "What's this about, Antilles?" he began, then peered more closely at Col. "Oh. Sorry."

Col knew his face was reddening even before the laughter began.

Puck slung an arm around his shoulder: "And that, Col Takbright, is why you are and will always be known around here as Fake Wedge."

In his calmer moments, Col knew the nickname had stuck for reasons beyond his superficial resemblance to Antilles.

During mission briefings, Antilles limited himself to a few specific questions, while Col wanted to know if Starfighter Command had analyzed all the alternatives. When things went wrong in the simulator, Antilles reviewed telemetry while Col vented his rage on helmets and furniture. Even their helmets were opposites—Wedge's a matte green, Col's a riot of yellow racing stripes.

Garven Dreis—Red Squadron's craggy-faced, sad-eyed commander—had lectured Col after his eruptions. So had General Merrick, who'd died with too many others at Scarif. And veterans such as Puck and John D. had tried to reinforce the message. Col knew Puck's teasing was meant to help him develop thicker skin.

Col had tried to be more like the pilots praised for their placid exteriors—pilots like Chan and Antilles. But inevitably, another feeling would steal over him as he lay in his bunk staring at the stone ceiling.

Every day, the Empire was devouring worlds for ore and fuel and murdering those who dared to oppose it. Col had watched in increasing agitation as evil crept across the galaxy, until he'd realized he couldn't spend another day on his placid homeworld doing nothing. He'd left Uquine that night with some credits, a duffel bag, and a vow to avenge those the Empire had wronged.

Maybe, he'd lie in the darkness and think, the Rebellion's problem wasn't that Col Takbright was too angry. Maybe it was that people like Wedge Antilles weren't angry enough.

The other pilots laughed, but Antilles looked pained and turned away—Col assumed he was embarrassed at being mistaken for the squadron's scapegoat.

Rue, meanwhile, had abandoned the caf line.

"Sorry, Takbright," he said quietly. "I wasn't trying to be funny. My mind was somewhere else, that's all."

"Forget it," Col said, knowing this time Puck hadn't set him up—the next practical joke Rue played would be his first.

John D. caught Col's eye and inclined his head—*sit*. Col choked down his anger and did so. A moment later, Antilles settled into the chair next to him with a sigh.

"I think it's time to switch things up," he said. "Hey guys, it's me— Fake Col."

Col's first instinct was to knock Antilles onto the floor and show the whole squadron the joke ended here. But Red Leader would arrive soon with the pilot roster for the Death Star mission—and Col would be an easy cut if found brawling with a fellow pilot.

And that wouldn't be right. Col had earned the right to be part of the most important mission in Alliance history. No, he hadn't flown at Scarif—the last place in the squadron had gone to Pedrin Gaul, who'd died there. But Dreis had praised his performance in recent raids, and Col had racked up patrols and recon missions. He just had to keep his cool and hope for the best.

"Takbright! You still haven't told us what the kid said."

That was John D. again, like a nek with a bone. Still, it was better than this embarrassed silence—or whatever torment Puck might think up next.

"He told me he used to bull's-eye some kind of varmint back home. In—get this—a T-16."

Biggs looked over and wagged a finger at Col. "Hey, don't knock T-16s. I learned to fly on them—if you can handle a skyhopper, you can handle an X-wing."

"Before Biggs crafts another ode to the galaxy's noble bush pilots, I wanna hear more about the varmint," Puck said.

Col furrowed his brow. "He called it a . . . a *womp rat*. Whatever that is."

Biggs turned so quickly that caf sloshed out of his cup.

"A womp rat? You're sure that's what he said?"

"Would I make up a name like that?"

"No way. It can't be."

And then Biggs was rushing for the door, nearly toppling Dreis as he entered the ready room with Zal Dinnes and Ralo Surrel at his heels. The squadron leader shot a curious look in Biggs's direction—pilots tended to rush in when the Old Man arrived, not hurry out—then shrugged.

Chairs scraped on the ancient stone floor as the pilots stood. Col spotted the muscles of jaws working and fingers tugging at uniforms. These men and women would be all business in their cockpits, but this part made them nervous. These were the moments in which they'd learn who'd fly and who'd be left dirtside, to lunge for control yokes and triggers that weren't there.

381

"At ease," Dreis said. "Save it for zero hour."

No one sat.

"Like that, huh? Can't say I blame you. Let's get to it. You all know we have more pilots than birds. Given our losses at Scarif, we're trying to figure out if we can even put Green and Blue squadrons together. I'd fly with anyone in this room—and you all deserve a place on this hop. But unfortunately that can't happen."

Silence hung over the room.

"First flight," Dreis began. "I'm flying lead. Theron, starboard wing as Red Ten. Puck, you're port as Red Twelve."

As usual, Nett had no reaction. But Puck blew his breath out and nodded to himself—the first time Col had ever seen him look nervous.

Col tried to think along with Dreis. Red Squadron's twelve X-wings were divided into four flights of three starfighters each. Dreis normally flew with Nett and Surrel as his wingmates. Since he'd subbed Puck for Ralo, in all likelihood he'd decided . . .

"Ralo, you'll lead second flight as Red Eleven," Dreis said. "Wings are Branon and Binli, as Red Four and Red Seven."

That wasn't a surprise either—John D. was a veteran and Harb Binli had flown well at Scarif.

"Third flight," Dreis said, and Col noticed eyes narrowing and postures growing rigid. Third and fourth flights were where Dreis had needed to make tough choices.

"Zal, you'll fly lead as Red Eight. Wings are Naytaan and Porkins, as Red Nine and Red Six."

Dinnes's only reaction was to nod briefly at Nozzo Naytaan and Jek Porkins.

One flight to go. Col's eyes skittered over Antilles and Chan, Rue and Quersey, and the other pilots on the bubble.

"Fourth flight will be led by the new kid, Luke Skywalker," Dreis said.

That was *not* expected. The pilots muttered and exchanged startled looks.

"The womp rat kid?" Col demanded, drawing an exasperated look from Puck.

"Is that what we're calling him?" Dreis asked. "He'll fly as Red Five—assuming his simulator run checks out. Before anyone else has something to say, remember that without Skywalker the princess would have been executed—and we'd be going up against that battle station with nothing but prayers."

Two slots left in the squadron. Puck fixed Col with a stern look that he didn't need to interpret.

"Darklighter will be Luke's starboard wingman, flying as Red Three," Dreis said. "Assuming someone can find Biggs by the time we fly."

One seat left. Col prayed that the Old Man wouldn't let him down.

"Wedge, you'll be port wing, flying as Red Two. But see Kelemah about your bird—he's got a couple of things to go over with you."

Col leaned against the wall and stared down at his flight suit, numbly registering the chest-mounted life-support unit and the band of signal flares around his lower leg. Both useless—he didn't need gear to sit and wait while others did the job he'd been meant to do.

"I'm not much for speeches, but seems like the occasion calls for one," Dreis said. "You know there's a tough target waiting for us. Just like you know that a lot of brave people—including friends of ours—gave their lives so we'd have a chance to take that target down."

Someone clapped a couple of times, stopping when no one joined in.

"You're every bit as brave as they were," Dreis said. "I saw that just a few days ago. I know in the next hour I'll see it again. We'll rely on one another up there, like we always do. And as long as we do that, I'll go up against anything in the galaxy and like our chances. All right, that's it. Techs have already started preflight. Get to your birds in ten minutes and I'll see you up there."

Col remained motionless as the other pilots and techs began filing out of the room.

"Tough break, kid," said Puck. "Stay sharp—if they can get more birds flying they're going to need pilots."

"But Red Squadron's got its twelve," Col said. "So even if that happens, I'll be at the back of the line."

Puck started to say something, but Col turned away. "Just leave me alone," he said, leaning his forehead against the wall. The ancient stone felt soothingly smooth and cool.

The room quieted and when Col looked up he was alone. The only sound was the hum of the air scrubbers fighting their rearguard action against the jungle moon's relentless humidity. The chairs were askew, and ration bar wrappers and half-empty cups of caf dotted the tabletops.

Someone needs to clean this up—if Colonel Cor sees the ready room like this the demerits will fly.

Except there wouldn't be a next briefing. Soon everything around him would be part of a cooling debris field in the earliest stages of becoming a ring of Yavin. What was the point of cleaning up? What was the point of doing anything except waiting to die?

The fury came all at once. Chairs flew, tables overturned and still Col raged on, looking for new targets. He spotted his flight helmet, hanging by its chin strap from a rack on the wall. That would do nicely, he thought, taking a step toward the helmet and the one hanging next to it.

The matte-green one hanging next to it.

Oh.

The door opened and Antilles stared at the wreckage and Col standing in the center of it, breathing heavily.

"I guess you forgot your helmet," Col said, his voice low and strange in his ears.

"Kelemah had to ask where it was," Antilles said, stepping carefully over a tangle of fallen chairs. "Not the best way to start a hop."

Antilles avoided Col's eyes as he made his way to the rack, took his helmet down, and picked his way back to the door. But then he paused and turned.

"I'm sorry you're not going up with us," Antilles said. "I mean that, Col. And I had nothing to do with that idiot nickname."

"You've got no reason to be sorry," Col said with a smirk. "You get to fly against the Empire, while good pilots like me sit down here and do nothing. Just remember that you're flying for all of us—and you better not let us down."

Antilles nodded, but his eyes had turned hard and flinty.

"I'll fly for you, Col. And for a lot of other people, too. The whole galaxy's counting on us, you know. You're not alone in this fight—and you never will be. Unless you insist on pushing everybody away."

The sound of Antilles's departing footsteps grew fainter and was lost amid distant voices, whining machinery, and muffled announcements—the activity of a rebel base ready for war.

Col listened for a moment longer, then began to right the tables and chairs.

When he entered the war room Col immediately spotted Princess Leia, a slim figure in white at the main command table with Dodonna and other rebel bigwigs. He scanned the room and found a knot of orange flight suits at an auxiliary display: Rue, Chan, Quersey, and Kelemah.

Col steeled himself for their reaction, but the others simply nodded, with Rue and Chan making room for him at the table.

385

"Battle station's orbiting the gas giant," Chan said. "Less than fifteen minutes to firing range."

"So when do they call Kay-One-Zero?" Col asked.

"Don't think they're planning to evacuate," Quersey said. "Most of the essential equipment left with the fleet. It's all in the hands of the pilots upstairs."

And there's nothing I can do about it, Col thought. The pilots were the last line of defense against the Empire's planet killer. They'd need every advantage they could get—and a lot of luck.

Kelemah tapped at a readout on the tactical display, muttering at what he saw.

"Problem with one of our birds, Kel?" Chan asked.

"Port stabilizer on Red Twelve's misaligned. But Naeco knows to compensate for it. I'm more worried about Red Two. We had to do a patch job on the stern hydraulic lines after Scarif."

"Wedge can handle it," Chan assured him.

Col retraced schematics in his mind and didn't like what he found.

"If those lines fail, his micro-maneuvering controls will go, too."

"Antilles knows that and still wanted to go," Kelemah said. "It was fly with the patches or don't fly at all."

"That's a big risk," Col said, which drew a bark of laughter from Quersey.

"Look around, Col. We're all part of the biggest risk in the history of the galaxy."

Over the speakers, Gold Leader announced the start of the Y-wings' attack run, with Red Leader directing his X-wings to cut across the battle station's axis and draw the Imperials' fire.

Col stared at the tactical display, trying to match the bright blips indicating the fighters' positions with the chatter on the squadron channel. The X-wings had broken into pairs and trios, raking the surface of the battle station with laserfire. They were a distraction, harrying the Imperial defenses while the Y-wings raced for the vulnerable exhaust port. Pilots he'd served alongside were risking their lives for a slight increase in the Alliance's odds.

"They're outflying those turbolasers," Kelemah grunted. "Those guns are meant for capital ships, not starfighters."

But then Porkins announced he had a problem, and the red dot that represented Red Six slowed. An agonized yell was drowned in static, and the dot vanished.

"So long, Piggy," Rue said quietly. "You will be avenged."

An alarm sent controllers scrambling. Kelemah waved a mottled hand at new lights blinking on the tactical readout.

"TIEs," Rue said. "If the Empire's jamming our sensors, those fighters will be right on top of our birds before they're detected."

A warning went out to the pilots, and the table became a shifting constellation of red and green. Col realized he was gripping the edge of the table so hard that his knuckles were white. He told himself to relax, then realized the other pilots were doing the same thing.

A green dot attached itself to John D., and a moment later the rebel veteran was dead. Then Skywalker took a glancing hit from a TIE just before flying into a heavy fire zone. Both the red and green blips vanished, and Chan leaned closer.

"Did we lose the kid?"

The two blips reappeared, and Skywalker called out for Biggs. But it was Red Two that vaporized the Imperial pursuer.

"That's Antilles's third kill," Kelemah said. "Wish he wouldn't ride those patches so hard."

"Shh," Chan said. "Gold Squadron's starting its attack run."

Col studied the telemetry from the Y-wings' sensors and shook his head.

"They've got no room to maneuver in that trench. With all those guns down there, their forward shields will take a beating."

The Y-wing pilots switched on their targeting computers, and numbers began counting down on one section of the readout.

"The guns—they've stopped," Gold Two said in disbelief.

A moment later, TIE fighters swooped in from behind. Col tried to will the targeting numbers closer to zero.

Then Gold Two was dead, followed by Gold Leader. Gold Five, doomed, was warning Red Squadron that the fighters had come from behind. And the Death Star was less than five minutes from clearing the planet.

Col realized he'd been holding his breath and let it out in a ragged stream. He stared at the tactical readout, trying to count the red dots.

"The other Y-wings are being chewed up," Chan said, seeing his gaze. "And Red Eight and Red Seven were shot down skirmishing TIEs."

Dinnes was dead, and Binli, too. Col remembered the pride on their faces after Scarif, how he'd ached for the chance to fly with them.

"The Old Man's up next," Rue said. "He'll make that shot, you watch."

Col nodded, trying to convince himself. Wasn't Dreis a legend, with a flight log dating back to the Clone Wars? And didn't he have Theron and Puck backing him up? He imagined Puck destroying the battle station and becoming a rebel hero—and choosing Col as his wing as the Alliance pursued more victories.

With the Death Star three minutes from firing, Dodonna told Dreis to keep half his group out of range for another potential attack run.

"We won't get a third shot at this," Col said, and Chan shushed him.

Dreis ordered Skywalker, Darklighter, and Antilles to hold their positions while Red Nine and Red Eleven kept skirmishing with TIEs.

As the three X-wings swung into the trench, Col found himself muttering under his breath, begging Puck to watch out and urging whatever cosmic forces had shaped the universe to guide Dreis's torpedo.

Rue stood stock-still at the tactical table, sweat running down his forehead. Quersey kicked relentlessly at the stone floor. Chan gnawed his lower lip.

"That's six kills for Antilles," said Kelemah. "I fix something, it stays fixed."

Col stared at the three dots approaching the blinking cross that marked the exhaust port, trying to speed them up.

"Keep your eyes open for those fighters," Dreis said. A chime announced that his targeting computer had the target marked and locked in.

"Come on, boss! Come on!" Col said.

And then there was a cry and the blip representing Red Twelve blinked out. Puck was dead. Col looked down, blinking hard.

"You'd better let her loose!" Naytaan urged. "They're right behind me!"

"Almost there," Dreis said, his voice almost pleading.

"I can't hold them!" Naytaan warned, and then wailed in anguish.

Another chime, Dreis yelled, "It's away," and a dozen conversations started at once.

"It's a hit!" someone yelled on the squadron channel. Col stared at Quersey, seeing the same wild hope he knew was on his own face.

"Negative," Dreis said as the green dots closed on his position. "It didn't go in. Just impacted on the surface."

He ordered Skywalker to get set up for his attack run. And then the Old Man's starboard engine was scrap. Dreis howled until his X-wing smashed into the station's surface.

A cool voice announced the Death Star's time to firing range: a minute and closing.

"Biggs, Wedge, let's close it up," said Skywalker, sounding far older

389

than the young man in dusty clothes who'd sat next to Col. "We're going in. We're going in full throttle."

The three X-wings raced into the trench with Skywalker leading and Darklighter and Antilles farther behind, to impede the fighters everyone knew were coming. At those near-suicidal speeds, Col knew, any mistake would send a starfighter careening into the trench wall—or another T-65.

Red Nine vanished, leaving Red Eleven as a solitary red blip surrounded by green dots.

"Get Surrel out of there," Col begged. "He can't survive those odds."

"No," Chan said. "But he can buy them a little more time."

"Fighters," Antilles said. "Coming in point three."

As Skywalker's targeting computer picked up its lock, something blinked on Kelemah's tactical readout and the tech's maroon skin turned a pale salmon.

"Antilles is hit," he said. "Shot severed the hydraulic lines. If he doesn't get clear he's as big a danger as those TIEs."

Col could almost see Wedge fighting a slewing and bucking starfighter while trapped in the narrow trench.

"Tell him, Kel!" Col urged.

"I'll never get through."

"I can't stay with you," Antilles said bleakly, and the red blip zoomed away from the trench. Seconds later, the dot representing Surrel disappeared. Red Squadron had been reduced to Skywalker and Darklighter.

"The TIEs are accelerating," Chan said. "Now it's a race."

"Hurry up, Luke!" Darklighter said, then hesitated.

"Wait!" he said plaintively, a split second before he died.

Thirty seconds to firing.

Col spotted the red blip that was Wedge—heading back toward the trench with a cloud of TIEs closing in.

"What's he doing?"

Kelemah studied his instruments. "He's charged the auxiliary hydraulics. But that'll only give him a minute of fine control at most. If he goes back in that trench he'll never come out."

Col silently begged Wedge not to throw his life away—not after having survived such odds. But he suspected he'd have done the same thing, recklessly trying to rejoin the fight rather than let people think he'd run.

Nobody who'd flown a T-65 would say that. But did Wedge realize that right now? And if their positions had been reversed—as Col had so fervently hoped—would Col have realized it?

And then everything seemed to happen at once. The Death Star cleared the planet. Skywalker's targeting computer shut down, and the Womp Rat Kid claimed nothing was wrong. The freighter that had returned Princess Leia to Yavin 4 came out of nowhere, scattering Skywalker's pursuers with a suicidal charge. And Wedge, instead of dropping into the trench using the last drizzles of hydraulic fluid, turned his X-wing away from the Death Star.

391

Skywalker's torpedoes fired—Col thought he heard the young pilot gasp as they ignited—and the noise in the war room rose in pitch and volume.

The Death Star vanished from the tactical boards, leaving just four red blips against a blank expanse.

Col and the other pilots stared down at the readouts. No one breathed. No one dared to speak.

"Target destroyed," a controller said, and the war room descended into pandemonium. Col found himself pounding Rue on the back, hugging Quersey and Kelemah and slapping hands with Chan so hard that it hurt.

Then he was swept up in the throng of pilots, soldiers, and technicians rushing for the main hangar. They arrived in time to see the freighter set down outside the temple, with a Y-wing landing nearby—and two battered X-wings easing into the hangar.

Most of the crowd headed for the T-65 with the five chevrons on each wing, but Col's destination was the X-wing attended by only a scattering of rebels. He was waiting at the bottom of the ladder when Wedge slowly descended, facing away from Col.

Wedge removed his helmet, his back still turned. His hair was matted with sweat and his shoulders rose and fell.

When Wedge turned he saw Col and took an instinctive step backward.

"There was nothing I could have done—"

And then Col wrapped him in a bear hug.

"You took out six TIEs, ran that trench at full throttle, kept your bird intact without its maneuvering systems—you did all that and then you tried to go back, you crazy fool," he said. "You did everything anyone could have done and more."

When he finally let Wedge go, the other pilot gaped at him.

"I just hope everyone sees it the way you do."

Col threw an arm around his shoulders.

"If they don't, tell them it was Fake Wedge up there," he said. "Because I'd be honored to be mistaken for you—for *any* of you. Now come on. There's a celebration waiting for us."

DESERT SON

Pierce Brown

The fear—which I know will last till I see the winged eyeball sil-
houette of TIE fighters tearing headlong toward me through black
space—metastasizes in my gut as Dodonna's briefing comes to an
end. But there's another feeling, the same that I felt before the mutiny
on the *Rand Ecliptic*.

Peace.

A feeling of serene completeness, as if the nomadic path that took
me to the Imperial Academy, to my first post on the *Rand Ecliptic*,
and to my subsequent defection to the Alliance, has brought me full
circle. As if, parsecs from Tatooine, billions of kilometers from Tosche
Station and the moisture farms of my family, I've found home again.

PIERCE BROWN

I heard his voice in the briefing.

I saw his farmboy face, the same that used to smirk at me before a run on Beggar's Canyon or when he'd waste a womp rat at full pitch.

But still I didn't believe my eyes.

The kid's sandy tuft of hair disappears out the tunnel from Dodonna's debrief like the rump of a fleeing bantha. I call after him, but he doesn't hear. I caught wind from Wedge that the princess had been brought back by a farmboy and a smuggler, but there's more agricultural systems under the Empire's boot than the grains of sand on a Mon Calamari beach. Even a top-of-the-line protocol droid couldn't calculate the odds of the farmboy being a son of Tatooine, much less the only bush pilot besides myself who's ever threaded his way through Stone Needle in Beggar's Canyon.

But it feels so purposeful. So fated.

Just as my path has led me here, to the point of crisis, where I can strike a blow for freedom, it's brought my best friend as well. What luck. It's as if all the stories we heard as children were true.

I push my way through rebel flight officers and pilots and get tangled with an astromech droid, banging a chunk of skin from my left shin. Shouting in pain, I hop sideways on one leg straight into Jek Porkins. I sink into the side of the man, and he throws an arm around my head to try to ruffle my mustache with his ham-sized fingers.

"Watch where you're goin, laserbrain." Porkins chuckles like a Hutt and I manage to wrench myself free of his squidgy embrace. Most of the Alliance veteran pilots—loose a term as that is—were accommodating to new recruits, especially given the nascency of their fighter squadrons. But Porkins, a cocky pilot from Bestine, seems to think it's his duty to institute ritual hazing, even on the brink of battle.

"Hope you're better off your feet than on them," he says with a grin.

394

"That sounds like an invitation." I snort a laugh. "Do you want to try that again, Porkins?"

He grins and pushes me to the side. "Oh, I'm far out of your league, nerf herder."

It's not till the hangar that I catch up to my old friend as he runs his hand along the fuselage of a T-65 with the same wistful expression he wore when we parted at Tosche Station just a few short weeks ago. He's dressed in a flight suit now.

"Hey, Luke!" I shout.

He wheels around, a bright farmboy grin already on his face. "Biggs?"

I laugh. "I don't believe it!" I throw an arm over his shoulder, questions tumbling out. "How are ya? How'd you get here? You coming up with us?"

He doesn't miss a beat. "I'll be right up there with you, and have I got stories to tell you."

Him and me both. How the hell did he end up in this? There's no time to ask, and even less time to tell him how happy I am he's here.

"Skywalker." Garven Dreis, Red Squadron leader, approaches from behind and nods to the rusted T-65. "You sure you can handle this ship?"

I see the panic in Luke's eyes, and I cut in before he can answer. "Sir, Luke is the best bush pilot in the Outer Rim Territories."

Garven grins, knowing I don't give compliments lightly. "You'll do all right."

Luke smiles. "Thank you, sir. I'll try."

Garven heads to his ship as Luke and I head down the line to our own. "Gotta get aboard," I say, wishing we had more time. "We'll hear all your stories when we get back, all right?"

He grins at me. "Hey, Biggs, I told you I'd make it someday."

He did, and I never doubted him once. Warm pride swells up in me like a twin desert sunrise, and I think how fitting it is that we are here. Two sons of Tatooine.

"It'll be like old times, Luke. They'll never stop us."

I leave Luke behind and find Wedge sitting on the boarding ladder to his cockpit. "Biggs," he says with a distant smile. "Who's the kid?"

"Friend from home," I say. "Always said he'd join the Rebellion."

"Shame we don't have more Corellians." He grins. "We'd have the Imperials running for Coruscant in a blink."

"We got them right where we want them!" I say. "Good luck out there, Wedge."

"And to you, Biggs." We shake hands.

I board my X-wing and begin the preflight checklist with my astromech. As nearby technicians sheath their hydrospanners and shimmy off the aluminum engineer ladders, I feel happy. Knowing that all my boyhood competition and camaraderie with Luke has led us here, prepared us for this moment.

We leave Base One behind, taxiing up away from the ancient temple, past the observation obelisks where sentries wave good luck, up from the sea of jungle toward the pregnant red hulk of Yavin. We breach orbit, and I feel space untether me from gravity. My heart rushes in my chest while at the same time it seems as if my stomach has made a migration up into my throat. I'm thanking the stars I passed on the jet juice that Porkins was dishing out last night.

Our squadron circles Yavin, and we see it for the first time. A pale-gray orb hanging in space like an untethered moon. Men built this. I'd say it was impossible if I didn't see it with my own eyes. Our thirty tiny ships are nothing but gnats on a bantha.

The joy I felt in the hangar is eroded by fear. So long as I was the only one exposed to this fight, the fear was something manageable. Something I could shove deep down into my stomach and forget like it was my private dark secret. But with Luke here, the fragile memory of home, friends, and family feels so very exposed, as if it could be broken at any moment. And the leviathan is what will do the breaking.

Garven's voice comes over the comm unit. "All wings report in."

"Red Ten standing by."

"Red Seven standing by."

"Red Three standing by," I say.

The confirmation rattles down the rest of the squadron until I hear Luke's voice. The fear fades. It might not be sand under our wings, but we've yet to face a run we can't manage together.

"Lock S-foils into attack position," Garven says. The Death Star expands till it consumes my entire viewport. There's still no sign of enemy fighters. Can they really be so arrogant? My ship begins to shake; the control stick bucks against my hands like an unruly eel. "We're passing through a magnetic field, hold tight. Switch your deflectors on double front."

"Look at the size of that thing," Wedge murmurs. I hear the fear in my friend's voice, the same fear that would steal the courage from me. It sweeps through the squadron as we coast toward the killing station. Inside are the men who destroyed Alderaan, a peaceful planet if ever there was one. How many more will suffer if this evil is not taken down here and now?

"Cut the chatter, Red Two," Garven says. "Accelerate to attack speed." I shake myself in my cockpit and push forward on the throttle. We race closer. Closer, till the station seems all there is, a hulking, impossible sphere of bone-hued metal and turbolaser towers and defense installations that jut up from the station's skin like ingrown hairs. "This is it, boys."

"Red Leader, this is Gold Leader. We're heading for the target shaft now."

"We're in position. I'm going to cut across the access and try to draw their fire." Garven's X-wing banks hard diagonally down at the surface of the Death Star. I bank my ship to follow in a lazy corkscrew. A fury of green laser bolts lance up from the gray landscape, burning through the black of space. They pass harmlessly, the towers too slow to track us as Luke, Wedge, and I skim close to the surface of the station.

"Heavy fire, boss, twenty-three degrees," someone says.

"I see it," Garven replies. "Stay low."

Our three ships dip and weave through the communication and antiaircraft towers. "This is Red Five: I'm going in," Luke says as he peels off from Wedge and me and dives toward a heavy turbolaser tower. His lasers burn across a trench line, digging furrows in the metal. But he's going in too hot.

"Luke! Pull up!" I shout. At the last moment, his ship pivots up from its collision course with the station and bounds away. "Are you all right?"

"I got a little cooked, but I'm okay."

I sigh in relief as Luke forms up on Wedge and me. There's hardly time to reorient. Fire from dozens of turbolaser cannons laces the dogfight. Garven, cool under pressure, identifies the source. "There's a lot of fire coming from the right side of that deflection tower."

"I'm on it." Luke says, hungry for another attack run. He was always the more eager of the two of us. Aunt Beru was more than half certain he'd end up engine paste on the side of a Beggar's Canyon rock shelf. To be honest, so was I. But I've never seen anyone with the run of luck Luke has.

I form up on his flank to help with his attack run on the laser towers. I look on the scope to see who is nearby to offer support. "I'm going in. Cover me, Porkins."

"I'm right with you, Red Three." The sound of his voice is a surprising comfort. Luke and I swoop low to the deck, weaving between towers, and concentrate our fire on the laser tower that was chewing up Garven's wingmates. It flashes and glows as our cannons melt into its reflector shields, and then detonates as Luke and I soar past. Just like bull's-eyeing womp rats. I whoop in exhilaration.

Then Porkins's voice comes frantic over the comm.

"I've got a problem here," he says from above. I watch him on my scope. He's pinned in a field of overlapping fire and hit bad in the fuselage.

"Eject . . ." I say.

"No, I can hold it." A second later, a laser enters the belly of his ship and detonates it from the inside. I look for sign of an ejection, but there is none. Porkins is dead. I barely have time to register the loss when Base One hails us.

"Squad leaders, we've picked up a new group of signals. Enemy fighters coming your way."

"My scope's negative, I don't see anything," Luke says. And neither do I. I crane my neck around to scan the space above me for the eye-balls.

"Pick up your visual scanning."

"Here they come."

"Watch it. You've got one on your tail!"

A cloud of fire ignites and dies as an X-wing disintegrates to starboard.

"You've picked one up, watch it," Luke shouts at me. I wheel my head around, juking and spiraling to confuse the TIE's targeting computer. I still haven't spotted him. "I can't see him." I veer away from the Death Star to gain room to maneuver. The TIE's lasers lick past me. The hairs on my arms stand up. A weight grows in my gut. I jerk on the control stick. This guy is good. "He's on me tight. I can't shake him."

"I'll be right there," Luke says. I even out, presenting the TIE pilot with a clean shot, making him an easier target for Luke. He drops in behind the TIE and sends a salvo of lasers into its rear fuselage for a clean kill.

"All right! Good shooting, Luke!"

"Thanks, Biggs, but we're not out of this yet!"

I swerve my X-wing back toward the Death Star and strafe several turbolaser towers that are peppering the Y-wing Gold Squadron. Two detonate spectacularly. Above me, Luke has picked up a TIE on his tail. Debris shears off the top of the X-wing, just behind the pilot's canopy. I shouldn't have gone for the laser towers. I left him exposed. "I can't shake him!" he says.

In a panic, I'm about to come at the TIE from underneath when Wedge vapes the ship with a bold head-on attack run and soars straight through the debris. Damn, that man can fly. I form up on the two and check out the damage done to Luke's ship.

"You got some damage there," I say. "How's the stick?"

"Still got maneuverability," Luke says. "We gotta stay tight. No more running off!"

"Copy that," I say, surprised and somewhat relieved that he's taken control of our flight wing. If Wedge hadn't been there, Luke would've been in some real trouble. That's on me. I got hungry for a kill and I left my wingmate. Not again. We form tight on each other.

"Red Leader, this is Gold Leader. We are starting our attack run."

"I copy, Gold Leader. Move into position."

Free from the harassment of the destroyed laser towers, the Y-wings dive into the trench. Slower and older than our T-65s, they're more vulnerable to the enemy fighters, and stronger against entrenched elements. Red Squadron provides cover for the Y-wings as they continue down the trench. Luke, Wedge, and I tangle with a trio of TIE fighters. Lasers splash against my front deflectors. I juke upward and let off a stream of fire, clipping the solar panel of the TIE. It careens sideways into its wingmate, which Luke shreds with his lasers. Wedge spirals downward and kills the last fighter as it heads for the Y-wings.

But as we tangle with them, three marks slip underneath our dogfight and dive into the trench after the Y-wings.

"Three marks at four ten," I say.

"We gotta keep them off the Y-wings," Wedge says. We never get the chance. Another squadron of TIEs appears on our sensors, swarming us and cutting off our path. There's no time to think. The chatter dies and Luke and I flow together wordlessly through the dogfight as if attached together with tow cables. Synced in perfect precision, one baiting the TIEs as the other hits them from the flank or rear. But even as we destroy the squadron, we hear the Y-wings dying over the comms.

"Gold Five to Red Leader, I've lost . . . Hutch. Came . . . from behind—"

"Red boys, this is Red Leader. Rendezvous at mark six point one."

Wedge and I both copy. There's only six Red Squadron pilots left. The rest of the squadrons have been wiped out by the guns and the TIEs and whoever killed Gold Squadron in the trench.

"Luke, take Red Two and Three. Hold up here and wait for my signal to start your run," Garven says as his two wingmates dive into the trench. We form up at the end of it, where a hole has been carved in the turbolaser defenses, and watch the skies for TIEs. Sweat stings my eyes. Our window is shrinking.

Garven's comms crackle, almost inaudible as he carries down the trench into the teeth of the turbolasers. One of his wingmates' comms gets through. "There's too much interference. Red Five . . . can . . . you . . ."

"Coming in at point three five," Luke says.

"I see them."

A flight of three TIEs diving down into the trench dozens of klicks away. One is larger than the others, swollen like a beetle with armor and advanced sensors. They disappear into the trench and all we can do is watch. Holding for our attack run, we're too far away to help. They're sitting ducks in there! I want to break free of our holding pattern and charge after them, but there's no time.

"Just hold them off for a few . . ." I hear through the chatter. "Almost there . . ." A ball of fire flashes far ahead in the trench. One of the X-wings disappears from my sensors. Then the second goes with it. Garven's alone, without wingmates, but he's in range. They bought him enough time.

"It's away!" he shouts and peels up out of the trench. His proton torpedoes fire at the exhaust port.

"It's a hit?"

"Negative, negative. Didn't go in. It impacted on the surface," Garven says grimly. The armored TIE that destroyed his wingmates has pursued him up out of the trench, spewing acid-green laserfire at his engines.

"Red One, we're right above you. Turn to point oh five and we'll cover for you," Luke says.

"Stay there," Garven orders. "I just lost my starboard engine." Wedge and Luke are silent in their ships. I feel a chill go through me. Garven knows he's going to die. If we go help him, we'll lose our chance. "Get set up for your attack run," he says bravely. The words are barely out of his mouth when he's clipped in the rear by a laser. He loses lateral controls and careens down into the surface of the Death Star, screaming.

We're alone. Our squadron gone. Out of thirty ships, only three of us remain, and the Death Star is drawing around Yavin, mere seconds left before it can fire down at the moon and obliterate the Rebellion as it obliterated Alderaan. We are the last hope.

"Biggs, Wedge, let's close it up," Luke says, more authority in his voice than I've ever heard. Before today, we were friends, equals as boys, though the world always put me above him. I was older, wealthier, better with the girls at Tosche Station. When I saw him in the hangar, I thought I'd show him the ropes. But he doesn't need me to teach him any longer. He's different today from the boy I knew on Tatooine. He's a man now, and something, some strange calm fills his voice and soothes my nerves. "We're going in, we're going in full throttle. That ought to keep those fighters off our backs."

"Right with you, boss," Wedge says.

"Luke, at that speed will you be able to pull out in time?" I ask.

I can practically hear him smile. "It'll be just like Beggar's Canyon back home."

Grinning ear-to-ear, I follow him into a dive toward the trench, my ship vibrating as the engines are pushed to their limits. Luke's in the lead now, and good for it. He was always the better shot.

"We'll stay back just far enough to cover you," I say, remembering how easily Gold Squadron and Garven's wingmates were picked apart. I have to buy him more time than they did. He has to have a chance at the shot. And a hell of a shot it'll have to be.

"My scope sees the tower, but I can't see the exhaust port. You sure the computer can hit it?" Wedge asks.

Lasers spray fire down the trench at us.

"Watch yourself. Increase speed full throttle," Luke replies.

"What about that tower," Wedge presses nervously.

"You worry about those fighters. I'll worry about the tower," Luke snaps.

We race through the trench like womp rats with their tails on fire. Lasers burn past us, their green lances filling our viewports as we juke manically within the narrow confines of the trench. It's a miracle we don't collide with one another or the walls. I spare a glance up

403

through my canopy to look for the enemy TIEs and almost careen into the wall. I correct myself and chance a look back up. Wedge spots them before I do.

"Fighters coming in point three," he says. They're directly on our engines, matching our breakneck pace. Their lasers flash between our S-foils before connecting with the engines of Wedge's ship. His X-wing bucks sideways, almost colliding with mine. I bank hard on my stick and skim a handsbreadth from the walls, nearly shaving off my right S-foils. I jerk back toward the center of the trench, wary of Wedge's wobbling ship. He could take us both out with his internal stabilizer malfunctioning.

"I'm hit. I can't stay with you," he says.

"Get clear, Wedge. You can't do any more good back there," Luke replies.

"Sorry!" Wedge pulls out, and I'm left alone. My sensors are scrambled from the interference of the trench. I crane my head around to see the TIEs behind me. They're accelerating, not just matching my velocity now but outstripping it. Reeling me in for the easy kill.

"Hurry, Luke," I rush. "They're coming in much faster this time. We can't hold them." I could bug out, like Wedge, and they wouldn't follow. I could shunt the remaining power from my overworked reactor to my rear deflectors to keep myself alive. But without power for the engines, I'd fall behind. They'd leap past me and shoot Luke down. What do I do?

I feel a sudden, inexplicable joy open up in me. A powerful feeling of purpose, of peace, urging me to make the choice I always would have made: to save my friend.

I strip all power from my deflector shields and guns and put it into my engines, gunning them past the redline. My ship leaps forward, a shield for Luke. But there's more power in the advanced TIE behind me than in my X-wing. It accelerates after me. I glance back and hear the warning of a target lock.

The calm disintegrates.

"Wait . . ." I hear myself saying. To whom, I don't know. Some man who cannot hear me. It wasn't supposed to end this way. I can't leave Luke yet. We have so much yet to do. First the Death Star, I thought when I saw him. Then the liberation of home, Coruscant, all the planets in the galaxy. Together, we'd be unstoppable. But a cold feeling of dread enters me now as I see the green lasers leap through space and collide with my engines. They shear through the hull of my ship and out the other side. A fire starts in my controls. Then another salvo eviscerates my ship.

But beyond the terror, beyond the flaring light of my disintegrating hull, beyond the dark reaches of the Empire and the endless black of space where stars burn like little promises of hope, I feel the wind of Tatooine sweeping across the desert, and hear the call of my mother for dinner, and I know beyond a shadow of a doubt that Luke will not miss.

The fear is gone, and then there is only peace.

GROUNDED

Greg Rucka

Nera Kase sat on an empty proton torpedo crate in the former Massassi temple on Yavin 4, in what the rebels used as their main fighter bay, with her boots dangling eight centimeters from the floor, and she stared at nothing, and waited for the grief to come again.

She'd been religious growing up, a gift from her parents, who had venerated the Force in the Phirmist tradition. Their home had been their ship, and they'd had no world, just the endless, repeating cargo runs from the Core Worlds to the Outer Rim to the Mid Rim and over and over. She'd been born on their ship. She'd lived the first half of her life on their ship. She'd imagined she would die on their ship.

Instead it was her parents who had died, and their ship had been impounded by the Empire. In the space of seven minutes, Nera Kase lost her home and her family.

In the space of seven minutes, the Empire had made her their enemy.

She couldn't remember any prayers, but that was all right, because an insincere prayer seemed to her less than useless at the moment.

She was a small woman, three years shy of thirty, and the combination of a decidedly youthful face and small stature caused people—in particular new arrivals to Base One—to mistake her for much younger than she was, and by extension, someone of little import and no authority. Her general appearance did nothing to correct this assumption. The mechanic's jumpsuit she habitually wore could, at best, be described as "stained," and only the greatest charity would have gone on to call it flattering to either her frame or her figure. When she was only seven she had discovered—the hard way—that long hair in a narrow crawl space could lead to getting hung up on the machinery, pain, and disaster. She'd shaved her head ever since, but the last week had been utterly relentless, and Kase had barely found time to bathe or eat, let alone groom or sleep. The result was now her scalp appeared as smudged and grimy as her clothes.

Despite all appearances, however, there were those in the Rebellion—and in particular, in the High Command—who would argue that Nera Kase was one of the most crucial people on Base One. Of those, at least two would have taken it further, and argued that she was one of the most critical people in the entirety of the Alliance to Restore the Republic. Mon Mothma and Bail Organa may provide the heart and soul of leadership, but Nera Kase, they'd have argued, puts the body in motion.

Kase shifted on her crate, sore and tired, and continued to wait. Her tool belt, overloaded to the extent it now rode her hips rather than her waist, clattered softly in response. She tightened her grip on the datapad in her hand. She didn't look at it. She would have to soon enough.

She would put that off for as long as she possibly could.

The bay wasn't truly empty, it just felt that way, the same way a closet cleared of clothes feels empty, no matter how many hangers have been left behind. There were service vehicles and cargo trolleys and loadlifters parked all around the space. Crates of ordnance, most of them as empty as the one she now sat upon, stacked up high against the walls. Fuel lines crisscrossed the floor of the bay, running from hastepumps and fuel cells, curled around the many scattered repair and fabrication stations used to keep the fighters fit and flying. A couple of droids idled, duties completed, lost in electronic standby dreams.

Aside from the droids, Nera Kase was alone. The flight crews, all sixty-seven sentients she coordinated and guided through every hour of the day, day in and day out, had left shortly after the last fighter lifted off. Most were now crammed into the pilots' briefing room, where they could watch the telemetry data come in live from the battle about to be joined. Those who hadn't gone to the briefing room were likely clustered in or around the command center itself, hoping to do the same. Anywhere they could see and hear the pilots flying into the mouth of Imperial evil.

They'd launched every fighter they could for the battle. There'd hardly been a point in holding anything in reserve, after all. Thirty fighters divided into two groups, Red and Gold—twenty-two Incom T-65B X-wings and eight Koensayr BTL-A4 Y-wings—against the largest battle station the galaxy had ever seen. Thirty fighters against a machine that could destroy a planet.

Thirty fighters against an Empire that would do it again, and again, and again if they weren't stopped. There wasn't a single person on the base, not a single pilot up above, who didn't know what had happened to Alderaan. There wasn't a single person on the base who didn't understand what was bearing down at this exact moment on Yavin 4, and what would befall countless other planets in its wake unless the Rebellion ended this, here, today.

It ended now. Or it would never end.

Only seven spacecraft remained in the bay, now: five X-wings, one Y-wing, and one U-wing. Two of the X-wings had been cannibalized for parts following the Battle of Scarif, and the other three, though flight-worthy, had no pilots to crew them. The lone Y-wing needed another thirty-six hours of dedicated effort just to get its repulsor engines back online, let alone its ion thrusters. The U-wing was another story entirely. It was ready to go, but had been left behind during the battle a week ago due to lack of available crew, and would've been utterly useless in the attack about to commence far, far overhead.

Far, far overhead, but coming inexorably closer.

As if in answer to the thought, the hangar's sound system crackled to life, speakers clicking on high above her where they'd been secured to the ancient stone ceiling. Someone in the command center, most likely the flight controller, was patching in the live audio from the fighters to the ground. There was a hiss that faded to silence, then a fresh ripple of static, and then Kase heard Red Leader's voice.

"All wings report in."

Red Leader. Flying Red One (*pilot: Garven Dreis, 21,082 flight hours, quadruple ace, twenty-four confirmed kills*), Kase thought automatically. Serious, sincere, precise. One of the most levelheaded pilots she had ever known. Professional, that was the word. She'd had a crush on him for the better part of a month after they'd first met, all because he'd taken the time to get down on his back beneath Red One where Kase had been trying to get the haptic feedback to properly compensate on the fighter's mag launchers. They'd spent twenty minutes under there, Dreis handing her tools and talking specs, and when they'd finished he had given her a nod and a smile and turned to go. As he went, he'd extended his left hand, stroked the side of the fighter's fuselage like he was petting a much-loved beast of burden. Kase was certain Dreis hadn't even realized he'd done it.

Over the speakers, one after another and in no appreciable order, each of Red Squadron's pilots called in.

"*Lock S-foils in attack position,*" Red Leader said.

In the same way that her mind tied each pilot to his or her ship, Kase immediately could picture the execution of the maneuver without any conscious thought. Each of Red Squadron's pilots on their sticks, each of them reaching out to flip the same switch in each of their cockpits. The current pulsing as the circuit closed, the charge redirected down the wiring that ran through the dorsal hull to the splitter, where the signal was redirected port and starboard, ordering the actuators to engage. The hydraulics coming to life in response, flooding fluid into the motivator channels, the strike foils opening as if each of the X-wings were flexing its biceps.

There'd been a problem with the hydraulics on Red Seven's fighter following Scarif, Kase remembered. Red Seven (*pilot: Elyhek Rue, 3,804 flight hours, ace, six confirmed kills*), not a hotshot but not a traditionalist by any means; the man could make any fighter you put him in twist, turn, and tumble. He flew hard, had flown hard at Scarif, and Red Seven always came back the worse for wear. Kase had lost count of the hours she and her crews had put into recalibrating systems on the fighter, on making certain that when Rue needed it the ship would answer as called.

They were passing through the magnetic field. She heard Red Two (*pilot: Wedge Antilles, 1,598 flight hours, ace, nine confirmed kills*) break comm protocol, heard the awe in his voice, and Red One told him to clear the channel. Kase understood that Garvin Dreis wasn't

411

so much admonishing Red Two as he was using the opportunity to refocus the pilots, all the pilots, on the task at hand.

Kase didn't know what she thought of Red Two. His time on the stick was misleading. He'd flown for the Empire, trained on TIEs, had flown before that doing what she didn't even know. He was one of the few pilots on Yavin who could claim to have logged flight time in an A-wing. General Syndulla vouched for him. Everyone who'd flown with him said he was the real thing. Whenever he spoke to Kase, he always called her ma'am, was always polite to the point of shyness with her crews.

And he was almost a double ace already. Kase could almost—*almost*—feel sympathy for any Imperial TIE pilot who found himself in Wedge Antilles's crosshairs.

Sometimes it was the quiet ones you had to watch out for.

The only pilot Kase genuinely wasn't sure about was the new Red Five (*Luke Skywalker, unknown flight hours*). Prior to Scarif, Red Five had been Pedrin Gaul (*952 flight hours, one confirmed kill*), awkward and eager and still rated as a cadet. He'd died over Scarif, disintegrated while attacking the shield gate.

Like so many others who had died over Scarif.

And high above them, at this moment, Kase knew that so many more would die over Yavin 4.

With an effort, she pushed herself off her perch, landed with another clattering of the tools at her waist. The battle was about to be joined. She needed to be in the command center for this part.

The grief followed her, waiting for its moment.

The pilots know the truth.

They are the women and men who test their skill, their mental fortitude, their physical strength in machines that reward even a moment's inattention or complacency with cruel—and oftentimes fatal—retribution. They put their lives on the line every time they go up, whether in combat or outside it. The glory they wear as a result is bought dear, and much-deserved.

To fly in combat is to tax the body in ways that even the most battle-hardened ground trooper will never understand. It is physically exhausting, the pilot responding to constant stress, acceleration, deceleration, the variance of artificial gravity and true gravity. The rank funk that rises from the cockpit after a battle is heavy with sweat and adrenaline and fear, all cooked in an atmosphere of recycled air and overheated electronics.

It is mentally exhausting, demands constant situational awareness and multitasking. It requires a mind's-eye picture of the battlefield in three dimensions, constantly in motion, a macro-level view that no computer will ever adequately replicate. It requires an obsessive, relentless attention to detail, a total understanding of not just the pilot's own vessel—how it is responding, what it is trying to tell him or her—but also of all those that surround it.

Yet when viewed from afar, the pilots and their ships are seen not as a cohesive unit, but rather as a mass of individuals. They may hunt in a pack, but the belief is that every pilot flies alone.

But the pilots know the truth. The pilots know this:

They *never* fly alone.

Every time they take to the skies or the stars, the pilots take their flight crews with them. Every flight, they carry with them the men and women who made it possible, the men and women who poured heart and soul into not just caring for their ship, but into caring for their pilots themselves.

On Yavin 4, at Base One, each rebel fighter was served by a crew of five or six personnel, depending on the needs of the ship and its pilot. Logistically, this meant that every flight crew worked triple,

413

even quadruple duty. Thus, a single ground team of five was responsible for Gold Two (*Dex Tiree, 3,237 flight hours, ace, five confirmed kills*), Red Nine (*Nozzo Naytaan, 1,060 flight hours, three confirmed kills*), and Red Twelve (*Puck Naeco, 5,879 flight hours, double ace, eleven confirmed kills*). These teams served both the fighters and, by extension, the pilots in a relationship that was intensely personal and oftentimes intimate.

Ship, pilot, and crew became one.

When a ship was lost, when a pilot was lost, the crew remained. And they grieved.

For Nera Kase, it was worse. Every ship, every pilot, and every member of the ground crew was her responsibility. From the astromechs to the ordnance loaders to the mechanics and up to the pilots themselves, they all belonged to her. That was her job.

Chief Nera Kase, Fighter Boss, Base One.

Her flight crews. *Her* starfighters. *Her* pilots.

She carried with her every pilot fallen in combat, and she carried their crews, as well, bearing their grief atop her own. Their sorrow when their pilots failed to return. Their self-recrimination and self-doubt, all the hours lost wondering if there was something more that could have been done, or should have been done, or—worst of all—something they failed to do. Another tweak of the deflector shields, an extra boost to engine efficiency, a higher cycle rate on the laser cannons.

Something, anything, that would have brought their pilots safely back home.

Nera Kase had lost fifteen ships and nineteen pilots and crew in the past week alone. It had begun with the mad scramble to put Blue Squadron onto target at Eadu, a flight of seven X-wings and two Y-wings quickly scrambled at General Draven's order for a hit-and-run.

Two never came back.

Less than thirty-six hours later had been the Battle of Scarif.

Two of Blue Squadron never made it past the shield gate protecting the planet. Another two were shot down over the beaches, including Blue Leader (*General Antoc Merrick, 22,542 flight hours, quadruple ace, twenty-four confirmed kills*). Eleven more fighters, mostly out of Blue and Red squadrons, had alternatively been shot down by Imperial emplacements, destroyed by TIEs, or taken by the pilot's worst enemy of all, bad luck.

Fifteen ships, nineteen pilots and crew. In just one week. Nobody under Nera Kase's command was untouched. Some of her crews had suffered multiple losses over the course of a single day.

She had suffered them all.

It was as still as a morgue in the command center. Kase entered quietly, moved around the edge of the room to where she could keep an eye on the tracking board. Three of her crew chiefs had made it inside, pressed against the wall—Benis, Ohley, and Wuz. They gave her the slightest nod of acknowledgment. Nobody else noticed her. Everyone was concentrating, listening. General Dodonna and Princess Organa, along with one or two others and a protocol droid, were gathered around the map display in the center of the room.

Kase looked at her datapad.

If the ships, the pilots, and their crews were the focus of her life, then the datapad was the nucleus. On it she kept everything relating to her duties. Manifests for equipment and munitions, a detailed list of spare parts for every make and model of fighter Base One could field, the names and assignments of every member of her crew, with notes on their specialties, their strengths, their weaknesses. Y-wing influx rephase not processing at full efficiency? Put Darton Bailey on it, he'd have it singing again in minutes. Stuck repeating blaster mount on a U-wing? Give Benis a hydrospanner, and if that didn't work, let her whack at the mount with the blunt end until it behaved. She even had an inventory of flight suits and helmets, and an icon guide just in case one pilot's helmet was ever mixed up with another's.

She also had the roster of pilots.

Kase switched her attention to the fighter tracking board, listening and watching. The initial attack on the station had begun, Gold and Red squadrons each making preliminary assaults to degrade the Death Star's defenses. Kase tracked the small dots and squares, the X-wings and the Y-wings, moving in two dimensions along the etched glass. Gold One (*Jon "Dutch" Vander, 19,997 flight hours, quadruple ace, twenty-two confirmed kills*) broke his squadron, taking Gold Two (*Dex Tiree, 5,062 flight hours, double ace, thirteen confirmed kills*) and Gold Five (*Davish "Pops" Krail, 7,603 flight hours, ace, seven confirmed kills*) on approach for the meridian trench. The remaining five Y-wings in the element split, holding back, as Red Leader brought his group across the axis, trying to draw their fire.

Then Gold Seven (*Gazdo Woolcob, 4,816 flight hours, four confirmed kills*) vanished from the board without warning.

Anti-ship battery fire, Kase told herself.

She checked her datapad, and marked his name, and added a note: *Flak.*

Red Squadron was engaging the surface batteries, now, trying to clear the way for Gold One's element. Red Three (*Biggs Darklighter, 5,874 flight hours, triple ace, sixteen confirmed kills*) called his target, Red Six (*Jek "Tono" Porkins, 10,499 flight hours, double ace, fourteen confirmed kills*) following him in and—

"*I've got a problem here,*" Red Six said.

"*Eject,*" Red Two said.

"*I can hold it.*"

Kase looked through the board to where Wuz had, even in the poor light at the edges of the room, gone pale. Red Six was one of his ships, tended by his crew. Porkins had only recently—very recently—arrived at Base One, brought in to take over for the grounded Wes Janson (*unassigned, 9,869 flight hours, ace, eight confirmed kills*). Janson had expressed concerns about the electricals on the fighter, in particular some of the glitching he'd been experiencing with his astromech's interface to the X-wing's augmented sensor package. Wuz had assured Kase he'd gone over the fighter millimeter by millimeter, that the ship was good to fly.

"Pull up!" Red Two, almost shouting now.

"No, I'm all righ—"

There was a flash of static as Red Six's comm channel flared out, almost in time, but not before everyone heard him start to scream.

Wuz looked to Kase, shattered.

Kase checked her pad, marked off *Red Six—Porkins,* and then added, *Mechanical?*

When she looked up again, Wuz had gone.

Then the Empire launched their fighters.

The battle over the Death Star lasted another seventeen and a half minutes.

Kase ticked the names on her datapad without emotion. She made a note with each loss, and where she was uncertain of the cause, she added a question mark. She concentrated on her job, moving her attention from the pad in her hand to the tracking board and back, over and over again.

TIE.

Flak.

TIE.

TIE.

TIE.

Flak. Flak?

TIE.

TIE.

Flak.

TIE?

TIE.

TIE.

Flak.

TIE.

TIE.

TIE.

TIE.

TIE.

TIE.

TIE.

TIE.

"*Red Leader, we're right above you,*" said Red Five. "*Turn to point five, we'll cover for you.*"

Kase looked up from her datapad.

"*Stay there,*" Red Leader ordered. "*I just lost my starboard engine. Get set up for your attack run.*"

Garven Dreis. She'd never had the nerve to tell him about her crush, to say anything, to do anything.

He was always a professional.

The whole command center heard his scream as he was shot down.

Kase made a note.

TIE.

There were four ships left, only four. Gold Three (*Evaan Verlaine, 3,637 flight hours, four confirmed kills*), Red Two, Red Three, and Red Five. Gold Three had tried to get around behind the element that had claimed Gold Leader and Red Leader attack runs, but her Y-wing didn't have the speed and it didn't have the maneuverability, and she was forced to do what she could from above, trying to stay alive amid the combined fire from the Death Star's turbolasers and the TIE fighters still hunting above the trench.

Then Red Two took a hit, and Kase moved her hand, ready to make her note, and she heard Red Five ordering him off. The regret in Wedge Antilles's voice came through loud and clear, but he did as ordered. Kase was mildly surprised that the TIEs let him go. Her eye tracked his travel on the board, watched as Red Two maneuvered to assist Gold Three.

The Death Star was in range of Yavin 4.

Kase watched the board.

Red Three vanished from the screen.

She checked the line *Red Three—Darklighter* and dutifully added the word *TIE.*

Red Five was somehow still flying.

He'd taken a hit earlier dogfighting a TIE, and the repair made by his astromech had now broken free. She imagined him trying to control the X-wing, wondering if he had ever, in fact, flown an X-wing before, or even anything like it. Wondering if he could keep the fighter, now with a broken port stabilizer, steady enough to make his shot at the exhaust port without at the same time turning himself into an easy target in the shooting gallery the meridian trench had become.

"His computer's off," someone said. "He's switched off his targeting computer. Luke, your targeting computer's off. What's wrong?"

Kase tensed. Red Five had been one of Benis's ships, part of her crew. If this was another mechanical—

"Nothing," said Red Five. *"I'm all right."*

If the command center had been as still as a morgue when Kase had entered it, it now had the silence of the same. Nobody moved, each of them processing what they had just heard.

There was a fizz of static, an electronic wail.

"I've lost Artoo!"

That would be his astromech, then.

Kase found the line on her datapad that read, *Red Five—Skywalker.*

There was truly no point in continuing, now. It was clearly over. The Death Star had cleared Yavin, was at this very instant preparing to fire on Yavin 4. In a few more seconds, a minute, perhaps, everyone and everything here would go the way of Alderaan: Pilots, ships, crews, datapads, all of them, *everything* would cease to exist.

The Rebellion would cease to exist.

But the Empire . . . the Empire would continue.

A voice cut across the comm in the command center, broke the silence. The voice was yelling, but it wasn't in pain.

It sounded to Kase an awful lot like glee.

"You're all clear, kid, now let's blow this thing and go home!" the voice said.

Her eyes went to the tracking board, to the callout for Red Five. She saw the notification flicker across the glass.

Torpedoes away, it said.

Nobody dared to breathe.

Then, just as silently and without any fuss, on every monitor that had shown the graphic representing the Death Star, the graphic winked out. The callout on the tracking board in front of Kase was the last to go, the image of the Death Star far too big to be shown on the glass, represented only by the simple words BATTLE STATION at the center of the board.

420

Then those two words vanished, as well.

The voice was saying something, but Kase couldn't understand it. Nobody could understand it, because suddenly everyone was in motion, and everyone was making noise. Hugging one another, jumping up and down as they laughed, as they screamed in triumph, as they poured out their relief and their joy. Kase saw the princess through the glass look skyward, mouthing something, then run for the exit. General Dodonna followed after her, into a scrum of men and women rushing to clear the room, to get to the hangar, to welcome the pilots home.

Benis and Ohley were waiting for her in the doorway.

"I'll catch up," Kase told them.

They nodded and rushed out, after all the others.

Kase was alone.

She stood still for several seconds, datapad in her hand. Then, very carefully, she switched it off and lay it on the nearby console. She tried to take a step, and succeeded, and tried to take another one, and failed, and she collapsed with the sob already rising out of her, and the tears already beginning to fall.

The grief caught her.

421

CONTINGENCY PLAN

Alexander Freed

In the very near future, no more than a day from now, there's going to be a battle above the fourth moon of Yavin. Scored and pitted X-wings will launch from the moon's jungle, condensation boiling off their hulls as they emerge from the atmosphere under the light of a red gas giant. The squadron will race toward a space station armed with nightmarish weapons dreamed up by bitter old men.

The X-wing pilots—young and ambitious and goodhearted youths who have already seen their share of bloodshed—will seek to exploit a vulnerability in the station and ignite its reactor core. But their hurriedly assembled plan will fare poorly against the designs of the bitter old men. One by one, their starfighters will be destroyed. The space station will enter the moon's orbit, where it will emit an obliterating beam that disintegrates every storied stone of an ancient and haunting temple.

Along with the temple's inhabitants.

Along with the rest of the moon besides.

This is not the future Mon Mothma hopes for, but it isn't an unlikely one.

"I could overrule you," she says as she diligently transfers a stack of datapads from her desk to a metal case. She double-checks the files on each device before stowing it—she reviews rebel cell listings, coded contact frequencies, safe house locations, stolen Imperial documents. *Twenty years of work reduced to a courier package,* she thinks.

"Overrule me to what end? Even if things go well, you can't help us. We'll need to dismantle the whole base." Jan Dodonna raises his hands haplessly in the doorway to Mon's office. "If things don't go well—" He works his lips before the words finally form. "Mon, you won't just be leading the Rebellion. You'll be all that's left."

Mon doesn't flinch. She learned to suppress that instinct in the Senate (back when there *was* a Senate). But she slams the case shut too hard. The snap of the latches echoes in the small chamber. "I want every droid in the complex ready to analyze those station schematics once the princess lands. If they're tracking her—if her signal was accurate—the Empire won't wait long to follow."

Did she give that order already? she wonders. She hasn't slept in over three days, and facts and intentions are blurring together.

She brushes past Jan, who follows her down stone steps toward the hangar and the jungle's tapering drizzle. Cianne appears at Mon's side with a pair of duffels slung over her shoulders. "Fresh clothes and small arms," Cianne explains, "along with a few mementos."

Cianne served Mon in the capital before Mon began moonlighting in treason; since then—since Mon's flight from the Empire and public endorsement of the Rebellion—she's barely left Mon's side. *She probably added the evacuation to my daily calendar.*

"I spoke to the comm crew," Cianne goes on. They move onto the tarmac and into a wet, tepid breeze. "We'll contact Base One every ninety minutes for updates."

"The Empire may jam our transmissions or try to trace incoming signals," Jan adds. "If you can't make contact, don't keep trying forever." He hesitates as they approach a passenger shuttle covered in fading pastel graffiti. Mon doesn't recognize the alien alphabet. "Do what has to be done, Commander."

He snaps a salute. Raindrops wriggle between his fingers.

Mon can't recall ever seeing him salute her before. She reads it as a final farewell.

"Give my thanks to the princess when she arrives," Mon says. *And my condolences,* she wants to add, because she knew the princess's father so very well. But it's no use thinking about Bail right now.

She would embrace Jan, but there are flight crews watching and they need to see her strength. Instead she climbs aboard the shuttle clutching her metal case in both hands. Cianne hauls herself in behind Mon, seals the hatch, and calls orders to the pilot. As the vessel rises from the tarmac, leaving the rebels of Yavin to fight for their lives against an impossible foe, Mon wonders whether Jan understands at all *what has to be done.*

Like Mon, Jan is simultaneously practical and idealistic. He may well understand, and that thought breaks Mon's heart.

In the future—or in *a* future, a not unlikely future—the obliteration of Yavin 4 will send the remnants of the Rebellion into a panic. Mon will try to reestablish contact with the surviving rebel cells, to implement some sort of coherent strategy, but she'll be left impotent amid the chaos. Her shuttle will jump from star system to star system, constantly fleeing pursuit, and she'll spend hours daily listening to static on her comm unit and watching her life's work fall apart.

The scattered rebels will seek refuge among civilians but will find no haven. The destruction of Alderaan—a peaceful world, a beloved world, home to billions—will have convinced the ordinary people of the Empire that they cannot afford to show complicity in rebel crimes. It's one thing to endanger oneself for a cause, after all; another to endanger one's entire home planet. Stormtroopers will massacre the last remaining insurgents, hunting them relentlessly through deserts and treetops and hollowed-out asteroids.

One day, a death squad will find Mon Mothma and Cianne hiding in their shuttle in the radiation belt of a black hole. The shuttle's engines will be nonfunctional, its fuel spent. Without scanners, they won't notice the TIE fighters until too late.

Within the decade, the Rebellion Mon built will be erased from history and erased from consciousness. Soon after, even the Empire's censors will begin to forget the past.

"There are four, maybe five safe houses in range that we believe are secure and well supplied. Also two habitable planets off the Imperial charts, if you're willing to go without infrastructure. The mobile squadrons haven't managed to regroup, so we shouldn't count on those . . ."

Cianne goes on as Mon's seat vibrates with the turbulence of hyperspace. Mon only half listens. She knows all this. There are *details* that escaped her mind—she lacks the encyclopedic knowledge of rebel assets that some of her peers in High Command possess—but no one is more aware than her of the Alliance's capabilities and limits.

The princess should be arriving on Yavin 4 any moment now.

"No safe houses." Mon dismisses the option with a wave. "No hiding in deep space. If there's any point at all in our survival, we won't prove it in isolation."

Cianne's first duty, as she sees it, is the safety of her senator. Mon knows this because Cianne has said so. But Cianne also knows when it's pointless to argue, and she doesn't argue now. "All right," she says. "We could try to contact ground forces in the Rim worlds—bit of a gamble, but it would be a start."

Because that's what this means. Starting over.

Exhaustion subsumes Mon like a rising tide. She remembers the metal case nestled between her feet—the twenty years of work in a courier package. She remembers her first meetings with Bail and the others, when she was practically a child and so certain of her own experience and ability. She had imagined toppling the Emperor in a matter of months, not decades.

"Not the Rim worlds," Mon says. Her voice is commanding, loud enough for the pilot to hear. He'll draw inspiration from her, even if Cianne won't. "We go to Coruscant." Heart of the Empire, heart of the galaxy.

The pilot swears. Cianne hesitates, mentally assembling the pieces and searching for coherence. "The Senate," she says. "Disbanded or not, it's a powerful voice. And after Alderaan, the senators will have to back you."

"Perhaps," Mon says, and adds nothing more. Because while she's good at lying, she never did develop a taste for it.

In another future, the Rebellion will live on in the days after the annihilation of Alderaan and Yavin 4—not just live, but *grow,* as the Empire's atrocities become public and Mon Mothma and the Senate-in-exile kindle support. The destruction of Base One will prove a blow to the structure but not the spirit of the Rebel Alliance.

There will be a true revolution. Uprisings unlike any the galaxy has seen will erupt on a thousand worlds.

Then the Empire will respond.

Every world that defies the Galactic Emperor will be destroyed. The space station—the planet killer—will be *used*, not as a threat but as a weapon of absolute terror. The Emperor and his bitter old men will prove crueler than anyone imagined.

How many worlds will die before blood quenches the Rebellion's fire? Will Mon Cala's endless oceans boil? Will the thorn-communes of Menthusa burn? Will the ancient cityscape of Denon turn to ruins? Will two, three, a dozen, a hundred worlds fall? The galaxy is large. The Empire is unimaginably strong. For its leaders, there is no sacrifice too great to ensure its survival.

Mon will give up eventually, of course. She's not a monster. She's learned to stomach sending children into battle, but she'll never abide the loss of whole planets.

Mon Mothma can't actually see the future. She used to know people who could, but the last of them is dead now, too.

"No word from base, Senator," Cianne says. She's arranging a meal on a serving tray: stewed beans and bread and a tin cup of steaming caf, all procured from who-knows-where. Utensils clink softly, and a loamy scent fills Mon's nostrils. "We'll signal again in ninety minutes. For all we know, Private Harge still hasn't figured out the comm unit."

"Harge? What about Lentra?"

"Went to Scarif," Cianne says. She doesn't say *and didn't come back.*

The notion of eating makes Mon ill. How often has she dined

while others fought for their lives? The wounds she sustains never bleed; she has no corporeal scars to assure her that she's suffered for her cause. She recognizes the indulgent self-pity in this line of thinking, but she can't entirely banish it.

She eats. Cianne does not.

"It's all right to mourn," Mon says softly. "We may not have another chance for a while."

Cianne taps her left temple. "Biochemical regulatory implant. It keeps my stress hormones in check." She doesn't look directly at Mon. "Besides, most of my—the people I know are still on Yavin. Mourning would be premature."

By now, it might not be, Mon thinks, though she knows Cianne is aware of this.

Still, she likes hearing Cianne act hopeful. It reminds her of Bail. Through the blur of sleeplessness she imagines his ghost and asks, *Was it painful, when Alderaan died? Did you know what was happening? Did you think we'd lost?*

Mon finishes no more than half the meal. She prompts Cianne multiple times until her aide finally dines on the beans and bread remaining, more eagerly than Mon did.

"We should have waited for the princess," Mon says. "Extracted her, as well."

Cianne only shrugs. "She wouldn't have come. And trying might have left us with no time to escape."

"I owe her father," Mon says.

"Bail owed *you.* So does she. She's paying off that debt now."

Mon has heard reasoning like this before. It's reasoning that can excuse any number of deaths, and it almost works.

But Mon has other reasons to wish Princess Leia had been evacuated. The girl is young, and the galaxy has enough bitter old masterminds trying to shape it to their respective visions.

429

In another future, Mon will walk the hallways of the Imperial Palace, her white robes in contrast to the dark tile and the crimson armor of her escorts. Perhaps she will ache from bruises sustained in her capture; more likely, she will be in perfect health.

After all, she will be there by choice.

The Emperor will meet her in his throne room not to interrogate her (though Mon has heard he conducts certain interrogations personally), but to look down upon her and smile that withered, wax-faced smile. "Senator Mothma. It is so good to finally be reunited." He'll say this, or something equally unctuous.

She will be at his mercy forever.

Her Rebel Alliance—the revolution she built on a foundation of bones—will cease to be. The murder of Alderaan, the defeat at Yavin, and the surrender of its commander in chief will be blows the organization cannot recover from. There will be Imperial cleanup operations, but no more planets will die. Why should they, when the Emperor has everything he's ever desired?

Mon will be humiliated. She will be asked to renounce her cause publicly, and she will do so. She knows the Emperor well enough to expect she won't be executed—rather, she will be kept alive on the off chance he needs to use her as a warning to his enemies.

In time, she will be forgotten.

In time, her mistakes will be forgotten. Her arrogance will be forgotten.

Her complicity in the deaths of billions on Alderaan will be forgotten.

Mon Mothma is responsible for her own failures. How can she believe she has the right to start the cycle over again—to rebuild the same Rebellion that was defeated once already?

In this future, she will live her life in darkness. In time, perhaps someone else will find a better answer.

Mon writes with furious urgency, tapping words into her datapad as her metal case trembles between her ankles. She needs to complete the speech before they reach Coruscant, though that isn't why she races through it. Instead she's driven by the overwhelming need to confess, to disavow her life's work and all the horrors it has bred.

The speech isn't one of her best, and it won't get much better—she doesn't have time to redraft. She doesn't have anyone to critique her style and rhetoric. She won't let Cianne learn the truth until it's too late.

She looks from the case at her feet to the cockpit, where Cianne and the pilot are hunched over the main console. Carefully, she sets her datapad to the side and opens the case. She transfers its contents to the gap under her seat. Cianne or the pilot will find the secrets of the Rebel Alliance stashed there after Mon is gone. They can judge how to use it all themselves.

431

Like the princess, they're young enough to choose their own future. Their own means of rebellion. Mon has abrogated any right to choose for them.

She's failed at her task. Maybe others will do better.

Unless . . .

No, she tells herself. *There's no time left for dreams. Jan said it himself: Do what has to be done.*

She still has the rest of the journey to change her mind. To find another way. She doesn't believe she'll succeed.

When laughter emerges from the cockpit, she can't entirely comprehend it. She hears Cianne's voice before the pilot joins in. Mon furrows her brow as her aide rushes into the cramped passenger lounge.

"We heard from Base One," Cianne says. Her eyes glitter wetly.

"And?" Mon asks.

"They destroyed the Death Star. We won."

In the very near future, Mon will reunite with her surviving colleagues in High Command. The Alliance will rally in the wake of its extraordinary victory, and its message will spread like starlight to a thousand worlds. Rebels too young to know democracy, regret, or a lover's kiss will strike at the Empire again and again under Mon's leadership.

She will never speak of her Yavin 4 contingency plan.

The conflict will not end swiftly. The destruction of the Emperor's space station will only amplify the violence. Mon will watch the carnage from safety—from hidden bases in the jungle and under sheets of ice—sending children to die with the swipe of a finger on a tactical map. If victory comes (and it may not, it may still all prove pointless; she may even go through this a second time, with a second space station) it will take many more years.

But Mon believes in victory again.

As her shuttle adjusts course, her newfound hope crushes her like gravity and steals the air from her lungs. She does not hesitate to delete her message of surrender, but she longs for its simplicity—the endless peace of submission to despair. A new scar is etched across her spirit now, the work of the Emperor's greatest weapon.

She does not weep at her burden. She gives orders to Cianne and steels herself for the years of war to come.

THE ANGLE

Charles Soule

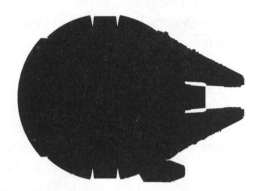

"**Y**ou ask me, Alderaan had it coming," Lando Calrissian said. "Playing it all high and mighty as long as they did."

"So you believe the rumors?" Jaff responded. "You really think the Imperials destroyed an entire planet?"

"Well, something turned Alderaan into a bunch of little rocks—and it seems like the Empire's style. You know what I mean, right?"

Lando flicked his gaze across the table, just a quick little scan across the pile of fleshy folds the Verosian called a face. Jaff Basan was strange looking, even in a galaxy with no lack of strange. Lando wanted to catch his reaction to that last statement—but, you know, without being obvious about it. You didn't want the other guy to figure out he was being played. Jaff was no amateur, though. His face maintained the same bland expression, the Verosian equivalent of a pleasant, noncommittal smile, that he'd kept on his face for the entire game so far.

Lando and Jaff sat across from each other at a low table, drinks in front of them, surrounded on all sides by a silent audience, wealthy degenerates from all across the galaxy. Activity at the other gambling stations in the casino had slowed to a crawl as word spread of what was happening here—an actual game of Klikklak between Lando Calrissian and Jaff Basan.

Klikklak was named for the sounds made by a large insect native to the forests of the planet where the game was invented. The bugs called out to each other *klik* and answered *klak,* the sounds traveling for kilometers through the trees. And that was the game: just a conversation. Each player got one card from a standard sabacc deck. Then, for a little while, they just . . . talked. Had a little chat about whatever they felt like. To an observer, Klikklak usually seemed pretty light, pretty casual. It wasn't.

When the allotted time was up, each player pressed a single button on the table between them, locking in the one decision required by the game's rules: whether they thought their card was higher or lower than the other guy's. That was it. The entire thing. You won by being right when your opponent was wrong. If you both guessed right, or both guessed wrong, the game was a push—but the house still took its 10 percent commission, the worst possible outcome. There was some dignity in losing, but when nobody won but the house? Forget Alderaan—*that* would be a tragedy.

The trick to Klikklak was the conversation. You had to use those ten minutes or so not only to try to figure out what your opponent had, high or low, but also to get them to guess the way you wanted them to go. You had to figure them out, and misdirect them at the same time. Lando loved it. If gambling could ever be called art—and as far as Lando Calrissian was concerned, it *absolutely could*—then Klikklak was its highest expression.

Jaff was a tough opponent, though. Lando didn't know much about Verosian physiology. Always a tricky situation, especially since humans were among the most common species in the galaxy. That made them underdogs in games like Klikklak. Jaff probably knew what most human facial expressions signified—but Lando was flying blind, trying to piece together what a little tremble of the antennae might mean, or a slow, languid blink of an ocular membrane.

Still . . . you know . . . exhilarating.

"What do you mean?" Jaff said.

"Well, didn't the Empire get all up in your planet's business, too?"

Jaff made the sort of wobbly snort that passed for a chuckle.

"They're in everyone's business, aren't they?"

"Not mine," Lando said. "I stay clear. That *is* my business."

"Oh really?" Jaff said. "I thought it was losing at cards."

A little held breath from the audience, as they waited to see how Lando would respond. But insults were part of the game, nothing to get all worked up about. Lando glanced around the room at the watchers. Beings from more than twenty different worlds, united by a single expression of rapt fascination. They were watching two masters at work, and they knew it.

Lando grinned self-deprecatingly, lifting one arm to the crowd, letting himself be the butt of the joke, giving the audience permission to laugh with him. He took over the moment, not watching Jaff's reaction, but of course he was absolutely watching Jaff's reaction, and there—there it was. The tiniest flush of green on the folds of his neck. The same flush he'd seen when Lando had mentioned the Empire.

Jaff Basan came from Veros, and Veros had once been an extremely wealthy planet. Technically, it was still a wealthy planet, but that wealth was now in the hands of the Empire, instead of the bank accounts of the familial alliances that had ruled the planet for centuries, one of which was the venerable House of Basan. It had all happened decades ago, and Jaff was still rich—very rich, or he wouldn't have been allowed entry to this room at all—but there had to be a twinge when he thought about what had been taken from his family. Frustration, expressed in a spray of viridian across the gill-like fronds on his neck.

The infuriating thing about Klikklak was that having a high card wasn't always good, and low wasn't always bad. Lando's card was precisely in the middle of the deck—he couldn't even use the odds to help him. But that didn't matter, really. In Klikklak, the cards were, in many ways, irrelevant. The game was about coming to a complete and thorough understanding of another being in the space of a single conversation, and if you couldn't manage that, you were lost.

But Lando was not lost. He had Jaff dead to rights. He'd pieced together that the little flush of green meant frustration, and he'd also seen it whenever he'd slipped references to things being high, or tall, or above into the conversation—little signifiers, meant to be perceived by Jaff as accidental—subconscious nudges to help him think Lando's card was on the high side. Every time he did it, another green flush, which meant Jaff was annoyed, which meant Jaff's card had to be high, too, because it was hard for him to decide whether Lando's high card was higher than *his* high card. Put all of that together and Lando's bet was easy. Low.

"Shall we?" Lando said, gesturing toward the buttons on the table's surface, hidden from the other player by a small screen, which were used to indicate the high/low bet.

Jaff nodded politely, and moved one of his appendages behind his own screen.

Lando kept his smile smooth and his breathing steady—no external signals for Jaff to read—but inside, he was already laughing. This was it. At last. With the credits he was about to win, he could pay off his more pressing debts, put some money down on a ship, get mobile again, see what sort of delights the galaxy had to offer a man of Lando Calrissian's unique abilities and sensibilities.

He touched the button on the table, caressed it, savoring the moment.

And then, a shout, a command uttered in the gravelly, compressed, inhuman tone that anyone living in the Empire's galaxy recognized immediately.

"Hands in clear view! Anyone who moves will be shot. There will be no second warning," the stormtrooper said.

The room froze as everyone slowly turned to look at the squad of Imperial troops that had entered the little space. Five ordinary troops plus an orange-pauldroned sergeant—but also, somewhat unusually, a black-clad Imperial officer. Lando thought it was a lieutenant, but he couldn't be sure. He'd never bothered to memorize the rank insignia—the Calrissian policy with respect to Imperial officers was the same top to bottom: avoid.

The officer's face was cold, icy, clenched tight. It read to Lando like barely restrained rage. Anger at some great personal injury.

"This is an illegal gambling establishment, in violation of Imperial Statute Seven-Five-Nine-Point-Eight. You are all ordered to vacate the premises immediately. Any credits you have deposited with the room's cashier are forfeit."

A rumble of discontent rippled through the room. *Everyone* had money stashed with the cashier in exchange for the credit chits they used to gamble. Lando himself, in particular, had the very large wager he had placed on the Klikklak game. Thousands of credits, carefully amassed over long nights at gambling tables much less reputable than this one, scraped together from gigs that were so far beneath his talents that it almost physically hurt to take them. About to evaporate like smoke.

Movement in the crowd as a large, robed gentleman stepped forward, rings on his fingers glittering in the low light, heavy jowls lifting to lavish a generous smile on the presumed lieutenant. Luck Luck Freidal, owner of the casino, and a man with potentially more to lose that evening than any gambler in his establishment.

"My friend, is there a mistake?" Freidal said. "Everything here is legal. People are just having a nice evening."

"Not anymore. This is over," the officer said, his tone colder than the dark side of an ice moon.

The smile on Freidal's face wavered, just a touch.

Oh no, man, Lando thought. *Don't do it. Don't you see? The man's just* looking *for an excuse.*

But Freidal apparently did not see, or decided the risk was worth it, in the desperate hope that this obvious misunderstanding could be cleared up, that there was a way to salvage his reputation and his business before word spread that Luck Luck Freidal couldn't keep his illegal gambling den clear of Imperials.

Freidal leaned in closer to the Imperial officer and uttered a few low words. Lando couldn't hear them, but he had a pretty good idea of what was being said: *Hey, man, I'm paid up this month. What the hell are you doing? Don't we have an arrangement?*

Lando saw the officer's face turn even colder, which he would have said was impossible. He saw Freidal pressing his case, saw the troopers taking a tighter grip on their rifles. He saw it all, and knew *exactly* what was about to happen.

Lando had a blaster under his cape, at the small of his back. Just a little thing, but it packed a wallop. He was better with it than anyone in this casino knew—than anyone *alive* knew, in fact. He could take out the lieutenant, the stormtrooper commander, maybe even one of the underlings, before they reacted. And by the time they did, some of the other illicit weaponry in the room would be out from under cloaks and hidden holsters. These idiot Imperials had no idea how outnumbered they actually were in here—they'd all be gunned down in no time. Someone just had to make the first move. Someone had to play hero.

Lando Calrissian loved heroes. They thought the galaxy owed them something. Like they mattered, somehow, in some bizarre way that meant the fundamental rules of reality were tilted in their favor. Heroes believed, honestly *believed* that things would just . . . work out for them.

Heroes were Lando's favorite opponents at the gambling table. The worse the odds got, the bigger they bet.

Because heroes were suckers.

Lando slowly, carefully moved his hands up above the edge of the Klikklak table. They were empty.

The Imperial officer nodded once, tightly. Two quick shots from a blaster rifle, and then a thud as Luck Luck Freidal hit the floor, a smoking hole where his heart had been. Lando would have to find his next game somewhere else.

The lieutenant looked out at the room. The murder he'd just ordered appeared to have done exactly zero to cool the rage seething behind his eyes.

"Disperse," he said.

Lando's eyes shifted to the safe across the room where Freidal kept the wagers on the various games until they were paid out. Millions of credits in that safe, many of which had, just minutes ago, belonged to Lando Calrissian.

Lando closed his eyes for a moment, sighed deeply, then dispersed.

Another bar, across the city, in a less desirable zone. The sort of place Lando had sincerely hoped he would never have to set foot in again. A place where work could be found, for individuals with unique abilities, sensibilities, and moralities. Work had suddenly become *very* important. Lando needed a gig to make up those credits he'd just lost, and quick, or he'd be in trouble. More trouble.

So much for hope, he thought, stepping through the door, immediately suffused by the miasma of spilled drinks and dead dreams that places like this always shared.

Lando walked to the bar, sensing the eyes of almost every being in the place watching him. He owed debts to at least half of them, ranging from credits to blood. He reached the bar, then turned around and smiled.

"Hey, guys. Long time," he said. "How about a round on me?"

The bartender, of a species with arguably too many eyes, tapped Lando's shoulder.

"You buying a round for the bar? How you gonna pay for it, Calrissian?" he said.

"Put it on my tab, Okkul," Lando said, not turning.

"Your tab? Your *tab*?" Okkul said, his tone rising into an aggrieved whine that could pierce durasteel. "You honestly think there's credit for you in this bar, after . . ."

Lando pulled a credit chip from his pocket and placed it down on the bar, doing it theatrically, making sure plenty of people saw him do it.

"That should handle it. Everything I owe you *and* the round for the house."

Okkul's attitude mellowed considerably after that, and, more important, it meant Lando was safe, at least for the time it took for the bar's patrons to obtain and consume their drinks. You don't shoot the guy buying the booze. Usually.

Lando moved toward the end of the bar, where a man sat reading from a datapad. Lando joined the man, lifting his glass to his mouth.

"Nice gesture," Lobot said. "So you won?"

Lando drained his drink—a barely drinkable local brandy, but what could you expect, really—and set the glass down on the bar, signaling to Okkul to bring him another.

"I'm gonna need to you to cover this next one, Lo, and all of the many others I plan to consume this fine evening. Those were my last few credits. Your man Lando is officially skinned."

Lobot's mouth tightened in an all-too-familiar note of resignation.

"I told you that Klikklak game was a bad idea. Too hard to calculate the odds. Too messy."

"It wasn't the game. I *had* the game. Bunch of Imperials busted in, killed Freidal, ran us all out of there. Technically, I didn't lose—let's be clear about that—but they confiscated my buy-in. Lost my credits, kept my skin—the Lando Calrissian story, just like always."

Lobot raised an eyebrow, the metal implants on either side of his bald head flashing rapidly as he processed this new information.

"You're kidding," he said. "Freidal paid up every month, right on time. It was a point of pride with him. He ran the cleanest illegal backroom casino in the city. That's why he could bring in the big fish. And also the smaller fish."

Lobot lifted his own glass—water, of course. Lobot never drank or consumed anything that might cloud his thoughts, for fear it might allow his Imperial-issue implants the window they needed to finally take over his mind. The things were useful, especially when it came to gambling and calculating odds, but they extracted a price, no doubt about it. He tilted his glass toward Lando in a mock toast.

"Such as you."

Lando ignored the comment and took a sip from his fresh drink.

The bartender was hovering, waiting to see if new credits were forthcoming, and Lando waved him away with a little shooing motion.

"The Imperials were riled up," Lando said once Okkul was out of earshot. "Furious, even, and it wasn't just stormtroopers. They had a ranking officer with them, too. Don't know what happened, but—"

"I do," Lobot said. "They're trying to assert their authority. Get a little pride back."

"Pride? What the hell are you talking about?"

Lobot called out to the bartender, "Okkul, can you run that feed again?"

The bartender nodded amiably and reached for a control stick for the large holoscreen mounted above the bar.

"Sure," Okkul said. "You know, I've watched that thing ten times, and I'm *still* not sick of it."

Grainy footage appeared on the screen, sharpening up after a few initial bits of static. It looked like it was shot from the point of view of a starfighter, something long-nosed, zipping through space.

"What is this?" Lando asked.

"The Rebellion just leaked it on the DarkNet—it's getting play all over the place."

"Not another one of their propaganda clips? I wish they'd give it a rest. The more they shout about their stupid cause, the less interesting it gets. That's just basic psychology. You'd think they'd figure that out."

"Just watch," Lobot said, his voice quiet, and his eyes focused on the holoscreen.

So Lando watched—it was footage of a space battle, a bunch of X-wings and a few other fighters of various models, all of them looking like they should have been scrapped years ago, deploying against the biggest space station he'd ever seen, a huge gray sphere, almost like a miniature moon, bristling with turbolaser defense turrets.

442

"What *is* that thing?" he asked.

"They call it the Death Star," Lobot answered. "A planet killer, if you believe the rumors. How they blew up Alderaan."

Lando watched the fighters make their attack runs, watched the X-wings being picked off by the endless swarm of TIE fighters, watched a bunch of heroes die the way heroes always died. Suckers, one and all.

"Why would they release this?" Lando said, taking another slug of the increasingly drinkable brandy. "Do they want us to feel sorry for them? Who's to say this is even real footage? Both sides put out these propaganda pieces all the time, and—"

And then Lando knew it was real, because another ship had appeared on the screen. A very, very familiar ship. A Corellian YT-1300 light freighter, old, sure, maybe a little banged up here and there, but . . . still beautiful. She was still beautiful.

"That's . . . that's my ship," he said, rising out of his seat a bit. "That's the *Millennium Falcon*."

He watched, stunned, his drink halfway to his mouth, as the *Falcon* swooped in from out of frame, behind a trio of TIEs—one a little modified, maybe a custom job—that were trailing some X-wings running through some kind of trench on the Death Star's surface. Its quadlasers fired, and it picked them off, vaporizing two and sending the last one, the custom, spiraling away into space.

The ship—*his* ship—pulled up and flew away, out of frame. Lando felt more than sensed everyone in the bar leaning forward, as if they were waiting for something to happen.

"Wait, can you run that back for a second?"

Okkul paused the feed, to a few groans from around the room, and looked at Lando incredulously.

"This is nothing, Calrissian. The best part's coming up."

"Come on. Just run it back for me."

443

Lando gave his best smile, the very best one, the one he reserved for extremely special occasions. The smile that promised whatever the recipient might want or need—credits, friendship, protection, short-term *or* long-term love, the wonders of the galaxy itself—if only they would do what the owner of the smile wanted. The Calrissian Special.

The bartender shook his head but rewound the footage. Of course he did.

"Stop," Lando said. "Right there."

He watched it again—the *Millennium Falcon* saving the day, then zooming up and away.

"Again," he said. Okkul didn't even protest this time, just ran it back.

Lando had been sure the first time he'd watched it, but needed the next two play-throughs to process what he'd seen. But there was no doubt in his mind. The tactics, the maneuvers . . . he'd seen it all before. No one flew the *Falcon* as well as Lando Calrissian—but one man came as close as anyone could.

"Han Solo is flying that ship," he said.

"Looks like," Lobot said.

"But that is *impossible*," Lando said.

He was dimly aware of the footage continuing, of an enormous explosion, of cheers in the bar—cheers that would probably get everyone in here killed if there were any Imperials within earshot—but he wasn't really paying attention.

What was Han Solo doing with the Rebellion? And not just, say, smuggling for them. That'd be fine, sure. A gig was a gig, and fuel wasn't free. But this . . . Han was *attacking an Imperial superweapon.* It just . . . it just didn't make sense.

Lando knew a lot of people, all across the galaxy—it was sort of his trademark. But very, very few people knew him. He could count them on one hand. Lobot, maybe a few others, and Han Solo. He'd have said that was mutual. He'd even have said they were the same, morally speaking—more than anyone else in the galaxy. They were out for themselves, because no one else was.

And then this Death Star thing. Now, Lando could understand helping people out from time to time—that made sense. Never know when you might need to call in a favor. But this . . . this was lunacy. It was like doubling your bet in sabacc when the other guy had the Idiot's Array. It was like kicking a sleeping rancor. It wasn't just pushing your luck, it was shoving it off a cliff and laughing while it hit every rock on the way down.

The Rebellion was a lost cause. The rebels were heroes, with all that implied. They were doomed, because the Empire was the house, and the house always wins. And yet there was the *Millennium Falcon*, his ship, right in the thick of one of the ugliest battles he'd ever seen.

Lando would have bet every credit he had—used to have—that Han Solo was neither a hero *or* susceptible to the sort of nonsense ideologies heroes subscribed to. But there he was, heroing it up. Troubling.

Lando stared moodily up at the screen. The bartender had started the clip over, and he watched the heroes start their impossible attack once again. He tried to understand, and couldn't. He couldn't see the angle in it. Why would Han do this?

Lando turned to look out at the bar and lifted his glass.

"To the memory of the greatest smuggler I ever knew!" he shouted, to some halfhearted cheers from the other patrons.

He looked back at Lobot, and pointed at the screen, where Han Solo was once again risking Lando's ship, his precious, beautiful *Millennium Falcon*, for no reason he could figure.

"If I ever do anything like that . . . shoot me."

"No problem," Lobot said.

As Lando watched the Death Star explode, he considered the one rule of confidence men, tricksters, gamblers, and scam artists the galaxy over: If you can't see the angle, it means you're the one being played. You are, in fact, the sucker.

Lando sat, and thought, and drank drinks he had no money to pay for, and wondered what he was missing.

BY WHATEVER SUN

E. K. Johnston

Story by E. K. Johnston & Ashley Eckstein

Miara Larte breathed in and remembered how much she loved real air. Sure, a large part of her heart was in the skies and the void of space beyond it, trained in an A-wing cockpit before transitioning to an X-wing and, eventually, a cruiser, but nothing recycled through a ship's O_2 scrubbers could match good, green air planetside. Even now, in the wake of battle and horror, one or two deep breaths was enough to steady her.

"Is now really the best time for this?" Jessamyn was red-eyed, but her voice was clear and Miara couldn't smell any alcohol on her. Her second in command was a professional to the end, it seemed.

"They have to do something," murmured one of the new gunners,

Hester or Heattens or something like that. He'd been assigned to Miara recently. Like her, he had been away from Alderaan when the Death Star attacked. Unlike her, he hadn't been with his shipmates at the time.

Behind them, rank after rank of rebel soldiers filed into lines. Miara and her Alderaanian crew had a place of privilege at the front, but that meant they had the longest wait while the room filled up. It was the first time they'd had to stand around and do nothing, so she had expected someone to crack.

"It's just so . . ." Jessamyn trailed off. Miara reached across the prescribed space between them and took her hand.

"I know," she said. "There's nothing anyone can say. We've lost too much for that. But this reminds us that we didn't lose everything."

Jessamyn was quiet. Miara wondered if she'd said the right thing. As a captain, she was sure of it, but she hadn't been born on Alderaan, and sometimes those who had been took it personally when she claimed the planet as her own. It was bad enough when the planet still existed. Miara imagined that, now, her grief might seem like a fresh insult, but Jessamyn only nodded and drew herself up to attention. They didn't speak any further, but Miara could feel her crew all around her and knew that they would hold it together just a bit longer.

At last, the great cavern at the rebel base on Yavin 4 was crammed full, though the orderly lines of uniformed troops belied the crush. Miara forgot, sometimes, how big the Rebellion was. Their losses in the past few weeks had been near-catastrophic, and yet here she stood, knees locked at parade rest, hands behind her back, shoulder-to-shoulder with what remained of the Alderaanian guard.

. . . what remained . . .

Miara felt herself drift toward memory and pulled back sharply. She could get away with fidgeting in the crowd—the twisting of her fingers hidden against the palm of her hand, and the shifting of her weight concealed by her already bent legs—but this was not the moment for her grief. The Rebellion was quick and tireless, moving from mission to mission with very little downtime, yet every now and then a yawning pause would appear. Miara knew they were on the edge of one right now—this was not the first time she had lost a planet—but they were not there, not yet.

Lost a planet didn't quite cover it. Miara could go back to Raada if she wanted. See it from orbit, walk the dead fields, and go to the caves where Neera had saved her life with a stun blast. There was nothing left of Raada but the planet itself. There was nothing left of Alderaan but dust and memory, and what survivors remained spread out across the stars.

Without turning her head, she looked sideways down the line of her crew. *Crew.* Once, that word had meant family and farming. As a pilot—and later an officer—Miara found it meant a team and a job to do in all the mess.

Her people looked good, which was what she'd expected. Every line of their uniforms was crisp, and their helmets gleamed. In the bright sun of the Yavin 4 morning, no bleariness or signs of unprofessionalism remained, despite the fact that many of them had been up late the previous night. The colony here welcomed refugees from any world savaged by the Empire, places like Fest, Raada, Jedha, and now Alderaan. There was no shortage of understanding, no shortage of means by which to remember the names beyond counting and a world that was no longer a world at all.

Antilles, who had scooped them up.

Organa, who had given them a home.

Organa, who had given them a mission.

Organa, who stood here before them now and had given them hope.

All eyes were drawn to Leia, even though the ranks of rebels

449

turned to face each other. Her small form, clad in a pristinely white dress, was impossible to miss against the unrelieved gray of the cavern walls. More than that, she was compelling in the way her mother had been, and gentle in the manner of her father, and even the most disciplined of gazes shifted to her: an orbit around a star. Miara had heard the whispers—ice princess, cold—but she could find no fault in how Leia chose to carry herself. The Rebellion had demanded nearly everything of the princess. If she wanted to keep her grief private, Miara was not about to criticize.

Miara's own grief bubbled up again at the thought of what the princess had lost, and again, as Leia must be doing in full view of all those assembled, she forced it back down. Soon, but not yet.

Home had always been a place that Kaeden made. On Raada, her sister had kept them fed and clothed by sheer force of will. On Alderaan, even in that first refugee camp, it had been easier. This felt like a betrayal, though Miara could not have said of whom, and it drove Kaeden to restlessness, and eventually to a medical program in one of Alderaan's over-pretty cities. She served on a Republic medical frigate, and the sisters didn't get to see each other very often. At least Kaeden was alive.

Miara's path to the stars had been more direct.

The A-wing pilots who had flown in Raada's skies as the moon was evacuated had been high on adrenaline when Miara found them—fourteen and, despite the carnage she'd witnessed, fearless now that she was in the sky—and they had told her all kinds of stories on the way back to Alderaan. By the time they'd landed, Miara was certain she was going to fly again, but next time with her own hands at the controls.

The Rebellion had been in dire need of pilots, so training had been easy to come by. Miara had risen through the ranks thanks to her own quick thinking and the prodigious death rate pilots faced in the early days, before the various rebel cells had coalesced into something more stable. Her promotion to captain had come at the request of Senator Organa himself, though Queen Breha had been the one to formalize it in a ceremony in the capital where several other promotions had been handed out. It was the first time Miara had seen the princess up close. At ten, Leia was tiny and filled with dignified fury, a seemingly perfect mix of the senator and queen, both. Miara had been young for a promotion, but she had understood why she received the honor the moment her first classified mission had come in: There was no mistaking the Fulcrum symbol attached to it. She'd had to tell Kaeden in person, words chosen carefully to avoid compromising a valuable secret.

They would need more pilots again, now. So many had died at Scarif and in the battle against the Death Star. Imperial defectors were already showing up, horror woken by the carnage the Empire's now destroyed superweapon had wreaked. Yes, there would be bodies for cockpits, hands for the controls, souls to stretch the limits of speed and agility, bending X-wing to will.

451

Music sounded from somewhere, a horn pulling Miara out of memory and musing and back to the cavern with the rest of her crew. She heard Jessamyn's breath catch as she recognized the song: another piece of Alderaan the Empire had not ruined. It was against protocol—and awkward, given that Jessamyn was currently standing behind her—but Miara reached back to her second in command again. For a brief moment, Jessamyn's fingers grasped hers, and then Miara returned to attention.

If it made Skywalker or Solo nervous to walk the entire length of the cavern with the eyes of the Rebellion on them, they didn't show it. Miara assumed the Wookiee was fine. She hadn't met Solo at all, had only heard what he'd done after the fact, but she'd been in the briefing when Skywalker had spoken up. He'd made her feel old, made her think of a girl on a little moon, building bombs because she could, eager to fight in a battle she didn't yet understand the true scope of.

That was the difference the Rebellion made. It had taken that girl and trained her, made her better and given her the tools she needed to survive. She had passed along as much of what she knew as she could—to her crew, to the other pilots, to the not-quite-random idealists she'd ferried about the galaxy on those missions she wasn't supposed to talk about. She had been alone, in the end, on Raada, and she'd been out of materials to explode, but she wasn't alone anymore. Neither was Skywalker, though she had no idea what he'd become as a result of it.

The trio passed in front of her and climbed the stairs to stand before Leia and what remained of the Alliance High Command. As one, the rebels on the floor of the cavern turned, facing front toward the princess. The music grew quiet as Skywalker and Solo bowed to receive the medals the princess hung about their necks. Miara could tell by the way Leia's mouth twitched that Solo must have pulled a face at her, but the princess remained cool under the scrutiny of hundreds. The light gleamed off her necklace—a traditional Alderaanian piece, Miara was sure. She wondered who had gotten it off the planet and how it had found its way to Yavin 4.

There was a shuffle on the platform as a little astromech unit pushed its way forward to stand beside the princess's gleaming protocol droid. It chirruped—oddly cheerful for a droid, Miara thought—just as the music swelled again, so only those at the very front of the cavern heard it. Everyone could see Skywalker laughing, though, as he, Solo, and the Wookiee turned around to face the crowd. The Wookiee roared as cheering broke out. Miara took another look to her side and saw tears streaming down Jessamyn's face. Her second in command looked at her long enough for a quick nod.

This was why it had to be now, why they had to stand in this place on this planet, and celebrate what they had while remembering what they had lost. It was for the balance of it, the good measured out to offset the bad, but neither of them forgotten or erased.

When Miara looked back to the platform, Leia was smiling, her face radiant as she stood at the center of attention. It wasn't a political smile; Miara had seen enough of those to know them. It was real.

Miara felt something in her own chest unclench, freeing the emotions she'd been holding back since Alderaan had disappeared in a blaze of fire, unsure if she was entitled to feel them. Raada was gone. Alderaan was gone. Her sister lived. *She* lived. She had her crew and her ship, and soon she would have a mission again. She stood on Yavin 4 and breathed green air.

With grief on her cheeks and hope in her heart, Miara Larte added her voice to those in the cavern who celebrated the living and re-membered the dead. It would be a long night, she knew. She had lived long nights before. But in the morning, by whatever sun, she would get up and she would rebel.

WHILLS

Tom Angleberger

At last it is time . . . I have heard every version of the story, viewed every holocron, and studied every artifact. A lifetime of preparation has readied me for this noble duty. May the Force be with me as I begin the sacred task of writing in the *Journal of the Whills* . . .

A long time ago in a galaxy far, far away. . . .

Well, I mean it's not really *that* far away, is it?

What are you talking about?

"Far, far away"? I'm saying it's "far," but not "far, far."

Uh . . .

I mean, if anything I'd say it's a long, long time ago in a galaxy far away.

Yeah, well the rest of the Whills asked *me* to write this, not you. So it's going to say . . .

A long time ago in a galaxy far, far away. . . .
It is a period of civil war.

A "period"? Wow, you really like to keep things vague, don't you?

Good grief, what do you want me to put: "It is a Thursday afternoon of civil war"?

No, that's stupid. Maybe the problem is that passive voice. "It is a . . ." Kinda weak! You should really start with an action verb.

It's the first sentence, dude. If you nitpick every single sentence of this journal, we aren't even going to get to the battles.

All right, fine. Keep it . . . It could be better, but . . .

Rebel spaceships, striking
from a hidden base, have won
their first victory against the
evil Galactic Empire.

Whoa, whoa, whoa . . . The Empire and the rebels?

Uh, yeah.

Already? What about the Republic?

What about it?

You're just going to skip over the Republic? Don't tell me you're skipping the Clone Wars and all of that stuff?

Well . . . yeah . . .

What about Anakin and Padmé and the sand and—

I figured I could just sort of make some mysterious references to all that.

Mysterious references? What about Darth Maul? He's just going to be a mysterious reference?

Actually, I'm not sure. I wasn't really planning on mentioning him.

Not mention Darth Maul?!?! *Darth? Maul?*

No . . .

Next you're going to tell me that you weren't planning to mention Captain Rex, Ahsoka, Ventress, Cad Bane, Savage Opress, Jar Jar, and the Mandalorians?

Well . . . I guess I could always go back and tell their stories later.

Out of order? That's just going to confuse everybody!

I think they'll figure it out.

Uh-huh, right. Wait, I know! Maybe you could add numbers to the beginning of each part. You know, like maybe this one starts out "A long, long time ago in a galaxy far away: Episode 4."

That seems kind of—

Ooh, I got an idea! What if you made it "IV"? That would be fancier. And you could give each episode a title. Like, uh, "Episode VII: Blue Harvest"!

Well, that's just weird, but if I promise to call it Episode IV and think of a great title, will you let me get on with this?

Yeah, cool, keep going. You're about to get to the good stuff: Jyn Erso, Orson Krennic, K-2SO . . .

During the battle, Rebel spies managed to steal secret plans to the Empire's ultimate weapon, the DEATH STAR, an armored space station with enough power to destroy an entire planet.

457

Wait, that was it? What about Erso? What about K-2SO?

I'm planning to start with R2-D2 and C-3PO.

Okay, now you're just being crazy. You're going to skip over K-2SO, the *Best. Droid. Ever.* And start with a protocol droid??? What the Hutt, dude?

I mean, R2—yes, he's awesome—but if you're going to skip anybody you should skip C-3PO! All he does is whine.

I can't skip him; he's really important on Endor.

Endor? Wait a minute, you're not putting in the teddy bears, are you?

They're not teddy bears! The Ewoks are fierce warriors. The top of the food chain on a savage planet!

Okay, first of all, they live on a moon, not a planet. Second of all—

Look, just save it! They're not going in this episode anyway.

Well, what *is* in this episode? You're skipping *everything*!

Well, Princess Leia will be in it if you ever let me get started.

Okay, cool, good. She's awesome!

Pursued by the Empire's sinister agents, Princess Leia races home aboard her starship, custodian of—

Custodian? Seriously? People are going to think this is a movie about a janitor!

Oh my Jabba! You are driving me *nuts*! Do you have to nitpick every single word?!

It's just constructive criticism. Can't you even take a little constructive criticism? I mean if you can't take constructive criticism maybe you're not the best Whill for the job.

Oh, I guess you think you can do better?

Honestly? Yes, I do.

458

Then why don't you go write your own journal and leave me alone?

Okay, fine, you know what? *I will!* I've got some great ideas for an episode about how Chewbacca's family celebrates Life Day!

Okay, great, off you go. Now, where was I?

Custodian.

Right . . .

**Princess Leia races home
aboard her starship, custodian of
the stolen plan that can save her
people and restore freedom to the
galaxy . . .**

ABOUT THE AUTHORS

All participating authors have generously forgone any compensation for their stories. Instead, their proceeds will be donated to First Book—a leading nonprofit that provides new books, learning materials, and other essentials to educators and organizations serving children in need. To further celebrate the launch of this book and both companies' long-standing relationships with First Book, Penguin Random House has donated $100,000 to First Book, and Disney/Lucasfilm has donated one hundred thousand children's books—valued at $1 million—to support First Book and their mission of providing equal access to quality education. Over the past sixteen years, Disney and Penguin Random House combined have donated more than eighty-eight million books to First Book.

BEN ACKER and BEN BLACKER are the creators and writers/producers of the Thrilling Adventure Hour, a staged show in the style of old-time radio that is also a podcast on the Nerdist network. In television, they have written for CW's *Supernatural,* DreamWorks/Netflix's *Puss in Boots,* and FX's *Cassius and Clay.* They've also developed original pilots for Fox, USA (twice), Spike, Paramount, Nickelodeon, and other entities. In comics, they've written for Marvel, Dynamite, Boom!, and others. Acker has written for PRI's *Wits*. Blacker is the creator and host of The Writers Panel, a podcast about the business and process of writing, as well as its spin-off, the Nerdist Comics Panel. He's the producer of Dead Pilots Society, a podcast in which unproduced television pilots by established writers are given the table reads they so richly deserve.

RENÉE AHDIEH is the author of the #1 *New York Times* bestselling *The Wrath and the Dawn* and *The Rose and the Dagger.* In her spare time, she likes to dance salsa and collect shoes. She is passionate about all kinds of curry, rescue dogs, and college basketball. The first few years of her life were spent in a high-rise in South Korea; consequently, Renée enjoys having her head in the clouds. She lives in Charlotte, North Carolina, with her husband and their tiny overlord of a dog.

TOM ANGLEBERGER is the author of the *New York Times, USA Today,* and *Wall Street Journal* bestselling Origami Yoda series, as well as *Fake Mustache* and *Horton Halfpott,* both Edgar Award nominees, and the QwikpickPapers series. He is also the author of the transportation picture book *McToad Mows Tiny Island.* Tom lives with his wife, Cece Bell, in Christiansburg, Virginia.

JEFFREY BROWN is the author of numerous bestselling *Star Wars* books, including *Darth Vader and Son* and the middle-grade Jedi Academy series. He grew up in

Michigan, where a lot of snow fell every winter. Unlike Neanderthals, he has never learned how to make stone tools. He lives in Chicago with his wife and sons.

PIERCE BROWN is the #1 *New York Times* bestselling author of *Red Rising, Golden Son,* and *Morning Star.* While trying to make it as a writer, Brown worked as a manager of social media at a start-up tech company, toiled as a peon on the Disney lot at ABC Studios, did his time as an NBC page, and gave sleep deprivation a new meaning during his stint as an aide on a U.S. Senate campaign. He lives in Los Angeles, where he is at work on his next novel.

MEG CABOT is the #1 *New York Times* bestselling author of the Princess Diaries series, with over 25 million copies of her books sold worldwide. Born and raised in Bloomington, Indiana, Meg also lived in Grenoble, France, and Carmel, California, before moving to New York City, after graduating with a bachelor's degree in fine arts from Indiana University. She is the author of numerous books for adults and children, but From the Notebooks of a Middle School Princess is the first series she's illustrated. Meg Cabot currently lives in Key West with her husband and cat.

RAE CARSON is the author of the bestselling and award-winning Girl of Fire and Thorns series. Her books tend to contain adventure, magic, and smart girls who make (mostly) smart choices. Originally from California, Rae Carson now lives in Arizona with her husband.

ADAM CHRISTOPHER is a novelist and comic writer. His debut novel, *Empire State,* was *SciFiNow*'s Book of the Year and a *Financial Times* Book of the Year for 2012. In 2013, he was nominated for the Sir Julius Vogel Award for Best New Talent, with *Empire State* shortlisted for Best Novel. His other novels include *The Age Atomic* and *The Burning Dark.*

ZORAIDA CÓRDOVA is the author of the Vicious Deep trilogy, the On the Verge series, and the Brooklyn Brujas series. She loves black coffee, snark, and still believes in magic. She is a New Yorker at heart and is currently working on her next novel.

DELILAH S. DAWSON is the writer of the Blud series, *Servants of the Storm, Hit, Wake of Vultures* (as Lila Bowen), and a variety of short stories and comics. She's also a geek, an artist, an adventure junkie, and a cupcake connoisseur. She writes books for both young adults and adults that range from whimsical to dark to sexy to horrific to adventuresome.

KELLY SUE DECONNICK got her start in the comic industry adapting Japanese and Korean comics into English. Five years and more than ten thousand pages of adaptation later, she transitioned to American comics with *30 Days of Night: Eben and Stella,* for Steve Niles and IDW. Work for Image, Boom, Oni, Humanoids, Dark Horse, DC, Vertigo, and Marvel soon followed. Today DeConnick is best known for surprise hits like Carol Danvers's rebranding as Captain Marvel and the Eisner-nominated mythological western, *Pretty Deadly;* the latter was co-created with artist Emma Ríos. DeConnick's most recent venture, the sci-fi kidney-punch called *Bitch Planet,* co-created with Valentine De Landro, launched to rave reviews in December 2014. DeConnick lives in Portland, Oregon, with her husband, Matt Fraction, and their two children.

PAUL DINI is a multiple Emmy- and Eisner Award–winning writer and producer who has helped redefine the legends of the DC Universe in such series as *The New Batman/Superman Adventures, Batman Beyond, Krypto,* and *Justice League Unlimited.* In doing so, he co-created one of the most popular characters in comics in Harley Quinn, who originated as a character in *Batman: The Animated Series.* In comics he has authored *The World's Greatest Super-Heroes,* illustrated by Alex Ross. Dini has also collaborated with Chip Kidd on *Batman Animated* for HarperCollins.

IAN DOESCHER, author of the William Shakespeare *Star Wars* series, has loved Shakespeare since eighth grade and was born forty-five days after *Star Wars Episode IV* was released. He has a BA in music from Yale University, a master of divinity from Yale Divinity School, and a PhD in ethics from Union Theological Seminary. Ian lives in Portland, Oregon, with his spouse and two sons.

Known to Star Wars fans as the voice of Ahsoka Tano on *Star Wars: The Clone Wars, Star Wars Rebels,* and

Star Wars: Forces of Destiny, actress and entrepreneur
Ashley Eckstein also founded Her Universe—the
groundbreaking fangirl fashion company and lifestyle
brand. Ashley has been widely recognized as a busi-
nesswoman and fangirl trendsetter. She was recently
chosen by *Good Housekeeping* magazine as one of their
25 Awesome Women for 2016. Her Universe is a proud
licensee for Disney/*Star Wars* and Marvel, BBC/*Doctor
Who,* CBS/*Star Trek,* Studio Ghibli, as well as a growing roster of properties.

Ashley is a recognized personality in the "geek
world" and an in-demand actress and host starring in
several TV specials, live shows, events, and videos for
Disney, HSN, Comic-Con HQ, and more. In addition
to *Star Wars*' Ahsoka Tano, Ashley is also the voice of
Mia the Bluebird on Disney's *Sofia the First,* Dagger on
Disney XD's *Ultimate Spider-Man,* and the voice of
Cheetah on *DC Super Hero Girls.* Ashley was also heard
on the big screen in 2016 as the voice of Yaeko in the
English adaptation of Studio Ghibli's beloved film *Only
Yesterday* alongside fellow *Star Wars* actress Daisy Rid-
ley and acclaimed actor Dev Patel.

In October 2016, Her Universe was acquired by Hot
Topic, Inc., and joined their stable of brands as a stand-
alone subsidiary, e-commerce and wholesale brand.
Ashley continues her role as founder and GMM of Her
Universe and in overseeing every aspect of the com-
pany.

Matt Fraction writes comic books out in the woods
and lives with his wife, the writer Kelly Sue DeConnick, his two children, two dogs, a cat, a bearded

dragon, and a yard full of coyotes and stags. Surely there is a metaphor there. He won the first-ever PEN USA Literary Award for Graphic Novel. He, or comics he's a part of, have won Eisners, Harveys, and Eagles, which are like the Oscars, Emmys, and Golden Globes of comic books and all seem about as likely. He's a *New York Times* bestselling donkus of comics like *Sex Criminals* (winner of the 2014 Will Eisner Award for Best New Series, the 2014 Harvey Award for Best New Series, and named *Time* magazine's Best Comic of 2013), *Satellite Sam, ODY-C, Hawkeye* (winner of the 2014 Will Eisner Award for Best Single Issue), and, oh, lordy, so many more.

ALEXANDER FREED is the author of *Star Wars: Battlefront: Twilight Company* and *Star Wars: The Old Republic: The Lost Suns* and has written many short stories, comic books, and videogames. Born near Philadelphia, he endeavors to bring the city's dour charm with him to his current home of Austin, Texas.

JASON FRY is a writer in Brooklyn, New York, where he lives with his wife, son, and about a metric ton of *Star Wars* stuff. He is the author of *The Clone Wars: The Visual Guide, The Clone Wars: Ultimate Battles*, and *The Clone Wars: Official Episode Guide: Season 1*, and has written extensively for the *Star Wars Insider* magazine and Wizards of the Coast.

KIERON GILLEN is a writer based in London. In terms of stories set in a galaxy far, far away he wrote the comics *Star Wars: Darth Vader* and *Star Wars: Doctor*

Aphra. Elsewhere in comics he has written basically every major Marvel superhero you've heard of and a lot that you haven't, and he's the co-creator of the award-winning *The Wicked + The Divine* and *Phonogram*. He is cursed by editors for his seeming inability to learn how to spell "Wookiee" and "Tatooine." He will be disciplined.

CHRISTIE GOLDEN is the award-winning, *New York Times* bestselling author of over fifty novels and more than a dozen short stories in the fields of fantasy, science fiction, and horror. Her media tie-in works include launching the Ravenloft line in 1991 with *Vampire of the Mists*, more than a dozen *Star Trek* novels, several movie novelizations, the *Warcraft* novels *Rise of the Horde, Lord of the Clans, Arthas: Rise of the Lich King*, and *War Crimes, Assassin's Creed: Heresy*, as well as *Star Wars: Dark Disciple* and the *Star Wars: Fate of the Jedi* novels *Omen, Allies,* and *Ascension*.

In 2017, she was awarded the International Association of Media Tie-in Writers Faust Award and named a Grandmaster in recognition of over a quarter century of writing.

CLAUDIA GRAY is the author of *Star Wars: Bloodline* and *Defy the Stars*, as well as the Firebird series, the Evernight series, and the Spellcaster series. She has worked as a lawyer, a journalist, a disc jockey, and a particularly ineffective waitress. Her lifelong interests include old houses, classic movies, vintage style, and history. She lives in New Orleans.

PABLO HIDALGO is a creative executive within the Lucasfilm Story Group, a resident *Star Wars* authority who helps ensure consistency across a wide array of *Star Wars* projects. He has written several DK titles, including most recently the bestselling *Star Wars: The Force Awakens: The Visual Dictionary*. He lives with his wife in San Francisco, California.

E. K. JOHNSTON had several jobs and one vocation before she became a published writer. If she's learned anything, it's that things turn out weird sometimes, and there's not a lot you can do about it. Well, that and how to muscle through awkward fanfic because it's about a pairing she likes. When she's not on Tumblr, she dreams of travel and Tolkien. Or writes books. It really depends on the weather.

PAUL S. KEMP is the author of the *New York Times* bestselling novels *Star Wars: Crosscurrent, Star Wars: The Old Republic: Deceived,* and *Star Wars: Riptide,* as well as numerous short stories and fantasy novels, including *The Hammer and the Blade* and *A Discourse in Steel.* Kemp lives and works in Grosse Pointe, Michigan, with his wife, children, and a couple of cats.

MUR LAFFERTY is a writer, podcast producer, gamer, geek, and martial artist. She is the host of the award-winning podcast I Should Be Writing, and the host of the Angry Robot Books podcast. She is the winner of the 2013 John W. Campbell Award for Best New Writer. She loves to run, practice kung fu (Northern Shaolin five animals style), play Skyrim and Fallout 3, and hang out with her fabulous geeky husband and their eleven-year-old daughter.

KEN LIU is one of the most lauded authors in the field of American literature. A winner of the Nebula, Hugo, World Fantasy, Locus, Sidewise, and Science Fiction & Fantasy translation awards, he has also been nominated for the Sturgeon Award. His short story "The Paper Menagerie" is the first work of fiction to simultaneously win the Nebula, Hugo, and World Fantasy awards. He also translated the 2015 Hugo Award winning novel *The Three-Body Problem*, written by Cixin Liu, which is the first novel to ever win the Hugo Award in translation. *The Grace of Kings*, his debut novel, is the first volume in a silkpunk epic fantasy series set in a universe he and his wife, artist Lisa Tang Liu, created together. It was a finalist for a Nebula Award and the recipient of the Locus Award for Best First Novel. He lives near Boston with his family.

GRIFFIN MCELROY is an Austin-based writer, video producer, and podcaster, and co-founder of the video game website Polygon. He co-hosts My Brother, My Brother and Me, an advice podcast, with—you guessed it—his two brothers, and serves as Dungeon Master for The Adventure Zone, a D&D Actual Play podcast he created with his family. He and his wife, Rachel, host a *Bachelor* franchise recap podcast called Rose Buddies and also recently co-founded a human baby called Henry.

John Jackson Miller is the *New York Times* bestselling author of *Star Wars: Kenobi, Star Wars: A New Dawn, Star Wars: Lost Tribe of the Sith*, and the *Star Wars Legends: The Old Republic* graphic novel collections from Marvel, among many other novels and comics. His website is farawaypress.com.

Nnedi Okorafor was born in the United States to two Igbo (Nigerian) immigrant parents. She holds a PhD in English and is a professor of creative writing at Chicago State University. She has been the winner of many awards for her short stories and young-adult books, and she won a World Fantasy Award for *Who Fears Death*. Okorafor's books are inspired by her Nigerian heritage and her many trips to Africa. She lives in Chicago with her daughter, Anyaugo, and family.

471

Daniel José Older is a Brooklyn-based writer, editor, composer, and author of the Bone Street Rumba novels, including *Midnight Taxi Tango* and *Half-Resurrection Blues,* and the YA novel *Shadowshaper*. He has been nominated for the Kirkus Prize, the Locus and World Fantasy awards, and the Andre Norton Award. *Shadowshaper* was named a *New York Times* Best Book of the Year.

Mallory Ortberg is Slate's "Dear Prudence." She has written for Gawker, *New York* magazine, The Hairpin, and *The Atlantic*. She is the co-creator of The Toast, a general-interest website geared toward women. She lives in the Bay Area with her laptop and her cat.

Beth Revis is the author of the *New York Times* bestselling Across the Universe series, the companion novel *The Body Electric*, a twisty contemporary novel *A World Without You*, and numerous short stories. A native of North Carolina, Beth is currently working on a new novel for teens. She lives in rural North Carolina with her boys: one husband, one son, and two dogs roughly the size of Ewoks.

Madeleine Roux received her BA in creative writing and acting from Beloit College in 2008. In the spring of 2009, Madeleine completed an honors term at Beloit College, proposing, writing, and presenting a full-length historical fiction novel. Shortly after, she began the experimental fiction blog Allison Hewitt Is Trapped, which quickly spread throughout the blogosphere, bringing a unique serial fiction experience to readers. Born in Minnesota, she now lives and works in Wisconsin where she enjoys the local beer and preparing for the eventual and inevitable zombie apocalypse.

Greg Rucka is the *New York Times* bestselling author of almost two dozen novels, including *Star Wars: Before the Awakening* and *Star Wars: Guardians of the Whills*, and has won multiple Eisner Awards for his graphic novels. He lives in Portland, Oregon, with his wife and children.

Gary D. Schmidt is a professor of English at Calvin College in Grand Rapids, Michigan. He received both a Newbery Honor and a Printz Honor for *Lizzie Bright and the Buckminster Boy* and a Newbery Honor for *The Wednesday Wars*. He lives with his family on a 150-year-old farm in Alto, Michigan, where he splits wood, plants gardens, writes, and feeds the wild cats that drop by.

CAVAN SCOTT is an author and comic writer for both adults and children. He has written for a large number of high-profile series including *Doctor Who, Star Wars, Adventure Time, Judge Dredd, Disney Infinity,* and *Warhammer 40,000.* He is the writer of Titan Comics' *Doctor Who: The Ninth Doctor* miniseries and currently writes *Minnie the Minx* and *Gnasher & Gnipper* for legendary British comic *The Beano.* A member of both The Society of Authors and the Dennis the Menace Fan Club, Cavan lives near Bristol with his wife, two daughters, and an inflatable Dalek named Desmond.

CHARLES SOULE is a *New York Times* bestselling, Brooklyn-based comic book writer, musician, and attorney. He is best known for writing *Daredevil, She-Hulk, Death of Wolverine* (inspiration for the film *Logan*), and various *Star Wars* comics from Marvel Comics, as well as his creator-owned series *Curse Words* from Image Comics and the award-winning political sci-fi epic *Letter 44* from Oni Press. His debut novel, *The Oracle Year,* will be published in 2018 by HarperCollins.

SABAA TAHIR grew up in California's Mojave Desert at her family's eighteen-room motel. There she spent her time devouring fantasy novels, raiding her brother's comic book stash, and playing the guitar badly. She began writing *An Ember in the Ashes* while working nights as a newspaper editor. She likes thunderous indie rock, garish socks, and all things nerd. Tahir currently lives in the San Francisco Bay Area with her family.

Elizabeth Wein was born in New York City, grew up abroad, and currently lives in Scotland with her husband and two children. She is an avid flyer of small planes and holds a PhD in folklore from the University of Pennsylvania. Elizabeth is the author of *Code Name Verity*, winner of the Edgar Award in the Young Adult category and a Printz Medal Honor Book; *Rose Under Fire*, winner of the Schneider Family Book Award; and *Black Dove, White Raven*, winner of the Children's Africana Book Award.

Glen Weldon has been a theater critic, a science writer, an oral historian, a writing teacher, a bookstore clerk, a PR flack, a movie usher, a spectacularly inept marine biologist, and a slightly better-than-ept competitive swimmer. His work has appeared in *The New York Times*, *The Washington Post*, *The Atlantic*, *The New Republic*, *Slate*, and many other places. He is a panelist on NPR's *Pop Culture Happy Hour* and reviews books and comics for NPR.

Chuck Wendig is a novelist, screenwriter, and game designer. He's the author of many novels, including *Star Wars: Aftermath*; *Star Wars: Aftermath: Life Debt*;

Star Wars: Empire's End; Blackbirds; Atlanta Burns; Zer0es; and the YA Heartland series. He is co-writer of the short film *Pandemic* and the Emmy-nominated digital narrative *Collapsus*. He currently lives in the forests of Pennsyltucky with his wife, son, and red dog.

WIL WHEATON began acting in commercials at the age of seven, and by the age of ten had appeared in numerous television and film roles. In 1986, his critically acclaimed role in Rob Reiner's *Stand By Me* put him in the public spotlight, where he remains to this day. In 1987, Wil was cast as Wesley Crusher in the hit television series *Star Trek: The Next Generation*. Recently, Wil has held recurring roles on TNT's *Leverage* and SyFy's *Eureka;* he currently recurs on CBS's *The Big Bang Theory*. He played Axis of Anarchy leader Fawkes in Felicia Day's webseries *The Guild,* and just completed writing, producing, and hosting *The Wil Wheaton Project* on Syfy. He is also the creator and host of the multiple award-winning webseries *TableTop,* now in its fourth season.

As a voice actor, Wil has been featured in videogames such as There Came an Echo, Broken Age, Grand Theft Auto: San Andreas, Brütal Legend, DC Universe Online, Fallout: New Vegas, and Ghost Recon Advanced Warfighter. He has lent his voice talents to animated series including *Family Guy, Legion of Superheroes, Ben 10: Alien Force, Generator Rex, Batman: The Brave and the Bold,* and *Teen Titans*.

As an author, he's published many acclaimed books, among them: *Just A Geek, Dancing Barefoot,* and *The*

Happiest Days of Our Lives. All of his books grew out of Wil's immensely popular, award-winning weblog, which he created and maintains at WIL WHEATON dot NET. While most celebrities are happy to let publicists design and maintain their websites, Wil took a decidedly different turn when he started blogging in 2001, when he designed and coded his website on his own.

Wil personally maintains a popular social media presence, including a popular Tumblr, Facebook page, and Google Plus page. His frequently cited Twitter account is followed by more than 2.75 million people.

Wil is widely recognized as one of the original celebrity bloggers and is a respected voice in the blogging community. In 2003, Forbes.com readers voted WWdN the Best Celebrity Weblog. Wil's blog was chosen by C|Net for inclusion in their one hundred most influential blogs, and is an "A" lister, according to Blogebrity .com. In the 2002 Weblog Awards (the Bloggies), Wil won every category in which he was nominated, including Weblog of the Year. In 2007, Wil was nominated for a Lifetime Achievement Bloggie, alongside Internet powerhouses Slashdot and Fark. In the 2008 Weblog Awards, Wil was voted the Best Celebrity Blogger, and in 2009 *Forbes* named him the fourteenth most influential Web celebrity. This is all amusing to Wil, who doesn't think of himself as a celebrity, but is instead "just this guy, you know?"

GARY WHITTA is the former editor in chief of *PC Gamer* magazine and is now an award-winning screenwriter best known for the explosive post-apocalyptic thriller *The Book of Eli,* starring Denzel Washington, and as co-writer of *Rogue One: A Star Wars Story.* He also co-wrote the Will Smith sci-fi adventure *After Earth,* and was writer and story consultant on Telltale Games' *The Walking Dead,* for which he was the co-recipient of a BAFTA Award for Best Story. Most recently he served as writer on the animated TV series *Star Wars: Rebels.* He also wrote the film adaptations of the Mark Millar comic *Starlight* and David Petersen's *Mouse Guard* for 20th Century Fox, and the David Fisher book *The War Magician* for StudioCanal and Benedict Cumberbatch. His first novel, *Abomination,* is now available, and his original comic series *Oliver* arrives via Image Comics in 2017. Born and raised in London, England, Gary currently lives with his wife and daughter in San Francisco.

ABOUT THE TYPE

This book was set in Minion, a 1990 Adobe Originals typeface by Robert Slimbach (b. 1956). Minion is inspired by classical, old-style typefaces of the late Renaissance, a period of elegant, beautiful, and highly readable type designs. Created primarily for text setting, Minion combines the aesthetic and functional qualities that make text type highly readable with the versatility of digital technology.